Hadford Howell was born in Barbados in 1956. He went to join his parents in England in 1968 before returning to Barbados in 1981. In UK and in Barbados, he worked both in the public service and in the private sector. Prior to his early retirement, he served for 33 years in a senior position at a diplomatic mission in Barbados.

He is continuing to fulfil a life-long ambition of writing novels. *Hung Out to Dry* is the follow-up to the successful publication of his first novel, *Connect the Dots...* Other novels in the Barbados Intelligence Bureau (BIB) series are in advanced stages of development. Hadford is a graduate of the University of the West Indies (Cave Hill Campus), has served on his local Church Council and School Boards and was awarded an MBE in 1998. He has been a Justice of the Peace for over 20 years. He currently sits on the Board of Directors of two Barbadian charities and is the appointed chairman of a national agency.

Hung Out to Dry is dedicated to those who have supported me in any way by buying and/or recommending purchase of my first fictional novel, *Connect the Dots*...to others. This was the book which established the ten-book Barbados Intelligence Bureau (BIB) series. Readers will be familiar with some of the characters established in that initial novel, but in *Hung Out to Dry* they will meet some new and exciting characters that will attract their curiosity and add to the book's intrigue.

Remember to *Live, Laugh and Love*. These exemplary attributes should lead you to gain solid friendships and ensure positive outcomes from the good deeds we endeavour to undertake in life.

–   HH

Hadford Howell

HUNG OUT TO DRY

A BIB Novel

AUSTIN MACAULEY PUBLISHERS™

LONDON * CAMBRIDGE * NEW YORK * SHARJAH

A CIP catalogue record for this title is available from the British Library.

ISBN 9781528993081 (Paperback)
ISBN 9781528993098 (ePub e-book)

www.austinmacauley.com

First Published (2021)
Austin Macauley Publishers Ltd
25 Canada Square
Canary Wharf
London
E14 5LQ

Hung Out to Dry could not have been written and finalised without the further support of my family (wife, Anne; daughter, Kelly-Anne; son, Graeme) close friends, supporters and my talented production team. To my editor Jackie Jones in particular, proof readers, commentators, publisher and printer, I extend sincere and heartfelt thanks for your assistance in helping to bring this second novel project in the BIB series to fruition. This work is better because of all your invaluable contributions.

– HH

Chapter One

Danos Fisico (Physical Damage)

SATURDAY, 14 APRIL

Senor Max Frequente ran Frequente's Automovil, a legitimate vehicle retail business in Acapulco, Mexico. However, he also operated a couple of others 'under the radar'. One of these ventures did business with *The Organisation*.

Frequente had gotten into trouble with *The Organisation* through owing what had become an eighteenth-month old US$750,000 debt, plus interest. His several promises to settle over this period had always fallen through, so Rhohan Castille had at last been dispatched by *The Organisation's* Head to pay Frequente a visit to collect what was due. Castille had clear evidence that Frequente could have long paid his debt, but had simply been stringing along *The Organisation*.

Castille's visit to Frequente's showroom was a surprise. Having spoken only a few days earlier with Castille, Frequente did not expect to see Castille on his doorstep as no indication had been given during their conversation that Castille would visit Mexico anytime soon.

"Mr Castille! Good...good to see you. What a pleasant surprise. Here on holiday?" Frequente asked nervously, suspecting otherwise while thinking about how quickly he might be able to get Castille off his premises without any commotion. Frequente was aware of Castille's reputation, so did not want to be hurt or in any way embarrassed by him in front of his staff or any of his customers.

"*Buenas tardes*, Senor Max. No holiday, just business. I'm here to collect. I'll go wait in your office, yes?" asked Castille.

"Yes, yes…please. My secretary, Maria, will show you the way," said a concerned Frequente.

Maria Soares did as she was told.

Five minutes later, after completing the required sales paperwork to a client for a traded-in two-year-old Mercedes SUV, Frequente made his way to his office.

"Can I get you a beverage – tea, coffee, beer? I have Corona and Victoria, or perhaps you'd like a Michelada? Paloma is also nice," stated Frequented invitingly but still nervous.

"Thank you, but none of the above. Just the money owed to us. US$750,000. No cash, so please call your bankers and make the arrangements. The outstanding interest can follow," said Castille tersely.

"The business doesn't have anything like that amount in its bank account, so I cannot send that to *The Organisation*. Perhaps in a couple of weeks I might be able to gather it up though. So how about I send you guys US$100,000 tomorrow, and the balance say, over a three-month period?" asked Frequente.

"Senor Frequente. You've played this game with us before, too many times. Make the call. We know you have the resources in your account. Otherwise, you should gather it together from other sources. I'm not a patient man. *The Organisation* wants its money. Will you deliver now or not?" asked Castille.

"I'm telling you, Mr Castille, I can't pay right now. You have to believe me. Please take my offer…oh, sure you won't change your mind and also accept my offered hot or cold beverage?"

This man isn't listening, thought Castille.

He decided to take some action to move things along. Standing up from his chair, he started to approach Frequente behind his large desk.

"Wait, wait, what are you doing?" asked Frequente, alarmed.

"Let's take a walk out back," said Castille, who while waiting had noticed and looked beyond the door that was at the back of Frequente's office. Castille had removed the key and now grabbed Frequente's right arm before leading him to the door. Inserting the key, he unlocked the door enabling them to venture outside into an enclosed private car park which obviously served as Frequente's private entrance to his office once the showroom was closed. Only one vehicle was located in the car park, a brand-new Mercedes-Benz C-Class Cabrolet.

"Make the call, Senor Frequente," said Castille in a soft but threatening voice.

"I told you –"

"Make the call," said Castille coldly.

Now gripped with fear, Frequente complied using his mobile.

Once Castille received the evidence from Frequente which confirmed that the outstanding sum sought had been paid in full by credit transfer (excluding interest), he thanked Frequente.

"Guess you'll be on your way now. I'll try to do better next time," said the relieved man.

"I'm sure you will, Senor Frequente. Let me leave you with my calling card."

Castille's unexpected blow to Frequente's left arm instantly broke it. As he whimpered, Castille applied a savage kick to Frequente's right leg. He obviously knew where to direct his kick, because Frequente crumpled in a heap to the ground. Groaning loudly as he was in great pain, Frequente cowered and begged for mercy. Unexpectedly, Castille took pity on him. A broken arm and a broken leg were enough *physical* punishment for this man. Castille knew it would take Frequente a while to recover from these injurie but for good measure, there was *The Organisation*'s final piece of justice to be administered. This took the form of Castille smashing the windscreen of Frequente's Mercedes Cabrolet using a sledge-hammer that for some unknown reason had been left leaned up against the fence that enclosed Frequente's private car park.

Throughout the beating, Castille did not speak. His actions would remind Frequente not to trifle with *The Organisation* or its merchandise going forward. Castille also believed that this would serve as an excellent lesson from *The Organisation* to its other Mexican, Central, South and North American east coast employees, clients and collaborators. To the few fledgling Caribbean persons who were already dealing with *The Organisation* too as they would in due course also hear of and take note of what had happened to Frequente. They would not want to play the non-payment game, especially with Castille around.

Before leaving Frequente's premises through the private car park exit, his mission accomplished, Castille had locked the back door to Frequente's office before throwing away the key. He could hear Maria Soares and other members of Frequente's staff responding to his cries for assistance by banging on the back door of his office. Castille knew they would eventually break down the door and reach Frequente, by which time he would be long gone from that location.

***

Chapter Two
Mexico Calling

MONDAY, 16 APRIL

One of several hundred overseas calls that were made to Barbadians on this Monday morning was to an individual living in a parish on Barbados' scenic east coast. This call originated from a Mexican city where it was clear to residents and visitors alike that it was going to be another warm day.

"Hello?"

"Hello back," answered a male voice.

"Oh, it's you."

"Yes, my friend. Time to go to work! Confirm goal is to recover the package. Box it and have it ready for my arrival at the agreed location no later than 3:00 p.m. on Wednesday. That's in…another forty-eight hours or so. Clear?" asked the overseas caller.

"Understood. Be jolly now, but there's one more thing. Do you want a…"

Click. The conversation had ended.

The desired message had been delivered in a clipped but unmistakable and commanding style. It was almost scary in its simplicity and directness. The message was not misunderstood by the recipient.

Removing the phone from his ear, the Barbadian realised that this was the third call he had now received from the overseas caller whom he had not met. All of their calls had ended abruptly.

Standing up from the rocking chair on the semi-secluded veranda of his house overlooking Bathsheba, he asked himself in a barely audible tone, "Why must he always do that?" After a further minute's contemplation and a shake of his head which demonstrated his frustration, the Barbadian recipient of the overseas call re-entered his house through the opened front door.

It was time to make three calls.

***

It was 9:00 a.m. across the beautiful island of Barbados. A typical Monday that marked the start of another busy work and study week for most working Barbadians and schoolchildren.

Retirees had already visited a local beach and taken their daily sea bath. Other such fortunate Barbadians were in the process of finishing up their work in personal flower or vegetable gardens as the sun became too hot to continue working under. The need to shower, relax and catch up on the day's local and international news and entertainment was attractive. They'd devour the local print and online newspapers and surf the internet for the latest. Other Barbadians were already enjoying a favourite national pastime of 'gossiping' on their phones, often about what had happened at or what they had learned from fellow congregation members outside of church the day before. Titbits like who was sleeping with whom in their district, who had died since their last conversation (and what from), and of any recent or significant developments that had occurred in the local political arena. Others still were preparing to tune in and even contribute to the two live daily local radio call-in programmes at 9:30 p.m. and 10:00 a.m. where issues discussed during the past week might again be addressed.

In the private and public sectors, most CEOs, Permanent Secretaries and senior managers, believing that it was 'the early bird which caught the juiciest of worms', had already caught up on e-mails which had hit their inboxes overnight and had already held their first meetings of the week with subordinates. Being a Monday morning, senior management meetings had either just gotten underway or were about to commence, while more junior executives were on their way out to appointments away from their offices.

Enterprising visitors to Barbados were also up and running, implementing their respective holiday plans for the day. Some were in the country with one simple purpose in mind, to relax on the island's attractive west and south coast beaches by sunbathing and reading a book. Others would pursue island safari tours, day-long catamaran cruises, fishing expeditions or go on shopping sprees at the various malls in search of that special piece of jewellery or souvenir item for themselves, a family member, friend or work colleague back home. Finally, the visitors who, having only gone to bed late last night or earlier that morning, were seeking to compose themselves before having a late breakfast in a restaurant before it closed off.

**

The overseas caller was known to most of his clients only as The Principal.

Castille wondered why the man he had just spoken with briefly always wanted to extend their conversation. Castille did not dislike the man for this but had never seen any merit in prolonging conversations with any of his Greater Americas' Corporation's, a.k.a. *The Organisation* US and Latin American clients and collaborators.

From early childhood, Castille had not been much of a talker. Even at school, chatting unnecessarily was never his style. While his teachers praised him for his quiet demeanour, they were also frustrated by his unwillingness to answer questions in front of other students in his class. He did not find any pleasure in engaging in team sports either. Since becoming an adult and in his particular line of work, Castille found speaking unnecessary. This was right up his street as it reduced opportunities for anyone – family, friends, accomplices or competitors, to remember a conversation with him, trace his calls or easily track down his whereabouts. Conversations, especially long ones, were dangerous, and talking too much could easily cost one their life. He sought to do his best to ensure that talking did not cost him his.

There was something else that Castille's deceased mother had told him on his first day at the primary school's gate, "Watch who you speak to and what you say. Walls have ears and people remember things."

He had carried those admonitions from that day on. He had interpreted them in his adult years to mean always be discreet in whatever you said and did. Hence, his practice of having 'short and sweet' conversations had become his trademark, part of his method and tradecraft.

With that in mind, Castille followed his well-established practise of disposing of the phone he had just used for a fourth time during his three-day stay in Mexico. This was just one of the several basic phones he always took with him on overseas trips. Once he had used one of them four times, he would disable and dump it in pieces. This was to be the fate of the phone he now held in his hand in another ten minutes or so, once he was clear of his current location, a third-floor room in one of the more popular four-star hotels in the Cuauhtemoc borough of Mexico City. Any of the three remaining phones he had would then be used for the remaining two items of business he still had to conduct for *The Organisation* before he left Mexico.

***

Demario 'Spend Big' Wharton was the Barbadian recipient of the call from Castille. Their third telephone conversation was, in a way, funny. Both men knew what to expect and believed that they understood each other. This latest call from Castille confirmed that Wharton's Pressure Group should proceed with the agreed project in another forty-eight hours. Wharton knew what the project was and intended for his team to execute it flawlessly on the day.

Without hesitation, he went to work. He spoke on his phone to the other three members of his Pressure Group. He advised them that the project had been green-lit and was in play for the fourth day of the week. Those listening to Wharton knew what this meant, having discussed it the previous Friday night after Wharton had received his first call from Castille. Nothing from their in-depth planning meeting last Saturday night had changed. They had no questions and made no comments except to acknowledge Wharton's instruction by stating 'Right', 'Okay' and 'Right on' before Wharton ended each conversation with his standard 'Be jolly now' rendition.

The project was safe between the four men. Each knew what had to be done, how, why and when. The *where* needed to be conveyed to them by late tomorrow (Tuesday) afternoon ahead of their assembly at 9:00 p.m. in the back room of Wharton's popular Spend Big's Bar & Grocery (SBB&G), located on the outskirts of St Michael. There, the Pressure Group would adjust the execution of its operational plan if necessary. Despite the noise that was always outside of the SBB&G's back room, inside would be quiet. This was Wharton's office, his private space. Here, no one dared interrupt them. As the owner and operator of SBB&G, Wharton had privileges. Not being disturbed was one of them.

***

15

Having checked out of his hotel, Castille took a taxi to Beniteo Juarez International Airport to catch American Airlines (AA) 1:45 p.m. flight to the USA. *The Organisation*, for which he had worked for ten years, had arranged for him to go to Barbados in thirty-six hours after his Miami stop-over for some much-deserved R&R. Castille saw this down time as his weekend, and why not? Most persons worked five days a week and got two days as their weekend, so why shouldn't he have a half-day less as his weekend?

Once in Barbados, Castille planned to follow-up on the execution of *The Organisation's* carefully devised plan. Everything was expected to go well before his arrival, making the impact of *The Organisation*'s plan over the following few days felt across Barbados by residents and visitors alike. *The Organisation*'s plan was three-fold. First, their package had to be collected. Second, it had to be kept in a particularly safe but unassuming place. Third, outstanding funds would be collected. As a bonus, causing some confusion for the local authorities should be easy to roll out and ensure his quick return to the USA.

Piece of cake, he thought.

Only time would tell how, and how well or badly the Barbadian authorities would respond to *The Organisation's* planned incident. It could become more challenging for *The Organisation* if friendly countries with international agencies based in Barbados decided to respond to and help the local authorities. Were this to happen, support personnel from *The Organisation's* fledgling Eastern Caribbean network might be needed to lend Castille some assistance but he did not anticipate this being necessary. However, should that come to pass, he would have to make some adjustments to *The Organisation*'s after-plan on the spur of the moment.

Castille smiled to himself as he reflected on that possibility. Yes, the local authorities' response to *The Organisation's* plan might be timid, awkward even incompetent, but based on his research and experience, that was not likely. If they were diligent, bold and unafraid in how they responded, he would be tested. Whatever happened, he had no doubt that *The Organisation* would achieve its set goals by the end of the coming weekend. His plan was to depart Barbados on Sunday afternoon at the latest, so 'cover' from the three sporting and entertainment events set to take place in Barbados within one week would be sufficient. With these activities set to take place on specific days, times and at different locations, flexibility to make revisions to *The Organisation's* plan was there. This was comforting to know.

Castille was always confident about anything he set out to accomplish. His boss, the Head of *The Organisation*, knew this and had great confidence in his ability to get any project allocated to him over the finish line. He achieved, by hook or crook. It was why he felt relaxed and had no doubts that *The Organisation's* Barbados project would succeed.

Castille made the last of his Mexican calls on behalf of *The Organisation* from the back seat of his taxi. He spoke in Spanish and quickly received an assurance that payment for the outstanding moneys owed to *The Organisation* would be made later that day by its client. He would ask *The Organisation*'s accountants to check requisite bank accounts later that evening to confirm that the promised settlement had been made.

Castille accepted the promise, but warned the client that should payment not arrive by mid-day tomorrow, he would return to Mexico *rapidamente* (quickly) to collect the much overdue payment for goods delivered by *The Organisation* which had the evidence that its goods had been received, sold and the benefits pocketed. For good measure, Castille suggested to this client that he should place a call to Max Frequente in Acapulco to see how he was doing. Frequente would verify that *The Organisation* did not make idle threats about collecting outstanding debts, especially if Castille had to visit.

***

Satisfied with his review of what was planned for the next forty-eight hours and that his Pressure Group members would keep their mouths shut, Wharton wandered down to his local corner shop to purchase a copy of one of the country's newspapers. As was his custom, Wharton first sought out the comics/cartoon page. After a few giggles, he turned to the sports pages observing that Mr Black had won himself another annual national road tennis championship, his fourth title on the trot.

"Good for you, bro," he growled.

Next, Wharton turned to page seven, which listed all the court cases that had been processed during in the past week. This page also listed where and when the High and Magistrate Court cases would be presided over during the current week. Wharton paid special attention to the entries for Wednesday, 18 April at the District 'A' Court in Station Hill, St Michael.

What he was looking for was right there, in black and white.

"Good, got cha' back, Stabs," he said softly.

With nothing else in the newspaper of interest to him, he tore out page seven before dropping the rest into the dustbin outside of the corner shop. The old adage about newspapers being today's news and tomorrow's garbage sprung to mind, except that in Wharton's case, both had taken place on the same day, indeed within minutes of each other.

"Be jolly now," he said to himself as he set out on the short walk back to his house.

***

Once Castille had checked himself in for his 1:45 p.m. flight to Miami in the AA area, he called one of his friends in Miami using the one phone he permanently kept with him. He firmed up the tentative arrangements earlier made for his thirty-six-hour stopover in Miami. Happy that the services of Frieda, Aisha and Sean (yes, all three) had been secured for the party that night at his apartment, Castille joined the line of passengers wandering towards the security check-point to gain entry to the inner side of the airport.

Minutes later, he placed his personal belongings onto the conveyor belt leading into the security machine. He was fifth in line to be scanned.

***

Chapter Three

Retirement

TUESDAY, 17 APRIL

At 9:00 a.m. on another bright and sunny Tuesday morning in Barbados, a cloudless blue sky greeted Petra Carmichael as she exited the front door of her four-bedroomed Gibbs, St Peter house on the west coast. She did not expect her journey into and across Bridgetown this morning to take more than thirty minutes, as most of the rush-hour traffic heading from the north of the island to offices in and beyond central Bridgetown had passed her by earlier. She hoped the customary build-up of traffic would also have dissipated once she got close to Bridgetown, enabling her to pass through the city centre quickly and arrive at Government Headquarters well before the 10:00 a.m. appointment she had with her successor and visiting British officials. Carmichael needed to fulfil a promise that she had made to the Prime Minister prior to starting her pre-retirement leave.

Truth be told, Carmichael did not want to leave her home until early evening when she would attend a two-pronged retirement function in her honour. She had arranged a Service of Thanksgiving at the Cathedral Church of St. Michael and All Angels in central Bridgetown to celebrate her thirty-five-year career in the Barbados Public Service. That would be followed by a reception at the Barbados Defence Force's (BDF) HQ at the insistence of and hosted by the Rt. Hon. Jeffrey Zachariah Motby QC MP, Prime Minister and Minister of Finance, Economic Affairs and National Security. He was also the current Chairman of the Caribbean Economic Community (CARICOM), the twenty-member Caribbean political organisation comprising of fifteen full and five associate member countries.

She carefully pulled out of her driveway into the flow of traffic. Once she got going, she kept a clear head but could not help reflecting on what had been a successful public service career and the new overseas assignment the Prime Minister had offered to her on her last day at work two weeks earlier. He had given her a fortnight to decide whether or not she would accept his offer, as he needed her answer before conclusion of the second part of her retirement function tonight.

Carmichael had decided to give the Prime Minister her reply today during her visit to Government Headquarters. She had taken the fortnight to consider his offer, discussing it at length with her husband and three grown-up children. The family had agreed that she should accept the offer. When she greeted Motby just before 6:00 p.m. that evening, the only thing Carmichael wanted to have on her mind would be enjoyment of her retirement function.

***

In Miami, Castille was a contented man. His carefully arranged R&R plans were going as smoothly as had his flight from Mexico City to Miami the previous afternoon.

Frieda, Aisha and Sean had joined him at his apartment around 8:00 p.m. the night before. They had played their roles with him to perfection, making the night a memorable experience for all concerned. Now exhausted, but fully satisfied, Castille turned his mind to what he wanted to do for the rest of the day. He needed to do some shopping in one of the nearby malls later that afternoon before taking a 9:30 p.m. meeting with his boss in downtown Miami. He did not expect that meeting to last long, so he would get a chance to relax on his own and have a good night's rest before travelling to Barbados the following mid-morning.

Castille disliked early starts to his day, but tomorrow would need to be an exception. He decided that, in another hour or so, he would ask his three friends to leave. He would then clean himself up and work to fit in his plans for the rest of the day. Tomorrow's AA flight from Miami should see him arrive in Barbados mid-afternoon. All things being equal, the proposed clandestine action should have been completed prior to his arrival on the island. That meant that he could not be directly connected to it. There would be sufficient time for him to collect his rented vehicle from the airport, drive to and check into his south coast hotel, shower, change and have something to eat before making his way to the agreed rendezvous location.

***

Dr Winston Peter Smith GCM, Cabinet Secretary and Head of the Public Service (HOPS), left his office to go down the corridor to see Sharon Evans, Executive Assistant to the Prime Minister. Joseph Medbin, recently promoted to be Permanent Secretary in the Prime Minister's Office following Petra Carmichael's retirement, was present. They were reviewing the final arrangements for the second part of the night's reception with Brigadier Michael 'Mike' Tenton, Chief of Staff, BDF and one of his junior officers who was acting as his driver today.

"Hi Winston. All seems to be in order for tonight. My only concern is that the reception must start promptly at 7:45 p.m., allowing it to end as planned at 9:30 p.m.," said Medbin.

"Why is there this concern? We spoke about this a week ago. Surely we've been able to nobble the Dean and encourage him not to preach too long on this occasion?" asked Dr Smith.

"We've tried, but I'm not sure that he will comply with our wishes. After all, it's his church. Also, he likes a grand stage and when he sees one, he will want to –"

Dr Smith cut across Medbin. "I don't care about his performances. Please speak with him directly. Use my name – the Prime Minister's too if necessary, to get our point across. The good Dean must understand what we're trying to accomplish here," said Dr Smith.

Medbin recognised the signs that Dr Smith was starting to get grumpy, and so he sought to put an end to it by speaking directly to Evans.

"Indeed! Sharon, please call the Dean and remind him that we have a tight schedule to keep tonight. His address must not be too long. I can speak to him later this morning after my meeting if you don't get through to him, or think he's not bought into what we want of him. Emphasise the *not too long* bit please," said Medbin.

"Sure thing. I'm on it," said an enthusiastic Evans.

"Thank you. Do let me know the outcome of your call with the Dean. I'm aware that we cannot tell God's mouth-piece what to say, or for how long, but just the same, we can try. I'll also make myself available to speak with the Dean to reinforce our message if all else fails," said Dr Smith.

"No need, Dr Smith. I'll handle it."

"Very well." Turning to Brigadier Tenton, Dr Smith continued. "Michael, your people will be ready to receive any early arrivals at BDF HQ from 6:45 p.m., right? Not all reception attendees will have gone to the church service."

"Yes, we are ready for that eventuality," said Tenton confidently.

"Good. I must again thank you and your people in advance for making the arrangements for tonight's do. You'll come to the service first, yes?" asked Dr Smith.

"Of course, I need to see Petra off in the proper way and then drink to her release from Government service. Her longevity is to be commended," answered Tenton.

"Indeed. See you later then," stated Dr Smith as he started to leave the room.

"Yes…it'll be a great night for everyone. Goodbye, Mrs Evans, thanks for the session," said Tenton turning to his BDF aide, intimating that they should be getting back to BDF HQ.

The three men followed Dr Smith out of Evans' office. She waved goodbye to them, having started to dial Dean Mercer's number.

"Take care, Mike," said Medbin as they entered the corridor. Once there, Tenton and his aide turned left and took the stairs which would lead them to the main car park outside Government Headquarters. Medbin and Dr Smith turned right to return to their respective offices as a young Royal Barbados Police Force (RBPF) officer greeted them as he headed in the opposite direction.

Medbin and Dr Smith passed the doorway to a small waiting room on their left which had a splendid view of Carlisle Bay through the closed window. Two military-looking men were observed speaking softly with Ryan Appleton, Chief of Protocol, Ministry of Foreign Affairs and Culture (MFAC). All three were obviously visitors to Government Headquarters, confirmed by the visitor's passes that hung from around their necks. They had been escorted up to the third floor waiting room earlier by the young RBPF officer Medbin and Dr Smith had just passed in the corridor.

Medbin recognised Appleton and the two men. They were British officials who were in Barbados conducting the second of their mandatory reconnoitre (recce) visits, before a member of the Royal Family would be allowed to make an official visit to Barbados and St Vincent and the Grenadines next month. Their job was to finalise the security arrangements for the first leg of the forthcoming Royal visit with the Governor General's Office, RBPF and Prime Minister's Office. Medbin knew that they would also travel to St Vincent the following morning on LIAT's first flight to undertake their second recce visit for that leg of the Royal visit. The Prime Minister had instructed that the two men be shown some Bajan hospitality, and so they had been invited to attend Petra Carmichael's retirement reception at BDF HQ later that night.

"Let me say hello to these fellows, Winston. They're early for our meeting," said Medbin.

"Knock yourself out, Joseph."

Medbin did not respond but noted Dr Smith's response. It was typical of the man, direct yet charmingly polite. He could be humorous at times, but one should never take Dr Smith's ready smile and humour to even *suggest* that he was an easy-going guy or a pushover. Quite the opposite. Most of his colleagues knew him to be one tough son-of-a-bitch to work for, even alongside. As Barbadians often say, 'he wasn't easy'.

Indeed, Dr Smith was a man of great ability, with seemingly the integrity to match. He took his responsibilities as Head of the Barbados Public Service very seriously, enforcing public service rules to the letter wherever possible. Continuing down the corridor to his spacious office, he wondered what the morning meeting with Motby he'd been invited to earlier was all about. In the five years since Dr Smith had been appointed HOPS, he had never gone into such a meeting with the Prime Minister without knowing what was to be discussed. Dr Smith consoled himself by noting that at least he did not have to prepare anything specific. Perhaps Motby simply wanted to pick his brains on something related to a new, wide ranging public service policy, for example on public servants' rules, roles and/or obligations? Or might it be about a forthcoming Budgetary initiative he was considering? Time would tell.

That was tomorrow. Meanwhile, Dr Smith thought, *I have a lot of work to do on my desk today.*

***

Chapter Four
Contact

Colonel Trevor 'TB' Burke, Director of the Barbados Intelligence Bureau (BIB), returned to his office around 9:30 a.m. after chairing his weekly BIB staff meeting with his eleven operatives of the now twelve-year-old security agency. It would soon be time to call Tommy Connell, Managing Director of the UK Trading Co. Ltd.

The previous afternoon, Colonel Burke (code number B1) had received a hand-written note from HE Balwin Tullock CMG, British High Commissioner to Barbados and the Eastern Caribbean, requesting that he call a Mr Connell on a specific number at 10:00 a.m. today. Colonel Burke had duly returned a hand-written note to Tullock confirming that he would do so, but had been informed by the MFAC that a local security Heads meeting had been set for Thursday with Connell.

This was to be the first time that Colonel Burke would speak directly with Connell, whose real name was Sir Thadeus Theolophus Thomas KCMG who was Head of MI6, Britain's Secret Intelligence Service.

***

Sir Thadeus was in Barbados (incognito) for a ten-day holiday with his wife Cindy Lady Thomas to celebrate their twenty-fifth wedding anniversary. A long-time lover of Test cricket, Sir Thadeus had seen at least one full day's play of the past fifteen home Test Matches played by England at the Lord's cricket ground in London. The nature of the various senior jobs he had held in Britain's

Government service had effectively prevented him from seeing England play any part of a Test Match overseas. This would be corrected during his Barbados sojourn. He would break his duck, as it were.

Sir Thadeus and Cindy Lady Thomas had earlier this morning spent some time lounging by the pool at their carefully chosen, quiet, secure and secluded west coast villa. While they had spoken generally before leaving the UK about what they would do during their holiday, it was only now after each had done a few laps in the pool that they were focussing on what their holiday activities should definitely include.

"Thad, I think the odd sea-bath will do us both good. Also, we must visit the picturesque east coast. I'm really looking forward to that," said Lady Thomas.

"Copy that. Add both to your 'activities list', plus our attendance at the second and third days of the England v West Indies Test Match at New Kensington Oval over the weekend. I'm excited about that. Balwin's got us included in his invitation. Each day we'll be in a different box," said Sir Thadeus.

"Hmmm. Exciting for you, a bit boring for me but I guess I must tag along and hope to find someone, another female that I can speak with from time to time. Will Andrea also be there?"

"I expect so. Getting back to our activities list. Why don't we eat out a couple of nights? I'll ask Balwin to recommend a couple of appropriate and safe restaurants. We can afford that," said Sir Thadeus with a chuckle.

"Well, I promise not to break the bank when I place my order," said Cindy Lady Thomas with a wry smile.

***

A fortnight prior to Sir Thadeus' arrival in Barbados, he had indicated to the British High Commission that he did not wish to have any formal calls with Barbados Government officials. An opportunity to hold an informal, roundtable session with the Heads of Barbados' law enforcement and security agencies would however be welcomed. A *Diplomatic Note* had been dispatched by the High Commission to MFAC requesting such a meeting for Sir Thadeus who was described in the correspondence as 'a senior British security official'.

A week later, at a reception held for the outgoing Chinese Ambassador at Ilaro Court, the Prime Minister's official residence, Tullock had taken the opportunity to have a quiet word with Motby about Sir Thadeus' visit, presenting a copy of the submitted *Diplomatic Note* to him. A verbal commitment was immediately given by Motby that the meeting would be facilitated and MFAC would confirm this shortly to the High Commission through a response *Diplomatic Note*.

The High Commission duly received MFAC's *Diplomatic Note* a couple of days later. It confirmed that a Thursday, 19th April meeting could take place at 3:00 p.m., with *'Ben Mar'*, the British High Commissioner's official residence, being the venue as Tullock had agreed to host the meeting. The *Diplomatic Note* also specified the five persons who would be attending, all being law enforcement and security agency Heads based in Barbados: Willoughby Jeremie, Commissioner, RBPF; Brigadier Tenton, Chief of Staff, BDF; Lt. Colonel Simon Innis, Head, Barbados Prison Service (BPS)/Superintendent of Her Majesty's Prison (HMP) Dodds; Colonel Burke, Director, BIB; and Commander Junior Samuel, Co-ordinator/Executive Director, Regional Security System (RSS).

There was to be no official agenda for the meeting and so no formal record of it would be taken, although all of the participants knew that their discussion would be reported on by two of the participants. Colonel Burke, as Chairman of *P.A.A.N.I.* would do so to Motby in the next weekly *P.A.A.N.I.* report. It was also anticipated that Tullock would do likewise to his London superiors in the Foreign & Commonwealth Office (FCO) after the meeting. No residence staff, not even Tullock's wife would be allowed on the premises during the meeting with Sir Thadeus. Andrea Tullock had therefore already issued instructions to residence staff to prepare afternoon tea, a variety of local juices, cucumber sandwiches, scones and sweet biscuits for the occasion. They were to lay these out on the dining room table, enabling the meeting's seven participants to help themselves as necessary during their discussions.

***

Joseph Medbin entered the waiting room in a business-like manner. With a broad smile of greeting and his right arm outstretched, he welcomed the three men to Government Headquarters.

***

"Good morning, Mrs Carmichael... I thought you'd fired this place! Anyway, it's great to see you. Are you enjoying your retirement so far?" asked the security guard standing at the main entrance to Government Headquarters as he offered to help her with the package she was carrying.

"Good morning, Donald. I'm happy to see you again. I can manage – just passing through for an hour or so. We'll see you this evening?"

"Yes, Mrs Carmichael, I wouldn't miss it for the world! You have a nice day now."

"You too, Donald. How's the wife and kids?"

"Everyone's well and thanks for asking."

"Good." Carmichael started to climb the stairs to the third floor where, until two weeks ago, her office was located across from the Prime Minister's.

A minute later, she was surprised to see Medbin standing at the top of the stairs. He'd left the two British officials with Ryan Appleton and was awaiting his former boss' arrival on what used to be her old familiar stomping ground, one last time.

"Hi, Petra. I can see in your face that retirement is starting to agree with you...but yet you can't keep away from this place of madness!"

"Hello, Joe. Thanks for your compliment – if it was one! You know I shouldn't be... I really don't want to be here, but the PM and Winston wouldn't let me go until I'd signed off on the final arrangements, pre-Cabinet, for our leg of the Royal visit."

"*I know that feeling.* Let's try to get your work here done quickly so that you can return to your retirement solace and get ready for tonight."

"That would be nice."

They entered the waiting room where Appleton and the two British officials had by now sat down.

"Gentlemen, this is Mrs Carmichael..." Medbin stated.

Both British officials stood up, hands outstretched. They had communicated with Carmichael by e-mail on several occasions and had also spoken with her on the telephone, but neither had met her in person yet. She had been away on overseas Government business when they had visited Barbados six weeks earlier on their initial Royal visit recce.

"I'm delighted to meet you both at last, gentlemen. Please tell me, which one is who? I like to put names to faces," said Carmichael, shaking their hands in turn.

"Mrs Carmichael, it's my pleasure to finally meet you too. I am Major Digby Moorhouse, Private Secretary to Her Royal Highness Princess Rowen. This is Inspector Brian Swetland, Royal Protection Unit, Metropolitan Police."

"Thank you. Ryan, how are you doing today?" asked Carmichael as she turned to Appleton, giving him a hug.

"I'm fine, Petra…just wishing that when I get to retirement, I'll also receive the sort of send-off you'll experience this evening," said Appleton with a broad smile.

"Don't rush your career, young man. Your time will come," she said, returning an equally broad smile.

"Well, now that the greetings are over, let's go to the conference room and get down to business. I'm sure our missing RBPF officer will join us shortly. Can I offer any of you some refreshments…tea, coffee, juice, water?" asked Medbin.

"Nothing for me, thanks," answered Moorhouse.

"Some water would be nice please," said Swetland.

"I'm fine, Joseph," chimed in Carmichael.

"Me too," said Appleton.

Medbin picked up the phone to ask Jean Cushion to bring up the requested glass of water to the conference room for Swetland, along with Medbin's 'usual'. Jean knew that meant a cup of tea in the morning and coffee in the afternoon (milk, no sugar in each case).

Shortly thereafter, Sergeant Billy Browne, Visiting VIP Close Protection Unit (CPU), Special Branch, RBPF, joined them in the third-floor conference room. As RBPF liaison officer for the Royal visit, Browne had overseen and accompanied the British officials on their earlier and current recce visits. He had picked up both officials from their south coast hotel at 9:00 a.m. and brought them directly to Government Headquarters for this wash-up meeting. Browne and the two officers had now completed their final inspections of the locations chosen for the Royal visit programme. On arrival at Government Headquarters, he had been asked to meet briefly with the Prime Minister before he left for Parliament. Browne had therefore handed-off the two British officials to the young RBPF officer standing in the reception area with instructions to escort them to the third-floor waiting room.

"My apologies for being late –" he started to say, but Medbin cut him off.

"No apology needed, Sergeant. Your timing's good, as we're only now getting started."

"My lucky day…" responded Browne.

Medbin asked if he wanted any refreshments but he declined the offer. With the conference room's doors closed, the meeting commenced. Five minutes later, Cushion arrived with the requested items. There was a brief pause in their discussion. Cushion departed quickly so it soon resumed apace.

***

Back in Christ Church, at bang on 10:00 a.m., Colonel Burke dialled the number he had been given.

"Hello."

"Good morning. This is Colonel Burke."

"Thadeus Thomas. Thanks for calling, Colonel. I thought I should speak with you as I'm on your patch. You have a beautiful country here, sir. I wish Cindy and I had visited Barbados sooner, as we've already fallen in love with your little island! Look, I'd like to catch up with you before I meet with your fellow security Heads on Thursday afternoon at Balwin Tullock's house if you don't mind, given that we run similar agencies. How about dinner tonight, just you and me?"

"First, it's my pleasure to speak with you, Sir Thadeus. Welcome to Barbados! While I'd very much love to join you for dinner this evening, unfortunately I have a previous official engagement that I must attend. Are you and your wife available tomorrow evening? If so, my wife Diane is an excellent cook, so we'd love to have you both over for dinner at our house. I promise that you'll get a great meal and we'll be able to chat securely. The ladies could also get to know each other."

"That sounds like a great offer to me, Trevor…may I call you Trevor? We accept your dinner invitation. I'll ask Balwin to have us picked up and brought to your place…and please call me Thad. My wife's name is Cindy."

"That's good. Trevor is fine, Sir Thadeus… I mean, Thad. See you tomorrow night. Shall we say 7:00 p.m.? The High Commissioner's driver knows where I live because he brought High Commissioner Tullock to our last Christmas party."

"That works for us, Trevor. Have a great day. Looking forward to meeting you in person."

"Same here. Enjoy the rest of your day."

"We plan to. Cheerio."

As Colonel Burke replaced the receiver, he was not sure what to make of his first conversation with the Head of MI6. The man was not officious and was pleasant, friendly even. Not at all what was expected.

He swung his high-backed executive chair around to look out his window. Across the road and beyond the beach was the glistening Caribbean Sea. The few fishing boats in Oistins Bay that had been late in departing that morning gently bobbed in the blue water. Colonel Burke decided that he would break off work slightly early today and do something he had not managed to do for a couple of weeks, take a sea bath at one of his favourite south coast beaches before he and Diane attended Petra Carmichael's two-part retirement function.

Colonel Burke realised that he had not enquired whether Sir Thadeus or his wife had any special dietary restrictions or requirements. Were they vegetarians? He would ask Tullock during the day if the couple had made any. What they could not eat could then be passed on to Diane and Sherman Broome to ensure that the meal they prepared was appropriate and enjoyable.

So that he did not forget the offer he had just made Sir Thadeus, Colonel Burke called Diane on his mobile to alert her that he had just invited two English visitors to their home for dinner tomorrow evening.

"Fine. Do they have any special dietary requirements?" she asked.

"Don't know yet, but I'm working to establish that. When and what I'm told, I will pass onto you."

"Okay. Hear you later. Bye."

"Yes. See you."

Colonel Burke swivelled his chair around to face his desk. He was happy that Diane had confirmed her willingness to host and prepare a meal for Sir Thadeus and Cindy Lady Thomas tomorrow night at their Christ Church home. He then turned his mind to completing preparation for that afternoon's weekly *P.A.A.N.I.* Heads meeting.

***

It was just before 11:00 a.m. when the final arrangements for the Barbados leg of the Royal visit were finalised and signed off by the meeting's participants. The concerns of Buckingham Palace on earlier drafts of the Barbados leg of the

Royal visit programme had been shared with Major Moorhouse and Inspector Swetland prior to their return to Barbados. They had diligently articulated them beforehand and throughout their second recce visit to Government House with Browne, who had in turn shared them with other senior Barbados Government officials. This resulted in the Palace's concerns being accommodated and a tight set of final Royal visit arrangements, subject only to the Cabinet of Barbados' ratification at its next meeting in two days' time. Once approved, the Royal visit programme would become 'green lit' and in due course be embargoed before publicly being disseminated a fortnight before the Royal visit was set to commence.

Finalisation of the Barbados leg of the Royal visit programme had been the reason for Carmichael's visit to Government Headquarters that day. She had been, until her retirement, the Barbados Government official most experience at making arrangements for major VIP (including Royal) visits. Both Prime Minister Motby and Medbin knew Carmichael would be far away from Barbados on her long-planned and well-deserved retirement cruise to Alaska with her family when the Royal visit took place next month. With Motby being keen on succession planning, he had earlier directed Medbin to understudy Carmichael during the final three months of her public service career. He had gone further and directed that Carmichael record and share her extensive knowledge of making such VIP arrangements in a webinar to and for fellow senior colleagues (including Medbin) before she left Government's employ. This had been successfully done, so ensuring that as far as possible, future VIP visits to Barbados would continue to be handled appropriately with successful outcomes always being the ultimate goal.

***

Chapter Five
New Appointment

Following the Royal visit programme meeting, Petra Carmichael asked Joseph Medbin to assemble her former (now his) staff from the Prime Minister's Office for a couple of minutes. There was one last thing she wanted to say to them, a personal gift of sorts. Carmichael felt tonight's reception would be too crowded for what she wanted to share with her closest former colleagues, although she hoped they would all attend her double-event that evening.

Carmichael went to the bathroom while the staff were being assembled in the conference room that had just been vacated. On her way back, she stopped by the outer door of the Prime Minister's Office. She knew he would not be there as he seldom was at this time on Tuesdays when the House of Assembly was usually in session from 10:00 a.m. Once Prime Minister Motby was in Barbados, he would be either in his seat in the House of Assembly or in his office on that compound.

Carmichael exchanged pleasantries in turn with Sharon Evans, Elizabeth Burkett, Motby's Executive Secretary and Debra Adams, his Diary Secretary. All three of her now former colleagues appeared happy to see her. They confirmed that they would attend tonight's reception. None mentioned attendance at her church service, so Carmichael assumed they would not be there. She believed she knew why. Neither Evans or Burkett were Anglicans and she recalled that Adams had never shown or mentioned any interest in religion. Seeing them all at the reception would be good enough for Carmichael.

She believed there was no better time than now to confirm her acceptance of the UK assignment that had been offered to her by Motby, so she decided to send him a simple text.

"PM, I accept. Carmichael."

She was most surprised to receive an immediate response from Motby in the form of a telephone call.

"Hi, Petra. I'm absolutely delighted that you've accepted my offer! You'll be a great success. I'm sure the Brits will accept you. Running, so see you at 6:00."

She barely got out "Thank you, Prime Minister…" before he hung up.

Carmichael did not have a lot to say to the dozen staffers now assembled in front of her in the conference room she had now returned to.

"My friends, thank you for joining me. Let me express heartfelt thanks to you for all of the support and hard work put in over the past ten years while I was your PS. It's been a real joy…an honour, pleasure and privilege to work with you over that period. We've faced and successfully overcome many a challenge by working together. We were a team, something I hope continues under Joe."

A few of Carmichael's former colleagues nodded in agreement as she spoke. Delaney Prescod, an Executive Officer known as the joker in the pack because he was always one to make wisecracks around the Prime Minister's Office, asked the person standing next to him softly, "You mean long days, sleepless nights and weekend working won't end under Mr Joe?" to which Jessica Bean, a Clerical Officer responded, "Nope. Just more of the same."

Carmichael noticed the exchange but persevered with her comments. "There is one last thought that I'd like to share and leave with you. It's in the form of a poem, a copy of which I have for each of you. I confess to not knowing the alleged author's name for a long time. Its sentiments have repeatedly inspired me throughout my career. I pinched a copy of this poem from a colleague's notice board in our High Commission in London on my first visit there back in 1998. I hope it comes to mean as much to you as it still does to me."

Carmichael looked at the ceiling for a few seconds to retain control of her emotions before concluding.

"I wish you all the very best that life has to offer in both your career, family and personal lives. Good luck and thanks again. Hope to see you all later."

With that, Carmichael distributed copies of the poem. Some of her more observant former colleagues recalled seeing a framed version of it on her office wall throughout her tenure as their PS. They could all now read it at their leisure. Carmichael had typed it up and gone to the trouble of framing twelve copies of the poem for them.

There were a few hugs and some tears before Carmichael picked up her notepad and handbag with the intention of heading out of Government Headquarters for the last time.

"Not so fast, Petra…" said someone almost jumping her.

It was Medbin approaching. Evans was walking beside him and they were carrying a large package between them.

"This is for you. It is just a little something from all of us who have worked with you here at Government Headquarters and elsewhere across the various Ministries and Departments of Government where you've served. We hope it reminds you of what's been done together over the years," he said.

Carmichael was surprised, because she'd already been presented with what she believed was her farewell present from her colleagues on her last day in the office two weeks earlier. She was therefore unprepared for this extra gift.

Managing not to cry, but still speechless, Carmichael invited Evans to help her open the package. Everyone looked on as they did so. The gift was a framed map of Barbados, showing locations of Government Ministries and Departments where she had worked and statutory corporations that had fallen under her responsibility during her long public service career.

This is a great reminder of what we all do, day by day, hour by hour, week by week, month by month, year after year not only for ourselves, but for the near three hundred thousand Barbadians and the over one million annual visitors to our shores we serve daily, Carmichael thought.

"Wow…! Seriously folks, this is beautiful. I'm absolutely blown away. Lost for words."

Struggling to speak, she continued, "Colleagues, please know that I'll treasure this collage forever, It will take pride of place in my home because it reminds me of you and the work you do. Thanks ever so much, everyone," Carmichael concluded uncertainly.

With that, there was an outburst of applause, followed by a verse of *'for she's a jolly good lady…'* before persons started to drift back to their desks and work stations amidst promises of 'see you later'.

Carmichael asked Medbin to help her take the collage to her car. He willingly agreed. It was only after she had gone down the three flights of stairs and passed through the reception area and had waved to those looking on and standing on the steps of Government Headquarters that she felt the tears she had earlier managed to hold back start to trickle down her cheeks. She looked away, hoping Medbin would not see her crying, but it was too late. He noticed and understood.

After helping her to load the collage into the back seat of her vehicle, he gently tapped her on the shoulder saying, "Thanks for everything, Petra. Go safely and see you later."

Once in her car, she thanked Medbin for his assistance and support over the three years they had worked together. He simply nodded and tapped the top of her car as she drove away. Carmichael was conscious that she was now driving away from Government Headquarters as a former top Barbados-based public servant for the last time. She also realised that she had a new and different opportunity before her to serve Barbados from a distant place. She would work as hard at that task as she had always done.

***

In Miami, Castille visited his local barber shop for a haircut before attending the local gym. There, he made himself undergo an hour-long workout. Keeping himself in tip-top physical condition was important to him.

Back in his apartment, Castille fixed himself a quick meal. In the process, he realised that he was low on some basic items, so he made a mental note of his needs with the intention of visiting the grocery store later that afternoon. Castille never liked leaving his apartment for even a few days and returning to it without having a good selection of items from which he could prepare a tasty meal for himself.

A lengthy afternoon stretched ahead of him. How to kill some hours before his late-evening meeting with the Head of *The Organisation*? Castille decided to spend some time reviewing his plan to quickly recover an outstanding sum of money owed to *The Organisation* from another one of its few but delinquent Caribbean clients located closer to the US. He anticipated completing that task (including any necessary 'clean-up' work) within two days. Post-Barbados, of course.

His review completed, there was still more than enough time for him to grab a late-afternoon nap before his visit to the grocery store. The late-evening appointment with *The Organisation's* Head should not last too long.

***

Promptly at 2:00 p.m., *P.A.A.N.I.'s* meeting commenced at its customary venue, BIB HQ in Christ Church. *P.A.A.N.I. (Police, Army, Air Force, Navy, Intelligence)* is Barbados' four-pronged security entity which oversees all national security matters, incidents and necessary investigations that take place in Barbados and in its coastal waters. *P.A.A.N.I.* met at least once a week, normally on Tuesday afternoons. Written reports on conclusions reached at the end of its weekly meetings were provided to Barbados' Head of Government within twenty-four hours.

P.A.A.N.I.'s size had been increased from its original three-member agencies (RBPF, BDF, BIB) to four, following the May 2016 general election with the addition of the Barbados Prison Service (BPS) which has responsibility for Her Majesty's Prison (HMP) Dodds. *P.A.A.N.I.*'s mandate remains to keep on top of Barbados' security situation through a minimum of once-a-week 'in-person' meetings (rather than the weekly teleconferences the agencies originally held). In exceptional circumstances where in-person meetings are neither practical nor possible, a preferably video, if not a teleconference would be arranged. Though all four Heads were busy running important law enforcement/security agencies this new, stepped-up and best-practice system put in place by Motby seemed appropriate after the earlier assassination attempt on his life.

P.A.A.N.I.'s usual participants were: Commissioner Jeremie, RBPF; Chief of Staff Brigadier Tenton, BDF; Superintendent Innis, Head, BPS/Superintendent of HMP Dodds; and Colonel Burke, Director, BIB. With Barbados having no full-fledged Air Force or Navy, its small air-wing unit, comprised of two C26 surveillance aircraft and Coast Guard unit made up of five motorised vessels, both air and sea units operated under and reported to Tenton. He was careful to leave the day-to-day running of these units to Captain George Collins and Commander Edward 'Ted' Madley respectively. Tenton held twice weekly (Tuesday and Friday morning) videoconference meetings with Collins and Madley to ensure he was kept up-to-speed with what both units were doing.

***

DON'T QUIT [Edward A. Guest: 1881–1959]

When things go wrong, as they sometimes will; When the road you're trudging seems all uphill; When the funds are low and debts are high and you want to smile, but have to sigh; When care is pressing you down a bit – Rest if you must...but don't you quit. Life is queer with its twists and turns, as everyone of us sometimes learn. And many a failure turns about when they might have won had they stuck it out. Don't give up, though the pace seems slow –you might succeed with another blow. Often the goal is nearer than it seems to a faint and faltering individual; Often the struggler has given up, when they might have captured the victor's cup. And they learned too late when the night had slipped down, how close they were to the golden crown. Success is failure turned inside out – the silver tint of clouds of doubt, and you never can tell how close you are. It may be near when it seems afar. So, stick to the fight when you are hardest hit. It's when things seem worst that you MUST NOT QUIT.

Evans had been kept busy throughout the morning, so it was not until mid-afternoon that she got to read Carmichael's literary gift over a late sandwich lunch, with a strong cup of coffee for good measure. She read the poem three times before understanding what Carmichael was saying to her former colleagues. DON'T QUIT was too simple. Most likely, Carmichael was telling them to *Just **DO** (N'T QU) **IT!***

Evans read the poem a fourth time, even more slowly. She became convinced that this was Carmichael's subliminal message. *Just Do It* – your job as a public servant: help Barbadians and visitors alike.

***

P.A.A.N.I.'s meeting was chaired by Colonel Burke. Jeremie and Tenton came up from their respective central Bridgetown RBPF and BDF HQs, while Innis came down from his BPS HQ at HMP Dodds in St Phillip.

The agenda for today's meeting was a short one. Nothing of great significance had changed on Barbados' security front from the previous week's *P.A.A.N.I.* meeting. Their approved plans for the week ahead now only needed their formal sign-off, having been carefully examined for any holes a week before. The nine-day extra cricket cover (ECC) security screen project, set to run from Tuesday night, 17 April to Wednesday morning, 25 April, would start with the England and West Indies cricket teams' arrival tonight ahead of the second Test Match being played at New Kensington Oval. The five-day game was scheduled to start on Friday, 20 April and end on Tuesday, 24 April. The security arrangements around the team's movements in Barbados had only been completed after extensive discussions between the England and Wales and West Indies Cricket Boards and the RBPF.

Last week's *P.A.A.N.I.* meeting had been a long one. Only minor last-minute tinkering with the ECC plan was needed. Thankfully, these were quickly dealt with. The carefully made plans by senior officers within the Heads' agencies were therefore signed off as being feasible, practical, applicable and appropriate. The ECC security screen project had passed *P.A.A.N.I.* Heads' stringent operational acid tests.

BIB's operational team leaders were James 'JJ' Johnson (code number P3) from Gold team, Alfred 'Fred' George (code number E5) of Blue team, and Kylie 'Joe' Callendar (code number S11) of Black team.

Beyond the ECC security screen project's arrangements, three other major public events were scheduled for the coming week and so these also formed part of the discussion. Minor adjustments were made to the first two before they were approved by the Heads. These events were to be a friendly international soccer match between Barbados and the USA at the National Stadium on Saturday night (21 April), and a concert by a top Canadian performer at the refurbished Garfield Sobers Sports Complex on Sunday night (22 April). The changes made to earlier plans were around the total number of island constables to be deployed at each event being increased from eight to twelve to augment the allocated compliment of RBPF officers and BDF soldiers already assigned to oversee these events.

No changes were made to the third public event – arrangements for a two-day Commonwealth Sports Minister's conference being hosted at Hilton Barbados Resort by the Government of Barbados on Tuesday (24 April) and Wednesday (25 April). Hon. Preston Grant MP, Minister of Tourism, International Transport and Sport would host a reception at the Hilton on Monday evening (23 April), but the hotel's experienced security team, supported by RBPF's Visitor CPU and a small contingent of regular RBPF officers, would run that event easily. They had handled a hemispheric Health Minister's meeting the previous October at the same venue without a hitch.

With *P.A.A.N.I.* Heads contented, their meeting ended in under an hour. Details of the final approved security arrangements for all of the upcoming events would be circulated later that afternoon by Jeremie as his RBPF was the designated lead agency for each event, enabling all relevant public and private sector entities involved and responsible for executing various aspects of the events, to kick into high gear. Emergency back-up plans for the ECC security screen project and three other public events were also signed off just in case something went drastically wrong, which called for additional security measures implementation. Jeremie, like his fellow Heads, hoped that none of their back-up plans would be needed over the nine days.

***

The *P.A.A.N.I.* meeting did not discuss the BPS or HMP Dodds' weekly prison run (PR) which enabled prisoners to have their day in court. Colonel Burke was aware that, for the following day's PR, BIB's Gold team would participate. Innis brought up no concerns about his BPS agency and so the four Heads had nothing further to consider.

In less than twenty-four hours, this would prove, with hindsight, to have been a big mistake.

Thursday afternoon's forthcoming meeting with the visiting British security official was also not on the *P.A.A.N.I.'s* agenda, so was not mentioned during the Heads' meeting. The Thursday session was to be a special stand-alone one, unprecedented in fact, as it was set to include Commander Junior Samuel, the Barbados-based Coordinator of the Regional Security System (RSS). Barbados and the six-member Organisation of Eastern Caribbean States (OECS) had set up the RSS as a collaborative response mechanism to help ensure state stability, emergency security and responses to national disasters over three decades ago, but the RSS had never been asked to join such a meeting before.

"Thanks for coming by, guys. See you later at Petra's double-farewell do?" asked Colonel Burke of his three colleagues who he knew Carmichael had invited. They all confirmed their attendance at the events. She had been good to all of the *P.A.A.N.I.* Heads and their agencies at various times during her tenure as Permanent Secretary in the Prime Minister's Office.

***

Once his fellow Heads had departed, Colonel Burke started to draft his weekly *P.A.A.N.I.* security brief. As he was attending Carmichael's double-function that evening, he wanted to finalise and submit his brief to Motby early the following morning from his office. As usual, Colonel Burke anticipated having to answer a few questions from Motby ahead of Thursday's weekly Cabinet meeting. The secure phone call normally came to him at BIB HQ around 3:30 p.m. each Wednesday afternoon.

Unknown to both men, the coming Wednesday afternoon conversation would be unlike any other they'd had before. In fact, it would be the first of several conversations they would need to have over the coming week. As for *P.A.A.N.I.* Heads, they could not have known that by late Thursday, all that they had carefully planned for and signed off on would have been turned upside-down.

***

Superintendent Innis returned quickly to HMP Dodds, Barbados' sole adult custodial facility. Having responsibility for this facility, he needed to do two things before he headed home for a shower, change of clothing and could set off to attend Petra Carmichael's double-retirement function. He would enjoy some of the excellent food that was sure to be available from BDF HQ at her farewell reception. A couple of stiff drinks would also help to wash away what had been a long day. Innis was also looking forward to his spouse joining him at the reception once her 10:00 a.m. to 6:00 p.m. shift had ended at a private south coast health clinic where she was the facility's administrator.

First, Innis wanted to visit the specially equipped, temporary ten-cell facility that had been prepared for catchments, e.g. pick-pockets, shoplifters, ticket touts, drug sellers, and prostitutes) who would undoubtedly make themselves known to law enforcement and security agency personnel during the Test Match (part of the ECC security screen project) and around the soccer game and pop concert. The facility he viewed looked fine and so he returned to his office to undertake the second task he'd set himself to do.

The PR exercise between HMP Dodds in St Philip and the various courts around Barbados normally went off smoothly and without a hitch. Tomorrow's PR was slightly unusual in that all the inmates being transported to and from HMP Dodds were set to appear at District 'A' court in Station Hill, St Michael, just outside of Bridgetown. Innis' goal remained, as ever, to operate the prison facility as simply and efficiently and effectively as was possible.

There was a slight complication about tomorrow's PR in that only one of HMP Dodds' three prisoner transport vehicles were working. This was the case operational-wise, going into a second week. It hampered his ability to run the tight ship he'd always strived to operate and was expected to be successful at doing by those who employed him. He had not mentioned the specific challenges that he was having to his fellow *P.A.A.N.I.* Heads at their meeting that afternoon. Yes, he had considered doing so, but felt his colleagues might find his concerns a distraction as they were focussed on the more immediate, extensive ECC secure screen project and other related arrangements instituted for this and the other public-facing events including the two-day Commonwealth Sports Minister's conference which were all more important than his internal challenges. His resource issues, specifically the lack of sufficient functional prisoner transport equipment, were not 'sexy' enough topics for discussion at today's *P.A.A.N.I.* meeting. He had said nothing, anticipating that his management team and staff would be able to muddle through and deal with the problem for another week or so until at least one of the broken prisoner transport vehicles would be back in use. Shouting his need from the rooftops would be a last resort.

***

Over in Miami, Castille's afternoon was taking shape. He was relaxed and felt comfortable about the Barbados project he had initiated and planned to see through over the next few days.

***

After reviewing tomorrow's PR activity, Innis saved an e-version of his approved PR document in HMP Dodds' electronic filing system. He then called in his secretary Melba Bodie, before printing off and handed her a signed hard copy of the PR document for filing. He knew that she would pass the document to George Telford, the Deputy Prison Superintendent who sat in the office next to her. Telford's job was to complete the second part of the PR exercise.

Though BIB and RBPF were each to provide a three-person team of officers to escort the PR from start to finish, neither team would be told what the route was to be for the next day's exercise until they arrived at HMP Dodds on the morning of the PR to receive their briefings.

On the way to his vehicle, Innis decided that he would share his concerns regarding the HMP Dodds prisoner transport situation with BIB's three-member Gold team when he briefed them on their arrival on the following morning. He knew James 'JJ' Johnson well and felt JJ would understand and even be sympathetic to his situation. Innis also decided to place HMP Dodds operations as an agenda item for next week's *P.A.A.N.I.* meeting. He felt he would be able to secure the full support of his fellow *P.A.A.N.I.* Heads once they knew what the HMP Dodds situation was. Word would then quickly reach Motby's ears through the weekly *P.A.A.N.I.* brief submitted by Colonel Burke. Motby would surely ask direct questions and probably make HMP Dodds an urgent issue to be discussed at the next Cabinet meeting. Who knows where such a discussion could lead to? Might he, or rather HMP Dodds get what they needed? Innis hoped that some short-circuiting of the funding jam could be done, resulting in resolution of some of the issues at HMP Dodds to positively impact its day-to-day operations.

Yes, that's the way to deal with my problem, he thought to himself.

Once in his vehicle, Innis commenced the process of exiting the HMP Dodds' compound. He expected to be back by 7:30 a.m. the next morning as usual, unless something unusual happened overnight on the compound that demanded his earlier return. The three things that would cause this, a mass prisoner uprising, escape or a major fire were not at all likely.

***

Unfortunately for Innis, his reasoning was off. He would later regret not sharing his HMP Dodds concerns with his fellow *P.A.A.N.I.* Heads.

***

George Telford examined the PR document Melba Bodie had passed to him for action. He checked to see which BPS officers were on duty from 7:00 a.m. the next morning, before selecting the five he would allocate to PR duty. Telford took a moment before also signing off the PR document and returning it to Bodie. She in turn checked to confirm that Telford had selected the correct number of

BPS officers required for the PR and that he'd also signed off on the document as was required. As he had done so, Bodie proceeded to file away the signed hard-copy of the PR document for 18 April in HMP Dodds' secure, combination-locked and fire-proof cabinets. Telford's action confirmed that tomorrow's PR should take place and was signed evidence that the PR would be undertaken. This document would subsequently become important.

Bodie gathered up her personal belongings, locked her office and wished Telford goodnight before started the process of leaving the HMP Dodds compound. On her way to her vehicle, Telford joined her. He, like her, was on the same mission of escaping from their highly-secured place of work. It was time to see someplace other than high walls, barbed wire, electric gates, electronic security systems and the like. ·

Well, at least for the next fifteen hours.

***

Dr Albert Lewis left the Dawson Clinic in a daze, to put it mildly. He was thinking… *How am I going to tell my wife Betty and our two children what I've just learnt from Dr Dawson? Where the hell should I even begin?*

Dr Lewis had not been feeling well for a week. Over the weekend, he had started to feel increasingly weak. His wife had urged him to go to a doctor and he had done so on his own. As a part of his overall examination, blood was taken from him for analysis, given his symptoms of weakness, high temperature and irregular near constant bowel movements. Dr Dawson asked him to return for the test results in a couple of days. Dr Lewis had returned home, taken the prescribed medication before going to his bed. After a couple of restful nights and feeling much better on Monday morning, he had decided to go into work where he somehow managed to get through the day. Surprisingly, he had a third restful night and so had decided to go into work again on Tuesday. This proved to be a much more difficult day. By mid-afternoon, he was struggling so badly that he soon left his workplace, telling his secretary that he was going back to the doctor to have his condition checked out. He would also collect his blood test results.

What Dr Dawson told him was unpleasant to learn. In his panicked state, might he have misinterpreted what had just been conveyed to him, the gravity of it? How he was feeling made him think not.

Oh God!

Dr Lewis sat in his car for a while, unsure at first of what he should do, before deciding that he would not go home, at least not straight away. Taking a drive up the west coast along Highway 1 would give him some thinking time before he could have a drink or two. Yes, he had taken medication, but it had not made him drowsy so what the hell, he could do these things. He had to have a serious conversation with himself before the subsequent and dreaded one at home with his wife and later their children. Both conversations were going to be rough and hurtful, especially the former since they had been together from their initial meeting in their first year at university a long, long time ago.

Dr Lewis usually reached home around 8:30 p.m. most week-nights, so getting home a little later would not raise any suspicion.

What a crummy day for me…what a nice afternoon for everyone else, he thought. Dr Lewis' brief internet research from a couple of days earlier had suggested what the problem with him might be given his symptoms, but hearing Dr Dawson's comments after gaining knowledge of his test results was somewhat surreal.

Not good. God, not that.

***

Unknown to Innis, shortly after his departure, but before Telford and Bodie left the HMP Dodds compound, a personal mobile phone had been used to capture and transmit an unsanctioned copy of Wednesday's approved PR document. This information, though never acknowledged by its recipient, was appreciated. This was the final confirmation required by Wharton's Pressure Group. It ensured that the plan could be executed the following day, Wednesday, 18 April now that they had a route. Last-minute adjustments to the plan would be made at a meeting later that night.

***

Dr Lewis started his vehicle, pointing it away from the direction of his St George home and towards the west coast parishes of St James and St Peter via central Bridgetown. He knew the exact place where he could think and plan his explanation to his wife while sitting in either his vehicle or on a bench looking out to sea. Since his return to Barbados from Washington DC, he had discovered this location and found it to be a good place to visit whenever he needed to think deeply and alone on an issue. He loved the experience of seeing the sun set on an evening from this spot. The words he would say to her would come there. Hopefully they would be from his heart, although he did not expect her to take his news calmly or compassionately.

Then it hit him. Why tell her anything? Not tonight anyway. He pulled his vehicle over to the side of the road, cut the engine and contemplated what this latest thought meant. Tell the truth or lie? No, he could not do so after all of these years.

Pulling back into traffic, he continued on to his intended location where he would seek to find answers to his current plight.

***

It was the end of another busy work day in Barbados. Office workers wearily trekked towards the nearby public and private transportation hubs on their way home. Some school children were belatedly doing likewise after having attended additional lessons or participated in after-school sports programmes. Older youths were also on the move, making their way to the various evening class institutions around St Michael including the University of the West Indies (UWI) Campus at Cave Hill.

What appeared to be a chance meeting at 5:00 p.m. in Independence Square, central Bridgetown went almost unnoticed. Three individuals appeared to be but were not tourists. One was a male Mexican in his late-forties, another a blond female American in her mid-thirties. The third was a black British woman in her early-thirties. Jose Jesus Sanchez, Amarouse Busbee and Zoe Markowitz had carefully and deliberately chosen this very public venue for their rendezvous.

These three individuals mixed in with local Barbadians and a visiting Canadian group was also there. Its members were in the process of capturing images of central Bridgetown: the imposing eleven-storey Tom Adams Financial Centre, picturesque Parliament Buildings, Chamberlain Bridge (once known as the Swing Bridge), Charles Duncan O'Neal Bridge, Fairchild Street Bus Stand, four-storeyed Treasury Building and the Careenage.

Sanchez, Busbee and Markowitz, casually dressed, were otherwise undisguisable when they had entered Independence Square from different directions. They had surveyed the Square prior to approaching each other before finally converging around the statue of Barbados' first Prime Minister and National Hero, the Rt. Excellent Errol Walton Barrow, known locally as the 'Father of Independence'. With visitor materials in hand, cameras strung around their necks and shoulders, they pointed fingers in different directions and appeared to naturally strike up a genuine, spur-of-the-moment conversation which went on for about five minutes.

The average Barbadian, even if they were closely watching these three individuals, might only have surmised that this was a genuine meeting between visitors to Barbados from different countries who had an interest in exploring elements of central Bridgetown. This meeting was surely pure coincidence.

Nothing could be further from the truth.

For here, in living colour, in real time and very much out in the open, international espionage was being practiced in its simplest, rawest, yet purest and at the same time cleverest form. Information exchanges between country operatives take place nowadays in the most obvious and public everyday places.

Like Independence Square in central Bridgetown.

What the three individuals were really speaking about to each other amongst the other genuine visitors would remain unknown to local law enforcement and security agencies for another seventy-two hours.

***

Just after 5:30 p.m., Angela Johnson answered the land line in the Johnson household in Christ Church.

"Hello, Johnson residence."

"Hi, Angela, Uncle Fred here. How are you doing today, young lady?"

"Pretty good, Uncle Fred. How you doing?"

"I'm great just for having had the pleasure of speaking with you. Is your dad around please?"

"Yep. He's in his music room surrounded by all that musical stuff, you know what I mean? Records, CD's, cassette tapes and more, all in final preparing for his show tonight. Guess you want to speak to him?"

"Yes please, Angela."

"Okay hang on. I'll get him for you…and bye, Uncle Fred."

"Thanks. We'll talk again soon, young lady," replied Fred.

Fred heard her move away, shouting, "Daddy, Uncle Fred's on the phone for you."

"Please bring me the extension, dear," said JJ.

"Coming, Dad."

A full minute passed.

"Hi there, Fred, sorry about that… I'm working on finishing up a couple of new mixes for my set tonight. What can I do for you? You know, you really must stop interrupting a professional when he's creating! And hey, why didn't you call me on my mobile?" asked JJ.

"Mine's not close to hand, so I used this, okay? Look, I've been hearing you talk about and sing along to your back in time stuff ever since I joined BIB. We coming down tonight to support you, that is Charlee, Joe, Stef and me. Our foursome will keep you company at the club for a few hours if no other patrons show up, so you'll have an audience to play for. No seriously, we wanted to let you know beforehand that we're coming down…wouldn't want to put you off your game when you look up from your toys and see us four staring right back at you," said Fred to end his monologue.

"Oh man, that's great! You won't be the only people in the house, I can assure you. You lot could never put me off my game as my stuff's pretty much ingrained in me. I may be new to DJing in public, but don't forget that I've been playing music to myself and for friends and my family for donkey years. I'll be there before 7:45 p.m. to start playing at 8:00 p.m. when the club opens. I'll be running things till midnight when the Resident DJ will take over till 3:00 a.m."

"JJ, you've really taken this DJing thing seriously, haven't you? Word of advice, don't give up your day job for it though because we in BIB can't do without you. Yeah, we know you've got the '70s' to '90s' music stuff down pat, so we expect you'll do okay. Sorry it's taken us three weeks to come down to hear and see you in action, but you know how our work goes…and what Charlee gives! Can't speak for why Joe and Stef haven't been to the club yet. I must go. Expect to see us by 10:00 p.m. Bye for now."

"See you all later, Fred, and thanks for calling. You lucky guys have tomorrow and Thursday off to relax, so go easy on the booze tonight, won't cha?"

"You know me, boss."

The three individuals who had masqueraded as visitors had forgotten one thing. Eighteen months earlier, the re-elected B.U.P. government had implemented its increased security (IS) policy in the country by systematically installing close circuit television (CCTV) cameras. These were centred in and around Barbados' main cities, built-up areas, main ports of entry and on major roadways. The specific locations were Greater Bridgetown, Speightstown, Holetown, Oistins, St Lawrence Gap, Warrens, Six Roads, Grantley Adams International Airport, Bridgetown Port and major intersections of the cross-country ABC highway and two main highways on the south and west coasts. All Government buildings and major landmarks around the above areas were also covered by CCTV cameras. In addition, CCTV security systems were increasingly being used by businesses.

In the manifesto, the third-term government had promised to increase the use of CCTV cameras around the country as a tool to significantly reduce crime. The above areas were chosen because of the high density of human and road traffic revolving within and around them. The government's actions had proven correct, with increased subsequent captures resulting in successful prosecutions of a host of petty criminals (muggers, bag snatchers, pickpockets) being caught red-handed, along with traffic offenders. This led to drastic reductions in petty and motoring crime overall. Barbados had become an even safer place for locals and visitors alike to live, work, visit relax and move around in.

BIB's ability to gain access to images captured by the various CCTV cameras had proved invaluable in helping the two information and communications technology (ICT) operatives who worked in the agency's secure intelligence room (SIR) to solve recent cases. The CCTV cameras overlooking Independence Square captured the three individuals (and a fourth individual) who all proved to be of subsequent interest to BIB operatives. Though the fourth individual did not link up with the other three who had carefully assembled, he easily stood out and drew attention to himself by his unusual height for a Chinese national. He appeared to be in his early-fifties.

Why were these four non-nationals in Independence Square, at the same time? What, if any, would be their roles in the situations that were soon set to start unfolding in Barbados over the next few days?

***

Alfred 'Fred' George, BIB team leader, ended his call with JJ. As a senior two-Dan Back Belt Sensei at Marine Garden Judo Club in Hastings, Christ Church, he was scheduled to take tonight's senior class between 7:00 p.m. and 8:30 p.m. Within his class were two excellent prospects who were clear potential candidates to qualify for and represent Barbados at the 2020 Olympic Games in Tokyo, Japan. Fred had started to spend an extra half an hour working with these two judokas after each Tuesday night session from the start of the year, his BIB work permitting, of course. Tonight's extra session would certainly take place as he had the next couple of days off. He knew of the ECC project arrangements that were in place for the five-day Test Match set to start in three days' time would prohibit him from taking his class on Saturday morning, so he had arranged for another sensei to cover it for him.

Now aged thirty-four, Fred was a Barbadian-born ex-British paratrooper. Besides judo, Fred had a passion for baking. A BIB operative now for six years, he had previously spent one year with the BDF's Special Task Force unit. Once known as a lady's man, he was now a one-woman man. Since he had first set eyes on Charlotte 'Charlee' Piggott at Queen Elizabeth Hospital (QEH) on the night of Motby's attempted assassination, he had fallen for her. There was a rumour around BIB that Charlee had *tamed* Fred's wild ways. He now professed to being monogamous, something only he knew for sure, for he still admired attractive women, though only from a distance, especially when Charlee was around.

Charlee was someone Fred could consistently call and rely on. Her presence was reassuring to him. Not a big music lover by any stretch, but he had gradually and grudgingly come around to accepting the kind of music she loved. His propensity to gamble on local race horses had also diminished under Charlee's influence, given that she considered it a waste of money.

Fred's visits to BIB's gym were now four days a week, down from six pre-Charlee. He used these visits to keep himself in excellent physical condition. Tonight, after his judo session but before they went to P's Disco, Fred would present the small box now in his pocket to Charlee. Hopefully, on opening the box and seeing what was inside of it, she would say one word, 'Yes'. He might even go down on one knee to pop the question on this special occasion.

***

James 'JJ' Johnson reflected on his conversation with Fred, one of his two fellow team leaders after he had hung up. *Yes, I know you. Don't get too sossled. Charlee better be your designated driver.*

JJ had become known throughout BIB as the boss since his strong, incisive but inclusive leadership style had come to the fore some eighteen months earlier when he had led the investigation into the attempted assassination of the Prime Minister.

Shortly after that incident, JJ found himself seeking a form of relaxation outside of BIB and family life activities. It took him a while, but eventually he found what he was looking for. He accepted a long-standing offer from Pierre 'Double P' Pilgrim, a friend from schooldays to DJ in Pilgrim's nightclub, P's Disco. JJ's long-time hobby of playing music to himself at home had at last found a public outlet. The arrangement was that JJ would play two four-hour sets per week, on Monday and Tuesday nights. Though the agreement had been signed six weeks earlier, JJ had only started DJing at P's Disco three weeks ago, with tonight being his sixth four-hour show. The music which JJ played at P's Disco was that which he loved and played at home. Timeless vibes (from upbeat dance tracks to mellow jams), where words meant something and excellent musicianship were the order of the day and what he appreciated. Music primarily from the '70s through to the '90s relaxed and made him feel good. JJ wanted P's Disco patrons to experience what he felt, forget their worries and enjoy themselves at his shows.

JJ retuned his mind to completing his preparations for tonight's show. His audience would be the pre-midnight crowd who came to P's Disco to relax, enjoy a meal and a drink while listening to his mix of back in time (BIT) R&B, Disco, Soul, Funk, Hip Hop, Reggae, Smooth Jazz and famed Calypso/Soca tunes. Most patrons hit the dance floor at some point during their stay but tended to leave P's Disco anywhere between 11:30 p.m. and midnight when the club's younger patrons would start to arrive. This suited JJ who would normally return to his Christ Church home by 12:30 a.m.

***

Despite it being well past their normal working hours, the four individuals had returned to their respective offices to record what had just transpired at their central Bridgetown rendezvous. Their collaboration had resulted on a consensus of what activities the six-known major, locally-based criminal entities had been recently pursuing. They had also collected specific views, based on findings from their lines of work, on what local criminals' activities were in the pipeline and so might occur.

It all made sense. One thing was clear. Criminal entities were upping their game. Indications were that they were developing new and possibly extensive links with international criminal syndicates. What this would lead to was unclear, but an alarming trend had been identified which concerned the four individuals. Their afternoon meeting had confirmed that there were no perceived imminent threats or last-minute updates to the preliminary position they had reached at the previous weekend meeting at their American colleague's residence. All that now remained for the four individuals to do was to formally sign-off on and dispatch their reports to their respective headquarters in overseas capitals.

As for the security activities that were being put in place by local law enforcement agencies to cover the public activities that were set to take place in Barbados over the next nine days, they believed that things were under control. The ECC security screen project for sure, was well thought out and resourced, as local law enforcement and security agencies had ensured that all potentially appropriate response mechanisms were in place to deal with any imaginable situation at any of the announced public events. As a result, their input had not been necessary, although they had been briefed on the main points related to the ECC. Nothing unusual was anticipated to affect the soccer match, concert or Sports Ministers Conference. However, should any requests be received from the Barbados authorities for assistance, their response would be a joint, rapid and collective one. Yes, each mission had its standard and potential 'off the shelf' response mechanism, but these could be easily adapted if situations warranted. Collaboration between them was taken for granted, so first thing tomorrow (Wednesday), each of them would separately review their standard security response mechanisms to be ready, just in case unexpected trouble arose.

Barbados had retained an overall low security threat level, despite the earlier attempt to assassinate Motby and so the diplomatic missions the four individuals belonged to remained confident that there would be no need for them to have to collaborate over the next nine days. No sudden spike in local criminal activity was anticipated and their 'ear to the ground' investigations had not suggested there were any plans to attempt an overthrow of the Barbados Government, nor harm locals or visitors alike over this period.

***

Chapter Six

Night Moves

Having reached his destination, Dr Lewis spent the time he had promised to himself, thinking and endeavouring to find an immediate solution to his problem.

After sitting on the bench for some time, he returned to his car. There, he retrieved his locked briefcase from the boot of the car and placed it in the front seat beside him. Unlocking it, he felt inside and found what he knew was there under his papers. *Why not end everything, right here and now on this beautiful evening? I'd save myself a lot of embarrassment*, he thought. Dr Lewis gripped and withdrew the firearm from his briefcase. He examined it, knowing from the weapon's weight that it was loaded. *Should I or shouldn't I,* he wondered to himself as he caressed the barrel.

After a couple of minutes, he stopped his action, ashamed of what he was considering.

He realised that he lacked the courage to do harm to himself. Suicide was not his thing, even under current circumstances. *I don't deserve such an end. My kids might understand, eventually but Betty never would. I can't do this to her, the kids or the Bank. I can't shed further shame on them because of what I have. I want the chance to contribute to this world and help make it a better place than when I entered it before I go*. These thoughts and realisation dragged Dr Lewis from his emotional imbalance and suicidal thinking. Treatment for what his test results indicated was available. He could afford the best treatment and receive it for as long as it took. Hs effort would be treated confidentially and that would buy him some time. Honesty might yet save his marriage, his family, his job and himself.

Carefully, he unloaded the firearm. No need to shoot himself by accident. He exited his vehicle and looked around. There was no one in sight, that he could see, so he quickly dug a hole in the sand and dropped the bullets in it before covering up the hole. On his return to his vehicle, he returned the firearm to his briefcase, locked it and returned it to the boot. *Look how close I came to killing myself*, he thought. He turned on the engine to leave but suddenly broke down, sobbing gently at first with trembling hands, before crying more audibly with his head in both hands.

It took him a while to gather himself and start thinking clearly. Thankfully, he had not found the courage to go through with the action that had briefly appealed to him. He also felt exhausted.

He recalled a Bajan phrase he had heard last week from a Central Bank of Barbados colleague along the lines of 'dead men can't run from their coffins', meaning that it is impossible to run away from one's responsibilities, or destination.

Dr Lewis could not run away from his now.

***

The magnificent sounds of the Cathedral Church of St Michael and All Angels' organ in the near two-hundred and fifty-year-old building on St Michael's Row in central Bridgetown was a sound to hearken. The accomplished organist and musical director of an experienced choir were on parade, so to speak. They were about to sing for one of their own, before a congregation comprised of distinguished persons in Barbados who would appreciate their efforts.

The 6:00 p.m. Service of Thanksgiving for Petra Carmichael's three and a half decades of public service to Barbados was scheduled to last no more than ninety minutes. The service was put together by Carmichael and the Very Reverend Dr Boyd Mercer, Dean and Rector of the Cathedral Church where she had previously served for many years as Sunday School Superintendent and, for the past ten years, as an eucharistic minister. Carmichael had been a member of the Cathedral since childhood. Her move to the north of the island following her marriage had not stopped her from continuing to worship and serve at her beloved Cathedral. The congregation had been invited to join her on this special night and a good crowd had turned out, along with most of the seventy-five specially invited guests. Carmichael's former work colleagues present included the Governor General and his wife, Prime Minister and his wife, Chief Justice, most Cabinet ministers, some members of both Houses of Parliament, senior Government officials, members of the judiciary, family and some of her closest friends.

The Service of Thanksgiving was beautiful. The choir sung lustily and well, delivering a special anthem of the Lord's Prayer. Hymns and Bible readings were celebration-themed, as was the Sermon delivered by Dean Mercer. He held up his end of the bargain by preaching for only fifteen minutes. It was clear that he wanted to go on longer, but there might have been consequences in doing so. This enabled Carmichael's specially invited guests to be able to get away from the Cathedral by 7:40 p.m. The short drive to BDF HQ enabled the second part of her Prime Minister-hosted retirement function to commence at 7:55 p.m. after parking, an acceptable scenario given all that was happening that evening.

***

It was just near to the end of Carmichael's Service of Thanksgiving that Dr Lewis awoke. He had fallen asleep and had only been awoken by a knocking on his car-window by a concerned young man who was walking home from his job as a waiter at a local hotel. It was dark now, which meant that he had missed seeing the sunset off the west coast that he'd badly wanted to view earlier.

Winding down his window, he thanked the young man.

"Time to go and face the music," he said to himself before realising that he was very hungry. This hunger could not wait the forty minutes it would take him to get home. He remembered a nice place where he could grab something to eat before heading home.

***

P's Disco opened its doors promptly at 8:00 p.m. Located on the famous St Lawrence Gap, Christ Church entertainment strip, JJ got to work on his DJing duties for the evening. He initiated his eight thru twelve (ETT) show by introducing himself over his signature tune. P's Disco staff and the early patrons who had entered the club at opening time were his audience.

JJ had searched long and hard for what he felt was the 'right' signature track for his four-hour show on Monday and Tuesday nights. The criteria for his choice were that it had to be joyous, up-tempo, exciting and funky. He wanted the chosen track to demonstrate the BIT era of music he loved and musicianship, something audiences do not always appreciate in the second decade of the twenty-first century. Ideally, he wanted his selection to be an instrumental so that he could use it as a backdrop when relating to patrons during the show.

JJ shortlisted George Duke *Brazilian Love Affair*. While he felt this was a great song, it did not quite have the groovy feeling he wanted, no disrespect to the late brother George. JJ also considered Mezzoforte *Garden Party* among other tracks when he had a lightbulb moment!

Sharon Redd *Can You Handle It*! Perfect. The near-instrumental specially remixed version. JJ had played it three times to be sure some three weeks earlier and found it had everything he wanted. Solid enthusiastic drumming, strikingly funky guitars, a simple but driving bassline, riveting brass (sax) sounds, groovy piano solo and an exciting orchestra overlay. It was a classic floor-filler, especially when Sharon's sultry voice kicked in late on, mischievously asking, "*Can you handle…it?*" Simple, suggestive, sexy. JJ's signature track simply kicked ass and was suitable for his BIT audiences. *They must be able to handle my groovy musical selections*, he thought.

In Hour 1, JJ sought to create 'the mood' he wanted to sustain. Known as H1C (the 'chillin' hour), he played some of his favourite and smooth jazz, funk, instrumentals and mellow cuts until 8:45 p.m. Tonight, tracks featured would be Shiva *Never Gonna Give You Up*, Donald Byrd *Love Has Come Around*, Sun Palace *Rude Movements*, Sea Level *Sneakers*, Fourplay *101 Eastbound*, Sumy *Funkin' In Your Mind*, Surface Noise *The Scratch*, The Crusaders *Put It Where You Want It*, Chicago *Street Player*, Steely Dan *Hey Nineteen*, The Isley Brothers *Here We Go Again*, One Way *Shine on Me*, People's Choice *Do It Anyway You Wanna*.

***

Around 8:15 p.m., a middle-aged man entered P's Disco and sat himself down at a corner table in the dining section.

Zelda Hughes, a young waitress approached him to take his order, thinking *first dinner customer for the night. Wonder if he'll tip me.*

"No. 7 on your menu please Miss, that's the steak fish and chips with a side order of salad and a rum and coke."

"Any particular rum, sir?" asked Hughes.

"Cockspur," the man replied.

"Okay. Ten minutes to delivery of your meal. I'll be right back with your drink," stated Hughes.

"Fine, and thank you, miss," was the man's response.

Looks like he had a long or bad day at work. Probably no big tip coming my way, she thought.

***

Caribbean Airlines flight BW 415 arrived from Kingston, Jamaica carrying the West Indies and England cricket teams, their support staff, local, regional and international media. On disembarkation, both teams and their support staff were led to the Grace Lady Adams Suite (a.k.a. the VIP lounge) by airport security officers. There, the Hon. Preston Grant MP, Minister of Tourism, International Transport & Sport, Neal Butler, President of the Barbados Cricket Association (BCA) who was also a Director of the West Indies Cricket Board (WICB) and Elizabeth 'Liz' Brathwaite, CEO of the Barbados Tourism Hospitality Inc. (BTHI) met, welcomed and hosted them at a small reception.

***

At BDF HQ, there were only two speeches to be made at Petra Carmichael's reception. One was by Prime Minister Motby, with the other being a reply by Carmichael. She had earlier indicated to him that this was what she wanted. At 8:30 p.m., a bell was rung to gain her guests attention in the Officers' Quarters where the reception was being held.

He took the microphone that was handed to him by Sharon Evans. The room fell silent as he started to address the reception's guests.

"Good evening. Sir Livingstone and Lady Murray, Madam Chief Justice, Cabinet, Parliamentary, Diplomatic and Consular colleagues, senior Government officials, Petra and the Carmichael family, Dean Mercer, other specially invited guests and of course our friends from the media.

"Tonight is a very special occasion. It is also a sad one for me. We are gathered here to celebrate the work of an exceptional Barbadian public servant, Petra Carmichael. You all know Petra retired a couple of weeks ago after giving three and a half decades of stellar and selfless service to our country. Government records will show that numerous Barbadians have served our country well and for long periods of time in the past. Few though, in my humble opinion, have made a greater contribution to Barbados' development or been more highly valued by people like myself, for the continued high standard of work they have done for our Government, than Petra. And she's done it all generally – well, most of the time, with a smile…and perhaps the occasional grimace."

That brought a ripple of laughter from the assembled crowd. Motby glanced at Carmichael who nodded her head in agreement with this sentiment.

"A statement which seems appropriate for this occasion that I shall repeat here – it's from a play I once saw on Broadway, which says that the two most important days of your life are the day you were born and the day you find out why. Tonight, we celebrate not only that Petra was born, but we now know why…it was to spend most of her adult life in true service to her beloved Barbados. For that, we are very grateful to and salute you Petra. We thank your family for lending you to the people of Barbados, and for so long.

"It therefore gives me great pleasure and is also my humble but high honour to host tonight's reception. Petra, we're sending you off, not forever into the sunset as it were, but for a well-deserved rest. I'm sure you'll face new challenges that we'll soon all be hearing about. Earlier, in church we sang Hymn 26 '*The day Thou gavest Lord, is ended*'. Petra, this journey has ended but I have a feeling that at least one other will follow. Verse three of that hymn might even be prophetic… 'as o'er each continent and island the dawn leads on another day…'

"And so, Petra…on behalf of all of us, I simply want to say, on behalf of all your former colleagues, family and friends present here tonight, a big 'THANK YOU'. Barbados also thanks you. Let's raise our glasses to this wonderful public servant…job well done."

With that, Motby raised his glass, signalling a toast to Carmichael in celebration of her years of dedicated and loyal public service. The toast was lustily cheered, before he handed Carmichael the microphone.

"Your Excellency Sir Livingstone Murray, Governor General of Barbados and Lady Murray, Prime Minister Jeffrey Motby and Mrs Motby, Madam Chief

Justice Dame Laura Sprigg, Cabinet Members, Leader of the Opposition Richard Dawson and Mrs Dawson, other Members of Parliament, Permanent Secretaries, Heads of department and statutory corporations, members of the diplomatic and consular corps, other former colleagues, family members, friends and media members."

Carmichael had deliberately not used the now popular 'Protocol having been established' phrase at the start of her response to the Prime Minister. She thought it was disrespectful and so had discouraged its use by any of her staff when they had to speak publicly.

"Wow! Glad to get that intro out of the way! What can I say after all of that!

"First, allow me to thank you all most sincerely for coming out to join my family and me this evening. I know some of you also attended the earlier service at the Cathedral before this reception, so I guess double thanks are in order from me to most of you for your endurance.

"Second, I've really not got much to say, except that it has been a real pleasure for me to serve my country and to work with some of the most enthusiastic, patient and committed colleagues one could ever hope to work with over my long tenure in the public service. Luckily, I've always enjoyed my work and encourage those of you who remain in this noble service, to at least try and do likewise. I confess that working with Ministers, former colleagues and members of the public over the years for Barbados' benefit has both been overall enjoyable and worthwhile.

"My sincere thanks to you Prime Minister, your Government and Barbadians all over for the opportunity to have served and for your generosity to me and my family in putting on and hosting this reception at such a special juncture of my life.

"Perhaps, as Arnold Schwarzenegger the actor used to say, and especially after what the Prime Minister has just suggested, I'll be back to help out Barbados again in some minor capacity, somewhere, somehow.

"But expect nothing to happen next week! I need a break and a cruise is calling me. Thanks again for coming out tonight. It's all been a wonderful experience for me and my family.

"I love and appreciate you all. Good night and please get home safely."

A loud and long round of applause broke out across the room. Roger Carmichael hugged and kissed Carmichael. Motby then presented her with a large retirement card which had been specially signed by all of the attending guests upon their arrival. As Carmichael's guests started to swarm around to wish her well (again), two BDF soldiers brought out a large retirement cake that had been made by the BDF's kitchen staff. The inscription on the cake read *'Congratulations Petra: Happy Retirement'*. With guests watching closely and cheering, Carmichael and her husband Roger cut and shared the first slice of her retirement cake. The media's cameras and mobile phones clicked away as Carmichael presented Prime Minister and Mrs Motby with their slices of cake.

Taking a bite, Motby stated, "It tastes good," before the cake was whisked away by the same two BDF soldiers to be cut up and placed into small boxes for delivery to each guest on their way out of the Officers' Quarters in an hour's time.

***

Between 8:45 p.m. and 9:00 p.m., JJ played his 'getting up' musical mix for patrons desirous of shaking a leg early: Kool & The Gang *Ladies Night*, Bruce Johnston *Pipeline*, The Chimes *Heaven*, Mystic Merlin featuring Freddie Jackson *Mr Magician*, Melba Moore *You Stepped into My Life*.

Bang on 9:00 p.m., JJ launched Hour 2, called H2G (the 'groovin' hour) by re-introducing himself to those who had entered the club since 8:15 p.m. He spoke over his signature tune.

"Can you handle what's coming at you tonight in P's Disco?" he asked while pointing at the patrons already on the dance floor. "The music's hot, so come trot with yours truly JJ, De Ole Time General, right through till midnight. George Michael liked to say 'gotta get up to get down', so let's go. Here's Billy Paul *Bring the Family Back*."

JJ was now well into his night's work at the DJ controls. The club's assembled mature patrons were in a mood to party. A title had been given to JJ, De Ole Time General on his second night as a public DJ at P's Disco by an intoxicated lady who was out with friends celebrating her fiftieth birthday. JJ did not like the name initially, but the following week the group had returned to P's Disco to not only re-use but spread the title. It stuck, and so JJ accepted and also started to use it. His foot-tapping, finger-snapping BIT jams were keeping P's Disco's early patrons more than contented twice a week.

Some of the dancing patrons responded to his invitation with a wave, while others gave him the thumbs up. Satisfied, JJ set about playing an Aurra double *You & Me Tonight/Checking You Out*, Michael Lovesmith *Ain't Nothin' Like It*, Incognito *Always There*, Chic *My Forbidden Lover*, Luther Vandross *Shine*, Steve Arrington *Dancin' In the Key of Life*, Don Ray *Got To Have Loving*, Stevie Wonder *Boogie on Reggae Woman*, Eddy Grant *Walking on Sunshine*, Bob Marley and The Wailers *Could You be Love*, Earth Wind & Fire *Boogie Wonderland* and Ronnie Jones *You and I*.

***

The England and West Indies cricket teams, plus their entourages were whisked away to a four-star beach-front hotel in Rockley, Christ Church in separate coaches, escorted by RBPF officers. Their hectic nine-day Barbados visit was underway.

***

Kylie 'Joe' Callendar, BIB operative and Black team leader (code number S11), knowing what her plans for tonight and the next two days were, was keenly looking forward to this break away from her busy job. It was something she had seldom gotten a chance to do since joining BIB.

Now aged 31, she was settled in her job and personal life. The petite, attractive, pet-loving woman known as Joe to her BIB colleagues and closest friends was no longer single. She had met her dentist boyfriend Dr Stephan 'Stef' Simmonds quite by chance five months earlier. Stef appeared to be her Mr Right, someone who loved her, her pets, and recognised and accepted that her work sometimes got her into dangerous situations. What helped to quickly cement Joe and Stef as a couple was their willingness to laugh. Both of them loved comedy shows, especially when early on they discovered their mutual love of classic black and white Laurel & Hardy videos, pictures and books. Marriage, starting and raising a family were not yet on the cards but as they had already become such a reliable unit, their families and work friends were thinking that a union was looking inevitable.

Joe and Stef had arranged to join Fred and Charlee at P's Disco later that evening. Joe was looking forward to the evening, having not visited P's Disco since JJ had started DJing there, so she expected tonight to be a happy occasion. She expected the foursome to give JJ their full support while enjoying a late meal and a few drinks.

Joe's four animals, two cats and two dogs named Nelson and Winnie and Sherlock Holmes and Dr Watson respectively, had been fed, watered and put to bed for the night. While Stef had completed his customary review of the day's completed examinations at his dentistry practice, Joe had taken a shower and gotten herself ready for the night's activity. She and Stef planned to view the latest double-DVD compilation of Laurel & Hardy comedy sketches that had arrived yesterday tomorrow night!

Tonight, they were going out.

***

Prior to his departure, Motby spoke briefly and quietly with Carmichael.

"Petra, would you be able to take up your appointment from the first day of September?"

"Yes, Prime Minister."

"Thank you. Many congratulations again. We'll talk soon, after you return from your cruise, not before. Good night."

"Good night, Prime Minister," responded Carmichael. She mused to herself what with the time difference between the UK and Barbados, she could expect to be speaking with Motby more about this same time in the foreseeable future once in her new position.

Dean Mercer had been invited to attend Carmichael's reception. Having spoken with her a couple of years prior to her intended retirement from the public service, he had indicated to her that he would have work for her to do at the Cathedral. Unknown to him, that would now have to wait.

***

Only when Fred was leaving the judo club following the extended class with his judokas, did he realise that, in his enthusiasm to assist and enlighten his students, he'd spent an extra thirty minutes with them rather than the fifteen he had intended. Nevertheless, he was happy to have done so.

Their discussion was around a profound statement Mohammed Ali, former Olympic and World Heavyweight Boxing champion had reportedly made. Fred's intention was to use this alleged statement as a motivational tool for his judokas going forward: "If my mind can conceive it, and my heart can believe it, then I can achieve it." The discussion went well and he was pleased with the response of his potential Olympians, so much so that Fred determined that he would find additional statements for discussion at his extended Tuesday sessions. Fred was already thinking how best to develop his three-step motivational line: Chase, Catch, Conquer.

His girlfriend's call reinforced that he'd lost track of time. Charlee reminded him that they were scheduled to meet Joe and Stef at P's Disco at 10:00 p.m. Fred apologised and confirmed that he was on his way home. Once he had cleaned himself up, they would go to the club and enjoy a meal there. Charlee advised him that she was already dressed and was awaiting his arrival.

Fred felt bad. He recognised that he had now messed up. His plan for tonight relating to Charlee would have to wait until tomorrow, unless an opportunity presented itself for him to do so tonight after all.

***

The well-dressed man sitting at table #4 in P's Disco dining area had taken his time over his meal. He had also ordered a second rum and coke from Zelda Hughes as she passed by. Once that drink had arrived, he downed it and asked her for his bill. On her return with it, the man settled it in cash. He placed an additional US$10 on the table for her as a tip before leaving P's Disco. Hughes collected the payment and pocketed the tip. "Thanks Mister, you really surprised me," she said softly as she walked towards the cashier.

Poor fella. Guts full, but he still doesn't look happy, she thought to herself a few minutes later while walking back to clear the table for newly arriving dinner patrons.

***

By 9:30 p.m., over one hundred patrons were now inside P's Disco. *This is shaping up to be a good night*, JJ thought looking up at the gathered mass of patrons. He anticipated that many of them would enjoy a nice meal, hold a few drinks and the music from yesteryear he was playing that was still very much alive today in Barbados would make them feel good. JJ understood playing such music often brought back happy memories for many of his patrons on the two nights he played at P's Disco.

Following his late-afternoon conversation with Fred, JJ expected to see him, Charlee, Joe and Stef at the club later rather than sooner that night. Meanwhile, his task was to keep patrons happy. A touch of Marvin Gaye *Got to Give It Up*, Narada Michael Walden *I Should've Loved Ya*, Phyllis Hyman *You Know How To Love Me Now*, Michael Jackson *Rock With You* and Arrow *Party Mix* kept his playlist pot boiling.

***

Castille's meeting with the Head of *The Organisation* took place in a downtown Miami wine bar.

That person was Emma Pilessar, an attractive, shapely forty-two-year old brunette. Though Castille had joined *The Organisation* before her, she had quickly risen up the chain of command to become *The Organisation*'s Head two years ago, following the accidental drowning of her sixty-seven-year old male predecessor. Pilessar knew what Castille's range of capabilities were. Shortly after becoming Head of *The Organisation*, she'd had the opportunity to witness him in action, dealing with clients in both New York and Los Angeles. As a result, nine months into her tenure, Pilessar had promoted Castille to take charge of *The Organisation*'s thriving Central American business interests. In this position, he effectively became *The Organisation*'s number three. By all reports, he had done well since his promotion and quickly became *The Organisation*'s top overseas fixer.

Pilessar retained all responsibility for *The Organisation*'s mainland USA operations. She allocated to Royce Thomas, her trusted Number Two responsibility for growing the South American elements of *The Organisation*'s business. Pilessar was intent on overseeing the embryonic Caribbean business *The Organisation* had initiated a couple of years earlier herself. An overdue face-to-face meeting with her potential Barbadian-based collaborator and co-ordinator for the Caribbean, scheduled some two months ago, was finally set to take place somewhere in Florida in another fortnight, though a specific venue was yet to be identified. Pilessar, Thomas and Castille worked out of *The Organisation*'s Miami headquarters, but her meeting with her Barbadian collaborator would not take place there. Barbados, an attractive alternative place for their meeting had been considered but overlooked in preference for somewhere which offered both potential partners opportunities for anonymity, enabling their discussions to take place under cover.

New circumstances in the next few days would change the meeting and timing arrangements.

***

The door leading to the windowless and secure room located in the middle of the house in St Joseph facing the east coast of Barbados was closed, although the light inside of this room indicated that it was occupied. Except for the security lighting surrounding the house and a side table lamp burning in the master bedroom, there were no other lights on at the property.

To anyone watching or passing by the house, it appeared as if the well-known but respected and accomplished owner of the home was in the process of going (or had gone) to bed, perhaps after a long day at their Belleville, St Michael office.

Nothing could have been further from the truth.

***

Pilessar did most of the talking. Castille listened and responded when necessary. The pina colada each of them had ordered was excellent. Both drinks lasted the duration of their meeting and helped to make up appearances. To onlookers, the well-dressed couple might have already had dinner elsewhere and were following it up with this drink before heading off to a hotel room somewhere for a fabulous night of lovemaking.

Wrong. That was never going to happen. In college and throughout her business career to date, Pilessar had never been one to mix business with pleasure, especially with persons she worked with. In Castille's case, she was aware of how fit, trim, muscled and yes, ruggedly handsome he was. She had experienced great difficulty on one earlier occasion in controlling herself and not breaking her strict rule of non-fraternisation with a subordinate. Now sitting across from Castille at this wine bar, that earlier lustful feeling for him had rushed up on her. Both the little person in her head and the itch between her legs told her to go with the flow for a change and break her longstanding rule. But her greater self-control and inner resistance fortified her determination not to give into her head and bodily desires and so she did not invite him back to her place for a second drink, or whatever. Common sense prevailed, as it had done back in Los Angeles.

Her golden rule prevailed. No fraternising with subordinates.

With such thoughts banished, Pilessar had led discussion on Castille's recent activities in Mexico, and Panama before that. She confirmed that their second biggest client in Mexico had paid his outstanding debt in full (with interest) overnight. That client had since ordered a new shipment of 'materials' from *The Organisation* which she was prepared to have delivered within a fortnight. Pilessar warned Castille that he should prepare himself to return to Mexico in another month or so to recover early payment if their second biggest client there did not pay promptly. His payment terms had been amended as a result of his past indiscretions with *The Organisation*.

Castille responded simply, stating only, "Glad that payment's been made. I'm available as required to undertake any follow-up tasks given to me."

"Tell me more about your visit to our other Mexican clients," Pilessar ordered.

Castille reported in short, clipped sentences on the outcome of his Mexican visit. It had obviously been successful, though had not been without its challenges. He'd had to personally 'encourage' one debtor to make payment.

"Max? How did you encourage him?" she asked.

Castille explained the methods he had used to secure the outstanding payment from Frequente a few days earlier. As Castille spoke, Pilessar's response was classic her – nods at reasonable intervals during his brief monologue. She showed little other reaction as he spoke. Castille also reported briefly on his visit to Panama the week before where again, *The Organisation*'s clients had all been 'encouraged' to pay up and had done so. The one case which had given him some trouble necessitated some arm twisting, but payment was eventually secured. This came after Castille had threatened to make a video of a Government official's longstanding proclivity for and interest in young children, particularly boys, public. That threat got the payment over the line. Castille was no sweet bread.

Pilessar said little to Castille about his upcoming Barbados assignment. Both knew what the assignment entailed and why he had to visit. The details had been left to him to arrange with his local cohorts doing the implementation. He confirmed 'all was set to go' the next day. That was good enough for Pilessar.

Their meeting ended at 10:00 p.m. Before leaving the wine bar, they pretended to have a whispered conversation for the benefit of anyone who may have been watching them for the past half hour.

They left the wine bar together, side by side but not holding hands. Once outside and out of sight of the wine bar's patrons and its security personnel, they went their separate ways without exchanging any final words. Castille continued walking up the street before he hailed a cab which took him back to his Hialeah apartment. Pilessar's chauffer driven limousine quickly pulled up to her location. Once she was inside, the driver gunned the limousine into traffic and headed in the opposite direction. Ten minutes later, Pilessar was back in her penthouse suite overlooking Miami Beach's cruise ship docking piers.

Though Pilessar was an attractive woman, Castille had never thought of her in any sexual way. He only saw her as his boss who, as Head of *The Organisation*, he worked diligently for.

***

JJ, P's Disco's early DJ, would recall a few days later that he had recognised but not paid any attention to the middle-aged man who had sat by himself at table #4 in the dining area. Even top people need time to relax, often by themselves. After all, that was what he was doing at P's Disco twice a week where he escaped from his demanding day job and line of work. JJ was therefore focussed on what he was at P's Disco to do that night. The middle-aged man was not unlike other similarly aged men who regularly patronised P's Disco during the early part of each night, often accompanied by younger female partners. JJ knew from experience that most of the females accompanying middle-aged men were seldom their spouses or usual partners. The difference was that this man remained on his own throughout his stay in Ps Disco. Having a female partner seemed to be of no interest to him. JJ made a mental note of the time while observing that the man was enjoying the music being pumped out, especially by the side to side head movements he had made to Eddy Grant *Walking on Sunshine*.

***

Half-way through his eight to twelve (ETT) set, JJ felt the need to raise the night's musical tempo. Hour 3 he called H3F3 (the 'floor fillin'/funk you zone' hour). During this hour, he endeavoured to get the majority of patrons in P's Disco onto the dance floor for at least one jam, up-tempo or mellow. His playlist tonight was Band Of Gold *Never Gonna Let You Go*, The Players Association *Turn The Music Up*, Grey & Hanks *Dancin'*, Aretha Franklin *Get It Right*, Archie Bell & The Drells *Let's Groove*, Geraldine Hunt *Can't Fake the Feeling,* Luther Vandross *Never Too Much*, Francis Joli *Gonna Get Over You,* Driza Bone *Real Love,* Teddy Pendergrass *Joy,* Stevie Wonder *Part-Time Lover,* Slave *Just A Touch of Love*, before cooling it down with a mix of Inner City *Whatcha Gonna Do With My Lovin'*, S.O.S. Band *Just Be Good to Me*, J T Taylor *Long Hot Summer Night*. To crank things up again, he played a mix of War *Galaxy*, Chic *Good Times*, The Sugarhill Gang *Rappers Delight* and Will Smith *It's All Good*.

The segment worked. The dance floor remaining almost filled to its capacity. Even those in the dining area, close to the bar were tapping their feet, clapping their hands, snapping their fingers or rolling their heads from side to side while conversing. JJ's masterful mix of BIT grooves kept patrons happy.

JJ didn't notice when, around 10:40 p.m. Pierre Pilgrim popped his head out of his office to see what all the hooting coming from the dancefloor was about. Pilgrim was delighted to see his patrons enjoying their night out by working themselves into a frenzy in response to the hot tunes JJ was pumping out. Pilgrim was delighted with himself for having made the decision to invite, no push, if not *demand,* that his school friend should play.

Good job JJ, Pilgrim thought to himself on his way back to his office. still commending himself for having made this to happen. Like JJ, he knew that tonight was going to be another great night at P's Disco, even though the night was yet young, with hours of music still to be played. He diverted into the dining area as he caught sight of a couple of familiar faces.

***

The Prime Minister and Jacklyn 'Jackie' Motby were having a nightcap on the patio outside their master-bedroom overlooking the expansive grounds of their official residence, Ilaro Court.

It had felt like a long day to Motby. He had gone to his office at Government Headquarters early as usual and after a couple of meetings, he had attended the House of Assembly (Barbados' Parliament). The House had been adjourned following the lunch break because of an ongoing water problem that had been affecting segments of the Greater Bridgetown area over the past two weeks. He had therefore returned to Government Headquarters to attend to some paperwork before he'd left at 4:00 p.m. for Ilaro Court to relax a little. Following a shower, he had changed and headed off to the first part of Petra Carmichael's retirement function at the Cathedral before attending the reception.

Jackie had gotten little real 'family time' to catch up on the revised plans for their daughter Kimberley's wedding, now seven weeks away in mid-June. She used this opportunity before they went to bed to update the 'father of the bride' on the new arrangements.

Motby listened attentively to what Jackie was saying. He could find no fault with what he heard. He was not worried about the wedding arrangements, for he knew that with Jackie, his sister-in-law Gillian Nowell, Kimberley and her very best friend from school Jenny Wisdom (her Matron of Honour) that all of the arrangements for Kimberley's big day would be splendid and well taken care of. Nor was he unduly concerned about how much the wedding would cost him. Jackie would be stylish but economical.

He was however worried about Kimberly's punctuality. She could easily be more than thirty minutes late getting to the Church. Being one for punctuality, with Kimberley somewhat being the opposite, he knew he would have his work cut out on her wedding day 'to get her to the church on time'. *Tradition be dammed*, he thought. Motby did not believe in brides being 'fashionably late', on their big day or otherwise. He decided there and then that he would find a novel way to get his daughter to the church on time on her wedding day, but would keep his method to himself as he knew that the country would be watching.

"All sounds good to me, honey. Once you and Kimberley agree, I'll concur. Ready to turn in?"

"Yep. Though I've not had as full a day as you've had, I think it was that glass of champagne at Petra's do we toasted with that has gotten to me. Don't get me wrong, it was very nice, but it certainly had a kick to it. For tomorrow night's dinner, I'll offer our usual wine, unless you want me to offer something different – like what we had tonight?"

"I agree that we should stick to the tried and proven…wouldn't want you to be nodding off while hosting Captain Selwick for our long-planned dinner with him!"

"Won't matter, he won't drink any of the wine we offer anyway, because he has to fly back to London on Thursday afternoon."

"You're wrong there, honey. BA changed their Barbados stopovers last month, I understand. Crews now get two days off after flying to Barbados. So, as he will arrive tomorrow afternoon, he won't fly again until Friday afternoon, no evening. He's taking up BA's late flight leaving Barbados at 8:30 p.m."

"So, you expect he'll have a glass or two?"

"Probably, well, I sincerely hope he does. I'd be most surprised if Captain Selwick doesn't take a glass with us. Whether he does or not, I would have kept my long-term promise to provide a meal for him here, just to say 'thank you' again for the beautiful flight he flew between London and Barbados after my September 2015 visit."

"Fine. Lights out?" asked Jackie.

"Yes indeed, tomorrow should be an easier day for me – long again but pleasant," replied Motby.

***

"Trevor, do you think you'll get a send-off like Petra got this evening from the Prime Minister, whoever he or she is, when it's your turn to retire?" asked Diane Burke, slightly the worse for wear as he lay in bed following their intense bout of lovemaking after their return home from Carmichael's dual retirement function.

"Not a chance in hell!" Colonel Burke replied. "Nor would I expect or want one, given the sort of work I do…but I'm happy that the PM did this for Petra. She really deserved it for all the hard work she's put into her job. She certainly made his task as PM easier since she took over as his PS. I've enjoyed working with her. She was, no is, efficient as hell. A friendly but thorough and no-nonsense individual."

"I've always found her to be pleasant. I hope she gets to enjoy her retirement, though from what the PM's suggested, I think he's got something lined up for her to do. Any idea what that might be?" Diane asked.

"No idea, though I wouldn't be surprised if he offered her a diplomatic job overseas…possibly the UN, Canada or the UK. London most probably, if I know the PM. He's not mentioned anything to me, and why or should he? After all, it's his appointment to make. I expect Cabinet will go along with what he wants."

"Okay, and by the way, I still don't know if tomorrow evening's dinner guests are vegetarians, or don't like seafood, etc. Can you please find out for me ASAP in the morning? I've pretty much decided on what I'd like to prepare, but I'd hate to get it wrong! If I do, they might send 007 to finish us off!"

"Come on, Diane, don't be so melodramatic…they wouldn't do that, would they? Seriously, to put your mind at rest, I'll call Sir Thadeus (he wants me – us to call him Thad) tomorrow morning to be sure that everything's fine. Why not let me know what you're going to put on the table and I'll ask him if it's fine with them. Okay?"

"Thank you."

"Can I get some sleep now please?"

"Sure, after some more of you know what!"

"Right. Round two it is. Let's do it, D –"

"Not very romantic, Trevor! Surely you can be more enthusiastic?"

"All right, 'let's get it on, baby,'" he said in his best attempt at a Barry White voice impersonation.

"I suppose that'll have to do," Diane mumbled.

***

Hon. Richard Preston Dawson MD, MP, Leader of the Opposition and his wife Dawn were already in bed. They too were discussing what Motby might have been referring to when he suggested that Carmichael would be used in some future Government role.

"Dawn, I think Jeffrey will offer, indeed might *already* have offered, Petra a diplomatic posting. I don't think she's in anyway political, so making her a Government Senator would make no sense and I don't think would be accepted if offered. What's your bet?"

Dawn shrugged her shoulders, "Well, the HC slot in London is available, but the UN Ambassador job is also up for grabs in a few months' time. Take your pick," said Dr Dawson.

"I'm going for the UN, that would give Petra a few months to herself before taking up her position."

"You may be right. We should know by weekend, as someone in Cabinet is sure to leak her destination, if indeed it's a diplomatic posting."

***

Pilgrim greeted Fred, Charlee, Joe and Stef. They did not try to signal their arrival to JJ in any way as he was busy keeping the club's patrons intoxicated with his musical mixes. Pilgrim, having been pre-warned by JJ that a couple of his BIB workmates and their partners were coming in any time after 10:00 p.m., had reserved a table for them for the evening. Pleasantries exchanged and drinks ordered before deciding what they would eat, Pilgrim excused himself to return to his office.

***

JJ acknowledged a waved greeting from a patron walking past his DJ station with a thumbs-up response. Where were his work colleagues? Running late, he guessed. Just then, a loving feeling came over him and he decided to play his favourite song Earth Wind and Fire *That's the Way of the World* before going up-tempo again ahead of his ten-minute 11:00 p.m. break.

"Nice tune. JJ knows his onions," said Stef, a music buff in his own right. "The song is all about love, humanity, compassion...brotherhood and the like. Again, I say, nice one JJ."

"Yeah, I've liked this song from the time I first remember my dad playing a CD of it to me in the car on the way to school on my seventh birthday," said Charlee.

***

Joe's contribution to the evening was, as usual, to tell a few jokes. For a serious young lady, she had never been opposed to laughing at a funny situation.

72

Her discovery of Laurel and Hardy clips on YouTube had given her situations she could laugh at and share with others. Laurel and Hardy jokes in particular were now regular features of conversation when away from official BIB duties with her closest friends, a few of which of course were her fellow BIB team leaders.

"This if from a 1933 film, *Sons of the Desert*, Ollie Hardy is lying on a bed feeling ill. As usual, his good friend Stan is close by, looking concerned and wanting to be of some help. Ollie says… 'You'd better take my temperature…get that thermometer.' Stan replies, 'The what?' Ollie responds, 'Thermometer! You'll find it on the shelf.' Stan places the thermometer in Ollie's mouth and starts to take his pulse, so Ollie asks him, 'What does it say?' before Stan replies 'Wet and windy…!'"

Everybody in the BIB group cracked up. Fred spilt his drink when he slapped the table too hard!

"Let's have another one, Joe, but keep one of your best jokes for the end of the night…sort of like our 'one for the road', as it were," said Stef. He knew a lot – but not all of her jokes by now, having watched several of the Laurel and Hardy films with Joe that she had gradually been acquiring in the six months since she and Stef had become an 'item'.

"Yeah, go on, Joe," shouted Charlee with a schoolgirl giggle.

"Well, since you're forcing me to give you another one…" said Joe.

"In *A Chump at Oxford*, Ollie and Stan somehow get enrolled at Oxford University in England. A student says to them, 'Pardon me, but haven't you come to the wrong college?' Ollie responds, 'Well, this is Oxford, isn't it?' The student replies, 'Yes, but you're dressed for Eaton,' to which Stan replies 'Well, that's swell…we haven't eaten since breakfast…'"

More cracking up!

Fred (not spilling any drinks this time) shouted, "Joe, that's another fine mess you've got me into."

Everyone at the table nodded and responded almost in unison, "Joe, Joe, Joe, girl, you de comedienne."

Joe raised her glass to them. She'd heard this before…she stood up and bowed obligingly. She had a good one for them to end the night with.

***

Before leaving the DJ area to take his ten-minute break at 11:00 p.m., JJ inserted a CD mix of smooth mix of tracks. Four Tops *Still Waters (Love)*, Bob James *Westchester Lady*, Eddie Drennon & BBS Unlimited *Let's Do the Latin Hustle*, Junior Walker and The All Stars *Walk in The Night*. This enabled him sufficient time to take a bathroom break and go in search of his friends. He was pleased to see they had made it to the club and were enjoying their evening out together. JJ small talked with them for a couple of minutes and challenged them to hit the dance floor at some time before he finished his set.

As a parting gesture, he summoned Zelda Hughes and asked her to put a round of drinks on his tab for his friends. JJ expected his BIB colleagues and their partners to stay on at the club long after he handed over musical proceedings to P Disco's Resident DJ, Grover 'GP' Price at midnight before going home. How long his friends stayed on in the club was of no concern to him. He was working the next day, they were not until Friday morning.

Back in the DJ area, JJ initiated Hour 4 (the 'final get down' hour) of his set. Patrons knew what was coming – some mellow tunes, one unusual hit followed by a mix of popular dance numbers they all knew. Tonight's playlist was George Benson *Love Is Here Tonight*, Keni Burke *Risin' To The Top* and Smokey Robinson *Tell Me Tomorrow*, Patrice Rushen *Feels So Real (Won't Let Go)*, Cerrone *Give Me Love*, McFadden and Whitehead *Ain't No Stopping Us Now*, Narada Michael Waldon *Tonight I'm Alright*, Michael Jackson *Blood On The Dance Floor*, GQ *Disco Nights (Rock Freak)*, Robin S *Show Me Love*, O'Jays *Put Our Hands Together*.

***

Later that night in Miami while Castille slept, Pilessar was trying hard to find something that she might entertain herself with into the early hours of the morning. There was nothing she felt like watching on any of the one hundred and fifty available channels on her cable television system. Pilessar, through *The Organisation*, was involved in supplying drugs but had never used them. Nor could a woman in her powerful position afford to have too many boy (or girl) friends in a place like Miami, so she'd often found herself isolated, somewhat unhappy. Resorting to personal devices for self-satisfaction had therefore become normal for her.

It was these devices that she now used to entertain herself, yet again. The equipment in her exercise room would get her started, before she would try out her new toy, bought in New York a week earlier. The experience should be rewarding if all she'd been told about this gadget was anything to go by. So, tonight, she would take care of herself.

Pilessar thought no more about Castille or the Barbados operation he was going to oversee from tomorrow afternoon. She expected him to complete it quickly and be able to return to Miami on Saturday, Sunday night latest, to be ready for the new work week.

***

It was coming up to 11:50 p.m. in Block #5, cell 10 in HMP Dodds. Besides the BPS officers, there was at least one prisoner who was still awake, despite the main lights in the institution having been earlier turned out promptly at 8:30 p.m.

The prisoner was Jasper Power. He had gotten word that tomorrow would be a big day for him. Yes, he would return to court for the legal system to most likely convict him for a range of offences. From his perspective, that potential experience was now far from his mind. His big day meant something completely different! He was sure that he would not sleep in HMP Dodds again for a long time, starting with tomorrow night. His 'friends' on the outside would hopefully see to that tomorrow morning.

Power closed his eyes tight as he lay on his bunk. He wanted to spend some time with Marcia Leach tomorrow afternoon once the initial commotion about him had died down. Two weeks earlier when they were last together, they had made love after midnight on Rockley Beach…

***

At 11:55 p.m., JJ initiated his sign-off routine by playing his 'out' song Three Degrees *When Will I See You Again*. He reminded patrons that he'd be back in the DJ's seat every Monday and Tuesday night, ETT. He then handed over P's Disco to DJ Grover 'GP' Price.

Price's usual intention after JJ's set was to shift the feel of P's Disco to more suit and satisfy its younger patrons who had been arriving in their numbers since 11:15 p.m. and would soon fill P's Disco to its capacity.

Price got his set up and running by thanking JJ for doing a great job over the past four hours with his BIT music. He normally played some contemporary dance music to keep the energy levels high in P's Disco. But tonight, his instinct told him to change things up a little with a couple of smooth jams before reverting to hype. First up, The Weekend *I Feel It Coming*, followed by Ne-Yo *Sexy Love*. Having got that itch out of his system, Price hit the up-tempo stuff, starting with a second Ne-Yo song *Because of You*, followed by another tune from The Weekend *Can't Feel My Face*.

Price was in his zone. JJ's BIB colleagues were left in his capable musical hands.

***

Chapter Seven
Upheaval

WEDNESDAY, 18 APRIL

One of JJ's greatest pleasures as a dad on returning home on evenings from work or at nights after P's Disco was to locate and kiss his children. Angela was thirteen and Andrew ten. Tonight, they were fast asleep. After kissing them on their foreheads in bed in their rooms, he tip-toed into the master bedroom so as not to disturb Vanessa. Her bedside lamp was on, so he undressed quietly before entering the bathroom and closing the adjoining door behind him. After urinating, showering, brushing his teeth and gargling he felt refreshed yet sleepy, so put on a pair of boxer shorts before returning to the bedroom and climbing into bed.

He kissed Vanessa lightly, not wanting to wake her up.

"How was your BIT show?" she asked, turning to snuggle up to him.

"Awesome. My preparations helped. Fred, Charlee, Joe and Stef came by. I left them there."

"Don't they have work tomorrow?" she asked him sleepily.

"Only Stef at his surgery. Fred and Joe have the next couple of days off and Charlie is on a week's leave from QEH. So, they're all entitled to be out late," said JJ, making himself comfortable next to Vanessa.

"Lucky them!"

"Yeah. I'm gone early in the morning, so the school run is all yours, V."

"No problem."

"Night, babe."

"Night back."

P's Disco was scheduled to close at 3:00 a.m. Fred, Charlee, Joe and Stef had thought of leaving around 2:00 a.m., but conversations with Pilgrim about the outcome of the forthcoming Test Match between the West Indies and England pushed back their departure.

Once Pilgrim had left them for a second time to return to his office to check on the night's takings, Stef ordered another round of drinks before speaking.

"Fred, Joe has the last of her jokes for the night, so don't tell me that that you know what it is and want to tell it to us rather than her," said Charlee.

"Nothing like that! I have something better to say."

Fred turned to look at Charlee and said to her, "I have a question to ask you..."

Dropping onto his left knee, Fred reached into his right pants pocket and retrieved an item.

"Charlotte Nadine Piggott, in front of these two good persons, in this place and on this 18th day of April 2018, will you please marry me?" he asked.

Shocked, Charlee stood up, both hands on her mouth which by this time was gaping open. She was also trembling, Joe, Stef and Fred noticed.

"I... I... Yes, Fred. Oh my God. Yes!" Charlee responded.

With that, Fred rose from his knees to hug Charlee. They then kissed for what seemed like an eternity. Coming up for breath, Fred pulled away and opened the box that was in his hand. He carefully removed the engagement ring and holding her shaking left hand, he placed it onto the appropriate finger.

"Well, it seems to fit," said Stef.

"On yeah, it sure does," said Joe in agreement.

Seemingly lost in wonder, Charlee just continued to stare at her hand, before bringing it up to her face for a closer examination of the diamond engagement ring. She burst into tears, mumbling, "Fred, you've made me so happy. I don't know what else to say –"

"Yes sounded pretty good to me, Charlee," Fred replied, hugging her again. He then shouted to P's Disco's remaining patrons.

"Hey everybody, this woman just agreed to marry me. I'm the luckiest man in the world, no, I'm on top of the world, at least in here tonight."

P's Disco patrons turned to look at him before letting out loud cheers. Individuals came over to offer their congratulations. Some slapped him on the back, others offered to buy the engaged couple a drink.

After another five minutes, Fred said, "Well, as it's past our agreed 2:00 p.m. witching hour folks, I'm ready to hear Joe's last L&H joke for the evening. After that, once her joke is not about me, or marriage, I'll go home to take in the full meaning of what I've just committed myself to with this young lady sitting by my side."

"Fine, okay." Joe motioned them all to be silent. "Well, I had one L&H joke left to tell you guys but, because of the special nature of tonight, I'll give you two. Here goes. In *One Good Turn*, Ollie and Stan discuss who should chop up some wood. Stan says, 'Well, I don't know anything about cutting wood,' to which Ollie replies, 'Well, you ought to! You once told me that your father was in the lumber business.' Stan replies, 'Well, I know he was but it was only in a small way.' Ollie asks, 'What do you mean in a small way?' Stan replies, 'Well, he used to sell toothpicks…' Get it?"

"Nice one, Joe. Small way…toothpicks!" said Charlee with her infectious giggle.

"And the last one, honey?" asked Stef, certain that this joke would be one even he did not yet know.

"This one's short and sweet! In *Another Fine Mess*, Ollie tells Stan, 'Call me a cab,' to which Stan replies, 'You're a cab.' Get it?" asked Joe.

The other three persons in her group looked at each other in puzzlement and for some form of comprehension of the joke that had just been told. Then they got it, and started to laugh as they collected their belongings to leave P's Disco.

As they made their way towards the club's exit, their laughter grew louder – so much so that one of the remaining patrons looked around sharply at them and said to his friend.

"That lot had a good night."

***

The 5:00 a.m. telephone call made by Mrs Lewis to her son Bertram Lewis in his upstate New York, USA apartment was, to say the least, unusual. Not only the time of it, but the content. What she told her son greatly alarmed him, so much so that he made a determination to get on the first available flight to

79

Barbados to be with his mum. Mrs Lewis was upset, though not yet at the point of crying. Lewis wanted to get to the bottom of this unusual and worrying situation. Nothing like this had ever happened to anyone in their family before, at least not to his knowledge. Also, as his mum was never one to panic easily, it increased his concern. Being unattached, it would be easier for him to respond to his mum's needs than it would be for his younger sister Caroline Lewis-Greenidge, who lived in Texas. She had a husband and two young kids to manage along with her busy job at a Texas University, so it would take her much longer to get home to their mum.

Lewis instructed his mother to contact his father's secretary first thing that morning and call him back on his mobile with any new information. Once she'd agreed to do so, Lewis set about making his arrangements to fly to Barbados as soon as possible. He knew his dad's office would not be available to the public before 8:00 a.m., so he did not expect his mum to call him back before 8:30 a.m. at the earliest.

Switching on his computer, Lewis checked to see whether there were any economy class seats available on the 1:00 p.m. AA flight to Miami. There were six open seats. He booked and paid for one of them on his personal credit card. His flight would arrive in Miami in good time to enable him to make AA's daily 6:45 p.m. flight to Barbados, once they were seats! His luck was in. Three first class seats were open. Lewis now also booked and paid for one. He knew from past experience that it was always difficult to get an economy class seat on that evening flight to Barbados unless you had booked it well in advance of your travel date. Lewis noted that he would arrive in Barbados at 10:05 p.m. He would take a taxi to his parents St George home as it would be too late for Mum to drive out to the airport for him.

How Lewis missed having the daily direct flights to Barbados from New York on AA. Yes, there was now a low-budget direct option thrice a week, but that airline only flew on Mondays, Thursdays and Saturdays. Even if this was one of those days, the flight usually left New York at 9:20 a.m. and he would not have had sufficient time to make it today. Hence his pursuance of the New York-Miami-Barbados option. Something told him to resist the temptation to book his return flights for Sunday afternoon/evening.

Today will be a long flying day for you Lewis boy, he thought to himself before starting to shave. He would call his sister from New York airport once he knew more from his mum, as Lewis-Greenidge would still be asleep at this time of the morning, given the time difference.

Lewis opened up his carry-on suitcase to start packing the few items he would need for the trip. He kept a set of clothes back in Barbados, including a dark suit, a couple of white shirts, half a dozen ties, training shoes and running shorts for the gym he frequented in the Sheraton Centre mall complex when he was at home.

Always a proactive person, Lewis anticipated that if nothing else, his presence in Barbados would give his mum some peace of mind. He also thought of his clients and his business contacts who would be affected by his absence for the rest of the week at a minimum. Lewis called his secretary Roni Garcia, at 6:00 a.m. when he knew she would be up. Lewis explained to her what his situation was and of his proposed absence from the country for the next few days. He would confirm to Garcia exactly what he was doing by 8:45 a.m. or so through another call. She should postpone his appointments with clients for the rest of the week and re-arrange them for the same time and day of the following week. He decided to write notes for Garcia to pass to his law partner who would, in turn hand them to the two judges whose courts Lewis was scheduled to appear in on Thursday and Friday respectively, requesting adjournments for the cases he was involved. Knowing the two judges concerned as he did, Lewis felt that the adjournments would be secured. Also, out of courtesy, he decided to prepare short explanatory e-mails to the prosecuting attorneys in both cases. No point in pissing them off too. Whatever new dates the court set, he would accept in the circumstances.

2018 had already been a challenging year! The winter had been long and harsh. Lewis would use this opportunity to get some warm sunshine on his back for the next few days. He fully expected the problem in Barbados to be solved quickly, certainly within the next forty-eight hours max., given the prominent position his dad held in Barbados' public service.

Lewis also recognised that, all things being equal, he might just get to see at least one day of the Test Match at New Kensington Oval during his brief visit. This was something he had not done for a while, as he certainly could not watch a Test Match in New York.

***

Jasper Power woke earlier than usual on this Wednesday morning. He laid on his bunk in clear contemplation of what he expected the day would bring forth. Power was optimistic that he would not need to spend another night in this St Philip facility, in this cell and on this bunk. Some place more comfortable was certainly beckoning him…

***

JJ left his Christ Church home just before 7:00 a.m. He was keen to arrive at BIB HQ in good time to link up with the other two members of his Gold team whom he had led for the past five years. They would leave in good time to receive their briefing from Superintendent Innis at HMP Dodds ahead of their rendezvous with the other members of today's prison run (PR) team (RBPF and BPS officers) at 9:00 a.m.

BIB's main task today was to accompany the weekly PR. Such assignments were still relatively new to BIB operatives. Over the past two months, BIB's three operational teams had undertaken a total of twelve PR assignments, accompanying Barbados' most dangerous and other criminals when called upon by prison authorities to help escort inmates housed in the institution. At BIB HQ, PR's were perceived as 'riding shot gun' exercises.

Today, JJ's Gold team would follow the RBPF and BPS vehicles from HMP Dodds, the island's sole prison facility in St Philip to the District 'A' Magistrate's court just outside of Bridgetown and back to the prison. Each PR exercise normally took around five hours. The Gold team planned to leave BIB HQ just after 8:00 a.m. to ensure arrival at HMP Dodds by 8:30 a.m. Anticipating no problems with today's assignment, they expected to be back at BIB HQ by 1:30 p.m. when they would complete the required paperwork. The rest of the day would be theirs along with tomorrow. They would then join the other two BIB operational teams at 9:00 a.m. on Friday morning, enabling BIB to play its roles in the elaborate nine-day ECC security screen. Set up primarily for the Test Match, the screen would also cover the international soccer match, a pop concert and a Commonwealth Sports Ministers' Conference.

Specifically, BIB operatives were to help with VIP security by keeping not only both teams' squads and officials, visiting International Cricket Committee (ICC) officials, thousands of local, Caribbean and British supporters plus local, regional and international media safe and protected over this period.

Mohammed Carr (code number F40) and Jayne Bixley (code number U21) soon arrived to join JJ in BIB's Conference Room. Following a review of their instructions, they headed for their vehicles to collect any personal equipment required for the PR exercise. They had agreed to travel in JJ's vehicle for the twenty-five-minute journey to HMP Dodds.

***

As JJ waited for Mohammed and Jayne, he found himself reflecting on the Christmas presents he had received from his work colleagues. One was a book from Colonel Burke that he had so far only managed to read the introduction and Chapter 1 of. **The Art of War** by Chinese military strategist Sun Tsu. A few lines from that first chapter had stuck with him on his initial reading late on Boxing Day night, and so he had re-read and underlined those lines with a red marker as they were relevant to BIB's work. JJ's Google search indicated that the book dated back to the fifth century BC. The version he'd been given was the first annotated English Language translation published by Lionel Giles back in 1910. JJ had wanted to read more but had not found enough 'quiet time' to do so recently. He now planned to spend part of the afternoon and tomorrow reading Chapters 2, 3 and 4 to understand the concepts presented therein. His underlined lines were in verse 18 and they explained what **The Art of War** meant:

"All warfare is based on deception. Hence, whenever able to attack, we must seem unable; when using our forces, we must appear inactive; when we are near, we must make the enemy believe we are far away; when far away, we must make him believe we are near…"

JJ had interpreted those lines to mean that all warfare is based on deception.

Mohammed's knock on his driver's side window brought JJ back to reality.

"Sorry!" stated JJ by way of apology. He unlocked his vehicle's doors to allow Mohammed and Jayne to get in. This enabled Gold team to depart from BIB HQ for the run to HMP Dodds.

***

Colonel Burke rarely used his RED team (his three team leaders), but one notable occasion was the investigation of the attempted assassination of Motby two and a half years earlier.

Mohammed and Jayne made up JJ's Gold team. Mohammed was thirty-eight-years old and had been with BIB from its inception. A former Barbados Fire Service officer, he had been spotted by Colonel Burke who had observed him responding to a major motor vehicle accident on the ABC highway. On being invited to try out for BIB, Mohammed had to be encouraged by his father, an old friend of Colonel Burke's, to grab the opportunity. Thankfully, all had gone well and Mohammed had quickly settled down in BIB and was soon doing a fine job. JJ had no difficulty in choosing him to be part of his operational Gold team when BIB had established its three teams.

Jayne had been with BIB for five years now. Aged thirty-four, she was a highly qualified secondary school teacher with a Master's degree in Physical Education and Coaching (on top of a Degree in Psychology). She'd come to Colonel Burke's attention during a conference for senior public-sector teachers at Erdiston Teachers Training College. Jayne had spoken on the psychology of teaching secondary school and university students properly to help them to maximise their productivity in today's fast-paced workforce. Colonel Burke was only there because Jeremie had asked him to fill in for him at short notice.

Jayne had impressed Colonel Burke with the way she had structured her presentation with visibly descriptive and helpful slides throughout and a two-way Q&A session to wrap things up. He'd decided on the spot to make it his business to find out as much as he could as soon as possible about this obviously sharp lady. His instinct told him she might be a great asset to BIB, not necessarily on its front line, but more-so behind the scenes undertaking varying types of analysis to enable BIB to solve its most challenging and complex cases more quickly. When he'd contacted her a week later (after checking her out with the Public Sector Oversight Committee or PSOC), Jayne had been surprised to hear from him. She'd agreed to consider his offer before, twenty-four hours later, calling to say that she'd be willing to accept it. The money would be more than that of a teacher. The dangers of the job were, strangely, not of concern to her, as Jayne was looking for something more interesting (if not exciting) than running secondary school classes. Being a keen markswoman and having represented Barbados at the Delhi 2010 Commonwealth and London 2012 Olympic Games, that part of her personality was also never going to be a problem for BIB.

As things worked out, when an opening came on JJ's Gold team three years ago, she'd applied for it and was successful. Diversity in BIB was alive and well, as was evidenced by Joe's appointment to lead BIB's Black operational team nearly two years earlier.

Jayne was on the frontline after all! Colonel Burke had not been surprised at her rapid development in BIB, so was happy to sign off on her promotion.

***

As the Gold team departed BIB HQ, they met Colonel Burke driving in. He waved at them, as he knew where they were going and why. *Should be a piece of cake*, he thought to himself as he parked his vehicle in the space reserved for DIRECTOR in BIB's car park at the back of the building.

For Colonel Burke's part, he had argued against and still remained unconvinced of the need for BIB operatives to be utilised on PRs. But his political bosses had determined otherwise. His reservations had been noted. Either way, when asked he would ensure that one of BIB's operational teams escort the weekly movement of prisoners between HMP Dodds and the courthouses in Barbados. He and his operatives were therefore fully committed to undertaking this new task once requested by Superintendent Innis. That call had been made to Colonel Burke on Monday morning, and so it was JJ's Gold team that had then been tasked to undertake today's PR.

But this morning, Colonel Burke had other things on his mind. A major one was to compile and deliver the security situation brief (SSB) to the Prime Minister following yesterday's *P.A.A.N.I.* meeting.

***

Motby arrived at Government Headquarters just before 8:00 a.m. He knew that he had another long (but pleasant) day ahead of him. After work, he and his wife would attend a 6:30 p.m. reception at the British High Commissioner's residence for the two visiting cricket teams and their officials but would leave after an hour to return to their official Ilaro Court residence for a private dinner engagement.

Over five hundred persons had been invited to High Commissioner Tullock's reception. Less than eleven hours before it was due to start, how many of those invited would turn up remained unknown. Barbadians were notoriously bad at confirming (or not) their acceptance of invitations to evening events, especially

85

receptions. Nevertheless, given past experiences, it was reasonable to expect that, with Barbados being a cricket loving nation and more importantly, with the past year's exciting renaissance of the West Indies who were now consistently starting to win Test series again, at least four hundred of those invited could be expected to turn up.

This latter fact alarmed the Prime Minister's two-member RBPF Close Protection Unit (CPU), Sergeant Peter Eversley and Constable Jack Marshall. They were uncomfortable, not because Motby had accepted the High Commissioner's invitation to meet the members of both cricket teams, but about any potential harm that might befall him among so many people. They knew that Motby was not one to shy away from mingling.

Following the attempt to assassinate him, Motby had insisted on retaining the services of Eversley and Marshall, despite an attempt by Jeremie to replace them with a new two-member CPU team. Thereafter, Eversley and Marshall had been extremely careful about allowing 'PRIM' to be out in the open, i.e. in public places, for any length of time, just in case someone ever tried to physically harm Motby a second time.

With Eversley and Marshall expressing their concerns to him about crowded public appearances, Motby had sought to calm their fears the previous weekend by speaking with Jeremie. He had then requested that a third officer from the RBPF's main CPU unit be also designated to attend the High Commissioner's reception. Hence yesterday morning's meeting between Sergeant Browne of the RBPF's Visitors CPU unit and Motby at Government Headquarters. Browne was set to join Eversley and Marshall later.

Motby couldn't get away from himself on media outlets that morning, participating in Petra's retirement function. He had read the second lesson in the church and addressed guests at the reception.

Once in his office, he also observed that he was on the front cover of both local newspapers. Petra and Roger Carmichael were pictured with him. The headlines read *I'll Be Back*…on one cover and *Further Assignment for Former Top Civil Servant Expected* on the other. Motby was always amazed how newspapers around the world were able to create catchy headlines to encourage potential patrons to purchase their rags.

In response to both headlines, he thought to himself, *That's for me to know and all of you to learn about in due course.*

Motby turned to the newspapers' back pages. Each carried pictures and reports of last night's arrival of the two Test teams and their entourage in Barbados. The High Commissioner's reception that evening for the teams, their support staff, media, supporters and locals alike was also mentioned. He would watch the first ball of the Test Match, having been invited to be the guest of honour for the day by Neal Butler, BCA President and WICB Director. He planned to spend most, if not all of Friday at the cricket because it was unlikely that he would get back to New Kensington Oval again before the match's scheduled finish the following Tuesday.

Such was the lack of 'down time' for a Prime Minister charged with the responsibility of running any small Caribbean country.

***

Chief Superintendent Johnny Vickers, Head of Crime, Special Branch, RBPF parked his vehicle in the RBPF HQ car park. *Another fine day in paradise*, he thought to himself as he collected his briefcase and lunch bag from the back seat. Locking up the vehicle, he strode across the busy car park towards the main building. He had attended Carmichael's reception at BDF HQ the previous evening, and planned today to catch up on some outstanding paperwork. The murder trial scheduled to start in the High Court next week Wednesday, in which he would be called as a witness, was on his mind as he entered his second-floor office, but he had decided to do his preparation for this case tomorrow when he expected to have a quiet day.

With the Test Match taking place from Friday for another five days, Vickers would not be at his desk much during that period. Tidying up his desk as much as he could of any pressing matters and getting an early night's rest would set him up for the drudgery of the next week and a half.

***

The Central Bank of Barbados (CBOB) is housed in the Tom Adams Financial Centre in Church Village, central Bridgetown. Constructed back in the mid-1980's, it is an eleven-storeyed building. It's one hundred and fifty employees and other renters of office space in the complex enjoy a panoramic view of Bridgetown, the Caribbean Sea or Barbados' countryside from any work

87

station, depending on where they sat anywhere from the fourth floor up. The higher one went the better, more beautiful and expansive became the view.

The office of the secretary to Dr Albert Lewis, Deputy Governor, CBOB was located on the eighth floor. She had just settled down at her desk for another day's work, when the phone rang.

"Good morning, Central Bank of Barbados, Deputy Governor's office. Marjorie Ruck speaking. How can I help you?"

"Oh, good morning, Marjorie, its Betty Lewis. Is Albert there please?"

"No, Mrs Lewis. I haven't seen him yet, in fact, we haven't seen him since yesterday afternoon when he left early. I assumed that the bug he's been suffering from was getting the better of him. He said he would go home to rest up, but might also stop by his doctor on the way for some medication."

There was a long pause.

"Mrs Lewis, are you there?" asked Ruck.

"Uh…yes, Marjorie. It's just that Albert didn't come home last night. I haven't seen him since yesterday morning when he left for work. So that's twenty-four hours ago! That's not like him. I'm very worried. Has the Governor got him working on something new? A secret initiative for the Government perhaps where Albert has decided to bed himself down at the office or at some nearby hotel room? I'm at my wits end," said Mrs Lewis.

Immediately alarmed, Ruck did not know what to say at first. Dr Lewis was at work for most of yesterday. He'd been coughing and blowing his nose throughout the day, in fact, since the back end of the previous week. When he'd told her that he was leaving early, around 3:00 p.m., she thought this a good idea as the air conditioning certainly was not helping his condition. He'd indicated that making a doctor's visit on the way home was his intention. An early dinner, getting his wife to rub him up and down before going to bed in an effort to start throwing off his bad cold were his goals.

Dr Lewis normally got in before her, so when Ruck had not seen him, she'd not been too worried, assuming that he had not quite made the recovery he'd expected to overnight. Ruck was not one to call Dr Lewis' home, unless it was work related and important.

"Well, Mrs Lewis, while I don't know that we can say he's gone 'missing', I'll notify the Governor immediately. I'm sure Dr Lewis will turn up shortly, and that they'll be a reasonable explanation for his overnight absence. I'll get the ball rolling right away and call you right back," said Ruck.

"Oh, thank you, Marjorie. It's not like Albert not to keep in touch. I'm afraid something may have happened to him. Something's very wrong," responded Mrs Lewis.

"Alright, Mrs Lewis." Ruck had never addressed her boss' wife by her first name before and even now did not seem to be a good time to do so. "Please stay close to your phone. I'll get back to you shortly."

"Thank you so much, Marjorie. Goodbye." Mrs Lewis hung up the phone.

Ruck did likewise and sat quietly at her desk for a moment. Then, rising quickly, she strode across the corridor to the outer domain of the Governor's office.

As the Governor's secretary was off for the day, she knocked on the Governor's door and waited for an answer. Hearing "Come in", she entered and informed Dr Rollerick Edwards, Governor, CBOB of the situation related to her missing boss, the Deputy Governor.

***

BIB's Gold team arrived at HMP Dodds at 8:25 a.m. Their journey had been uneventful. They were ushered into the outer office of Superintendent Innis. JJ was presented with details related to the day's PR by Melba Bodie. Details included the number of prisoners to be transported, who they were, what they were going to court for, their criminal activity records (as known) and the eight-member team (three RBPF, five BPS officers) who would be on today's PR along with JJ's Gold team.

The PR document provided brief details on the five prisoners to be transported:

PR 18 April – 5 inmates (HMP Dodds to District A court/return)

LYNCH, Jessica (Mrs): a 47-year-old Barbadian female accused of jewellery shoplifting one week earlier in a west coast duty-free shop. Lynch had a long history of shoplifting clothes, food and small electronic items, but had now graduated to jewellery, so this was new territory for her.

MORADI, Franchesca (Miss): aged 21. Moradi was an Italian female drug mule who had been caught at the country's sole airport the previous Thursday attempting to smuggle cocaine into Barbados. She'd been charged with possession of cocaine, intent to supply, trafficking and importation of illegal drugs, specifically fifty-five kilograms of cocaine which had a street value of Bds$500,000. She was a first-time visitor to Barbados, was not a user so was simply a transporter.

FIELD, Warren (Mr): a 35-year-old unemployed Barbadian male had been sent to jail for repeated non-payment of child support. These offences related to his five children (three of which were from different women). Field's long history of non-payment of child support had seemingly finally forced the court's hand.

FOULKES, Orrin (Mr): a 67-year-old British male national on a day visit to Barbados via a cruise ship. Foulkes was caught trying to sell cannabis to locals on one of central Bridgetown's back streets. He had brought the drug (50.2 kilograms with a street value of Bds$250,000) with him off the ship. He had therefore imported it. Prompt police investigations found that Foulkes had no record of any kind back in Britain, so this was out of character and perhaps a 'spur of the moment' action. Obviously, the cruise ship he had arrived on the previous Wednesday, had sailed without him that night.

POWER, Jasper 'Stabs' (Mr): a 38-year-old Barbadian on a variety of firearms, ammunition and drug charges: conspiring to import six firearms without a licence (two Smith & Wesson Model 60 pistols, two Glock 17 pistol, one Heckler & Koch USP .40 pistol, one Taurus pistol); attempted sale of unlicensed firearms); unlawful possession of the above six firearms; fifty rounds of ammunition; possession of apparatus; trafficking in cannabis; possession of cannabis with intent to supply; resisting lawful arrest; shooting at a police officer. Power's past criminal activity also included wounding with intent and previous drug dealing activity. He is the most dangerous of the five prisoners being transported.

By order of/Signed: *S Innis – 17/4/2018*

Lt. Colonel Simon Innis, Head, Barbados Prison Service (BPS)/Superintendent, Her Majesty's Prison (HMP) Dodds

***

Marjorie Ruck's conversation with Governor Edwards prompted him to immediately call Commissioner Jeremie. He advised him that the Deputy Governor, CBOB had been missing for well over twelve hours – in fact his wife had not seen or heard from him for over twenty-four hours. Edwards requested that a senior RBPF officer – he mentioned one by name, be sent over to his office as soon as possible to initiate an investigation into the apparent disappearance.

Jeremie listened carefully, before agreeing to respond appropriately by sending over such an officer.

***

It was 8:40 a.m. when JJ, Mohammed and Jayne were shown into Superintendent Innis' inner office.

Following the usual pleasantries, they got down to business. The final plans for the day's operation were confirmed. All of the prisoners were scheduled to make their second appearances in Criminal 'A' Court at Station Hill, St Michael between 10:15 a.m. and 12:15 p.m. The PR expected to leave HMP Dodds no later than 9:15 a.m. to comfortably make the forty-minute journey and arrive at the courthouse's holding point by at least the minimum fifteen minutes required before the first prisoner was due to appear before Barbados' strict Chief Magistrate, His Honour Martin Taylor.

Innis spoke briefly about the first four prisoners. He then explained who Power was and why he was the most dangerous prisoner being transported in today's PR.

"Power was remanded to HMP Dodds a week ago following a shootout with RBPF officers after he was captured for unlicensed gun importation and possession of same. His police record is three pages long if you ever want to read his full criminal activity record."

Mohammed put up his hand and asked a direct question.

"Given what you say Superintendent, have you requested any additional protection for today's PR?"

"No."

"Why not?"

"Well, I believe your team and the RBPF boys can adequately handle the usual escort duties. My BPS crew will also be there of course. They will directly handle the prisoners."

Innis handed JJ a one-page document which was accepted. "This is a one-page summary of Power's record. You guys can read it through before you leave. Among his previous arrests were charges for stabbing up people that he did not like. Happened in nightclubs and at house parties. The nickname 'Stabs' came from one of his early victims," concluded Innis.

"Got it. Now, is there anything else you want to tell us about today's PR before we get going?" asked JJ, glancing down at the document he held. He was not expecting an affirmative answer.

"Well, yes, there is…" Innis said reluctantly.

***

Chapter Eight
Missing

Commissioner Jeremie's personal telephone call instructing Chief Superintendent Vickers to come to his office immediately was a surprise. Jeremie seldom used the telephone inside RBPF HQ to speak with him, as it was his practice to walk around HQ as much as possible to chat with or bump into his officers – especially his senior ones, at their stations. Jeremie did not like standing on too much ceremony. This came, Vickers felt, from Jeremie having started out at the bottom of the force as a beat cop where he loved being 'out and about' among the population. As he rose up the ranks of the RBPF, Jeremie had broadened this communication style of engagement with the public to include all officers under his command, whether inside or outside of RBPF HQ.

Vickers and Jeremie had, over the years, therefore usually chatted in Vickers' office. So, something was different today, no wrong. Something potentially serious must be afoot.

He hustled up the stairs to Jeremie's office. On reaching Jasmine Boyt's door, he knocked and opened it, thinking to himself, *Here goes my plan for a quiet day.*

Boyt, who had been Jeremie's secretary for the past year, directed Vickers towards the half-closed door beside her desk saying, "Go through. He's expecting you," so Vickers complied.

***

Dr Winston Smith's meeting with the Prime Minister did not require him to have done any preparation. As a result, he was back in his office within five minutes.

Motby had asked him what the big-ticket activities coming up between 1 May and 30 June were and their dates. Dr Smith wondered why he was being asked such a mundane question, because he suspected that Motby already knew the answer. They compared verbal notes on the subject for a couple of minutes. When Dr Smith asked Motby if he could have till close-of-play that day to provide a written, more accurate response to the request, Motby had agreed.

"Very well, Winston. Close-of-play it is. I anticipate leaving here around 4:30 p.m., 5:00 p.m. latest."

"I'll provide my written response well before you leave, Prime Minister," said Dr Smith.

"Thank you."

Motby knew that if anyone could confirm his information on what engagements would involve all elected Cabinet members and House of Assembly MPs, it would be his Cabinet Secretary. He didn't tell Dr Smith that he had already decided to present his annual Budget during the last week of May. But he wanted someone reliable to also check with. He anticipated announcing when Budget Day would be to the House of Assembly in mid-May.

***

Surprised, JJ looked up sharply. Normally, there would not be much else that a BIB team would need to know about the day's PR in general or their charges in particular.

"Well, due to vehicle shortages, all four prisoners will have to be moved to and from court today in one vehicle. You know that it is customary, though not mandatory for us to transport females separate from our male prisoners. We have only one available prisoner transport vehicle so have to make do," said Innis.

"Superintendent, why didn't you alert Colonel Burke about this at yesterday's *P.A.A.N.I.* meeting? Or even ask Commissioner Jeremie to borrow one of his police transport vehicles?"

Innis answered neither question.

"JJ, this is the position. We'll just have to make do. Luckily, the vehicle we'll be using today has three compartments in it. Males and females will be in the first two sections, while the third section is where we will place Power on his own as he is the most dangerous of the five prisoners to be moved. He'll be shackled hand and foot to the vehicle. He will know that other prisoners will be in the vehicle but will not be able to physically reach them. We've done this before when we've had to pre-BIB involvement with PRs. It worked out then as I expect it to work out today. My five prison officers will, as usual, be seated upfront in the double-cabbed vehicle," explained Innis.

JJ shook his head. "I don't like it. It sounds, feels and smells wrong whichever way you slice it."

"Look, can we just try and get through today please? I'm also short-staffed. I've not had time to write minutes to anyone expressing my every problem or concern about this place, or the whole prison service. My Minister is seldom available to listen."

"Make him," said JJ.

"That's easier said than done. Anyway, yesterday's *P.A.A.N.I.* meeting was otherwise focussed. I've tried my level best each day to run as tight, effective and efficient a security facility as I possibly can since I took over this office three years ago."

Innis' tone then changed.

"Look, if your team can't handle today's PR job JJ, just tell me so and we'll ring ahead and alert everybody that we can't bring the cons down to court today. That won't be pretty and when Chief Magistrate Taylor finds out that it was a BIB team that decided not to escort prisoners to his courtroom, he won't be pleased. There might even be hell to play. So, what I'm proposing is a solution to our problem! If we do it my way, all well and good. You'll have to explain to the powers that be if you do otherwise. The court backlog will simply continue to get worse if you fail to collaborate with my people today. JJ, it's BIB's call, or rather *your team's call*. What's your position? Is BIB in or out?" Innis asked.

Innis was trying to blame BIB for this situation and JJ could not let him get away with that. Damn the man.

JJ counted to ten.

Jayne, knowing JJ, gently touched his arm to stop him from verbally exploding at Innis. Mohammed also glanced sharply at JJ before interjecting.

"JJ, we're here already! Let's work the situation, not the personality. We'll report this problem later. It's close to our departure deadline anyway for getting this show on the road. Not moving in another ten minutes or so will mean that we not make the journey downtown in time, and we all know Chief Magistrate Taylor gets vex if people scheduled to appear in his courtroom are not punctual."

JJ did not respond immediately, so Jayne nudged him firmly. Innis was waiting.

JJ usually got on with Innis but right now, he wanted to reach across the desk separating his Gold team from Innis and knock some sense into his thick skull. He acknowledged Jayne's nudge, deciding to keep his cool and play ball.

Taking a deep breath, JJ said, "Fine, Superintendent. You win. We'll do today's PR your way but I'm not pleased. Once this PR is done, I'll report whatever transpires today to the powers that be. Hopefully some action will be taken to see that you get the resources (funding, equipment, bodies) required to run this place properly. I hope nothing stupid happens on today's PR, for everyone's sake."

"Fine. Thank you, JJ." He picked up the phone and spoke into it to get things moving. When he finished, JJ asked him a question.

"I'm curious. Have you participated in a PR since you became Superintendent of this place?"

"No, JJ. I have a lot to do here and elsewhere. Today is no different. My second will take it from here. Thanks for understanding and cooperation. Good morning to you all."

BIB's Gold team, having been summarily dismissed by Innis, rose from their seats and left his office. Deputy Superintendent George Telford was waiting for them in the outer office. He led JJ, Mohammed and Jayne over to the small prison loading area where the prisoner transport vehicle stood awaiting the five prisoners' arrival who were to be taken to court that morning. There, along with the three RBPF officers detailed to help escort today's PR and the five chosen BPS officers who were to accompany the five prisoners, met and introduced themselves to each other. Most knew one other from previous PRs, socially or from schooldays.

Mohammed pulled JJ aside while they waited for the prisoners to be brought out. He whispered to him, "I don't like this but there was no point in fighting him in there, so let's do what we came here to do."

"I guess you're right, Mo," said JJ, still unhappy.

"I agree with Mo," said Jayne who had joined them.

"Well, let's get this PR over and done with. We'll brief the chief fully once we're back at BIB HQ. He'll be able to formally raise it at the next *P.A.A.N.I.,* if Innis doesn't, if not before to the political class," responded JJ.

"Sounds good," said Jayne. Mohammed nodded in agreement. Gold team was ready to go.

***

A few minutes later, as the prisoners were being loaded into the prisoner transport vehicle, JJ slipped away behind a wall. Having now read the document Innis had presented to him, he made two quick calls.

The first was to briefly inform Colonel Burke of the nature of Gold team's situation with regard to the day's PR. He promised to share full details on their return to BIB HQ sometime between 1:00 p.m. and 1:30 p.m.

The second was to a reliable friend and colleague.

"Morning RED 2. Clear your head. I need you to be ready in case I call on you later. Please also alert RED 3. I've a feeling that Gold team might need some assistance from both of you during the day. I hope my sense is wrong and you guys are left to enjoy your two days off."

"Right, JJ, but what's this all about?"

"Can't specify because I'm not sure. I just have a strange feeling about today's PR. Must go, so we'll speak later." On that note, JJ ending the call.

RED 2 wondered what to make of that conversation. It was not like JJ to panic or be too concerned about any situation, certainly not a PR. JJ was always calm and confident at, about and with his work.

But something was different about their conversation. As he'd been called by JJ, he would do as he had been asked and notify RED 3. They would make themselves available to respond should JJ call.

***

Colonel Burke briefly pondered on JJ's situation. It was not good, but he did not dwell on it. JJ was his most reliable and experienced operative and so he felt confident that JJ would find a way to make the PR work. Lessons would be learned from this experience by BIB's Gold team and practices upgraded.

Colonel Burke focussed on completing the *P.A.A.N.I.* security situation brief (SSB). He knew the Prime Minister read every SSB that was submitted to him. As the SSB's author, Colonel Burke was never surprised to receive a call from Motby on the secure red phone in his office, seeking clarification on any unclear points before Motby would file away each SSB. Questions about an agreed *P.A.A.N.I.* strategy related to an important forthcoming event prior to its implementation were not unusual.

At 9:28 a.m., using BIB's secure e-system, Colonel Burke dispatched *P.A.A.N.I.* latest SSB to Motby.

***

After the second of his calls, JJ returned to his team and passed Innis' document onto Mohammed to read. Having done so, he in turn handed it on to Jayne to do likewise.

Shaking her head, her only comment was, "Power is a nasty piece of work, fellas."

"Too right! Let's get this over and done with. Once he's convicted and sentenced, he should go away from society for a good while given his track record. Hopefully others like him can follow suit and also be put away," was Mohammed's response.

"Okay people, let's do this. I have other things to do this afternoon at home," said JJ.

***

Being sent away today for a long prison term was not on Power's agenda. When he'd gotten word the previous evening at dinner that he would be 'sprung' during today's PR, Power was happy. He wondered who was behind it. *Once it's not those overseas people I owe significant sums to for the guns and drugs imported in recent months that remain unpaid for*, he thought he would be okay. Yes, he had promised to pay them last week but once he'd been caught by the RBPF, that went out the window. His reason now for not making payment was clear and excusable. Anyway, his operational expenses were high and he needed to take care of those before he could be in a position to repay his suppliers in full.

Being an optimist, Power believed that there was more importing for him to facilitate. More 'merchandise' and 'product' to retail that was separate from what the RBPF had captured from him a week earlier. He intended to continue living well and to enjoying the freedom of doing so. He was still a young man with the best years of his life ahead of him. A long period of imprisonment would prohibit all of the above and would not be an appealing prospect.

Hence, today was the day he and his business associates would be ameliorating both his and their situations. He hoped not but did not care if anyone got seriously hurt in the springing process.

***

POWER, JASPER (a.k.a. 'Stabs')

. Aged 38.

. <u>11 April 2018</u>: Remanded to HMP Dodds after Magistrates Court appearance (re-appearance date set for 18 April 2018).

. <u>10 April 2018</u>: captured and arrested by RBPF after a shootout for having illegally imported without the relevant license and having possession of a cache of firearms, ammunition trafficking in illegal drugs namely cannabis a.k.a. marijuana, all found in his house.

. <u>16 February 2016</u>: beat up a girlfriend, Marcia Leach – broken wrist, swollen face and grazed her right arm with a gun shot in a fit of anger over her refusal to have sex with him during her period. Leach attended a private clinic for treatment but refused to identify Power or press charges even though RBPF investigations identified Power as the culprit.

. Power had long been considered as a major local drug dealer, but insufficient evidence had not been gathered to enable RBPF to arrest, let alone prosecute or potentially gain a conviction in a court of law against him for such activity.

. <u>January to September 2013</u>: Power spent nine months in HMP Dodds for stabbing his supposed good friend, apparently over money supposedly owed to him at a bar.

. <u>25 October 2009</u>: Power stabbed a man at a night club after fighting over a girl (RBPF was called by the owner but as they no witnesses came forward, nothing happened).

. <u>February to September 2002</u>: Power spent six months in HMP Glendairy for breaking, entering and stealing electronic equipment from a home.

. <u>February 2001</u>: Power stabbed a woman at a night club after a drink was accidentally spilled on him (RBPF called but again victim did not pursue charges – it is believed that 'money passed hands').

. <u>August 1999</u>: Power stabbed a man at a house party who danced with the girl he took to the party (RBPF involved but victim declined to press charges).

. <u>November 1996</u>: Power was suspended and reported by his school principal to RBPF for selling drugs (marijuana) from the 6th form classroom at the school.

*****

Twelve years earlier, Motby had charged BIB, wherever and whenever possible, with wiping out corruption, no matter how it had raised its ugly head in Barbados. Colonel Burke, as Head of BIB, took this task very seriously.

At the time, having been a long-term supporter of Tottenham Hotspur Football Club, the North London team (a.k.a. *Spurs*) from England's Premier League since his student days at City University in London, Colonel Burke had liked and now chose to copy that club's motto for the new but small BIB security agency. He wanted something that would inspire his operatives. Looking back now, with *Spurs* having won the last completed (2016-2017) Premier League championship, he was pleased with his choice. Sharing *Spurs* club's motto of **'To Dare Is to Do'**, had worked out well. It corresponded with the challenge Motby had given to him way back then. BIB operatives had all come to learn, think of and appreciate this motto as their very own. Even Motby had become a part-time *Spurs* supporter once the motto had been explained to him. He considered Colonel Burke to have chosen well so yes, it was an appropriate motto for BIB.

All these years later, Colonel Burke remained more than content with the way BIB had gone about and successfully completed its various assignments. This was important to him. As part of that success, he had made two things paramount to his political bosses. The safety of his BIB operatives, tied to his ongoing wish to secure increased resources (preferably funding as additional staff was unlikely) would enable his operatives to be trained to the highest standards possible. Also, acquisition and use of the highest quality technological equipment that the Government could afford should enable BIB to maintain high standards of professionalism and performance. Simply growing BIB's size was never his concern.

Colonel Burke suspected that the Prime Minister appreciated these virtues, though they had not spoken directly about them, but had discussed the importance of BIB operatives trusting their instincts on investigations. At one of their earlier meetings, Motby had told Colonel Burke that experience had taught him not to believe everything he heard, even with his own ears. Also, he should never take anything for granted, or too seriously, always keeping his guard up. Ultimately, Colonel Burke should trust *his* instincts and only make judgments which led to *his own* reasonable conclusions.

BIB's refined mandate since 2007, '...*to root out evil, corruption, espionage and misdeeds affecting Barbadian society, elsewhere in the Caribbean too, once Barbados' national security interests were threatened...*' had served the agency and the country well. BIB's well-appointed HQ in the three-storey **Stand Firm** building at Welches, Christ Church also housed the Barbados Fire Service's (BFS) south coast fire station which was a co-tenant. BIB occupied the third floor which catered to the ongoing administrative side of BIB's work.

The well-secured, expansive basement floor served many purposes – as BIB's training/exercise area with full bathroom facilities, a sound-proofed shooting range, an interrogation centre featuring special 'accommodation' spaces for BIB's VIP clients, i.e. persons requiring special protection and or undesirable characters who needed to be kept for interrogation by BIB and other law enforcement/security agencies. Also housed in the building's basement floor was BIB's state-of-the-art ICT facility platform, the envy of most other Caribbean law enforcement agencies. The secure intelligence room (SIR), often the nerve-centre of any major ongoing BIB operation, was also located here.

BIB's twelve operatives were carefully chosen, experienced men and women. All operatives had seen 'action', completing several missions in and out of Barbados. Colonel Burke had once read a story in a US security magazine which stated that the USA's intelligence network was made up of sixteen agencies, 100,000 agents and operated on an annual budget of US$6.6 billion! Colonel Burke did not know how true this was, but he had used these alleged facts, along with the results from the final review after the attempted Motby assassination, to engineer a twelve and a half per cent budget increases in BIB operational funding over the past two financial years.

Colonel Burke had on more than one occasion told his operatives, *BIB is an ordinary Government Department whose top operatives regularly do extra-ordinary things.* His belief and passion were regularly shared with BIB's operatives. It meshed nicely with the **Spurs** Motto, ***To Dare Is to Do***.

The close-nit and reliable team of operatives were Colonel Burke's pride and joy. All of them held 'SECRET' clearances from the Cabinet Office following in-depth investigations by the RBPF's Special Branch. Colonel Burke and his three team leaders also held special 'TOP SECRET – EYES ONLY' clearances from the Prime Minister.

***

Chief Superintendent Vickers knocked and pushed the half-opened door to Jeremie's office.

"Good morning, Commissioner," he stated on entry.

He found Jeremie staring out of one of the two windows at the back of his third-floor office. Beyond the windows stood the Tom Adams Financial Centre which housed the CBOB.

Turning around, Jeremie spoke hurriedly.

"Thanks for coming up so quickly, Johnny. I've a big problem. The CBOB's Deputy Governor is missing. No one knows his whereabouts. His staff say he left work before close-of-play yesterday afternoon and they haven't seen him since."

"Sir, I take it he has a wife? When did she last see him?" asked Vickers.

"Yesterday (Tuesday) morning when he left home for work. Look, I'd normally get one of your people to work with the Station Sergeant at District B, that being the appropriate police station as the Deputy Governor lives in St George, to go over and speak with the staff at CBOB before visiting his wife at home. But Governor Edwards called me directly five minutes ago to request that I put one of my top sleuths on the case. Let me correct myself. Dr Edwards asked for you by name, Johnny," concluded Jeremie.

"Really! I didn't know the Governor knew my name," stated a surprised Vickers.

"Well, now you know that he does. Now, I'm told that the Deputy Governor is not known to be unreliable. He's a strict work to home sort of guy, a family man. No vices that I've been told about…at least so far. I can understand Dr Edwards' concern. I'd like you to pop over to the Bank and speak with him, the Deputy Governor's secretary and other staff who work closely with him. That's all appropriate. Try to gain some more background on the good Deputy. Was he working on something special for the Bank, the Ministry of Finance, etc.? Has he been ill or absent from work lately? Then go see his wife. Once you've done that, come back here and let's discuss what you've found. We can then decide what our, I mean your next step should be. How's that sound?" asked Jeremie.

"No problem, sir, but you haven't mentioned the Deputy Governor's name yet, although I think it's Lewis. Have we had any dealings with him before?" asked Vickers.

"My bad! Sorry Johnny, you're right. His name is Dr Albert Maurice Lewis. He's a dual national – Bajan born, lived in the US for many years. He worked at the IMF and the World Bank before re-locating to Barbados three years ago, initially on a one-year secondment from the World Bank to CBOB. When the Deputy Governor's position came up, Dr Edwards offered Dr Lewis a two-year contract with an option to renew for a similar period which was accepted."

"I take it that he accepted without hesitation?"

"Yes. Dr Lewis resigned from the World Bank and became a contracted CBOB employee. Dr Edwards told me that around that time, Dr Lewis had indicated that he had welcomed the chance to get away from the cold, hopefully for good. He also wanted to make an enhanced and ongoing contribution to Barbados' economic development. Dr Lewis is married. He has two grown children who both reside in the United States. The boy is a successful lawyer in New York and his sister's a management lecturer at a Texas university."

"Good for them. Tell me something. Is his first contract close to an end and if so, any word on if it's expected to be renewed by CBOB?"

"*Good* questions. Dr Edwards and I did not get into that, so why don't you ask him about the state of Dr Lewis's contract when you meet him shortly?"

"Will do, sir. I'll visit the Bank and speak with Dr Edwards. After that, I'll visit Mrs Lewis. With luck, I'll be back here by late lunchtime with something for us to munch on. Can I take Inspector Moss along with me? I suspect he'll end up being our lead 24 x 7 person on this case if we don't find Dr Lewis by nightfall. I'd rather not tie myself down on this one, just in case something big breaks on the ECC security screen project. Remember, the Test Match and ECC project we're already running," said Vickers.

"Yes, of course. By all means take him along. I'm up to my neck in paperwork with special security requests from Ryan Appleton for all these cricket VIPs who start arriving around lunchtime for the Test Match. So, you're right, just in case I need you to deal with something bigger over the next week or so, get Moss in on this. Pop across and show Governor Edwards that our force takes the disappearance of his Deputy seriously."

"Okay. Speak later."

"I guess I'll have to alert Colonel Burke of this situation at the Bank. He needs to be made aware, as he'll probably want to mention it to the PM in an updated SSB before tomorrow's Cabinet meeting. It would be great if we could have this all cleared up by then, Johnny – or at least to be close to solving this problem."

"Yes, Commissioner."

Once out of Jeremie's office, Vickers passed by Inspector Byron Moss's desk. Tapping him on the shoulder, he simply said, "Come with me, young man."

Two minutes later, the two senior officers headed out of RBPF HQ in central Bridgetown to commence the three-minute walk over to the Tom Adams Financial Centre and Governor Edwards' eighth-floor office.

Vickers briefed Moss along the way.

***

Five minutes later, after making a brief call to Elvis Springer, Permanent Secretary in the Ministry of Finance & Economic Affairs, Jeremie left his office to speak with Jasmine Boyt. Once their conversation had ended, he returned to his office and called Colonel Burke to inform him that the CBOB's Deputy Governor was missing.

Jeremie was surprised at the quiet way Colonel Burke received this information. *Trevor's in a good mood*, he thought after replacing the receiver. Perhaps after his dozen years as BIB Director, he was used to receiving and processing difficult news or information on national situations. *Comes with the territory.*

That caused him to briefly reflect on his position as Barbados' top cop.

***

Okay, thought Colonel Burke to himself. This is different! Senior Government officials in Barbados were not known to disappear into thin air for no apparent reason. Today was definitely *not* going to be as they say, another day in paradise.

There was work to be done. Colonel Burke placed a call to Valerie Holloway, Permanent Secretary in the Ministry of National Security (MNS). He wanted to learn some more about Dr Albert Lewis.

***

Hon. Preston Grant MP, Minister of Tourism, International Transport and Sport sat in his office reviewing the points he should make during a pre-arranged television interview that he would record with Britain's Sky Sports lead cricket correspondent in another half an hour. He was to be joined in the interview by Elizabeth 'Liz' Brathwaite, CEO of Barbados Tourism Hospitality Inc. (BTHI), the Government agency responsible for executing the tourism policy set by Grant's Ministry. An interview would also be taped with Neal Butler, President of the BCA at 3:00 p.m. that afternoon in New Kensington Oval's boardroom.

The knock on his door caused him to look up.

"Come in."

In strode Eunice Atwell, his secretary.

"Mr Minister, the Sky Sports people have arrived. I've placed them in the conference room where they can set up for the interview."

"Thanks. Eunice. Any sign of Miss Brathwaite yet?"

"Reception rang just before I came into you. She's on her way up, sir."

"Very well. Please show her in once she reaches. I need to ensure that we're both on the same page for this Sky Sports thing."

"Of course, Minister," said Atwell as she left his office.

A minute later, Atwell knocked again and opened the door. She did not wait for an answer this time. In walked Liz Brathwaite.

"Good morning, Miss Brathwaite, are you interview-ready?" asked Grant, looking up from behind his desk.

"I think so, Minister," Brathwaite responded with a disarming smile.

Atwell closed the door behind Brathwaite and retreated to her outer office.

Now alone, Minister Grant spent a few seconds admiring Brathwaite before stating, "My God, Liz, you look lovely today."

"You too, PG, if I may be allowed to say so in a Minister's innermost sanctum," replied Brathwaite.

He came from behind his desk and went over to Brathwaite. They exchanged a long and passionate kiss that ended with them patting each other on their respective backsides. Once they were apart, she immediately reached into her handbag for a tissue to wipe away her lipstick that was on Grant's mouth.

"Darn, now that you've got me going, I must make some running repairs!" said Brathwaite.

"Sorry. Please use my bathroom," said Grant, reaching for his tie to check that his immaculately tied knot had not been moved out of place during their embrace.

It was not yet public knowledge that Grant and Brathwaite were 'an item'. They had been seeing each another discretely for a couple of months now and had managed to keep family, close friends, colleagues and staff unaware of their romantic involvement. Truth be told, they'd been surprised that their relationship had not yet been discovered. Both were young (late thirties), single and attractive. They knew this situation would not last for much longer, Barbadian 'gossip and rumour mongering' within its society being what it was.

Both officials were very good at their jobs. They were well-qualified, suited, committed and dedicated to the task of presenting the best side of Barbados' tourism and sporting attributes to an interested overseas international and local audience.

Having regained control of themselves, they sat down to focus on the core messages they would seek to get across to their British audience in another fifteen minutes.

"You're going to be great in this interview, Liz," said Grant who had returned behind his mahogany desk to sit in his executive chair.

"You too, PG. We're both going to tell the Brits about our wonderful country, its tourism and sports policy initiatives, including the new initiatives we'll be launching ahead of the next winter season at this year's World Travel Market in London in November," she opined from her seat opposite Grant's desk.

"Indeed. Question. Has the *Advanced Tourism* policy paper you took to Cabinet two weeks ago been approved yet? I mean, are you sure we can mention it today?" asked Brathwaite.

"Not approved yet, but I fully expect that paper to be ratified shortly. It's on tomorrow's Cabinet *Agenda*, so I hope to be able to push it through because it has been discussed at the last two weekly Cabinet meetings. The *Sports Are Us* paper, well, that's not on this week's Cabinet's *Agenda* for tomorrow, but I'm advised by the Cabinet Secretary that it will be there next week. At Petra Carmichael's retirement reception on Tuesday night, I secured the PM's approval to mention both papers during my interview," responded Grant.

"Great," said Brathwaite.

Ten minutes later, Grant and Brathwaite left his office.

Waiting for them was Rosalyn Dalrymple, Grant's Permanent Secretary. Together, they journeyed to the Ministry's conference room. Each of them carried a copy of the prepared opening statement Grant would make at the start of the interview which would 'air' on Sky Sports television network during the lunch break on Day 1 (Friday, 20 April) of the Test Match. He was also scheduled to give a live, follow-up solo interview to Sky Sports during the tea interval on Day 3 (Sunday, 22 April) of the game by which time he hoped West Indies would be in an advantageous, if not a winning position.

***

Marjorie Ruck was awaiting the arrival of Chief Superintendent Vickers and Inspector Moss on the ground floor reception area of the Tom Adams Financial Centre. Ruck quickly signed them into the guest book before leading them to the lift. They ascended to the eighth floor and were led into Governor Dr Rollerick Edwards SCM's office.

After the introductions, he addressed the two RBPF officers directly.

"Thanks for coming over so quickly, gentlemen. I'm most grateful to Commissioner Jeremie for his prompt response to my request for assistance. Deputy Governor Lewis' disappearance is of great concern to all of us here at the Bank. It is unlike him not to make contact with his wife, Marjorie or myself during any twelve-hour period. So, something is *very* wrong. How can you gentlemen help us get to the bottom of this situation?"

"Can we see his paper diary or, if he doesn't keep one, the electronic calendar on his computer showing his appointments for the past two weeks up to this coming Friday? Also, was Dr Lewis working on anything sensitive that you know of – secret even, that someone outside of this office might want to obtain?"

Edwards responded.

"Nothing that I'm aware of, but…" he looked at Ruck enquiringly, in case she knew something he didn't.

"No, nothing out of the ordinary, sir," was her response.

"Good. Now let me see Dr Lewis's diary and the electronic calendar on his computer that would be a start. We'll see what they suggest to us. We'll then head over to Dr Lewis' residence to speak with Mrs Lewis. After that, depending on where we stand, we'll probably return here to speak with staffers who have worked most closely with him and who interacted with him on his last day at the office on yesterday. Depending on what our investigation show, we hope to report back to you before close of play, say around 4.00 p.m. Is that okay with you Governor Edwards?" asked Vickers.

"Yes, yes. Happy for you to get cracking on this matter. I'm available should you need me anytime today. Either Joyce, my secretary or Marjorie here can break into anything I'm doing if either of you gentlemen wish to speak with me should that help any part of your investigation."

"Thank you, Governor Edwards. That's good to know. We'll try not to disturb you unless we have some good news to report. So, until later, sir."

"Very well. Thanks again gentlemen."

The meeting was over. There were handshakes all around, before Marjorie led the two RBPF officers out of Edwards' office and into her own. She kept Dr Lewis' paper diary and so, once this was reviewed for any potential leads, she would then go into Dr Lewis' office and switch on his computer to see what was in his calendar for the previous and current week.

As she did not know his password, CBOB's Systems Administrator was requested to retrieve Dr Lewis' two current passwords from the safe that contained all CBOB employees' passwords in case of an emergency, which this now was.

Fifteen minutes later, with access having been gained to Dr Lewis standalone computer, nothing out of the ordinary appeared that would shed any light on his possible whereabouts. Nevertheless, armed with pages of the past fortnight's entries, Vickers and Moss left the CBOB and headed for the Lewis residence in the secluded Rowans Development in St George which was a twenty-minute drive away, traffic permitting.

***

Edwards was in a reflective mood.

Following his meeting with Vickers and Moss, he tried hard to return his mind to the second draft of the CBOB's First Quarter 2018 economic report on Barbados that was set to be released to the country in another five days (on Monday morning, 23 April). While it was not his practice to amend the drafts of any of the Quarterly or Annual economic reports, he liked to see each draft as it was being worked on by what he considered to be an excellent and experienced team of technocrats. He was of the opinion that he should be informed of, but would not interfere with any of CBOB's economic findings or conclusions on the country's economic performance. The truth should always be told to the country. Politicians were, of course, entitled to their views on CBOB's work and output, but it would always and only present the facts under his watch. The chips would fall wherever they did.

Edwards was fortunate in two ways. The economy was doing fine, with steady if not spectacular growth of 2.7% per annum for the past two years. Also, since taking up office he had discussed, but never gotten any pressure to enhance the economic figures, whatever they were, from the Minister of Finance and Economic Affairs (also the Prime Minister) or his Permanent Secretary. This had not been the case, going back to when the now Opposition Progressive Barbados Party (P.B.P.) was in Government.

Edwards pushed aside the draft of the First Quarterly 2018 economic report and swivelled his large executive chair around to take in the view out of his eighth-floor window towards the St George valley in the distance. It was really Dr Lewis' department which oversaw collection of the data used and undertook the analysis before compiling these and other reports issued by CBOB. In his absence, and until his return to work, he would have to pay closer attention to them.

So where is Albert? It's not like him to skip work for any part of a day, let alone parts of two. Edwards sincerely hoped that Dr Lewis was okay and would be safely back at work soon. A return tomorrow would be ideal.

Edwards swung his chair around to face his desk. Across the room, he noticed the three-word collage located on the wall directly in front of him. *Love… Laugh… Live.* This had been presented to him five years ago by his former economics faculty at the London School of Economics on his being appointed CBOB Governor.

Sight of the collage drew him to look across his office to his right near to the door leading to his secretary's office. There stood a second collage on his wall, with slightly different words which spoke to his personal philosophy of *Think… Reflect… Act.*

Edwards picked up his desk phone to speak with his secretary, Joyce John before quickly replacing it.

Silly me, he thought. He'd forgotten that John had taken the day off to be with her retired sister Gloria Griffith who lived in St Lucy. Today was Griffith's birthday. The two sisters had always been close, so much so that their family members referred to them as 'the twins', even though they were born five years apart.

He called Ruck. "Marjorie, please come in for a minute."

"On my way, sir."

109

Ruck quickly appeared. Edwards initialled the second draft of CBOB's First Quarter 2018 economic report on Barbados before closing the file containing it. He gave the file to her.

"Please pass this to Claire Parnell. In Dr Lewis' absence and as Head of the Research Department, she should proceed with any later updates to the proposed report."

"I'll take it to her right away, sir."

"Many thanks and, Marjorie, let's keep Dr Lewis' absence as quiet as we can for as long as we can today please. If asked, just say he's not in yet. If he's not back with us by tomorrow morning, then I guess we'll have to go public to staff, media and whoever."

"Yes, Governor, fingers crossed that we see Dr Lewis shortly, and in one piece."

"I second that, Marjorie," responded Edwards as Ruck left the room.

Edwards returned his mind to the next item sitting in his inbox. In another half hour, he would receive a courtesy call from HE Stephens Rowley III, USA Ambassador to Barbados and the Eastern Caribbean. Would Ambassador Rowley be aware that Dr Lewis was missing? Unlikely, so he would not tell him.

Edwards had sufficient time to call his fellow Central Bank Governor in Port-of-Spain, Trinidad on another matter before Ambassador Rowley arrived.

***

Vickers now had what he considered to be the back-story to events prior to the non-appearance (he preferred to use that word rather than disappearance) of Dr Lewis. A visit to Mrs Lewis for her side of the story would further help him. Due to the importance of Dr Lewis' position at CBOB, and of him being one of the Government's main financial advisers, it was decided to keep this issue under wraps for as long as possible, certainly from the media.

Vickers hoped Dr Lewis would turn up shortly, ideally before day's end and could explain his absence. If he did so, this would all quickly go away and become 'yesterday's news', though it would never be forgotten by his family or employer.

***

Chapter Nine
Breakout

Incidents of attempted prisoner escapes in Barbados while being transported by law enforcement agencies between the prison and court for appearances were far and few between. Successful escapes just did not happen.

Ten minutes into today's journey out of HMP Dodds, this would all change.

Just after the leading RBPF escort vehicle had rounded a slight corner, two loud noises were heard. Gunshots. Nothing seemed to happen for a few seconds until, almost as if in slow motion, the prisoner transport vehicle swerved across the road before slamming into the ten-foot high rockface through which the road had been cut fifty years earlier.

Randolph Perch, the BPS officer driving the prisoner transport vehicle, felt the steering wheel escape both of his hands. He could do nothing about what was happening to his vehicle. Clarence Rouse, the senior BPS officer on the day's PR was sat in the front passenger seat. He screamed an obscenity that should never be repeated in front of children but was acceptable given the circumstances. He was sure that Perch had not hit anything on the road. As the vehicle hit the rockface, Perch's head smashed into the side of the cab. He also received several cuts from fragments of glass emanating from the shattered windscreen and driver's side window.

Perch and Rouse started to gather themselves, but quickly became aware of further imminent danger. There was the noise, then through Rouse's window they saw a six-wheeled truck heading directly for their vehicle. It appeared to Rouse that the truck coming their way had been specially rigged for the task it was set to perform. Both men screamed and looked away just before the truck slammed into Rouse's side of the prisoner transport vehicle, driving it into the rockface for a second time before reversing. A few seconds later, the now badly damaged prisoner transport vehicle righted itself by falling back onto what was left of its wheels.

Perch, now in agony, was slumped over the steering wheel and recognised blood on himself and around the cab. He did not know what to do next and so did not move. Rouse on the other hand, wanted to exit the vehicle and get away from the vehicular carnage as soon as possible. He soon realised that movement was impossible for him. His left arm felt broken and his feet had somehow gotten tangled up with the shattered door on his side of the vehicle from the truck's impact. Swearing even more loudly again, Rouse could only look over at Perch. They pitied each other.

They could hear their passengers, three fellow BPS officers and the five prisoners shouting and banging the vehicle's sides for help in the back of the prisoner transport vehicle. Just a few minutes ago, all ten occupants of the vehicle had been travelling safely (if not comfortably). That now seemed an eternity ago.

***

Leading the three-vehicle PR convoy was the RBPF vehicle. In it were three officers. Their vehicle had already rounded and cleared a slight corner in the road when they had heard what to their experienced ears were gunshots. Checking his rear-view mirror, driver Paul Reece noticed that the prisoner transport vehicle travelling behind them was not there.

"Heard that?" asked Sergeant Malcolm Holder. He was the senior RBPF officer on today's PR.

"Sure did, Sarge. Something's up," responded Reece, slowing down the vehicle.

"Okay. Stop. Better still, let's get back there quick to see what's going on, Paul," ordered Holder.

Rather than turn the vehicle around, Reece put the vehicle into reverse. The weapons of Sergeant Holder and the third RBPF officer were already drawn.

The RBPF vehicle never reached the scene of the damaged prisoner transport vehicle. The six-wheeled truck had anticipated the RBPF vehicle's return and so was ready to undertake its second destructive action. As the truck smashed into the RBPF vehicle, the sight and sound appeared to be even more fearsome than had been the case when the truck had hit the prisoner transport vehicle.

***

The RBPF vehicle, having been hit by the oncoming six-wheel truck, was rammed with such force that it toppled onto its side and rolled over a couple of times before ending up in the roadside's ditch.

Holder was the first to react inside the vehicle. Though his nose was bloodied, he shouted at his two fellow officers.

"You guys okay? We're in real trouble boys, so keep your head's down," he ordered.

There was no answer at first, so Holder looked around inside the overturned vehicle. Luckily, he was otherwise fine, but Reece had not moved since the vehicle had come to a halt. Holder suspected that Reece might have received a blow to his head during the collision and aftermath. The third and youngest officer started to moan.

"What's your condition, son?" asked Holder.

"My left leg's caught behind Reece's seat Sarge and I can't move it," he responded.

"Okay. Stay still. I'll see what I can do for you once I've assessed what's happening outside. Remember, stay down," he ordered again. Gun in hand, Holder poked his head out of the damaged vehicle.

What he saw confirmed his first thought and fear. *This was a breakout. How many men are involved in it were unknown but Jesus, did it have to happen on my PR?*

Just then, further explosions were heard. More gunfire. Where was it coming from, Holder wondered?

***

BIB's Gold team was the third vehicle in the day's PR convoy. As per protocol, JJ had driven thirty yards behind the BPS prisoner transport vehicle and so had seen it suddenly swerve and hit the rockface for no apparent reason. Alarm bells went off when they noticed a six-wheeled truck's appearance and its first action.

113

"Something bad is happening team. Let's get ready to respond. Where's the lead escort?" JJ asked, slowing down his vehicle, only to observe the damage that was then done to the RBPF vehicle by the same truck.

"What the hell –" shouted Jayne as the RBPF vehicle ended up by the roadside's ditch.

***

A car was also rapidly approaching the scene.

They were three masked persons in it. The car screeched to a halt where, in the blink of an eye, the person in the back seat opened his door. Jumping out and, he headed directly towards the prisoner transport vehicle. He had a metal-cutting tool in his hand which he used to completely open the prisoner transport vehicle's back door which was already half-open from the earlier collisions. The man proceeded to cut away the inner metal door containing Power and also released him from the prisoner restraints that had secured him to the prisoner transport vehicle before giving him a stern directive.

"Run like hell to the open back door of that car."

Power needed no second invitation to escape and so did as he was told.

The metal-cutting rescuer followed Power into the getaway car. Power was alarmed when the car did not move off immediately but understood why when a fourth masked man joined them in the back seat. He appeared winded from his run to the getaway car, managing to drag his right leg into it.

Power, in true Bajan dialect, wondered to himself: *Where de hell he come from?*

"Hurry up, hurry up man. All in?" asked the driver.

The car door slammed shut.

"Yes," said the fourth masked man breathlessly.

"Then let's get the hell out ta here boys," said the driver, moving the getaway car away from the scene.

It was now time to ensure its safe getaway from the scene. Those in the getaway car knew that neither the RBPF and BPS officers were able to stop their escape because they were incapacitated and had no working vehicles to pursue them with. The other agency was unlikely to pursue them, given the carnage that the getaway car's occupants had left behind. There was one way to ensure that there would be no immediate pursuit.

114

"You know what to do," said the driver to his front seat passenger.

"Yeah," was the response as he would down his window and reached for his rifle.

Power, knowing the getaway car's driver, engaged him. "Thanks for the rescue, man."

"Just doing a job, Stabs. Be jolly now."

***

It was Mohammed who spotted what turned out to be the getaway car.

As the Gold team pulled up on the confused scene, they were greeted by several gunshots which appeared to be coming from the getaway car as it started to speed away.

In response, Mohammed and Jayne exited JJ's vehicle with their weapons drawn. They knew they could not save this situation. But they had witnessed what had gone down and picked up that the last person who had ran from the truck to the getaway car's back door had a problem with his right leg. Did he get hurt during today's prisoner rescue or was he carrying a more long-term injury which made him run so gingerly to the getaway car? They filed away this nugget of information in their minds in case it helped them later on in any investigation tracking down the persons responsible for today's event.

The six-wheeled truck used to ram the prisoner transport vehicle into the rockface and push the RBPF vehicle off the road now stood, engine still running where it had been abandoned at the scene. It was the starkest of reminders of what had just taken place.

Why had JJ's Gold team not responded to the getaway car's gunfire or even gone after it at speed? That was not their primary goal during any PR exercise. This was to secure the prisoners that they were charged with escorting. It was also time to check on their law enforcement colleagues on the scene.

Given all that had transpired, JJ had a good idea which one of the five prisoners would not be here.

***

The breakout had come as a shock to the three law enforcement agencies involved in the convoy. It had taken place quickly, efficiently and successfully, though it had not been as clinical as its executors had anticipated. Nevertheless, it had been a carefully calculated and yes, vicious event.

During the assault, the RBPF officers in their escort vehicle had all been hurt. Their vehicle had also been badly damaged if not destroyed. A bloodied Sergeant Holder was shaken up but had managed to exit his vehicle to return fire at the gun-toting rescuer sitting in the front seat of the getaway car. Holder's shots had not prevented its escape.

The five BPS officers were also hurt, though they had no injuries that would not heal over time. Sensibly, the three officers in the back of the prisoner transport vehicle had made no attempt to prevent the removal of Power from his segregated area in it. Maybe they were afraid of getting hurt. Senior BPS officer Rouse had no way of doing this given his physical state. This situation was a first for them.

Investigations would later reveal that the prisoner transport vehicle's front and rear left sided tyres had been shot out, causing it to leave the road and crash into the rockface. Everyone inside of the vehicle had been thrown around. The BPS officers and remaining prisoners all had a few cuts and bruises.

Whereas Jessica Lynch, Franchesca Moradi and Orrin Foulkes had been able to stumble away from the much-damaged but now right-sided prisoner transport vehicle and now sat close together on the ground, Warren Field had taken the opportunity to make a run for his freedom through the deep brush that lined both sides of the road not far from the rockface.

***

Once the shooting had ended, JJ reported immediately to Colonel Burke on BIB's communications system what had just taken place. Colonel Burke agreed to inform Jeremie and Innis immediately and to send appropriate back up personnel to JJ's location forthwith.

The Gold team checked on the status of the prisoners. They confirmed that of the five prisoners they had left HMP Dodds with, Power was gone. So too was Field. The three remaining, Lynch, Moradi and Foulkes were accounted for, had no life-threating injures and were obviously not keen to go anywhere.

Next, the Gold team checked on their RBPF and BPS colleagues. While JJ would normally have expected the senior officers from both agencies to have already contacted their superiors through their respective communication systems about the incident, given their respective conditions, this had not been possible on this occasion. JJ's team did what they could to assist and comfort their injured law enforcement colleagues in the knowledge that 'back-up' and medical help was on the way.

JJ had just finished his second update to Colonel Burke when an old man came down the road in his donkey cart. Approaching them somewhat curiously, he looked at the confused scene.

"What's going on here? Need some help?" he asked.

If JJ had not witnessed this incident for himself, he'd not believe it. It could have been a scene from one of those Hollywood movies he'd seen more than once before.

***

Superintendent Innis and George Telford, his deputy, were in their mid-week senior BPS management meeting for officers responsible for running each cell block at HMS Dodds. None of Telford's colleagues thought much about it at the time, but would later recall that during their meeting, he had frequently looked at his watch and had seemed somewhat distracted when once asked about the maintenance contract for the compound's security fences, providing an initial incoherent answer before pulling himself together to respond appropriately to Innis' question.

Forty-eight hours later, Telford's BPS colleagues began to understand why he might have been distracted.

***

Vickers and Moss drove up to the well-appointed residence of Dr Albert and Betty Lewis. She stood at the front door, waiting to greet them once they had ascended the steps.

Moments later, Vickers and Moss sat down across from Mrs Lewis in comfortable chairs in the family room of the Lewis home. Mrs Lewis offered them tea, coffee or a cold drink. Vickers accepted the cold drink, Moss the tea.

Ava Prescod, maid to the Lewis family, quickly brought the requested items and left the room, enabling them to get down to business.

***

The media in Barbados, like the media in most countries, listened in on all police radio frequencies. Efforts over time to stop this practice had failed, so toleration by the authorities had been accepted.

It was therefore no surprise that within twenty minutes of the prisoners escape incident, local media had descended on the area. Thankfully, within ten minutes of the event's conclusion, the area had been secured by three joint four-member RBPF/BDF teams. They had been a couple of miles away on roving patrol as part of the ECC project. Media respectfully stood behind the RBPF **DO NOT CROSS** incident tape line that had been put in place by still arriving RBPF officers in their attempt to secure the entire area. The damaged BPS transport and RBPF escort vehicles were visible for everyone to see. Pictures were being taken of them by RBPF personnel, along with the broken glass, the remaining three assembled prisoners, and injured BPS and RBPF officers. The positions of spent gunshot shells were noted, photographed and collected. JJ's Gold team had sought to prevent pictures being taken of the scene, injured or shaken-up prisoners and law enforcement officials (including themselves), but they could not be sure that enterprising journalists, or anyone else at the scene with a phone which all have cameras, had not already done so intending to post captured images of the incident on social media. Indeed, this might already have been done.

Quickly on the scene to help out was Inspector Melanie Gray, the RBPF's newly-minted public relations officer. She spoke first with Sergeant Holder, the senior RBPF officer responsible for escorting the day's PR before speaking with Clarence Rouse, lead BPS officer before finally coming over to speak with JJ.

Gray and JJ had some history, she was the Station Sergeant in charge of Worthing police station when the attempt had been made to assassinate Motby and had accommodated JJ, Fred and Joe's interrogation of Miles 'Sugar' Roberts, a well-known snitch.

"Not good," stated JJ.

"Nope. My Commissioner is going to be pissed that all three of his men were hurt. The media will have all sorts of questions but let them wait awhile," said Gray. "What can you tell me?"

"Not much more than what the BPS crew and your officers have already told you. It was a slick operation. We couldn't stop the escape. It was well planned. Must admit, the execution wasn't bad either."

"Thanks. I better speak with these people before they write what they want to write," stated Gray before wandering off to face the assembled media crowd.

The RBPF media podium had been set up by Gray's support team. Microphones and mobiles were placed on it to capture her statement. Cameras took pictures of Gray as she started to speak.

"Good morning. I am Inspector Melanie Gray, Public Relations Officer of the Royal Barbados Police Force. This morning, at around 9:45 a.m., a Barbados Prison Service prisoner transport vehicle carrying five prisoners to District A Magistrates Court, was ambushed at this location. The BPS vehicle was escorted by RBPF and Barbados Intelligence Bureau personnel in their vehicles. It was a standard operation which happens on a weekly basis, sometimes twice a week. Three of the five prisoners are back in, or should I say never were out of custody, while another two have escaped. Details of the two escaped prisoners will be made available to you shortly on our RBPF website. Five BPS officers and three RBPF officers received various injuries in the incident. All are receiving medical attention as I speak. Please note that none of their injuries are life threatening. Two vehicles, one from BPS and one RBPF, have been badly damaged. That's as much as I have for you now. There'll be regular updates for you from RBPF HQ at we have and can release them, but at 5:00 p.m. this afternoon I'll speak with you again from RBPF HQ. Now questions. Please identify yourself and your news organisation," asked an authoritative Gray.

There was silence.

Don't all rush to speak at once, thought Gray as a couple of hands eventually went up. She pointed to the closest raised hand.

"Cornelius Pickett, Star News Corporation. Tell me, for these PRs, do you think sufficient security is provided for this activity?"

"It has been so far. May I remind you that this is a first in Barbados," answered Gray.

"So, will changes be made to the security level for future PRs?" was Pickett's follow-up question.

"I cannot say right now, but I'm sure it will be looked at," Gray answered.

"Barbara Jarvis, Barbados News Corporation. Can you tell us who the missing prisoners are? How dangerous are they? When would the authorities hope to recapture them – tomorrow, the weekend?"

"You've asked me multiple questions there. The names of the prisoners will be provided as soon as we have the appropriate publicity materials to do so. Yes, of course we know who they are but please be patient with us. We will endeavour to recapture both prisoners as soon as."

"You're not telling us if they are murderers, housebreakers, drug dealers…the public will be worried at today's developments. Should the country be worried? What were these escapees at Dodds for?" persisted Jarvis.

"Look, we'll give you what information we can as soon as we can. As you are aware, the public's safety is our ultimate concern. That's it, folks. I'll see you again at 5:00 p.m." With that, Gray left the podium and media huddle.

Jayne, who was watching Gray's performance from a distance, turned to Mohammed and stated, "Not a job I'd want to do day after day."

"Funny you should say so. Nor would I," he responded.

"Come on you two. If you progress upwards in this or another other Government organisation, dealing with the media is just another thing you'll need to do, though not perhaps every day like the Inspector. Let's finish up what we can here and head back to BIB HQ. I suspect we, well, at least I might not be on leave now for the rest of today and tomorrow after all," said JJ.

Members of the media who had not yet taken pictures or video of the scene now did so for their publications.

***

The Deputy Governor's disappearance was already set to be on next Tuesday's *P.A.A.N.I.* Agenda when it was anticipated that the matter would long have been resolved in a positive way. Given the immediacy of the now underway ECC project, Colonel Burke had felt no pressure to hold an emergency *P.A.A.N.I.* meeting before then.

As two new national security incidents were developing, Colonel Burke decided at 11:15 a.m. to place an urgent call to Motby to brief him on the morning's two incidents. Thanks to the media, the prisoners escape was already trending in the public domain. Once that call was completed, he decided to hold an emergency *P.A.A.N.I.* teleconference for 3:00 p.m. that afternoon at which only the Deputy Governor's disappearance and the prisoners escape would be Agenda items. As usual, he would chair the session before appraising the Prime Minister of the latest developments in both cases sometime prior to his attendance at the 6:30 p.m. cricket reception at the British High Commissioner's residence, before Motby returned to Ilaro Court for the night.

Colonel Burke was unaware of the long-planned Motby family dinner with Captain Rodney 'Rod' Selwick. Motby's private engagements at Ilaro Court were not part of BIB's normal portfolio, so there was no need for him to know about this event.

***

After receipt of Colonel Burke's call, Motby was more concerned about the Deputy Governor's disappearance than the prisoners escape. After all, it was not a breakout from HMP Dodds. He was confident that Commissioner Jeremie and Superintendent Innis would work quickly to recapture the two escaped Barbadian prisoners.

The Deputy Governor's situation was something completely different. He did not know what to make of Dr Albert Lewis' disappearance. He knew him, but only in his official capacity. Like most people, Motby had questions. Was it mischievous? Had Dr Lewis simply lost his mind? Was this related in any way to his Government? Only time would tell.

Motby returned his focus to the matters of state he had to deal with during the day and preparation for tomorrow's Cabinet meeting. Motby expected the two escaped prisoners to be recaptured and the Deputy Governor to be found by the time he went to bed that night, if not by the following morning.

***

Lewis had spoken with his mother on his way to the airport.

Mrs Lewis had updated him of a visit to her home by two senior RBPF officers that morning. She confirmed that she, her husband's office nor the RBPF had seen or heard from his dad since Tuesday (yesterday) afternoon. The RBPF officers indicated that they would not make Dr Lewis' apparent disappearance public before tomorrow morning. Mrs Lewis' thoughts of kidnapping were pre-

121

empted when she indicated that neither she nor the CBOB had received any request for money to secure her husband's safe return.

At least not yet.

Lewis informed his mother that he was coming home and was already on his way to Barbados. He told her not to even think about picking him up on arrival. He would grab a taxi and so she should expect him to be with her by 11:30 p.m. tonight latest once his two flights were on time.

Mrs Lewis thanked him for responding so quickly. He detected a few soft sobs from her, but deliberately did not ask her whether she had been crying. He knew his mum. She would have cried but would, as usual, try to cover it up from both of her children. Mrs Lewis asked him if he had spoken with his sister. Lewis stated that he had not done so because he was waiting for her to update him on everything. He would now call his sister shortly.

Thirty minutes later, having parked his vehicle at John F. Kennedy International Airport, Bertram Lewis self-checked himself into the AA system in New York for his flight to Miami and onward journey to Barbados. It was time to call his sister.

Caroline Lewis-Greenidge lived in Texas. It was a hard conversation for them to have, but they got through it. Lewis agreed to call Lewis-Greenidge on his arrival in Barbados when their mum would also speak with her.

Lewis-Greenidge in turn called her husband to notify him of the situation back home in Barbados. She then called her mum. She would then wait until her brother got home to do so again.

***

Castille arrived in Barbados on the AA flight from Miami at 1:40 p.m. Once clear of Customs, he went to the car hire facility where he had booked a car using his own name, producing his USA driver's licence. He paid cash for the week-long rental, collected the vehicle and set off for his south coast hotel. It helped that he was not a first-time visitor to Barbados. He understood the complex road network for an island of its size. However, as insurance, he would use the GPS that came with his hired car to get him to his rendezvous destination. He would not take the most direct route by choice, but follow a more circuitous route to arrive at his location well before the scheduled 5:30 p.m. meeting time. This plan should allow him time to grab something to eat, even relax some before setting out for his east coast rendezvous with Power.

Thereafter, Castille had one more engagement to complete that night before returning to his hotel. He would order in room service, watch some television, shower and turn in for the night. Before leaving the east coast, Castille also planned to collect the item that he had asked Wharton to secure for him. It would be needed later in his Barbados visit.

***

BIB's Gold team arrived back at BIB HQ around 2:00 p.m. They were an unhappy bunch. Three of the prisoners on the PR had been returned to HMP Dodds by RBPF officers – Jessica Lynch, Franchesca Moradi and Orrin Foulkes. Their day in court would now come later through no fault of their own. The injured and traumatised RBPF and BPS officers had been transported to hospital by a couple of ambulances to receive further medical attention.

The search for Warren Field and Jasper Power was underway. So too was that for the persons (it looked like four men) who had made the prisoners escape possible by their actions. It was felt from the outset that Field would quickly be recaptured. However, as it was unlikely that the breakout had been arranged for *all* of the prisoners, Power had clearly been the target. It was obvious that Power, being the most dangerous of the two escapees, would be the hardest prisoner to track down and recapture, especially given his past record of interaction with law enforcement and his ongoing penchant for doing bad things.

The prisoners escape, the way it had occurred, signalled to JJ's Gold team that there must have been some preparation and planning. Technical ability, skill and nerve had all been required to enable the successful execution of what would have been a complicated escape to pull off. Because shots had been fired by the rescuers during the incident, it was clear that the persons involved did not mind hurting anyone who got in their way.

That brought a heightened dimension to the incident. It was too early to be certain if any inside assistance had been provided to make the escape a reality, but JJ and his team suspected as much following the incident. Tracking down the culprit would be the task of the BPS and RBPF, with BIB assistance if necessary.

***

During the 3:00 p.m. teleconference, *P.A.A.N.I.* Heads were provided with updates on the prisoners escape and the CBOB official's disappearance. Superintendent Innis apologised to his colleagues for the escape of the two prisoners who were now causing all their agencies extra work on top of the ECC security project that was now up and running.

He explained HMP Dodds' recent transportation, equipment and staff shortage challenges and acknowledged that these issues, separately and/or together, had contributed to the prisoners escape. He refused to accept that the BPS should not take sole and full responsibility for the escape.

Colonel Burke, having spoken with JJ prior to the PR, following the escape and again on JJ's return to BIB HQ, was aware of these things, but was glad that Innis had at last laid them out for *P.A.A.N.I.* Heads' consideration. Innis was upbeat about recapturing both escaped prisoners within the next twenty-four hours. *P.A.A.N.I.* Heads raised the possibility of an inside job. Might someone in a trustworthy position at HMP Dodds have leaked today's PR details, including the routes, to those who had executed the escape? Innis thought this highly unlikely but could not rule out that possibility. The question was then raised as to who might have done so, but it was not pursued as this very point was the subject of an ongoing internal investigation Innis had already initiated and was leading.

Jeremie reported that senior RBPF personnel were on the case of the missing CBOB Deputy Governor. Background information had been secured, but no strong leads developed to date. He expected an update from Vickers, his lead investigator, around 4:30 p.m. and promised to share developments with his fellow Heads.

***

Once the teleconference was over, Colonel Burke called the Prime Minister to update him on the escaped prisoners' situation. They agreed to speak again at 6:00 p.m. that evening, by which time he also hoped to have something positive to report on the Deputy Governor's investigation from Jeremie.

***

By 4:30 p.m., the British High Commissioner's official residence, built in the 1920s and located on Erdiston Road, Pine Hill, St Michael, was a hive of activity.

Preparations for the evening's cricket reception were now near completion. In another two hours, around five hundred guests were expected to descend on the residence and its grounds. Though the two earlier events of the day were of concern to some of the senior officials in Government because they were of national importance, only one of them, the prisoners escape, was generally known to the public and the media. But these were not the issues on the mind of the expected guests and so would not dampen the spirit of fun, frivolity, relaxation and sporting delight they hoped to experience at tonight's function.

Between 6:30 p.m. and 8:30 p.m., the High Commissioner and Mrs Tullock would host one of the residence's largest receptions for the year. Five well-stocked bars were already set up to serve expectedly thirsty sports-mad guests. Five food stations were also being stocked to feed those who would need to soak up what they drank. Four tents of varying size were in the final process of being assembled on the residence's grounds and fitted with lighting. In the kitchen, residence staff who had taken delivery of a variety of foodstuffs from sponsors during the day, were also finalising their preparations of the goodies to be served up later.

Guests at tonight's reception were set to include ICC officials, the West Indies and England cricket squads for the second Test Match, both teams' support staff, visiting UK family members who were in for the Barbados Test Match, local, regional and international media, sponsors, cricket tour group and club representatives, local businessmen and women, politicians, senior public servants and diplomats from Barbados-based High Commissions, Embassies and Consulates.

To help ensure that all went well, the full staff of the British High Commission would be 'on parade'. They would have particular hosting duties to perform across the reception's duration. The High Commission had been closed at 3:00 p.m. that afternoon to enable staff to get home, clean themselves up, dress and arrive at *Ben Mar* no later than 6:00 p.m. They were all part of the 'home team', as Tullock, his wife and the residence staff liked to refer to all High Commission staff on such occasions. The experience of organising similarly sized receptions at *Ben Mar* over the years suggested that though 8:30 p.m. was the scheduled time for the reception to end, the last guests might not depart before 10:00 p.m.

Were this to happen tonight, Tullock would not complain, since his sole goal for the evening was to ensure that Andrea and himself, supported by their home team, hosted an incident-free and enjoyable evening for their attending guests. The attending UK story-seeking media in particular, should only see evidence of a successful reception. Parts of the event could then be shown on television, locally and back home in the UK. Positive images of what guests did could also be captured on mobile phones for subsequent posting on social media.

***

Vickers reported back to Jeremie at RBPF HQ just after 5:00 p.m. The investigation had not discovered Dr Lewis' location or why he had disappeared.

"Sir, his wife, his secretary and others in CBOB that we've spoken to also don't know. A check of his diaries, electronic and hand-written, revealed nothing helpful. Alarm has however grown throughout the day for his well-being. The media remain unaware of his disappearance," stated Vickers.

"Alright. What have you learnt about Dr Lewis the man, his family, his daily routine, his past fortnight's office movements?" asked Jeremie.

"Well, we've looked over everything about the man and the areas you're asking about. Nothing unusual. Overnight, we will review what we have learnt and done today and will seek to pursue new leads – real, potential or imagined, in the morning."

"Okay, Johnny. I'll advise Colonel Burke that we're making slow progress, but tomorrow hope to achieve a lot more. The PM will have to be satisfied with that when they speak, I think at 6:00 p.m."

"Sir, we're going to find Dr Lewis in the usual way. Through hard detective work. We'll shake some trees and see what falls out," concluded Vickers.

"Got it, Johnny. It's why you're in charge of this case. Governor Edwards wanted one of my best men on the job and that's why he wisely asked for you. You've notified him of progress to date?"

"I'll do so shortly, sir."

"Very well. Please keep me posted on how you go."

"Right. Have a good night sir," said Vickers.

"You too, Johnny. Let's speak again by lunchtime tomorrow," ordered Jeremie.

"Will do."

Once away from Jeremie's office, Vickers said to Moss, "We'll sleep on what little we know and think of a few new angles to pursue by morning."

"Agreed."

***

Before leaving RBPF HQ for the evening, Vickers called Governor Edwards as he had promised to do earlier that day. He apologised for calling him later than expected, reporting what they had done and indicating that Dr Lewis' whereabouts were still not known, nor was there any plausible reason for his absence from his family or the CBOB.

Edwards was disappointed but thanked Vickers for the efforts he and Moss had made so far. He hoped tomorrow's efforts would discover Dr Lewis' whereabouts.

Vickers and Moss went their separate ways. As he neared home, Vickers thought of a way BIB might help Moss and himself. The next day would also see them raise their efforts to find Dr Lewis.

***

Chapter Ten
Payment Demand

It was around 5:40 p.m. when Castille and Power sat down for a chat at Spend Big Wharton's home.

As was Castille's intention and practice, the discussion was not a lengthy one. He explained that he was *The Organisation*'s representative, to which Power owed a substantial sum of money. Power's non-payment had prompted *The Organisation* to dispatch him to Barbados to recover the outstanding sum, with interest. He presented Power with a sheet of paper which itemised the items that had been supplied by *The Organisation* to Power over the past twelve months. Dates, specific items and the individual sums involved were shown, culminating with the total outstanding being shown at the foot of the A-4 page.

Power examined the itemised list carefully, a second Banks beer in his hand. He swallowed several times while he read.

What's this? he wondered. Power knew that he owed *The Organisation* something but was not quite sure how it had gotten so high. This interest thing he'd never understood. It appeared to double what he thought was his debt to *The Organisation*. Anyway, he'd believed that it was one of his old collaborators, Wharton and his Pressure Group gang who had been responsible for breaking him free, simply as a favour because Wharton knew Power would reward him sometime later for his efforts. Perhaps as soon as a couple of weeks once Power was back on his feet and in full operation…

But this situation around his escape, was clearly something else! Power was now acutely conscious that his escape from the prisoner transport vehicle and by extension the confines of HMP Dodds, had been completed by Wharton's

Pressure Group. However, it had been done under the direction of and at the instigation of *The Organisation*. Power had only made a down-payment on the latest items he had acquired from *The Organisation* three months ago. He had not paid anything to *The Organisation* for two months, so he understood why a representative had been sent to directly collect in Barbados.

Castille's task was to get Power to make the outstanding payment due to *The Organisation* quickly now that Power was out of HMP Dodds. Castille believed that Power only had to say the word and one of his runners would be able to make arrangements to gather the sum owed from either one of his major local bag-men (or a collection of them). With that in mind, payment should be possible within a twenty-four-hour period. Power also had the choice of transferring the sum owed to *The Organisation* from one of his overseas accounts directly into its offshore 'client accounts' in the Cayman Islands.

"Look man, I know I owe you guys some change, but with my being inside the can for the best part of a week, I've not been able to make any payment arrangements to settle up. I guess you know how it is once you go on the inside."

Shaking his head slowly, Castille spoke coldly.

"Mr Power, I've never been *on the inside*, so don't know what you mean. You haven't paid us anything for a while now my friend, so I'm here to collect, one way or the other."

"Alright. I'll need some time, so give me say forty-eight, no seventy-two hours to secure your funds. I'll pay everything I owe your people."

"Mr Power, I want *The Organisation's* money. I'm here to collect what you owe us in full. Not in seventy-two. Not in forty-eight hours. Now. It's not the first time you're not paid us promptly, or in the agreed way. I'm here to sort this out quickly, once and for all. Full payment, or you could find yourself six feet under. Get me? It's your choice," said Castille staring at Power.

Power had seldom felt threatened by man, woman, child or animal. Certainly not in the circles he operated in. He was therefore not a man easily frightened by anyone, at any time, in any situation, circumstance or location. Furthermore, he'd never backed down from anything in his life, not from school teachers, gang leaders or armed RBPF officers (as was evident from the week before in a St James seaside village when he had been engaged in a shoot-out which had ultimately resulted in his capture, arrest and being taken into custody).

But there was something about the man sitting across the table from him in this small room in a house on Barbados' east coast which had him *worried*. It crossed Power's mind that he might, at last have met his criminal match. Shorn of any weaponry, he didn't think he would get the better of this man if they were in a physical contest. Even with a weapon of some kind, Power was uncertain that he would win the day against this man. Power realised that by having not paid *The Organisation* the overall US$1M he owed it, he was now in big trouble. The guns and ammunition recently acquired could not now be sold because of their capture by the RBPF. Also, the drugs that had earlier been provided to him for onward sale that he had sold but not yet repatriated the profits for after taking his cut, were also of concern.

Power decided to play ball with Castille.

"Twenty-four hours. Okay. Give me that time to get your money, man. Can we agree to meet back here tomorrow evening at this time? I promise I'll have it all for you then," said Power softly, trying not to show Castille his fear.

There was a minute's silence, during which Castille considered Power's offer. It was rare for Castille to make exceptions with debtors when demanding outstanding payments. He had only ever done this twice, the last time being earlier this week in Mexico.

Hat-trick, he thought.

After a minute's silence, Castille took a deep breath and spoke. "Your last chance, Mr Power. Be here tomorrow at…" he looked at his watch "…5:30 p.m. with my money. If you're not here, don't have it or can't show me that you've arranged to pay up from one of your two overseas accounts we know you to have access to, it'll be game over."

"Wait a minute –"

"No, you listen. Get this done, or we'll dance in a way you won't like. I'm advised that you're a resourceful man, Mr Power. Make this happen and I'll go away. You're free, and sit here because we sprung you to pay us what you owe."

"Ah –"

"Don't let *The Organisation* down. Pay up and live. Don't and die. Twenty-four hours. Clock's ticking."

With that, Castille rose from his chair, opened the door and left the room. He almost fell over Wharton who had obviously been eavesdropping just outside the door on Power/Castille's conversation. The television that was on had the sound-level turned down. Castille knew Wharton had overheard his conversation with Power, but decided it didn't matter if Wharton had heard even all that he had said.

"Here," said Castille, pulling a brown envelope out from his jacket pocket and dropping it into Wharton's lap.

"Your people did a nice job earlier today. I'll be back here tomorrow at 5:30 p.m. Your friend inside will have something for me to collect," he said.

Wharton stood up to shake Castille's hand. "Thanks, man. Be jolly now."

"Don't you also have something for me?" Castille asked.

Smacking his forehead, Wharton said, "Oh, yes sorry, I nearly forgot."

Wharton lumbered across the room to the food cupboard. He rummaged around for a while before handing Castille a brown paper bag. "Be careful with that thing, although I have a feeling you know how to use it. I don't want it back. It's got no prints, serial numbers or other markings on it. Silencer too. It's clean, just as you asked for," Wharton stressed.

"Thanks. Until tomorrow," said Castille, moving towards the door.

"Sure thing. Be jolly now," responded Wharton.

Once outside, Castille headed for his hired vehicle. He again wondered why, whenever he had a conversation with Wharton, he always ended their conversation with that stupid phrase. It annoyed Castille. Still, he hoped to converse with this idiot just one more time. Once he had what he'd come to Barbados for, he would not have to speak or deal with this man again.

Unless he had to return to Barbados for an as-yet unknown reason.

***

From the opened door, Wharton watched the vehicle disappear into the distance, before looking at the envelope. He knew what it contained. Wharton quickly placed it *inside* the Bible which lay on the stand beneath the large colour television that hung from the wall. He kept a couple of Bibles around his house and one at Spend Big's Bar & Grocery (SBB&G), his main place of business. Anyone hoping to read a passage of scripture in any of his Bibles would have been sorely disappointed – distressed might be a better description. For, once his Bibles were opened, there were only a few pages at the front and back. Everyone, except his Pressure Group friends, would have been surprised to learn what else he kept there.

Wharton would give what was due to the other three members of his Pressure Group for the work they had done earlier that day when they later met him that evening in SBB&G's back office.

***

Power sat quietly for another five minutes following Castille's departure from the room. He had now worked out what he could and would not do. He had no intention of being recaptured by Barbados' law enforcement agencies who were already hard at work seeking out his location. A quick return to HMP Dodds was not on his agenda. Though he felt inclined to find a way to pay off *The Organisation* within the twenty-four hours allotted by Castille for him to do so, he decided that he would not go that route. Yes, Power had always paid his debts – eventually, but to find a way to pay up by tomorrow would be very difficult. His alternative plan was therefore to run away, meaning that he would not pay up on this occasion. The question was how to get himself off Barbados before 6:00 p.m. the following day?

Power was honest enough to admit to himself that he had not fully comprehended one thing until his meeting with Castille had started. He had felt safe inside Wharton's 'safe house' earlier that afternoon, but the reality that Wharton was really working for *The Organisation* had hit him hard. Wharton's insistence on Power's arrival at the house that *someone* wanted to meet with Power "later this afternoon" had made no sense at the time, so he was not unduly worried.

He was now.

He could not blame *The Organisation*, but now knew for sure that Wharton had sold him out. The message he'd received a few days earlier in HMP Dodds was that 'his' associates would help him see true daylight on Wednesday. Power would not provide Wharton with any expected reward because he suspected that Wharton had already received such from *The Organisation*.

Power's earlier thought about seeing Marcie Leach, ideally sometime tonight, had deserted him. In his rationalisation, he had clean forgotten about her. Once he was safe and away from Barbados, Marcie's image might return to him again.

Survival, avoiding capture from the search by local law enforcement agencies and escaping *The Organisation's* clutches now pre-occupied him. Arranging repayment to the Organisation would be difficult anyway, if not impossible within twenty-four hours. Recapture and a return to HMP Dodds, not exactly a hospitable place, would almost be un-bearable to him. Death by *The Organisation*'s man Castille would be worse and so was unacceptable.

Power felt out of options and so decided to call in a favour tonight, as death didn't appeal to him, certainly not this early in his life. Being found somewhere in Barbados, be it at the bottom of a well, in a cane field, burnt in a house fire, or dying in a car accident. With payment out of the question, he needed to fashion a novel way out of his predicament by calling a former business associate.

Power worked out a tentative plan on how and who he would ask to help make his plan become reality. He could no longer trust Wharton as he was clearly no longer in Power's corner like when they had worked together six months earlier.

Power decided to rest up for the next few hours before making his move. As Wharton had earlier indicated that he would go to SBB&G for the evening and would not return to his house before morning, Power would use the night hours to firm up his moves for the next day. The fridge was well stocked with food and drinks, so after he had gotten some sleep, he would take a shower, get himself something to eat before initiating his plan.

***

Chapter Eleven
Reception, Dinners, After-Party

Promptly at 6:00 p.m., Sergeant Billy Browne arrived at the gates of *Ben Mar* ahead of the night's reception. His task was to be two-fold. He made himself known to the High Commission staff on duty. Initially, he would help protect the Prime Minister. Thereafter, he would help his fellow Visitors CPU unit colleagues who would also attend the reception offering protection to the cricketing VIPs from the ICC once the Prime Minister had departed.

At 6:15 p.m., the two coaches bearing both teams and their support staff arrived outside the residence. The teams had been asked to be inside the residence ahead of the first guests' arrival. They would not be part of the official receiving line, but would be visible to arriving guests.

Prime Minister and Mrs Motby were originally scheduled to arrive at 6:30 p.m., but this was adjusted on the morning of the reception to 6:40 p.m., just in case the teams arrived late for some reason, e.g. due to traffic congestion. No one wanted the PM's entry to clash with the first guests to arrive. As a result, Constable Marshall, with Sergeant Eversley beside him, drove the Prime Minister's vehicle through the opened gates of the residence and stopped just before the front door. Marshall and Eversley quickly exited the vehicle and opened the vehicle's rear doors to enable the Prime Minister and his wife to exit. While the flow of guests was temporarily halted by High Commission and security staff, Prime Minister and Mrs Motby were greeted by the High Commissioner and his wife Andrea. Browne had stationed himself just inside the doorway before the four principal personalities at the evening's reception spoke before quickly entering the residence's hallway and headed towards the High

Commissioner's spacious downstairs study where they would receive both teams.

Five minutes later, after drinking a glass of refreshing coconut water which was awaiting their arrival in the study, the players of both teams, led by their captains, began their procession into the study for their moment in time with the four dignitaries. Team management followed them. This process was marshalled by two senior High Commission staffers. During the presentations and picture-taking exercise, Browne stood in the hallway outside of the study door's exit. Eversley was already in the study, standing just behind Motby. Meanwhile, Marshall reconnoitred persons standing closest to the podium from where Tullock and Motby would later address the assembled guests.

***

Once Wharton had left the house, Power had the place to himself. He set an alarm on the old clock he found on the kitchen table for 10:15 p.m. His plan on waking up would be to make a call, shower, change and eat before making his way on foot to the individual he had decided to approach and ask, no *demand*, help from.

This individual was one of society's most respected and apparently upstanding personalities. But unknown to the vast majority of Barbadians, this individual had been a collaborator/co-ordinator of activities related to Barbados' underworld for over ten years. As it happened, the individual also lived on Barbados' east coast, not that far from Wharton's home. Luckily, they lived alone, so Power felt that making an approach to this individual under the cover of darkness should not be difficult. Securing their assistance might be trickier, even though he believed they owed him a favour.

So, given the circumstances, Power felt it was the right time for him to 'cash in' on the owed favour. Power knew exactly how he would endeavour to secure what he wanted.

***

Colonel Burke left JJ, Mohammed and Jayne at BIB HQ around 7:15 p.m. to go home and help host Sir Thadeus Thomas and Cindy Lady Thomas over dinner. He instructed JJ not to hesitate to call him during the evening should anything break on the prisoners' escape case.

The missing CBOB Deputy Governor's case was of less concern. RBPF was on that, with Vickers as lead officer. Colonel Burke knew Vickers well, so felt quietly confident that he might be able to solve and wrap up that case within another twenty-four hours or so. Colonel Burke promised to return to BIB HQ around 11:00 p.m. by which time his guests were sure to have left his house for their west coast hideaway. At that time, he would review any new leads that would have come in since his departure regarding the escape itself and any new developments on the search to recover the missing prisoners, with all available BIB operatives.

***

Around the same time, with presentations to the players and team management completed and photographs having been taken, High Commissioner Tullock and Prime Minister Motby headed off towards the podium and microphone located on a raised platform to deliver their speeches. As they arrived, Constable Marshall took up a position at the back of the platform. Sergeants Eversley and Browne stood alongside Motby at one end of the platform as Tullock started to address his guests by welcoming everyone to his official residence. The assembled throng, except for those who were standing at or near to the five bars, appeared to cut their chatter to listen to what he was saying. The music had been killed to facilitate the speeches.

Tullock broke the agreed protocol timelines by speaking for five minutes instead of two, rambling on about all sorts of things. No one stopped him from doing so. He was, after all, the evening's host and was at *his* house, as he and Andrea affectionately saw *Ben Mar* as their 'home away from home'.

Once it was the Prime Minister's turn to speak at the podium, Eversley and Browne adjusted their positions to stand at opposite ends of the raised platform facing and studying the large crowd. Motby also welcomed the guests to Barbados on behalf of himself, his family, Government and all Barbadians, particularly to overseas guests who were visiting the country for the first time. He encouraged everyone to enjoy the Tullocks' party and all the various attractions Barbados had to offer. He felt certain of the high level of cricket that would be played at New Kensington Oval between two of the world's top Test teams. Motby concluded his remarks by apologising for having to leave the party early because he'd somehow double-booked himself that evening, so had to 'show his face' at a second function.

***

Speeches over, the Prime Minister started to walk-through parts of the assembled crowd, accompanied by Tullock. His CPU team knew that Motby seldom wasted an opportunity to meet and greet his people and visitors alike. Whether the locals were persons who had already or might yet vote for him in the future, Motby used the opportunity to mingle. As for visitors, his engagement with them meant he was doing his bit to shore up the tourism sector.

Motby was aware that some of the night's guests did not know much about or understand the game of cricket. That included several of the Heads of diplomatic missions in attendance. He knew this because they had so informed him in previous conversations. Nonetheless, he was delighted that they had accepted Tullock's invitation and appeared to be enjoying themselves. Perhaps some of them might even decide to attend at least one day of the Test Match to see what all the sporting excitement was all about.

His entry into the crowd was therefore not unexpected by his CPU team that evening. Thankfully, the exercise went smoothly. He moved quickly through the friendly crowd, offering handshakes, smiles and mouthing pleasantries like "Hello, how are you?" and "Good to see you…" Responses were of the nature of "Good night Prime Minister…" and "Good to see you PM…"

Sarah McPiers, President of New Beavers Cricket Club (NBCC), a long-established but small cricket club from North London, was leading a ten-member group to Barbados for the Test Match. Four members of the group had been given invitations to the reception. She was speechless when she realised that she was to be one of the guests who would get to shake the hand of Barbados' Prime Minister. For McPiers, this was not something that she would have gotten to do back home. Luckily for her, Glen Aitken, a member of her group captured the moment on his phone camera for posterity. That picture would ultimately find a place of honour in NBCC's clubhouse on their return to the UK. A second print of the moment would adorn the living room in her house. An e-copy would also appear in her local UK newspaper.

***

Eventually, Motby reached the residence's hallway, closely followed by Tullock. Their spouses were already standing by the door in conversation.

A nod from Sergeant Eversley sent Constable Marshall heading through the front door to bring around PM1, the Prime Minister's official vehicle. With departing pleasantries having been exchanged between the hosts and their principal official guests for the evening, Marshall, with Eversley beside him and with the Motbys in the back seat, manoeuvred PM1 down the exit driveway and out of *Ben Mar's* gates, before commencing the five-minute drive to Ilaro Court for a private function the Motby family would host.

Back inside the High Commissioner's residence, the cricket party continued apace, with Browne now undertaking the second part of his night's assignment. He was delighted that the first part of his work that evening had gone off without incident. He hoped the second part would also be trouble-free.

***

A few minutes later, PM1 arrived at Ilaro Court. There, the Prime Minister and his wife joined other members of the Motby family in hosting a long-promised dinner for an old acquaintance.

***

Diane Burke met their guests on arrival. Colonel Burke was still dressing as he had rushed home from BIB HQ to take a shower before dressing in the clothes Diane had carefully laid out for him.

The Thomases and Diane Burke were having drinks by the time Colonel Burke joined them. He introduced himself to Sir Thadeus and Cindy Lady Thomas saying, "Good evening and welcome to our home. I see Diane is looking after you. I do apologise for running late, but I've had quite a day at the office."

"I gather you've had a day like those I usually have at my office back home, Trevor...but we learn to deal with them, eh what," said Sir Thadeus.

"Yes, indeed we do," responded Colonel Burke.

"Work aside, Trevor, I must really say that I've very much enjoyed my few days in Barbados already. What a lovely country you live in. I have a Bajan on my staff back in London, a very nice, bright and friendly fellow. Knowing him as well as I do, I had an inkling of what I was getting myself into by coming down here. Makes me wonder now why it took us so long to visit."

"Why thank you, Sir Thadeus… Thad. I really hope you'll have some fun while you are here. Balwin's mentioned to me that you expect to take in part of the Test Match. Cindy, how's it been for you so far? Are you as excited to be in Barbados as your husband is?" Colonel Burke asked.

"Oh yes, Trevor, very much so! I've wanted to visit for about five years now, but could never get Thad away from his work. One crisis or another always seemed to put a spanner in the works, until now. Diane and I both know what you men are like once you commit to your jobs. I'm glad he's finally managed to get some time away. Oh, and before I forget Diane, thanks for having us over this evening. We've brought you a small gift to show our appreciation for the trouble you must have taken to prepare a meal for us," said Cindy, taking the package now being held by her husband and presenting it to Diane.

"Thank you ever so much, but this really was not necessary. We enjoy entertaining, though we do not do much of that nowadays given Trevor's unpredictable schedule. I sincerely hope that you both enjoy what we've prepared for dinner, speaking of which, let's all have another drink before we sit down to eat."

"Sounds good to me," responded Sir Thadeus. "The aroma from your kitchen is delightful."

Just then, Sherman Broome, Diane's home helper for nearly ten years, appeared and took their second drink order.

"The usual for us please, Sher," said Diane. That meant a coke for her and a large glass of chilled coconut water for Colonel Burke.

"Once you've brought the drinks, give us ten minutes and then we'll sit down to eat," stated Diane.

"Very well, Mrs Burke," said Broome, disappearing from the room.

***

The Motbys found Selwick being entertained by their daughter Kimberly and Anton Zendon, Kimberly's fiancé. Selwick had been collected from Hilton Barbados at 7:30 p.m. by a RBPF officer and so had arrived early for their dinner engagement. Other members of the Motby family would join them for dinner at 8:00 p.m. that would be in his honour.

Motby expected tomorrow's local newspapers' back sports pages to carry pictures of High Commissioner Tullock and himself with players from both teams. UK papers would even have some of the pictures up on their websites before tonight was over. A selection of the pictures taken by the High Commission's photographer would also be forwarded to the management of both teams for circulation to the players and their families.

Motby wondered how this would look to Barbadian given the day's story on the successful ambush of the PR and resulting escaped prisoners. Tomorrow's front pages would certainly feature that story.

"Ah well, what's done is done. I'll not spoil Captain Selwick's evening with us," he said softly to himself.

***

The two men met for the first time at their pre-arranged meeting place in the unlit car park of an Anglican parish church situated just off the ABC highway.

Their meeting was brief, barely three minutes in fact. After introducing themselves, the visitor to the island thanked the Barbadian for providing requested information on a critical matter at the appropriate time. The meeting ended with the exchange of a small white envelope and an agreement that they would meet again the following evening at another venue around the same time to finalise their future potential and ongoing relationship. Their farewell was even shorter. The visitor would call the Barbadian the next afternoon to advise their meeting location.

The men then went their separate ways. The visitor's hired vehicle turned onto the ABC highway and headed for the south coast where he planned to spend a quiet night in his hotel room, having already pre-ordered with room service to deliver a meal to his room at 9:15 p.m. His work was done for today.

The Barbadian also turned onto the ABC highway, but in the opposite direction, going towards the north of the island. He viewed tomorrow's meeting as the start of an ongoing engagement. How quickly the two men could establish a collaborative mechanism for future activities would need to be finalised. *Yes, this was good*, the Barbadian thought to himself as he patted the envelope now sitting nicely in his left pants pocket. He could not wait for tomorrow night's meeting.

Once he got home, the Barbadian planned to have a drink alone on his balcony after his wife and children had gone to bed. That would be his small reward for what he had done. His real 'celebration' could follow later, once he was properly set up. For now, he'd call his 'better half' to tell her he would be home soon.

***

Eight persons sat around Ilaro Court's main dining table in Motby, Jackie, Jackie's sister Gillian Nowell and her husband Franklyn, Kimberley, Anton and Captain Michael 'Mike' Motby, the Motby's son who was a senior ATR Captain with LIAT, the Caribbean airline and their special guest of honour.

Motby had excused himself from the dinner table on three occasions during the meal to receive updates on the unfolding national security situation. Two calls were related to the prison escape from earlier that day, while one dealt with the ongoing search for the missing CBOB Deputy Governor. Nonetheless, he and members of his family were able to chat amiably with Captain Selwick about his family, career in aviation, security trends in aviation, Brexit and of course, cricket.

***

Colonel Burke, Diane, Sir Thadeus and Cindy had very much enjoyed the excellent meal prepared for them by Diane, with Broome's assistance. Their conversation over dinner had been light-hearted and surprisingly open and friendly for two couples who were only meeting each other for the first time. It took nearly two hours for the four-course meal and dessert to be slowly devoured. Dessert was home-made vanilla ice cream, a light fruit flan pastry and freshly prepared mixed fruit to complete the meal. The bottles of red and white wine that were available throughout dinner had barely been touched.

Throughout the meal, the day's two security incidents were on Colonel Burke's mind, although he was able to keep his thoughts on them latent during what turned out to be a pleasant and stress-free evening.

***

It was around 9:50 p.m. when the last guests exited the British High Commissioner's official residence. Among them were Sarah McPiers, her boyfriend Glyn Aitken, himself a former England Test all-rounder and Timothy Rickson, the club's fast-talking but ageing opening bowler.

On exiting the official residence, they saw a young lady standing alone. They were not sure, but it appeared as if she was waiting for someone, or her transport back to her hotel had already left. She looked lost, prompting Rickson, the most talkative member of the New Beavers Cricket Club (NBCC), to ask a question on the subject to which she confirmed that it was the latter.

Rickson, being well 'oiled', stated, "Gallantry is not dead! How may I be of assistance to you, young lady? Where do you need to get to this beautiful evening? Do I need to call you a taxi or can we drop you off somewhere in ours whenever it gets here?"

"I'm staying at the hotel closest from the Hilton, about seven minutes away," was her reply.

Just then, Gina Crosby, the English-born British High Commission media liaison officer descended the residence steps, heading for her vehicle.

"Good night. I hope you've all enjoyed your evening with us. We enjoyed having you here. Get home safely."

"We will, once the taxi we've ordered gets here."

"Where are you going?" asked Crosby.

"We're staying in Hastings, but want to go to St Lawrence Gap for a night cap before turning in. Oh, on the way, our young lady friend here needs to get to her hotel by the Hilton. Our ordered taxi from inside the High Commission's house has not arrived to pick us up."

"Don't worry, I can drop you all off by making a slight detour on my way home. I live in Maxwell, just before Oistins so you're all on my way."

"Many thanks, ma'am. I'm obliged to you," said Rickson. His gift of the gab had won the day again, and saved his group a few dollars.

On the way, the discussion turned to what exactly they might do in St Lawrence Gap after dropping off the young lady. Aitken mentioned that on the last England cricket team's tour to Barbados, there was a new club that had a great atmosphere where you could get a late meal, a few drinks and do some dancing if you were so inclined which he now wanted to do. So, aware of this, they agreed to go to that club, once they could find it. He could not recall the club's name.

"I think you mean P's Disco. I know it's location and can drop you off there," said Crosby.

She did just that some fifteen minutes later.

The young lady who had been standing outside the High Commissioner's residence and was now a member of the NBCC group was Rhonda Ziegler, a sports reporter for the Daily Dispatch, a well-known English newspaper. Rhonda had been assigned to cover the Barbados and Trinidad legs of England's 2018 cricket tour of the Caribbean. She did not need to file her story until 10:00 a.m. tomorrow, so why not have a couple more drinks with her newly-found friends and a meal to boot before she turned in for the night?

A few hours later, Ziegler started to wish that she had gotten Crosby to drop her off at her hotel. But then again, she also realised that she could get her first major front-page story which was not exactly a sporting one. Her sojourn to St Lawrence Gap might have been worth it after all!

***

Selwick thanked the Prime Minister for the excellent meal and opportunity to meet other members of the Motby family in person and in more pleasant circumstances than when he and Motby had first met. As anticipated, Selwick had allowed himself two glasses of wine during dinner, although he was careful to advise those at the table that he would not be flying any aircraft before Friday afternoon. That got a chuckle out of everyone.

When it was clear that the evening was coming to an end, Captain Motby asked if he could be excused along with Selwick so that they could spend a few minutes together to discuss a couple of 'pilot-related' matters.

"No problem, son," said Motby.

Just then, his mobile phone rang for a fourth time that evening.

"Excuse me again please, I really must take this, but please go on with Mike. We'll all say goodnight to Captain Selwick before he leaves us."

Leaving the dining room, he said. "Prime Minister Motby…"

Jackie had noticed that Selwick and her son had not spoken much to each other during dinner, but she sensed that they wanted to.

"Yes, I guess you two pilots have a lot in common to speak about. Please use the balcony," she stated. She only hoped her son remembered that Selwick's body clock was past 3:00 a.m., given the four-hour difference between UK and Barbados at this time of the year.

The unmarked RBPF vehicle which had brought Selwick from Hilton Barbados, stood ready outside to return him there whenever he got around to saying goodnight and goodbye to everyone.

***

The Head of Britain's Secret Intelligence Service (MI6) and the Director of Barbados Intelligence Bureau (BIB) sat on the balcony of the latter's home overlooking part of the restored expansive and peaceful Graeme Hall swamp. They held night-cap drinks in their hands, in Sir Thadeus' case it was a Johnny Walker Black whisky neat (his third such drink for the evening), while Colonel Burke nursed a small (Cockspur) rum and coke with loads of ice, his first shot of alcohol that night having used coconut water throughout dinner.

Sir Thadeus spoke first.

"Trevor, I know it's none of my business, but are your colleagues making progress on recapturing the two escaped prisoners?"

"Yes and no. This has not happened here before – I mean prisoners escaping while being transported between our prisons compound and a courthouse. Three of the five prisoners did not go anywhere so were back in HMP Dodds by mid-afternoon. Of the missing two, one has a long history. A local gang leader of sorts. He's been involved in stealing, gun importation, drug sales, stabbings and more over the years. The other prisoner is what our police colleagues call *small beer*, he's not paid his child support."

"Do they expect to capture both men quickly, possibly by morning or at worse by this time tomorrow?"

"We hope so. There aren't many places in Barbados where one can hide from law enforcement."

"That's good. Hey Trevor, before I meet tomorrow with your fellow Heads of security agencies, I wanted to share something with you, as our organisations do a similar job. I'll not mention it tomorrow in our general meeting with your security colleagues. As we both know, there'll be no *formal* record of tomorrow's session, but I wish, no *need* your thoughts on if you can give me your word or 'buy in' to what I say. If you agree, once I'm back in London I'll ask our Ministers to formally request of your Ministers, through my FCO to your

Foreign Affairs Ministry, that we commence activity along the lines I'm about to put to you. How's that sound?"

"I'm listening, Thad, but can't promise anything until I hear what you have to say."

***

Power had gotten himself a few hours' sleep after Wharton's departure. When the alarm woke him, he took a long shower. After cleaning himself up, he found a change of clothing from Wharton's wardrobe. Power was lucky that Wharton and himself were of a similar height and size. Power was hungry, so went to the fridge to find something to eat. He took up one of the large pizzas he found and warmed it up in the microwave. Once he had devoured it, he washed it down with a cold Banks beer. He was now clean, refreshed, refuelled and ready to go on his journey dressed in Wharton's all-black outfit.

There was one thing left for him to do. Make that phone call.

***

Unknown to members of the Motby family, Captains Selwick and Motby had started to communicate, just by chance, six months earlier through Facebook.

Captain Motby had heard from one of his pilot friends from UK flight school that British Airways, because of Britain's soon-to-be formalised exit from the EU as at end-March 2019, might soon start hiring senior qualified pilots for its various jet fleets. Having now been with LIAT for fourteen years, Captain Motby was ready to make a move overseas to work for a large international airline. As his ambition had always been to fly with BA, this could be a chance for him to make his ambition a reality. He had been told by Selwick that they should discuss his current career when he was next in Barbados and so this was their private meeting. Of course, Captain Motby had agreed to this once his flying schedule could be amended accordingly and tonight, luckily, was the back-end of his off day. Captain Motby had to fly in the morning and would be away for the next couple of days on a three-day rotation with intervening nights in different countries. His return to Barbados would not be before Saturday morning, by which time Selwick would already be back in the UK.

145

Once both men were settled in two comfortable chairs on the balcony overlooking the gardens at the back of the family quarters at Ilaro Court, the younger Motby hoped Selwick had something good to tell him, for example would confirm what his friend had told him about potential openings at BA by year-end. Captain Motby knew he'd have to give LIAT three months' notice, so should any BA offer be made to him by November 2018, he would be able to get to the UK anytime from the end of February.

***

Wharton and his Pressure Group pals assembled around 10:30 p.m. in the back room at SBB&G. He paid each member of the Group in cash for the work they had done earlier that day. There were no complaints. Wharton ordered in four Banks beers for them to toast what they certainly felt had been a job well done, though it had unfortunately not been flawlessly executed.

The shooting at law enforcement officers during Powers' break out was not originally planned but had become necessary. The explosions heard during the melee were necessary for distraction. The blowback from Power's escape was bad in that it had been made worse by the shots they had fired. Pictures of the area where the break out had taken place looked bad. The RBPF was, according to media reports, already hard on the track of the two escaped prisoners. Their photographs had been passed by BPS to the RBPF who had released them during Gray's promised 5:00 p.m. media briefing at RBPF HQ. They would be in tomorrow's newspapers and were already on television news programmes and across social media. The escaped prisoners' pictures were also now posted on law enforcement agency websites, meaning that the public could see what the faces of the escaped prisoners.

There were no media stories to date about who was responsible for the escape. Wharton and his gang members had tried their best not to leave behind any traces of who they were at the scene, having worn gloves and masks and so they were not worried about their identities being discovered.

Pressure Group members felt confident that once they continued their normal day-to-day work routines, their identities and respective roles in today's prisoners' escape would go unnoticed by family and friends. They each had what they felt were excellent 'cover' stories for where they were between 8:00 a.m. and 1:00 p.m. that day. As for the two vehicles that had been used to execute

Power's rescue, the stolen six-wheeled truck had been abandoned at the scene of the incident, while the getaway car now lay at the bottom of a gully three miles away from where the incident had taken place. They were careful not to leave their fingerprints anywhere on or in either vehicle. They did not think about DNA evidence that might have been left behind, although Power's fingerprints might, on reflection, be somewhere inside the getaway car.

Prior to the Pressure Group members leaving the back room of SBB&G, they allowed themselves another drink. This time they used something stronger than beer to celebrate their achievement and pay-day.

***

It was around 10:30 p.m. when Power dialled the number he'd memorised after being given it two days earlier by a fellow inmate.

A phone rang in an ocean-facing house in Bathsheba, St Joseph. The individual answering the phone sounded not too happy to hear from him. They wondered how and where he had gotten their number from, but agreed to meet him at their home at midnight. They did not ask where he was or how he would get to them.

There was no vehicle at Wharton's house for Power to use, so he knew he would have to walk the distance to the individual's house. That age-old Bajan saying of 'when you ain't got horse, ride cow' sprung to mind. He estimated having to make about a thirty minutes trek to his destination. Looking at the clock on Wharton's dining room wall, he realised that he would need to get going within the hour if he was to be punctual for his midnight rendezvous. The individual had warned during their brief conversation not to arrive at their house after 12:10 p.m. The residence's heavy security measures would be relaxed to facilitate entrance to their home.

***

"Trevor, I'm here on holiday, but I must confess that my visit coincides with a project we've been quietly working on in and around the Eastern Caribbean sub-region for about four months. To effectively bring it to the boil over the next year or so, I think it's going to be imperative that our two organisations, MI6 and

147

BIB start working closely together, sooner rather than later. Can that happen?" asked the Head of MI6.

"It depends on what you're trying to achieve, why and how," answered the Head of BIB.

"Good answer! Here's the what and why. Over the past six months, our people have noticed a significant uptick in criminal activity, not only in Barbados, but across the Eastern Caribbean sub-region. They and our American friends on the ground here all believe that they've identified some, but not all of those involved. We've not been able to establish why and around what, for example any major activities taking place that criminals might be building up to taking advantage of," said Sir Thadeus.

"Well, I can only think of our EEC, sorry Extra Cricket Cover security project that was initiated last night after planning it for well over six months. It runs until midnight next Wednesday," stated Colonel Burke.

"Why next Wednesday? The Test Match ends on Tuesday, that is if it goes the five days given the way England are playing nowadays. So why Wednesday?"

"Thad, the teams leave here mid-Wednesday morning for Trinidad and the 3rd Test. We also have a few other events that are in play around the cricket, ending with a two-day Commonwealth Sports Ministers Conference on Tuesday and Wednesday," said Colonel Burke.

"Where's that meeting being held?" asked Sir Thadeus.

"Hilton Barbados," responded Colonel Burke.

"What specifically are the *few other events*?"

"Two of them. On Saturday night, the USA's football team play Barbados at our National Stadium. On Sunday night, there's a big concert by a Canadian singer at the Garfield Sobers Sports Complex."

"You and your security mates have your hands full, Trevor! I'm sure the prisoners escape thing today isn't helping, in fact I suspect it will complicate your people's work. But back to my ask. The criminal activity we've been monitoring is different to what we've seen in the past few years in the Caribbean. That, is all about our drug interdiction/prevention programme aimed at stopping all kinds of major drugs, guns and other illegal contraband from primarily reaching UK, Europe and USA shores via Caribbean Sea and air ports from their originating points in Venezuela and the tip of Columbia," said Sir Thadeus.

"Yes, yes, but what's so new now, Thad? And how do you know that local groups are involved in more criminal acts now than they ever were before, and in different ways too where my people haven't picked up on that yet?" asked a puzzled Colonel Burke.

"Great question. There are new linkages with established international crime syndicates who are looking to spread their influence and reach all parts of the world, including new areas where they have not been seriously active before, such as the Caribbean. Small countries like Barbados and its neighbouring Eastern Caribbean countries, are particularly ideal for these syndicates to spread themselves into."

"Why?"

"Well, they believe local law enforcement and security agencies are not going to bother them because they are too insignificant. How so? By way of being insufficiently trained and or being understaffed to do anything about them, especially once they have fully extended their hooks into the local communities through their top professionals, politicians, public service officials, businessmen and even a few well-known sportsmen and women."

"You're kidding me, right Thad? I mean, we believe we have a handle on our local criminals and the overall situation…who they are, what they're involved in, where they keep their money, etc. But you're telling me that, by our not recognising this 'significant uptick' in the supposed activities of local criminals, we've in effect, dropped our own balls?"

"Not exactly, Trevor. But there is now much more going on in your country and your neighbours than I think your people are fully aware of, my friend. That old phrase 'live by the gun, die by the gun' is back. We should like to help you of course, but we'd prefer to do so formally and in fact must have political cover for our actions, otherwise my next House of Commons appearance before our Joint Security/Intelligence Committee will see me put away for all kinds of breaches. I don't want that for Cindy and myself. I'm sure as hell neither Diane nor you would want that for us either. Should that ever happen, we might just have to return to Barbados and have you hide us out, that is, if I managed to escape Dartmoor Prison."

"Indeed."

"So, Trevor, do you think your Prime Minister would be willing to sign off on an approach by our Secretary of State (SOS) seeking enhanced collaboration between the UK and Barbados' law enforcement/security agencies in general –

MI6 and BIB specifically? Of course, in a perfect world, I'd rather such collaboration not be publicly acknowledged, but I gather that it may have to be presented to, discussed in and be ratified by your Parliament."

"Damn right. That's for sure. Knowing my PM, he would insist on it, probably after an initial face-to-face meeting, ideally between himself and your PM (SOS might do) before anything can be formalised. My PM would have lots of questions about how any such arrangement would work between our two countries and organisations. For example, how would he deal with an investigative journalist or deliberate leak from a senior security official who dislikes the idea? My PM would at least have to first inform and discuss it with his Cabinet colleagues. I doubt any of them would be the source of a leak, but who knows?"

"Fine. We've dealt with such situations before with other friendly countries like Barbados. We've always managed to work through any problems they may have had with this sort of thing effectively. I don't think here would be any different."

"One, no two final considerations for you, Thad."

"Yes, Trevor?"

"I think you're aware that Barbados is part of and provides the headquarters for the Regional Security System (RSS), comprised of us and several Eastern Caribbean countries. The RSS is located next door to the airport. If this increased criminal activity you've just told me about really exists and is expanding and is so likely to engage other Eastern Caribbean (EC) countries, my PM will also have to speak with his fellow EC PMs. That would increase the risk of a new collaborative security agreement having to be more widely known, with debates being held in Parliaments, with the top public servants in these countries also having to be in the loop. Therefore, to avoid leakage, everything would have to be made public," reasoned Colonel Burke.

"Believe me, this can all be addressed. Like I've said already, we've worked out similar deals before, and I fully understand the UK's longstanding and established working relationship with the RSS that has helped to build up its current operations," said Sir Thadeus.

"Okay. Next, you've mentioned neighbouring EC countries, but haven't specified any in which what you've told me are rampant from your investigations. So, besides Barbados, which ones have shown an enhanced propensity for increased criminal activity by its local gangs, in concert with international criminal gangs or syndicates?" asked Colonel Burke.

Sir Thadeous thought for a minute.

"Trevor, a recent Director of the CIA has inferred that in order for their organisation to be successful, it must be aggressive, vicious, unforgiving and relentless. MI6, BIB and similar organisations, must do likewise with those who threaten our countries well-being, institutions, people – indeed our very way of life. I believe you to be the right man, in the right job, right place and time! They are a quadrant of countries where we've noticed activity that is gathering momentum: St Vincent and the Grenadines, Grenada, St Lucia, Antigua and Barbuda," answered Sir Thadeus.

"Thanks. That's most interesting," mused Colonel Burke.

"Before I leave you, I'm curious about one thing. How does BIB work? It's a small department that does not even number in total a section in one of my operational units," Sir Thadeus stated.

"It's simple. Barbados is tiny compared to your country. BIB has three operational teams of three, myself and two persons on the technical side of the house. Operational teams are called *Gold*, *Blue* and *Black*. All three teams are set to play a role in the ECC security project. Team names come from the colours of Barbados' national flag. *Gold* represents the sand on Barbados' beach. *Blue* (or ultramarine) represents the sea surrounding and sky overlooking Barbados. *Black* reflects the broken trident – the symbol of Neptune, a mythical sea god. The latter also speaks to Barbados' break with Britain in November 1966 when the country gained its independence after being a long-standing colony. We are a very integrated and flexible organisation. We work closely together, occasionally with assistance from RBPF and BDF personnel who support the operations we pursue."

"I think I understand BIB more clearly now. You are specialists and operate, more often than not, behind the scenes," said Sir Thadeus with a nod.

"You got it," said Colonel Burke. "Anyway, it's been good to have you over."

"Cindy and I are grateful to Diane and you for your kind hospitality…and our after-dinner chat."

***

Just after 11:15 p.m., Power slipped out of Wharton's back door to commence his journey. Some two years earlier, he had visited the heavily fortified residence he was now going to. Back then, he had approached the property by car, from the west and in daylight. Tonight, he would arrive on foot, from the east and at night.

Power would request the individual's assistance in one of two ways. Either provide him with the sum he needed to settle his debt to *The Organisation* by noon of the following day, or facilitate his departure from Barbados (and the clutches of its law enforcement) agencies by 4:00 p.m. Both situations would result in the *favour* the individual owed to him being wiped clean. His preference was the latter option.

Power knew the individual he was going to meet had the ability to deliver. They owed him big time for the favour he had done for the individual that hampered one of their main competitors. That was two years ago. Power and the individual had not spoken about that favour since, but neither had either of them forgotten about it. In his long criminal career, he knew that having someone being indebted to you was not always a good position to be in. They might want to bump you off so as not to have to repay their favour or debt of gratitude. You had to be careful to keep the *chit* you held somewhere safe for a time such as this when you would try to cash it because you most needed to do so.

Power's need was now. It was time to cash in his chit with the individual. Money would be good, but escape from Barbados would be far better. Power and the individual would be square. Both would know that should Power be recaptured he could decide to spill his guts to the authorities and the individual would go down big time. Great embarrassment to people in high places might also result from what he knew. Power's death would, of course, eliminate this worry to the individual but what he might leave behind might also hurt them and open up a can of worms. It was therefore advisable for the individual to give him what he wanted.

Power felt confident that he and the individual would come to a sensible arrangement tonight. Neither of them wanted to lose what they believed they had.

***

The media had not yet broken the news that CBOB Deputy Governor Lewis was missing, but this was expected to leak sometime soon, perhaps overnight. That meant that this subject did not come up during the one-to-one after-dinner discussion between the two security agency leaders. While the role, size and funds available to their respective agencies were far different, the thinking, understanding, willingness and desire of the two men to work together was clear and so boded well for the future.

***

Following Sir Thadeus and Cindy's departure, Colonel Burke reflected on the evening with Diane for a few minutes before setting off for BIB HQ. He would see Sir Thadeus again tomorrow afternoon.

Once back at BIB HQ, Colonel Burke went straight to his office. After checking to ensure that he had not received any calls from Motby or Jeremie on his red telephone line, he went in search of JJ, Mohammed and Jayne who he knew were in the building. Not finding them at their work stations, he went to the conference room where he found not only them, but also Fred and Joe.

"Did I call you two? Can't you sleep? You're off today and tomorrow."

"No chief, is the answer to your first question…and not anymore, is our answer to your second," said Fred.

"Very funny, Fred," responded Colonel Burke dryly but nonetheless nodded acceptance of Fred's position.

He looked over at Joe. "You're also back on the job?"

"Yes sir, I surely am. Can't keep me away," was her prompt reply.

Colonel Burke knew what that meant! He accepted that BIB's best operatives were here to help out. Come to think of it, he wondered why he hadn't seen them sooner!

Up to this point, there was still no word on the whereabouts of the CBOB's Deputy Governor.

***

Lewis had enjoyed a smooth flight from Miami to Barbados. Sitting in seat 15C (thankfully it had extra leg room) on what was a full AA flight on one of its newest A321 jets, was very comfortable. No turbulence was felt during the three-hours and forty-minute flight. He therefore slept like a baby most of the way.

After clearing Immigration, Lewis exited the Customs hall from the Arrivals hall of Grantley Adams International Airport (GAIA). He caught the first available airport taxi assigned by the dispatcher. He gave the driver his parents' address before settling back into the taxi's back seat as it rolled out of the airport. Once on the ABC highway, it headed off into the countryside.

Twenty minutes later, the taxi pulled up at the address he had been given. Lewis paid the driver before walking up the six steps to the house's front door to ring the bell.

Mrs Lewis quickly opened the door, holding out both of her hands before hugging her son closely. Without speaking, she pulled away to look him over. Satisfied, she hugged him again, this time standing on tiptoe to kiss him on both cheeks.

Once their embrace had finally ended, Lewis simply said, "Hello, Mum, it's good to be home."

"Good to have you home, my son."

Lewis picked up his backpack and overnight carry-on bag before entering the house behind her. He would call Caroline in half-an-hour or so to let her know that he had arrived safely. He knew she'd also want to speak to their mum as well.

***

Wharton closed-up SBB&G just after midnight. He would make his way back to the east coast early in the morning to see what Power had gotten up to overnight. Wharton's son would open the shop in the morning around 9:00 a.m. as usual.

Wharton hoped Power had made some progress on securing the funds he understood were being demanded from him by *The Organisation*. Failure to do that would mean real trouble for Power, not Wharton. *Some serious shit might then come down the tubes and tomorrow might not end well for Power if he was not able to deliver*, he thought. He felt that would not be good news for anyone, given Castille's unfriendly disposition at his first meeting with Power. Wharton did not want to get himself or any of his Pressure Group members caught up in any of that business.

Before he fell asleep, he said his prayers. He hoped all of the RBPF and BPS officers who had been shot at from their getaway car during Power's escape were okay. Media reports had indicated that none of them had been shot which was good news. He had only instructed his Pressure Group colleague to fire off a few shots to prevent the undamaged law enforcement vehicle that was also at the scene from chasing them. Thankfully, no chase had ensued.

Wharton ended his prayers by hoping for a better tomorrow and stating his usual 'be jolly now'.

A few minutes later, he fell into a deep sleep.

***

Chapter Twelve
All Hands-on Deck

THURSDAY, 19 APRIL

It took Power longer than he thought to reach the individual's house. The dogs had been put up. Only the house's security system was on.

The individual watched Power's careful approach up the driveway to the house from a darkened upstairs bedroom window. As he neared the front door, the individual started down the stairs as the doorbell rang and opened the door.

The reception Power received was a cold one. He was not surprised, as it was what he'd expected following their earlier phone conversation. But given his circumstances, Power knew that only this individual could help him out of the predicament he was in.

"Hi there," said Power.

"Hello, Jasper. I see it didn't take you long to get out," the individual responded.

"That's right! Most people I know would prefer to see me still on the inside for a long, long time to come, if not with a rope around my neck. I'm absolutely sure that you don't fall into either category."

"Try me," responded the individual.

"My, how you've *changed* since our last encounter. Anyway, what 'cha got here to drink? I'm thirsty after my long walk. Can I have a large one and I'll explain my situation, after which I'm sure you'll want to help me out," Power stated.

The individual turned away, frowning. "You may have come to the wrong place."

Power's response was irritating. "I don't think so."

There and then, the individual regretted not having had Power 'dealt with' early last year after he'd botched one of their newest fund-raising ventures. His failure had embarrassed the individual and cost them some money. Power's death would not have been mourned by many as punishment. The individual, in a moment of weakness, recalled that Power had previously done them a big favour, so had decided not to deal harshly with him as in the right circumstances, he might be of some use to them in the future.

The individual was wrong. Look how times had changed.

Power was now standing in the individual's house after midnight with a smug look, demanding a drink and seeking a favour. This was not what Power or the individual had anticipated when both awoke yesterday morning. The prospect of Power spending a long period of time in a prison cell had been a strong possibility, though it had been tempered by the improbability of his escape. With the latter now being an unfortunate reality, the individual was paying for their compassion.

"Damn!" the individual said softly.

"What's that you say?" asked Power.

"Help yourself, the bar's solid," said the individual pointing to its location.

"Cheers. Much appreciated. I'll tell you the two things I'd like you to consider helping me out with."

So, despite the individual's disdain for Power, tonight was going to be one of reckoning for both of them.

Power disappeared down a corridor and through the kitchen before entering a small entertainment room where a large counter with a wide array of alcoholic drinks were displayed.

The individual followed him.

"What if I can't help you with either thing?"

"That's not going to work. Got any ice?"

"Try the fridge."

A few minutes later, Power spoke again after a long pull of the drink he had mixed. He did not ask the individual if they wanted one.

"As I was saying. I need some cash."

"How much and for what reason?"

"Let me also tell you what might be a cheaper and preferred alternative," said Power playfully.

"Go on, but I'm still waiting on the answers to my first question. Then I'll compare that to your other ask," said the bored individual.

Power stated the figure he wanted and why.

"That's not going to happen, even if I had it here," responded the individual.

"Why am I not surprised? Okay. Can you quietly get me out of Barbados by late tomorrow afternoon? Then I swear, we'll be clear with each other."

"Gosh, I can see why you're in a real pickle, desperate even."

"Guess I am."

The individual thought for a few seconds before deciding to help Power with the second option. The individual grabbed a pad and wrote a west coast address on it.

"I'll make the arrangements to get you out, but you must be there no later than 5:00 p.m. tomorrow –" the individual looked at their phone before continuing, "...no, I mean later today. Miss the rendezvous and you're on your own, right? They are no second chances on this deal. Remember, you're very much a wanted item."

"Tell me about it. Thanks. I'm be going then."

With the individual nodding in the affirmative, Power downed the last of his drink and headed for the exit. The individual followed him to the door. That was meant to be their last exchange. Neither intended to say goodbye.

However, once the door was opened, they saw that it had started to rain. That simple observation caused them to re-engage about what happened next.

***

Colonel Burke, JJ, Mohammed, Jayne, Fred and Joe again reviewed everything that had happened on the previous day, from the Gold team's arrival at BIB HQ until when Colonel Burke had left them around 7:00 p.m. the evening before.

Colonel Burke telephoned Jeremie from BIB HQ around 1:00 a.m., just in case there were any updates on the Deputy Governor's disappearance. There were none so around 1:15 a.m. Colonel Burke and his BIB operatives decided to call it a night and go home to get some rest. They agreed to re-assemble at 8:00 a.m.

***

Jeremie wondered why his good friend Colonel Burke could not have waited until morning to call him. After all, Jeremie had advised everyone relevant that he had placed one of his sharpest men on the missing Deputy Governor's case. He knew Colonel Burke and his team were also working hard on that case, probably throughout the night, and to get to the bottom of the prisoners escape case. This did not surprise him. If one team could find any potential connection between these two incidents, hopefully before the Test Match element of the ECC security project fully got underway, it would be Colonel Burke's BIB boys and girls. Jeremie felt certain that he would speak with Colonel Burke again before he left his home for RBPF HQ in the morning, perhaps before he even got out of bed.

Jeremie turned off his bedside light for the third time that night. Colonel Burke was the latest person to call him since he'd climbed in around 11:30 p.m. The calls had come from Vickers, Motby and now Colonel Burke.

"No more calls tonight please," Jeremie said softly to himself ahead of drifting off to sleep for the fourth time that night. He was glad that his wife Sandra was not a light sleeper. Once the overhead fan was on, she was out for the count – in fact, she would sleep through most things until morning.

***

The last four English patrons to enter P's Disco that night had eaten their meals. Three of them had also had a couple of gin and tonics each. Rhonda Ziegler had taken a large coke with her meal. It was time for them to join the majority of the other fifty or so English and local patrons now bumping and grinding, some were even 'wuckin up' on P's Disco dancefloor to the latest Calypso and Soca songs being pumped out by DJ Price.

Sarah McPiers, Glyn Aitken and Timothy Rickson were having their own 'after-party' in St Lawrence Gap. Ziegler, stomach full, now wished that she had been dropped off at her hotel after all, as sleep was starting to get the better of her.

***

It was just before 2:00 a.m. when Power returned to Wharton's house on Barbados' east coast. He was happy to unlock the door and get inside.

He'd been lucky. As he was about to leave the individual's house to start what was probably a forty-minute walk back to Wharton's house, the rain had started to fall, gently initially but them more heavily. He'd requested a ride back from the individual, but there was resistance, with the individual fearing that someone might spot them dropping off a much sought-after escaped prisoner from their vehicle.

After ten minutes of non-stop rain, the individual gave in and consented to provide the requested drop. Power's ride was to the end of the road, not exactly to Wharton's house. That meant that he still had to walk the best part of fifty yards to Wharton's back door in the now driving rain. He did not bother to look back at the vehicle driven by the individual whose help he had just secured as it disappeared into the distance up the winding road.

Once inside Wharton's house, Power took a hot shower. Thereafter, he made himself a ham sandwich, and mixed himself another stiff drink before heading to the back bedroom that had earlier been allocated to him by Wharton. There, he quickly fell asleep on the bed.

***

It happened shortly after the NBCC's group of three, plus Ziegler had left P's Disco in search of a taxi. They found one not far away. The driver seemed half-asleep, so Rickson tapped on the front passenger's half-opened window.

"Want a job, mate?"

Instantly alert and rubbing the sleep from his eyes, the taxi driver replied, "Always. Where to, skipper?"

"The hotel before you get to the Hilton, then back to Hastings Main Road, you know the all-inclusive hotel opposite Jeepers Restaurant," responded Rickson.

"I know the hotel you mean. Hop in," said the taxi driver, starting the vehicle.

Now fully awake, he introduced himself to his perspective passengers. "My name's Francis, by the way."

The four passengers got into the taxi.

Rickson had learnt from his previous overseas travels to do two things before the start of any taxi or mini-cab journey. Secure a price up front from the driver, and keep his wits about him throughout the journey.

"How much?"

As Francis was about to reply, two men suddenly appeared on either side of the taxi with what looked, in the semi-darkness, to be handguns which were being pointed at the vehicle. McPiers, Aitken and Ziegler were in the back seats.

Rickson, up front with the taxi driver, was the only one in the vehicle switched on to what was happening. He shouted to Francis, "Drive." Francis immediately put the vehicle into gear, thinking, *This guy is in one hell of a hurry to get to his bed*, just as the window next to Rickson was shattered.

Francis did comprehend what was happening, but Rickson did not although he was unsure at first whether the broken glass had been the result of the butt of a gun coming through the window on his side of the vehicle or a gunshot fired by the assailant closest to him on the left side of the vehicle.

Francis picked up the imminent danger to his passengers and pressed the vehicle's accelerator hard to try and make their escape. By now McPiers and Ziegler were screaming, but Aitken noticed that Rickson had slumped forward in his seat holding his left arm, moaning and swearing in-between.

Pow. Pow. McPiers, Ziegler and Aitken heard two further gunshots. Assuming that these were being fired upon, they ducked for cover in the back of the vehicle in case further gunfire was to follow.

In Francis' frantic efforts to move off, he only managed to broadside the taxi that had been parked in front of him. It was also in the process of pulling away from the kerb with a couple of young Barbadians who were P's Disco regulars. Following a noisy bang, both vehicles came to a standstill. Terrified screams from inside both vehicles, shouts and cussing from onlookers started to reverberate in the immediate area.

The two assailants, as if by magic, quickly disappeared from the vicinity of the shooting and resulting accident. A RBPF officer, accompanied by a BDF soldier, came running towards the confused scene in St Lawrence Gap. The officer's weapon was drawn, suggesting that he had also heard the fired shots. On reaching the scene, he made a quick assessment before listening to descriptions of what had just taken place from the assembled onlookers. He then recounted their recollections to RBPF control on his radio requesting back-up and that an ambulance be dispatched to the scene to cater to the hurt persons.

"On the way, be there in two," said a voice over his radio. Obviously his RBPF backup was close-by in the Gap.

Within five minutes, St Lawrence Gap was awash with security and law enforcement personnel.

McPiers, Aitken, Ziegler and Francis stood outside of the latter's damaged taxi but close to the front seat where Rickson sat. The BDF soldier accompanying the RBPF officer announced that he was a trained first aider and quickly went to work on examining Rickson. The soldier confirmed that Rickson had received a gunshot to his upper left arm. He was bleeding. The soldier pulled what looked like a large but clean personal washcloth from one of his uniform pockets and applied it as a tourniquet to help stop the bleeding.

Meanwhile, the taxi that had been hit by Francis had not moved. The young couple in it still sat in it, dazed and unsure of what exactly had happened, not knowing what they should do next. They and their driver were in shock.

"This is clean, so don't worry. You'll be fine, man," said the soldier to Rickson. Turning to Rickson's English companions and the gathered bunch of onlookers, he added, "He'll live."

"An ambulance is on its way, sir. Hold on," said the RBPF officer.

Rickson, ever the funny man, spoke. "What else do you want me to do? God, this hurts in a sort of sweet way! Man am I glad I've had a few drinks this evening to help with this situation. Some after-party!"

McPiers and Aitken were concerned. As Rickson's close friends, they felt his pain and so urged him to keep quiet. This was not how their – no, not the way *any* after-party was meant to end.

The journalist in Ziegler was alert and thinking differently to McPiers and Aitken. *Story,* was her only thought. She mumbled to herself, "Christ, I think I might have myself an exclusive of sorts here."

With that, Ziegler withdrew her phone from her clutch bag and started taking pictures before video recording the scene around her. Boy did she have a story to tell, with pictures and video to boot. If she played this right, her on-the-spot report, pictures and video of the attempted robbery and shooting at a main tourist spot in Barbados would be newsworthy back home, perhaps across the world. Ziegler saw a big promotion coming if she did this just right. *When opportunity knocks, take it.* Social media would send her coverage to another level if she got things right, but she had to start now. She had truly been in the wrong place, but at the right time. A couple of comments from eye-witnesses would not hurt either.

Ziegler later gave descriptions as best she could recall of the two robbers/shooters to RBPF interviewers when they subsequently visited the scene. What a night! What a story she could tell.

***

The call Commissioner Jeremie anticipated came a lot earlier that morning than he had expected However, it did not come from the BIB Director.

It was 4:30 a.m. when Jeremie's land line rang. It was Assistant Commissioner (Administration), Jethro Smith. He apologised profusely for waking-up his boss so early, but he had felt the need to report what was a potentially damaging incident for the country that had taken place a couple of hours earlier in St. Lawrence Gap, Christ Church. AC Smith then passed the telephone to Station Sergeant Robert 'Bob' Black, in charge of the close-by Worthing police station.

He briefed Jeremie on the night's St Lawrence Gap incident.

When Black was finished, all that the startled Commissioner could say to him was, "Thank you Station Sergeant Black. This is crazy. Put AC Smith back on the phone please."

Once AC Smith was back on the line, Jeremie said, "Jethro, what the hell's going on in Barbados? This makes, let's see one, two, three unusual incidents that have occurred on this island since 10:00 a.m. yesterday morning. As far as I can see, none of them have anything to do with our ongoing ECC project. Dammed if I know why this is all bubbling up now. The PM will have my head for breakfast if I'm not careful and can quickly get to the bottom of at least this latest fiasco," he said.

"Sir, let me assure you that we're on the case to catch the perpetrators of this crime. It appears to have been 'an attempted robbery gone wrong'. The shot man has been transported to QEH. I'm no medic but am told by those who have seen him that they see no reason why he should not pull through. He was only shot in the left arm," said AC Smith.

"Thanks, Jethro. Please have SS Black e-mail me a full report of the incident at home by 6:00 a.m. I expect this will be one of the top news items this morning, if it's not already out there, so I'll need to be ready to make a statement to the media and answer some questions by the time I get to HQ. I suspect I'll also have to visit the scene this morning."

"Will do, sir. Night, I mean good morning to you and to Mrs Jeremie. Again, sorry for waking you up."

"No worries, Jethro! Being woken by my staff at all hours comes with the territory I occupy. Oh, please alert Inspector Gray too about this. I'll need her tomorrow morning. Goodbye."

"Will do, sir."

Sarah Jeremie was surprisingly awake. He guessed that his raised voice had woken her from her deep slumber. He quickly told her about the St Lawrence Gap incident and that there were now three unusual incidents that had taken place in Barbados over the past twenty-four hours. She was not amused to hear any of this, or at having to wake up so early this morning to police business. *I'm used to Will being called at night a lot more since becoming Commissioner but Christ, even at this early hour*? she thought.

AC Smith knew the St. Lawrence Gap incident might have to result in some re-jigging of the RBPF's manpower allotted to cover Day 1 of the Test Match starting on Friday. For sure, the PM and the Minister of Tourism, International Transport and Sport would be on Jeremie's case by daylight. They would want him to re-assure everyone who visited St. Lawrence Gap that it was, is and would continue to be a safe place for patrons, locals and visitors alike, to go for relaxation and entertainment over the coming week and beyond.

Jeremie also knew that he would need to give this assurance. Local politicians would be in a tizzy once news of this incident hit local airways and newspapers. It was already out there on social media. They might not now be any way to avoid new travel advice notices being issued by local Embassies, High Commissions and Consulates, particularly the Brits, given that their national cricket team was on island with thousands of supporters and one of their sports journalists had been directly involved in the incident. She would no doubt be providing a first-hand account of her unfortunate experience – if she had not already done so. Pity, because this would now negatively counter-balance the positive stories that were already in circulation as a result of last night's successful and incident-free cricketing party.

Jeremie would now beat Colonel Burke's anticipated call to him later this morning, only in reverse. His wake-up call to Colonel Burke would be around 6:00 a.m. After that, he would also need to speak with the Prime Minister. Right now, he wanted another hour's sleep, unless the phone rang *again*.

***

164

The individual living on the East Coast rose 5:45 a.m. It was an alien time for them to do any business, but following Power's visit the previous night, the individual needed to make four short but important calls. One was to a businessperson in Miami. It was now time for them to make an urgent visit to Barbados to discuss their proposed new Eastern Caribbean (EC) relationship *in person*. A two-day visit would be sufficient to finalise the arrangements.

Another call was to a businessperson on Barbados' west coast who ran a couple of businesses, including a fishing boat operation that was part-owned by the individual who was calling. A request was made to arrange a special fishing boat journey that would include an overnight visit to deliver a special cargo as part of one of its five-day fishing trips to the southern Caribbean. The individual would 'reward' the businessperson for making this extra overnight journey. The 'package' would be delivered to their home later that afternoon.

The third call made was to a soft-spoken man in a well-to-do residential district in a neighbouring southern Caribbean country. Could he receive and look after a package being sent his way for a while if it was dispatched to him overnight? The usual arrangements would apply.

"No problem."

"Fine. Thank you."

"Collection arrangements at my end will be in place for the morning. Early?"

"Yes."

"Call you back on receipt of package?"

"No. Less conversation is better."

"Okay."

It was obvious that the two persons had conducted this kind of business transactions before.

The east coast individual knew what Power had on them could be damaging if even a small part of their activities were ever to be made public. The individual did not want, could not afford to let that happen. Their professional life and position in Barbadian society, good covers for their 'other' underworld business endeavours, had to be protected. Hence the agreement to *off-load* Power that afternoon.

The fourth and final call made by the individual was to someone in authority.

"Hello," answered the official.

"Good morning. I need a favour?" stated the individual.

"My you're early. Pray tell me what you need," was the response.

"A distraction of sorts, within the next thirty-six hours."

"No kidding. Why?"

"Look, I have a situation here. Doesn't involve you – yet. You don't need to know the why. You up for this?"

"I'll see what can be done."

"Appreciate that. Have a nice day."

"After this start, how can I?" asked the person in authority.

"I'm sure you'll find a way." The east coast individual ended the conversation.

***

Colonel Burke was awoken by Jeremie at 6:01 a.m.

Once he had been informed of the early morning shooting incident, Colonel Burke got the distinct impression that his good friend and fellow *P.A.A.N.I.* Head had just gotten his own back on him for the call he had made to Jeremie five hours earlier. He also recognised that Jeremie had been considerate enough not to have called him a few hours earlier.

***

The 6:30 a.m., 7:05 a.m. and 7:30 a.m. radio news programmes on various radio stations had all carried a story on the overnight attempted robbery and shooting of a British visitor in St. Lawrence Gap. The middle report had stated that Commissioner Willoughby Jeremie would visit the incident's location and make a statement to the media between 8:30 a.m. and 9:00 a.m., well before the Test Match started at 10:00 a.m. tomorrow. Jeremie's comments were expected to re-assure everyone that Barbados remained a safe place to live, invest, work and play.

There was no new word on the two escaped prisoners from the day before. Efforts by the country's law enforcement agencies were continuing to apprehend them and they would hopefully be recaptured before nightfall if they did not turn themselves into a police station before. The public was warned not to approach either of the two escaped prisoners, particularly the most dangerous of them, Power, a known repeat criminal currently on gun, drug and other charges too numerous to mention. His long criminal record dated back twenty years. The prisoners were not thought to be together but their details were widely available.

***

Lewis' mobile phone alarm had woken him up at 6:30 a.m.

Damn! He was not pleased. That was his wake-up time when in New York, not Barbados! He regretted not having remembered to turn off his phone alarm before he went to bed early that morning. As he was up, Lewis knew he would not be able to get back to sleep as the brightness of the morning was already shining through the pulled curtains of the bedroom he used whenever he came home.

He decided to get up and go for a walk and a run. He used the bathroom, washed his face and brushed his teeth before pulling on his exercise gear that he kept in one of the drawers when on such visits to Barbados. Lewis made a check on his mother. He was glad to see that she was sleeping soundly. He left the house quietly for his half-an-hour walk and run around the neighbourhood. He felt this would help to clear his head. He'd had an uncomfortable night, just four hours sleep in the end because he could not help but review and reflect on the fond relationship he had with his dad. Lewis noticed some of the subtle changes that had taken place in the neighbourhood since his last visit. The walk and run helped to freshen up his mind.

On re-entering the house, Lewis decided to call the mobile number shown on the business card that his mother had presented to him, given to her by the two RBPF officers from the previous morning. Lewis wanted to start finding out what the latest was from the leading investigators on his father's disappearance.

"Chief Superintendent Vickers. May I help you?"

"Yes, hello. Good morning, sir. Bertram Lewis here, Dr Lewis' son. I'm here from the States, staying at my parents' residence. Came in last night."

"Thanks for calling, Mr Lewis. Nothing I want to tell you over the telephone. Can we meet at RBPF HQ around, say 9:30 a.m.? I have a stop to make but should be there around that time."

"Fine Mr – I'm sorry I mean Chief Superintendent. 9:30 a.m. is fine."

"You know where our HQ is located, Mr Lewis?"

"Think so…in the old Barclays Bank building in Roebuck Street?"

"Correct. See you later, Mr Lewis."

As Bertram rang off, his mum appeared and gave him a hug.

"Good morning son. Who are you speaking to this early?" Mrs Lewis asked.

"Morning, Mum," Lewis said, kissing her on her forehead. "Just one of the policemen who came to see you yesterday. I have a meeting with him this morning," he replied.

"Which one?" she asked.

"Chief Superintendent Vickers. I called him to find out if they had any new developments on Dad's investigation. He didn't say, but invited me to come and see him at RBPF HQ at 9:30 a.m. today. I'll get cleaned up and come back to join you for breakfast."

"Okay, son."

Twenty minutes later, Lewis had done the three morning S's and casually dressed. Breakfast, prepared by Ava Prescod, was already on the table in the family room.

***

Power did not see Wharton until the morning when he returned to the house. When asked if he had gotten a good night's rest, Power claimed to have done so.

"Slept like a baby, although I went out for a walk and got caught when a heavy shower fell around 10:00 p.m.," Power said so to explain to Wharton why there were a set of his still damp clothes hanging up in the bathroom.

Wharton thought that had been a strange thing for Power to do but said nothing. Of course, given the way rain falls in Barbados, while it had apparently rained on the east coast, not a drop of water had fallen in St Michael where SBB&G was located and where he had spent the night. It did not matter that the time Power told Wharton that the heavy rain had fallen on the east coast had actually taken place more than three hours after.

Wharton had earlier that afternoon told Power that he visited his mother in St John most weekday afternoons for a couple of hours. He usually returned home around 4:00 p.m. to change, before setting off for his SBB&G shop to spend the evening. That knowledge had enabled Power to work out a tentative escape plan prior to his meeting last night with the individual. Power had later fleshed out his plan once the early morning meeting with the individual had ended.

Power planned to depart Wharton's house at 2:00 p.m. He would head for his initial rendezvous point where transportation to his west coast destination would be provided. Escape from Barbados was on. Payment to *The Organisation* was not.

***

Dr Richard Preston Dawson, Managing/Medical Director of the Dawson Clinic, was also a Member of Parliament (MP). In fact, he was Leader of the Opposition P.B.P.

Dr Dawson arrived on the compound of his Dawson's Clinic just after 7:30 a.m. This was much earlier than he usually arrived on any Thursday. He'd come in especially earlier today because he planned to attend Day 1 of the Test Match at New Kensington Oval tomorrow as a guest in a box belonging to one of the main medical companies operating in Barbados. He therefore wanted to clear up some outstanding paperwork on his desk to make time to attend the Test Match.

As he was parking his vehicle, he saw a young woman standing at the clinic's entrance. He did not know who she was, so anticipated that she might be one of his constituents in need of his urgent assistance. Wednesdays was his announced week-day to see constituents at his clinic when he would try to deal with their problems and concerns, so this young lady was a day late or six days early. Nonetheless, as an experienced politician, he knew that he could not always determine when, or the circumstances through which he would encounter and have to deal with his constituents.

After parking his vehicle, Dr Dawson approached the clinic's entrance.

"Good morning, miss, how may I help you? My constituency surgery is on Wednesdays. The clinic does not open before 9:00 a.m. on the other weekdays," he told her with a smile.

"Good morning, Dr Dawson. Sorry, but I'm not one of your constituents. Nor am I here for an appointment at your clinic. I'm also sorry to approach you in this way and so early, but I have something that I feel I must share with you, but not out here. Can we go inside please?" asked the young woman.

"Slow down, slow down, young lady. I do not even now your name," Dr Dawson stated disarmingly.

"Sorry! My name is Evadne Scott. I live in Black Rock and work at Precision Laboratories," the young lady replied, before quickly continuing.

"Once you see what I have, I think you'll be glad that I've come. It's likely to get me in trouble, fired even from my job, but I felt compelled to share what I know with you," Scott said uncomfortably.

"I'm sure it cannot be that bad! Alright come on in, but give me a few minutes to open up this place. We can then have a chat and see what you have. You'll also have to show me some i.d., okay?"

"Thank you. No problem on the i.d. I know you'll want to be sure that I'm who I say I am," said Scott.

"Yes, indeed."

Dr Dawson unlocked the door. He had a strange feeling something bad was about to happen. He used Precision Laboratories, but did not know this young lady. Nevertheless, he was intrigued to learn what she so desperately wanted to share with him. He kept his apprehension under wraps.

"Well, Miss Scott, let's see what you have that's got you so excited, or is it upset? From your statement, it could be either or both. I'm sure neither of us want to end up in any trouble, do we?" Dr Dawson asked.

Fifteen minutes later, Dr Dawson, for the second time in three days, settled rather uncomfortably back into the executive chair in his office. Scott had shown him clear evidence that the blood test results he had received earlier that week from Precision Laboratories for six of his patients were erroneous. They had been mixed up. As such, potentially negative consequences for his patients were in play. Delivering the blood test results had been his responsibility and he had already done that. He felt guilty for having passed incorrect information to them. How now could he correct what were very difficult situations?

Dr Dawson decided he had to contact and invite his six patients to return to his office for an urgent consultation. But three of them were out of the country (two on business, one on holiday). That left three in Barbados and he had learnt from the morning's news, that one of them was now missing. It suddenly crossed his mind that there may be a link between his missing patient and the results he had given him.

"OMG," he said quietly.

"Dr Dawson, what was that?" asked Scott.

"Uh, I'm sorry, Miss Scott. Look, thank you for bringing this to my attention. You say that your manager will decide what action to take this morning? Seems to me that he has a big job on his hands if all the blood test results from last week and the weekend past have been given to the wrong doctors. They, in turn have probably also provided erroneous results to their patients. I'll wait to see what happens publicly on all this, but worse-case scenario, your manager should urgently start contacting the involved doctors about this mix-up – today. This is nothing short of criminal behaviour," stated Dr Dawson.

"I won't disagree with you, Dr Dawson. I'm really sorry about all this."

"Don't be. It's not your fault. I appreciate your honesty and integrity in coming to see me. Who else knows about this and why did you come to me?"

"Besides me, my manager and our receptionist, I think. She arranged dispatch of the results, but I'm not sure if she read any of the results as she placed them into the envelopes. I do remember that she did them all in a rush just before going to lunch on Monday with her boyfriend. That way she would catch the courier. She had other duties to do on that afternoon and so would only have gotten around to filing away copies of the results on Tuesday. That's when I noticed the errors."

"Why did you come to me?"

"You're a doctor and a politician. These things should not happen. Someone's life could be ruined by such careless mistakes. I would not want to get the wrong results, would you? Can't you get a law passed that punishes people for such mistakes?"

"It's not that easy –"

"Look, Dr Dawson, I could be fired for coming and telling you this... I'm breaking company policy."

"Yes, I guess so, but don't worry about that right now. Just let me know if you are threatened in any way and I'll do my very best to help you."

"You mean you'll help me to find another job?"

"Let's not 'rush the brush' on that, Miss Scott!"

Noting her deflated look, Dr Dawson quickly sought to rectify the situation with a more calming comment. "Come and see me again if ever you need to Miss Scott, however this all pans out."

"Very well and thanks. You know, my Gran voted for you. I can see why. I must be going," said Scott.

"See you around. Thanks for coming by Miss Scott," Dr Dawson said, shepherding her out of his office into the reception area and out of the clinic's entrance.

Dr Dawson returned to his office and reviewed the copy of the blood test results document from the lab Scott left with him, before unlocking his file cabinet to retrieve the confidential files of the affected patients. He focussed on Dr Lewis' file. According to the morning news, he was missing. Dr Dawson carefully placed the information Scott had given to him, i.e. the correct blood test results for Dr Lewis, onto his file. He did likewise for his other five patients. Dr Dawson felt mightily aggrieved. *How could Precision Laboratories have gotten their blood test results mixed up?*

Luckily, Scott did not know that Dr Lewis's blood tests was among those that had been mixed up. Her explanation for the mix-up at Precision Laboratories was worrying. It was reasonable to assume that there were other doctors and patients who had also been mis-informed by these wrongly allocated test results from that lab. How involved doctors would deal with their patients in this situation was unclear. He could only try and protect himself from any of his patients should they subsequently deciding to take legal action against him for malpractice. The damage to his medical *and* political reputation would be severe.

Dr Dawson briefly wondered if he was deliberately being set up! *Unlikely*, he thought. Even his political opponents would not be so wicked as to come up with this scenario.

He opened his computer and pulled up Dr Lewis' records, before transcribing the new (and hopefully correct) results, memorialising a short version of what Scott had told him on the original entry. He decided *not* to reach out to Dr Lewis' family on this matter. Once he re-surfaced, they would need to have an urgent conversation.

He then took similar action on the records of the other five affected patients before instructing his secretary at the clinic to contact the two patients known to be in Barbados and invite them to return to see him at the clinic urgently. Finally, he messaged his three overseas patients about coming in to see him on their return home.

***

Lewis enjoyed breakfast with his mum. Ava Prescod had prepared his favourite Bajan breakfast: some old-fashioned bakes, fried salted fish with lots of onions, some fresh pear and scrambled eggs, the usual faire whenever Lewis was visiting.

"Want me to come along?"

"Not necessary. I'm planning to come right back and report what I learn. I promise, if I'm told anything urgent, I'll call you straight away."

"As you wish, son. Anyway, I should probably stay here by the phone, just in case Dad calls."

"I agree, but Mum, don't forget that you have a mobile. In fact, I guess you now have two such phones if you've gotten Caroline's Christmas gift set up."

"Bertram, I know. I use the old one. I haven't bothered to get the new one set up yet."

"Okay. If you give it to me, while I'm out, I'll pop into the store and have it sorted out. If Caroline bought it locally, it should be ready to use. Whereas if she brought it with her from the States, I think we might need to get it unlocked before you can use it."

"She brought it with her."

"Then you might have to be with me when we sort it out. Let's work on that this afternoon after lunch once I'm back."

"Sure, but what if Dad turns up here after I've gone out with you?" Mrs Lewis was being stubborn now.

"Look, Dad's a big boy. He has a key to the house, remember!"

"Fine, but I'm staying put. How soon before you leave?"

"Around 9:00 a.m., traffic from St George into town should have died down by then if my memory serves me correctly. The big push is from around 7:00 a.m. to 8:30 a.m., so I should be able to get down to town in the thirty minutes I'm allowing myself."

"Ava tells me she's happy to see you home again, even under these difficult circumstances."

"Yes, she's made that clear! Mum, I picked up something special for her at Miami Airport yesterday afternoon. I'll give it to her before I leave for RBPF HQ."

"Oh, Bertram, that's very nice of you. I'm sure she'll welcome your gift."

***

Following breakfast, the West Indies cricket squad would leave their south coast hotel at 8:00 a.m. under police escort for the excellent net and medical facilities at the New Kensington Oval complex. There, they would practice and train between 9:00 a.m. and mid-day.

173

The England team would later do likewise, leaving the hotel at 11:30 a.m. Their net session would take place between 1:00 p.m. and 4:00 p.m. after they had taken lunch between 12 noon and 1:00 p.m. with the West Indies players in the spacious players' restaurant at the ground. It meant the West Indies then had the afternoon off, with the England team having had the morning to themselves.

Meanwhile, preparations for the Test Match at one of the world's most famous cricket grounds were near to completion. Sponsors signage were up outside and inside of the stadium, television and radio set ups were done and the final rolling and watering of the pitch (or wicket as some purists preferred to call it) were ongoing. New Kensington Oval was almost ready to stage another great Test Match.

***

Jeremie arrived at St. Lawrence Gap at 8:15 a.m., accompanied by Inspector Gray after first having gone to RBPF HQ for half an hour. They were met by AC Smith and Station Sergeant Bob Black.

Representatives of the local media were awaiting Jeremie's arrival. He was shown the location of the attempted robbery and shooting. The damaged cars were still in position. Following a further five-minute closed-door briefing away from the assembled media and growing number of members of the public, he approached the podium on which stood a variety of recorders from radio, television and print journalists' (including phones from the growing band of local citizen-journalists) as well as television cameras.

Before Jeremie could speak, the questions started coming.

Inspector Gray, raising both hands intervened, "One at a time please." This resulted in the journalists quietened down, though their hands remained raised.

"I have a statement for you, after which I'll take your questions," said Jeremie.

He read a prepared statement, which he skilfully adjusted slightly following the updated briefing he had just received on the incident. He then tried to answer all of the questions asked, responding honestly and as openly as he could without giving away key aspects of the several investigations the RBPF were now engaged in.

***

It was around 8:30 a.m. when Vickers parked his vehicle in the car park in Belleville, St Michael. Exiting his vehicle, he noticed another well-known vehicle was already parked in the MD space.

That was a pleasant surprise. He had expected to have to wait a while for Dr Dawson to arrive. Vickers knocked on the still locked door.

"Good morning, sir, may I help you? We're not open until 9:00 a.m.," said a middle-aged lady, unlocking the door, but not allowing him to enter.

"Good morning ma'am, I'm here to see Dr Dawson."

"Do you have an appointment, sir?" she asked.

"No. But please show him this," said Vickers producing one of his official business cards.

The woman looked at and read the card. "Just hold on a minute please sir," she said, re-locking the door.

A minute later, a smiling Dr Dawson opened the door himself.

"Top of the day to you, Chief Superintendent. What brings you to my clinic so early today? I'm sure you don't want me to give you any sick leave." They of course knew each other from previous official encounters.

"Not today, Dr Dawson, but I'm working a case that I think you might be able to help me with. May we speak privately please?"

"Sure. Do come on in." Dr Dawson noted the last sentence was rather formal.

A couple of minutes later, they sat in Dr Dawson's well-appointed office. More of the Dawson Clinic's staff had started to arrive to be in place for the official 9:00 a.m. start of business. Luckily, Dr Dawson's first patient appointment was not until 9:30 a.m. He would normally spend the first part of any day at the Dawson Clinic reviewing e-mails that had come in overnight and preparing to see persons listed as his patients for that day. The start to today had already been different. Now this!

Vickers wasted no time in coming to the reason for his visit to the Dawson Clinic.

"I understand Dr Albert Lewis from the Central Bank came to see you earlier this week. Please tell me exactly when and why he came to see you?"

Dr Dawson was unsure how to answer this simple question.

"Chief Superintendent, please tell me what this is all about, before I decide if I can answer your question or rather, how best I might do so."

"Why are you so concerned, Dr Dawson?"

"Well, I'm a physician after all. Doctor/client patient relationships are confidential. So, I'm asking again – why are you here?"

"Very well. Dr Lewis is missing and I've been tasked with investigating his disappearance. This was mentioned on this morning's news. I'm told Dr Lewis visited you late on Tuesday afternoon. True or not? Also, what was the purpose of his visit please?"

"Look, can you please tell me what this is really all about? I don't like games."

"No games, sir. Dr Lewis has not been seen since Tuesday afternoon. Our investigations so far suggest that you might have been one of the last persons, if not *the* last, to see him after he had left the Central Bank that afternoon and headed for your office, hence I need confirmation of his visit."

"Yes, of course. I'm usually in the House on Tuesdays so the clinic closes at 2:00 p.m., an early day for my staff. Last Tuesday, the House finished sooner than anticipated, so I stayed on in Parliament to do some work in the Leader of the Opposition's office. However, on receipt of Dr Lewis' call, around 2:45 p.m., I agreed to meet him here at 3:30 p.m.

"Let me back track though. I had seen Dr Lewis a week earlier. He had a cold and so came to see me to get checked out. He said his wife had forced him to come to me. I suggested that he take the remainder of that week off…three working days, get some rest and use the medication that I had prescribed for him. I gave him an appropriate doctor's certificate to cover his few days away from work. Before leaving, Dr Lewis asked me to take some blood from him and run some appropriate tests. He said that he had been feeling 'a little run-down' recently and wanted to check that all was well within himself."

"Okay. You mentioned tests, Dr Dawson. What were these for?"

Dr Dawson hesitated in answering.

"Look, this is a *serious* investigation. The Governor of the Central Bank has personally asked my Commissioner to investigate this matter and he has put me in charge. It wouldn't surprise me if the Prime Minister hasn't spoken to both men about this case, since Dr Lewis is a top public servant in our country. He's also a dual citizen, so for all I know the US is probably also speaking with our Government for news on his disappearance. I need answers, Dr Dawson, *now*. So, please…"

"Okay, but I'm loathed to tell you all of the man's business."

"Dr Dawson, I'm getting tired. I could go get a search warrant and come back with some men and start digging up your clinic until we find what you're not telling me. But I'm sure we can avoid that –"

"Superintendent, surely you're not threatening me. Are you?"

"Perish the thought, sir."

"Good. Then we understand each other."

"We sure do. That's what I wanted to hear."

***

Chapter Thirteen
Cabinet

Just after 8:40 a.m., Colonel Burke assembled his full team in BIB's conference room to consider where they stood on the operations they were now engaged on. The ECC project had gone well to date and was not expected to deviate much from the featured plan over the next six days. But the prisoners' escape, the disappearance of the CBOB's Deputy Governor and the previous night's St. Lawrence Gap incident meant that this discussion was necessary at the start of the day to harness BIB's efforts at solving the three problems as quickly as possible.

***

Dr Dawson took a deep breath. He stood up, took the few steps to close and lock his office door to ensure they were not disturbed.

He then told Vickers all he knew.

"Oh my!" exclaimed Vickers.

It was not just Dr Lewis who had been affected. Several of Dr Dawson's patients had been given the wrong blood test results and there were other physicians and patients who would have to go through this ordeal later today, otherwise soon.

Stunned, Vickers leaned back in his chair with his mouth slightly opened. After a minute of silence and staring blankly at each other, Vickers finally spoke.

"Dr Dawson, thanks for this! For my part, I promise to keep it as quiet as I can, for as long as I can."

Vickers placed himself in Dr Lewis' shoes. Had he received similar results from his doctor after tests were done on him, he might also have wanted to get away, at least for a while if that was what was in play here.

***

By 9:00 a.m. Jeremie was able to get away from St. Lawrence Gap. He headed back to his Bridgetown office to take part in an emergency *P.A.A.N.I.* teleconference that had been called for 9:25 a.m. by Colonel Burke.

With new work streams' having been allocated to BIB operatives by 9:10 a.m., Colonel Burke prepared himself for the *P.A.A.N.I.* teleconference he had instigated with his fellow Heads. He wanted an update from each of them in order to provide a special up-to-date SSB to Motby before the start of the day's 10:00 a.m. Cabinet meeting.

***

Going forward, Vickers' challenge was going to be discovering whether Dr Lewis' disappearance had been deliberate, and of his own doing (because of the results he had received), or if it was at someone else's behest. If the latter, the why would become important to establish quickly. Knowing this would start helping him figure out how best to retrieve the situation and hopefully find Dr Lewis in a good, safe and normal condition.

Vickers left the Dawson Clinic compound for the short drive to RBPF HQ to meet with Bertram Lewis. He would not share what he had just learned from Dr Dawson with Lewis. Nor would he, at this stage, tell his Commissioner, Dr Edwards or others in the Lewis family what he knew, though he realised that he would at some stage – probably within the next twenty-four hours, have to share this information with them all if Dr Lewis was not recovered within another forty-eight hours or so.

Meanwhile, he would tell Moss, his partner on this case sooner rather than later, but swear him to secrecy.

***

The emergency *P.A.A.N.I.* teleconference was short and sweet, as was often stated in Barbados, so it was all over ten minutes later.

Colonel Burke had spent the time between the end of his meeting with BIB operatives and the start of the short *P.A.A.N.I.* teleconference conceptualising what he might place in the security situation brief (SSB). He actually had a draft already typed, which he would expand and update as necessary shortly after he had chaired the *P.A.A.N.I.* meeting.

Colonel Burke observed that this was a good example of his often spoken of concept – 'walking and chewing gum at the same time'. He was therefore able to quickly finalise the special SSB for Motby. Ten minutes after the meeting's end and a final review, Colonel Burke dispatched the special SSB to the Head of Government.

He did not anticipate hearing back from Motby until after today's Cabinet meeting. He knew that he would have to make himself available to him once the Cabinet meeting was over – even if it meant him having to step away from the meeting with Sir Thadeus and fellow security Heads at the British High Commissioner's official residence scheduled to commence at 3:00 p.m. that afternoon. Elizabeth Burkett had his mobile number and knew where he would be, should Motby wish to speak with him before the Cabinet meeting ended. Colonel Burke would answer the Prime Minister's call, whenever it came.

***

It was 9:35 a.m. at Government Headquarters on Bay Street, St Michael. Members of Cabinet were starting to assemble for the 10:00 a.m. Cabinet meeting. As the Prime Minister had made it clear to his Ministers that they should not be late for his prompt start to their weekly Cabinet meeting, his Cabinet colleagues had for the past few years made it their business to never be late. He had made it easier for all of them by laying on tea, coffee, juice and biscuits from 9:30 a.m. to 9:55 a.m. when he would expect them to have at least assembled just outside the Cabinet Room's door – or rather be seated.

The Cabinet Meeting's *Agenda* for the day was as follows:

1. Minutes of previous Cabinet meeting – 12 April 2018
2. Matters Arising
3. Royal Visit – Final Programme

4. The Extra Cover Cricket (ECC) security project – 17 to 25 April 2018
5. The Commonwealth Sports Ministers' Conference – 23 to 25 April 2018
6. National Security – at 19 April 2018
7. 2018 Hurricane Plan – 1 June to 30 November 2018
8. New Tourism and Sporting Initiatives
9. New Diplomatic Appointment
10. Any Other Business

**

Hon. Walter Thompson MP, Minister of Foreign Affairs and Culture, Hon. Sebastian Smith QC MP, Attorney General and Minister of Residential Affairs and Hon. Preston Grant MP, Minister of Tourism, International Transport and Sport held a brief ten-minute meeting while they drank tea and nibbled on the biscuits provided. Anyone seeing them could easily guess what the subject of their conversation was: the previous night's St. Lawrence Gap attempted robbery incident which had already received heavy local, regional and international media coverage.

It was fair to say that Barbados was not being projected in any positive light. The British High Commissioner had made it his business to call Minister Thompson promptly at 8:00 a.m. to ask how he, or rather the Government of Barbados, was going to respond to the incident.

While there had not been any direct threat by High Commissioner Tullock to change the Advisory notice on Barbados, one could only imagine that, by simply making his call, Tullock had at least *implied* that it would shortly be reviewed if no visible response was taken by Barbadian authorities. There was probably a window being allowed to see what that action would be, given that thousands of additional British visitors were now in Barbados for the Test Match, due to start the next day. Aware of all this, Minister Thompson had promised to speak with Tullock following the day's Cabinet meeting, once discussion on the incident had taken place. He knew that having escaped prisoners on the run was not helping matters.

All three Ministers were determined to speak with Motby during the luncheon recess about holding a post-Cabinet meeting media conference to help settle things down in the country. They would offer to join him at this media conference, assuming that he agreed to their initiative.

On their way into the Cabinet room, they noticed that Motby and Giles Archer, Communications Director in the Prime Minister's Office, were in deep conversation. Perhaps Archer was thinking like them, or the other way around? Broaching this matter with Motby over lunch might be easier than they had originally thought!

***

"Sorry to keep you waiting, Mr Lewis, I'm Inspector Moss," the man quickly approaching Lewis stated.

"That's okay, I was a little late myself, parking was an issue today."

"No kidding – more like every day in Bridgetown. Best way of getting a good parking spot is to come into Bridgetown early and leave late."

"I'll remember that!"

"Let's go meet the person you came to see. Follow me please."

***

Castille, having had a late breakfast following a sea bath, contemplated how he would utilise some time until he had to return to the east coast around 5:00 p.m. that afternoon.

Never being one to go sightseeing in any of the countries in the Americas that he had visited over the past few years, he was intrigued by something he had read in a 'Barbados: Love It & Return' booklet that lay on his bedside table. At page seventy was an article about a restaurant at the Animal Flower Cave in St. Lucy, the northern parish in Barbados. He had to have lunch somewhere and thought why not visit to kill part of the day. He estimated that the journey from his hotel to the Animal Flower Cave would take around fifty minutes each way. If he took one hour over lunch, that would still allow him to be back at his hotel by 2:00 p.m. at the latest. That would allow him more than sufficient time this afternoon to recce the place where he was looking to meet his Barbadian contact tonight after his expected conclusive meeting with Power on the east coast. Leaving lose ends around were not his practice.

***

Vickers was sitting in one of the two small RBPF HQ conference rooms on the second floor awaiting their arrival. He stood up when they entered.

"You must be Bertram Lewis. I'm Johnny Vickers so happy to meet you, though I wish the circumstances were more pleasant. Mrs Lewis said you were on your way in when we met with her yesterday."

"It's my pleasure to meet you too, Chief Superintendent. Mum told me that you were both very kind during that meeting," said Lewis.

"I guess you want to know what we know?"

"Yes please… I want you guys to find my dad, and soon, because my mum is a complete mess now and my sister Caroline who lives in Texas, is equally disturbed."

"I understand. Let's get going then."

Vickers explained that it had only been twenty-four hours since the police had been notified about Dr Lewis being missing. Vickers had been tapped to head the investigation into Dr Lewis' disappearance and Moss was assisting him.

"To date we've discovered that Dr Lewis left his office on Tuesday afternoon not feeling too well, apparently with a bad cold. His staff had suggested that he go visit any of the doctors located close to CBOB. We've since confirmed that he did visit a doctor, but where he went thereafter remains unknown to us at this time," said Vickers.

Looking at his watch, he added, "It's actually now thirty-six hours since his disappearance."

"Which doctor did my dad visit?" asked Lewis.

"Dr Richard Dawson, the Dawson Clinic just there in Belleville," answered Vickers.

"Well, as far as I know, he's not my dad's usual doctor. He certainly isn't our family doctor. I'll ask Mum if Dad changed his doctor recently, as they have both used the Central Bank's panel of doctors since he joined the organisation," said Lewis who was puzzled by this revelation.

"Be that as it may, I met with Dr Dawson earlier this morning. He confirmed that he saw Dr Lewis late on Tuesday afternoon. He examined your father and provided him with a prescription for appropriate medication for the bad cold he had. Where he went next, Dr Dawson doesn't know and has not heard from him since.

"So, Inspector Moss and I have some more work to do. We're working with other officers in the Force, with some help from our Barbados Intelligence

Bureau or BIB friends. Can I call you later today, no tonight? Even if we've not found your dad by then, I'm hoping that we will be able to provide an update on the progress we're making."

"Guess I've made a wasted journey to see you then, Chief Superintendent," said Lewis.

"No, your journey wasn't wasted, Mr Lewis. I wish more people with reported missing family members would take an interest in the investigation like you have. If you or your mother think of anything unusual which was noticed in the few days before your father went missing, just give either Byron or me a call. Sometimes, the smallest pieces of information help turn investigations on their head," said Vickers.

"Much appreciated, Chief Superintendent. I'm a lawyer from New York, but I've always thought that you guys in the RBPF were good and, based on my first impressions from this meeting, I stand by that. Gentlemen, please find my dad, and soon. Our family love and are missing him very much already. So, if I can help you in anyway, please call me," said Lewis.

"Well, thanks very much for your vote of confidence, Mr Lewis. Yes, we'll certainly keep you posted. What time is best for us to call you tonight, at your mother's place, I presume?" asked Moss.

"Yes, I'm there. Anytime is fine," responded Lewis.

"Fine. Thanks again for coming in. Inspector Moss will show you out."

***

Meanwhile, Motby had received and read *P.A.A.N.I.*'s special SSB from Colonel Burke on the situation at 9:50 a.m. That brought him as 'up to speed' as he could have been on all national security developments when he entered the Cabinet room at 9:57 a.m.

Given the events of the past forty-eight hours, Agenda Item #6 was now likely to require more discussion than would normally have been the case, so he had asked Elizabeth Burkett to immediately bring him any updates received from Colonel Burke, or any of the other Heads of the country's security agencies during the Cabinet meeting.

***

Moss found Vickers back in his office.

"What next, skipper? My read is that you found out some more from Dr Dawson than you told Mr Lewis," stated Moss.

"Perceptive, aren't you?" Vickers asked him.

"I've known you for close to fifteen years and have now been working closely with you for the last couple, so I know when something's up," said the younger sleuth.

Vickers did not take the bait.

"You sound like my wife. Look Byron, I need to make a couple of calls. Then we'll hit the road again."

"Okay, but don't forget that you're meant to meet, or at least call Dr Edwards around 4:00 p.m."

"I hadn't forgotten."

With that, Vickers picked up his phone and started to dial. "Close the door on your way out please…thanks. Hello?"

Moss left the room. Once outside, he realised that the old fox had not responded to his question about meeting with Dr Dawson. He sensed that the skipper had something up his sleeve – he knew him well enough to know that he would share it with him before the day was over.

***

By 11:45 a.m., with the Prime Minister having secured unanimous Cabinet approval for the Royal visit programme to Barbados (final version), the EEC security project and Commonwealth Sports Minister's Conference, he turned to the sixth item on Cabinet's *Agenda*.

Having not been informed of any updates from Burkett, Motby initiated the National Security discussion. As expected, the Cabinet meeting had gone along pretty quickly and smoothly so far, though everyone around the table knew that Agenda Item #6 would be tricky to deal with. The shock of the escape from a prisoner transport vehicle was not only a first for Barbados, but had alarmed the population and primed the local and regional media to raise concerns about the country's security. Truth be told, they went somewhat overboard with their concerns. Both major newspapers carried editorials (one on its front page) about the state of the country's security. Was the airport secure from terrorists (recalling the attempted assassination of Motby thirty months earlier)? Was the country's main seaport safe for the thousands of cruise ship passengers who joined cruise ships or visited each week on them? Was HMP Dodds, the island's sole prison facility good enough to prevent any attempt at a mass escape by inmates? Should more prison officers be recruited, etc.

In addition, the early morning radio call-in programme on the Government-owned Barbados News Corporation (BNC) had apparently captured callers' concerns not only about the prisoners' escape, but also the overnight attempted robbery of two English visitors in one of Barbados' most popular tourist locations, St. Lawrence Gap. That led to questions being asked about the security of the visiting England and West Indies cricket teams, their supporters, international cricket officials and media. This all prompted Neal Butler, President of the BCA and AC Smith to call in, one after the other, to reassure both Barbadians and visitors to the island that all was well as far as security arrangements for the Test Match at New Kensington Oval was concerned. Both teams and the other public activities which were set to take place during the coming week in Barbados were expected to go off as planned, free of incident.

Ministers had heard some of these concerns that morning on their way to the Cabinet meeting. They had not heard what was similarly being expressed on Star News Corporation's (SNC), the non-Government radio station whose call-in programme started at 10:00 a.m. Some Ministers felt this 'excitement' would be another 'one-day wonder' and not be the topic of conversation by the weekend once the Test Match got underway and the two escaped prisoners were recaptured. Others had concerns that these issues might 'have legs' because of the presence of the visiting international sports media contingent who were going to be on island until the middle of the following week. Therefore, early action was needed – and had to be seen as being taken, to calm down an excited populace and smooth over any bad press the country might be receiving as a result of these developments. Hence the expectation that discussion on National Security could be lengthy and might get hot, prompting this Agenda item to extend beyond the meeting's scheduled luncheon adjournment.

"As you know…" commenced Motby. He outlined, in his matter-of-fact, frank way that colleagues called his 'unvarnished method', deployed when he spoke with his Cabinet and others at his Parliamentary Group meetings, that there should be no serious concerns about the country's security.

"First, the ECC security project is already 'up and running' successfully.

"Second, the current HMP Dodds situation is indeed worrying. Recent shortages of staff, equipment and materials was unfortunately not widely known to us in Cabinet. This situation needs to be fixed quickly, perhaps with some extra funding being put at HMP Dodds' disposal in the forthcoming Budget. As Minister of Finance, I will see to this. Escape from HMP Dodds facility, police stations or courts by prisoners is unusual. Prisoner escapes from an escorted mobile detail was unheard of prior to yesterday.

"Third, efforts to recapture the two remaining escapees are ongoing. Security agencies anticipate recapturing both men shortly, certainly by this weekend. The robbery attempt in St Lawrence Gap last night was just that, an *attempted* robbery gone wrong. It's a pity that those attacked included a journalist from a major UK newspaper, a former Test cricketer and their friends. Potentially, these persons make the country's response trickier to deal with, but respond we must. Finding them equally quickly is essential.

"Fourth, the disappearance of the Deputy Governor of the Central Bank is of great concern. We don't know yet if there was mischief here, i.e. he's been kidnapped, or if he's just gone to ground for a while to get away from the presumed pressures of his job. If it turns out to be the first option, that would mean some form of terrorism, local or otherwise, but to date the security forces have nothing to suggest that. So, we hope to recover Dr Lewis sooner rather than later, alive, physically and mentally unharmed.

"Our best people are working on all of these cases. Minister Thompson, I think we…you need to work particularly on the British High Commission to ensure that they do not issue any Travel/Security updates on our country, especially with all these Brits around, plus several of their top media house representatives. Catching the perpetrators is therefore vital. Commissioner Jeremie knows this, hence his visit to St. Lawrence Gap this morning. I hope that in any interviews you give by the middle of the Test Match, colleagues will be able to announce success on this…perhaps all these fronts. Any comments please, ladies and gentlemen, on what I've stated?" Motby asked.

There were many which made the ensuing discussion robust. Why was HMP Dodds in a mess? Specifically, what were the shortages? How much would it cost to put things right re money, manpower, equipment? On Dr Lewis, was he working on anything specific leading up to the Budget to be delivered in late-May? Did he have personal problems with CBOB, work colleagues, at home or health challenges?

Motby recognised that more questions, often uninformed opinions and rhetoric, were being stated by his Cabinet colleagues, with few solutions being offered on any of the four subjects he had mentioned in his national security presentation. The one thing everyone agreed on was the hope that these issues would somehow get resolved by the weekend. So Motby requested that over lunch, his colleagues seek to identify potential quick but realistic 'fixes' to the national security issues they were currently facing.

**

Lunch was taken between 12:30 p.m. and 1:30 p.m.

Three Cabinet Ministers descended on Motby prior to their re-entry into the Cabinet Room. Motby listened to their spokesman, Minister Walter Thompson's opening pitch about holding a post-Cabinet media conference before holding up his hand.

"Already organised, gentlemen. Giles is on the case. I trust 4:00 p.m. suits everyone?" asked Motby.

"Ah. Yes, Prime Minister. Thank you," said Minister Thompson.

"No problem." With that, Motby drank a glass of water that was on the table before him and pushed back his chair. As he set off for the Cabinet room, he nodded to Giles Archer across the room, who was getting ready to issue the appropriate media release and invitations to the post-Cabinet media conference.

**

The twenty-inch television the man had owned for the past ten years had finally packed up two weeks earlier after being in decline for a while. He and his girlfriend Iris McCarthy loved watching the American 'soaps' but had been unable to do so recently. Normally, he would have taped them for her to watch once she got home from working as a maid for a well-to do family. They did not pay much truth be told, but it was income since he had lost his job as a truck driver at a construction firm.

His windfall from last night would allow him to replace the broken television.

So, the man had journeyed into Bridgetown Thursday lunchtime and bought himself a forty-two-inch colour television from one of the country's leading appliance retail stores. He had long desired a television set of this size in his home and was now satisfied. He expected one of the store's handymen to collect and deliver and place his new purchase in his vehicle waiting at the back of the store. This was not to be, as he was informed that as there were no more televisions of that size at the store, he would have to go to the store's warehouse in Fontabelle, St. Michael to collect his purchased item. Reluctantly, the man had driven his aged but functional and distinctive looking open-backed vehicle to the location to collect it.

He had made the purchase without telling anyone in advance. He knew he would have to explain to McCarthy why and how he had managed to buy such a large television once she got home that evening. He decided to make up a story that he'd won some money playing Betto, a local lottery game. McCarthy knew him to play Betto regularly, so would most likely not disbelieve and be happy for him. She would ask him how much he had won and he would say $2,700. The television was on special, so he'd gotten it for $1,400. *A good and creditable story*, he'd thought to himself. He decided to give her $300 as well.

The man's vehicle was captured by one of the CCTV cameras located on a Government building's roof across the street. The camera had been set up to capture traffic flows up and down the busy Fontabelle area and vehicles approaching and exiting the front of the Government building. But during the regular sweeps of the area, the CCTV camera also captured ongoing activity on the premises of the appliance store's warehouse across the road.

To the man's dismay, there was no help with collecting or placing his purchased item into the back of his vehicle. Eventually, he managed to complete the task using a wheelbarrow that he had borrowed from one of the store's workers.

Returning to his vehicle, it appeared as if the man might have injured himself in the process. If not, was a previous injury the reason for his limp? Was not one leg shorter than the other one? During his exertions, he was oblivious to the CCTV camera across the road capturing his every movement.

As he drove away, the man thought none of his fellow Pressure Group members would ever need to know what he'd just done. None of them had ever been to his house. Nor did he plan to invite them either. Business and pleasure did not mix. Anyway, he wanted to keep them well away from McCarthy.

***

Around 1:35 p.m., Wharton left his house and headed towards his vehicle. It was that time of day when, three times-a-week, he visited his seventy-five-year-old mother's residence in rural St John.

"Stabs ma boy, see you when I return," said Wharton.

"Sure. I'll be here. Have a good trip," responded Power.

"Should be back around 3:30 p.m., latest. I hope you get through with your ongoing collection effort. Don't rub that man Castille up the wrong way. Have whatever he wants ready for him when he turns up in…under four hours, right?"

"Look man, I think I got it covered."

"Thanks! Be jolly now."

With that, Wharton gunned the engine and steered his vehicle onto the road to start his journey.

Wharton had earlier picked up the two daily newspapers for his mother who loved to read them in the afternoon. He also decided that he would purchase some cou cou and steamed flying fish to take for her from Boyd's Shop. The shop was at the end of the street where his mother lived, so the meal would still be hot.

Wharton disliked having the smell of food in his vehicle for even a short period of time. His mother loved cooked food, "Not the fast-food rubbish being sold all over the country," she'd often told him. She particularly loved 'soft' food, soup, mashed potatoes and of course cou cou since she had started to lose her teeth about five years ago. She disliked the dentures that she had acquired to replace her missing teeth and so generally only used them when she went to church on Sundays or when she was otherwise in public view. Wharton knew that, should she reach the great age of one hundred, she would surely put them in for a home visit from the current Governor General of Barbados (HE Sir Livingstone Murray KA would be long gone by then).

***

It was around 1:50 p.m. when Castille passed through Bridgetown on his way back to his south coast hotel. He reflected on his enjoyable visit to the Animal Flower Cave and its restaurant where he had eaten some of the finest and tastiest Barbadian foods on offer. It had all reminded him somewhat of the food he had occasionally eaten in the Cuban quarter of Miami. Yet the local food was different – in its preparation and in its presentation.

***

Once Wharton left, Power knew it was time for him to make his move. He had a small 'window' to get to his pick-up point, for if he was not at the rendezvous by 2:30 p.m., he'd miss his escape route opportunity and that wouldn't do.

Power would travel light. After taking a shower, he made himself a cheese and cucumber sandwich before washing it down with a cold soft drink. He then put on a large hat and a pair of baggy trousers and shirt that he had found in Wharton's closet. A pair of soft shoes, obviously not Wharton's, were lying at the back door which Power's keen eyes had noticed. He now also put them on – they were most comfortable. As there was not much else that he needed for his journey, Power stepped out from Wharton's house and started walking to the first of his pick-up points. After being transferred to the second pick-up point, he would be taken to the third and final pick-up point on the west coast of Barbados. There, Power's remaining journey would commence later that evening.

Goodbye Spend Big, Goodbye Mr Castille, he thought satisfyingly to himself.

***

The Cabinet meeting recommenced its discussion on the National Security situation after lunch. As hoped for, there were now a few solution-orientated concepts that were discussed. Cabinet formally agreed that the Prime Minister and three of its most senior Cabinet Ministers – Attorney General and Minister of Residential Affairs, the Minister of Foreign Affairs and Culture and the Minister of Tourism, International Transport and Sport should hold a joint post-Cabinet media conference in the Cabinet room at Government Headquarters to calm things down and push back against recent media reports about Barbados' national security situation. Sebastian Smith was also specifically directed by Cabinet to look into the HMP Dodds situation and bring a correction plan to Cabinet in a fortnight's time (to include budget, timelines, personnel and equipment requirements) to fix the problems related not just to HMP Dodds, but the entire BPS. The Government would ensure that the two escaped prisoners and two attempted robbers/shooters were recaptured and identified respectively. The missing CBOB Deputy Governor would also be found safely and hopefully unharmed.

Plans for the 2018 hurricane season were quickly disposed of. They would be re-examined in mid-May when the final hurricane plan for the country should be ready for approval and implementation.

The new Tourism and Sporting Initiatives, discussed ad nauseam at an earlier Cabinet meeting, were also now approved by Cabinet. This pleased Minister Grant no end, for it allowed him to mention some of the initiatives in his second Sky Sports television interview with Oswald King. He would make a full Ministerial Statement to Parliament a week on Tuesday on these new initiatives.

The item before Any Other Business (AOB), saw Motby announce to his Cabinet colleagues his intention to put forward Petra Carmichael, former Permanent Secretary in the Prime Minister's Office, for an Ambassadorial post. He reiterated her attributes and virtues as an excellent and longstanding public servant who, though now formally retired from the Public Service, remained willing to serve Barbados in a diplomatic capacity. He sought his colleagues' approval (though the decision was his and his alone as Head of Government) to offer her a three-year overseas assignment, with an option of a further two years should Carmichael and the Government of Barbados be willing to continue this relationship.

"Prime Minister, which country are we looking at? You've not said, but I don't think you mean to send Carmichael to New Zealand, Australia or India." It was Hon. Walter Thompson MP, Minister of Foreign Affairs and Culture.

"Ladies and gentlemen… I sincerely apologise to you all. In my enthusiasm to submit this recommendation for your consideration, I neglected to say the country to which I propose to appoint Mrs Carmichael. It is the United Kingdom of Great Britain. Mrs Carmichael will be accredited, once accepted by Her Majesty's Government, to the Court of St James. I've had the appropriate paperwork drafted but not finalised. Do we agree that I should submit her name? I'd like to do this tomorrow, with your consent of course. Are they any objections to my proposal?"

There were none. Mrs Carmichael's appointment was affirmed unanimous by nods around the table. Motby motioned to Dr Winston Smith who knew this signal meant that he was now to finalise the document following the Cabinet meeting and submit it through the relevant official channels to the Brits on the following working day.

***

Chapter Fourteen

Assemblies

Ben Mar now looked nothing like it had done the previous night to host the cricket reception. Gone were the 'clutter' of tents, drink and food areas, entertainment stand, performing stage and podium. In fact, by mid-day the entire facility was back to looking in its usual pristine condition.

Sir Thadeus was picked up from his west coast location by the High Commissioner's driver at 2:05 p.m. The twenty-minute drive to the residence meant that the Head of MI6 arrived there for his meeting with the five Barbados-based officials just before 2:30 p.m., where Tullock met and welcomed him. No one else was on the compound, except for two security men at the main gate.

With pleasantries over between Tullock and Sir Thadeus, they held a ten-minute conversation in Tullock's downstairs study before going out onto the back balcony where the 3:00 p.m. meeting was scheduled to take place.

The five special guests had been asked to assemble between 2:45 p.m. and 2:55 p.m. to enable a prompt start of their meeting. Keeping 'Bajan time' was specifically discouraged today! First to arrive, promptly at 2:45 p.m., was Colonel Burke. He was followed two minutes later by Brigadier Tenton. Next came Lt. Colonel Innis and Commander Junior Samuel who walked into the High Commissioner's residence together. Ten minutes later, Jeremie appeared.

All of them, along with Tullock and Sir Thadeus, were deliberately dressed casually. In fact, it was the first time Tullock had seen the five Caribbean men looking so unofficial. *I won't see these men dressed like this again before my tour of duty ends and my retirement from the FCO in nine months' time,* he thought. Tullock hadn't yet mentioned it to Motby, but it was his and Andrea's intention to purchase a west coast property in which they planned to eventually retire in Barbados, possibly in another couple of years.

***

As expected, the weekly Cabinet meeting ended just before 3:00 p.m. This enabled Ministers to return to their offices to complete their day's work and prepare for the following day and any forthcoming weekend activities they had in the pipeline for their ministries or respective constituencies.

Today was different. A post-Cabinet media conference featuring three Ministers was scheduled for 4:00 p.m., with the arrangements for this having been set up Giles Arthur. It was uncertain whether any of the international media would attend the afternoon's media conference, but preparations were made to include them in case they showed up.

Motby and Ministers Walter Thompson, Sebastian Smith and Preston Grant prepared themselves to deal with the three issues – yesterday's prisoners escape, Dr Lewis's disappearance and the previous night's St. Lawrence Gap incident involving four British visitors.

***

The seven men sat comfortably in large chairs around a circular table on the spacious back patio of the British High Commissioner's residence. The patio overlooked a green lawn that was half the size of a soccer pitch. Luscious, colourful gardens surrounded the lawn. It was all a sight to behold, especially with the six-foot fountain at the far end of the garden.

Tullock welcomed his guests before introducing Sir Thadeus. Next, he invited everyone to introduce themselves and the agencies they headed. Yes, everyone (except Sir Thadeus) knew each other, but that was part of Tullock's normal method of starting meetings he was going to be involved in. Formalities over, he offered them their choice of hot and cold refreshment items that were laid out on the dining-room table inside the residence.

Once each person had selected their eats and drinks, they reassembled around the table on the patio. Tullock explained that though today's meeting was not official, it was an important…a somewhat unique one and a first of sorts, since to his knowledge a meeting like this had not taken place before. To have Heads

195

of Barbados' law enforcement and security agencies, the Head of the RSS, the Head of MI6 and him all together was therefore special. Tullock encouraged those gathered to speak frankly during their discussion, as no formal record would be taken (they all knew that was not exactly true, but it had to be said).

He then gave Sir Thadeus the floor.

"Thank you, Balwin. I must say that I envy your home. Where I come from, I don't get anything like this. Not even my PM does!

"To our business. Thank you all for coming. I'm delighted to be in Barbados. My first time. Given your lines of work, I have assumed that you've all seen *Mission Impossible 3*. That's where Ving Rhames' character asks Tom Cruise's character, 'Whatever happened to those who can't do, teach?' Also, early on in *The Wedding Planner*, Jennifer Lopez tells her assistant, 'Those who can't wed, plan.'

"In my special and unpredictable line of work, I have translated these statements to mean *'those who commit major crimes against us will be engaged, legally apprehended and face the courts, or otherwise occasionally terminated'*. We'll use all legal means available, but that's not always possible or enough.

"I'm in Barbados, not specifically for this meeting but for a long aspired-to holiday with my wife. However, I know it would be a missed opportunity if I did not meet with the Heads of your island's major local law enforcement and security agencies on a subject that's dear to my heart: *'Future Co-operation and Collaboration Between Friendly Law Enforcement and Security Agencies, Size Being Irrelevant.'*

"I've been in this business a long time," Sir Thadeus continued. He went on to explain how and why such cooperation and collaboration between such agencies must change and be enhanced.

***

Wharton had started the return journey to his Bathsheba home when his phone rang.

"Hello?"

"Castille. Is our man there with you?"

"I'm on the road man, not at my house, but he should be there," answered Wharton.

"Do you know if he has secured what I came for?" asked Castille.

"I left him working on it… I suspect he's, you know, trying to pull in one or two favours so as to be able to deliver. I expect he'll have everything ready by the time you arrive."

"Fine. See you at 5:30 p.m."

"Right. Be jolly now."

There he goes again, thought Castille…this *damn 'be jolly now' nonsense is pissing me off.*

Castille called the person he'd met just off the ABC highway the previous night, as he'd promised to do. He had just returned from scouting the specific location he'd carefully chosen for tonight's follow-up rendezvous. He recognised the need to plug the first of the 'loopholes' in Barbados. Others would follow as necessary before his scheduled departure from Barbados on Sunday afternoon.

***

Around 3:25 p.m., Colonel Burke's mobile phone vibrated. He had warned the others present before the meeting started that he might have to take an important call and, should that happen, could they please hold off their discussion until he re-joined them. He'd promised up-front that he would not be away for more than a few minutes.

And, so it was. He excused himself from the group to take the call.

Motby asked him if he had anything further to report before he conducted a post-Cabinet media conference on the national security situation. Colonel Burke advised that there was nothing new, at least nothing that the Prime Minister should report to Barbadians within the next couple of hours. He knew he would probe, but simply asked for a few more hours to see if what his BIB team were already working on would bear any fruit. They agreed to speak again that evening, at a time convenient for Motby.

Colonel Burke returned to the meeting to find the others topping up their the refreshments that had been laid out for them in the Residence's dining room. Being discussed were memories of the glory days of West Indies cricket (mid-1970s to mid-1990s).

Noticing Colonel Burke's return, sandwiches and drinks were taken and everyone returned to the large patio to resume their seats. The discussion on future co-operation and collaboration then continued in earnest.

Recent developments in Barbados – the prior day's prisoners escape, the now public knowledge that the CBOB's Deputy Governor was missing, the previous night's robbery and shooting incident and the ongoing ECC project were not discussed, although they were vaguely alluded to during the afternoon's exchanges, sort of like…the 'silent elephants in their midst'.

***

The post-Cabinet meeting media conference commenced at 4:05 p.m. It was surprisingly not as well attended as expected, but there were still a good number of journalists, photographers and cameramen present. Only one non-regional television crew from Sky Sports had shown up unexpectedly and so had joined local and regional journalists in the third-floor conference room at Government Headquarters.

Motby, surrounded by his three fellow Cabinet ministers, wasted no time in getting down to business. His statement was short and direct as it related to the three incidents.

"First, the prisoners escape had been somewhat thwarted in that only two of the five prisoners remained on the lose thirty hours after they had gotten away. Local law enforcement and security agencies are hard at work tracking down the two missing men. Due to what had happened, Cabinet have just asked the Attorney General and Minister of Residential Affairs to undertake a review of the entire prison system operation and report back to Cabinet with recommendations two weeks from today. The review would include (but not be limited to) an examination of current HMP Dodds procedures, enhancing the mechanisms used in transporting prisoners to and from court, the existing security protocols, what new or additional equipment, personnel and funding might be required to enhance the BPS' capacity, efficiency and effectiveness going forward. I stress that the re-capture of the escaped prisoners remains our priority and is expected soon.

"Second, I acknowledge but will not at this time shine any new light on what progress had been made to date following the sudden disappearance of our Central Bank's Deputy Governor.

"Third, it is still too early to say any more than has already been stated by our Commissioner of Police on last night's St. Lawrence Gap incident. However, be advised that having visited the scene first thing this morning, Commissioner Jeremie has since also met with the four British visitors involved in the incident. Both he and Minister Thompson have also spoken with British High Commissioner Tullock today. To summarise, all hands were on deck to quickly and satisfactorily resolve all three incidents by close-of-play-Monday in cricketing parlance. Once these targets are achieved, I will address the country. In the meanwhile, our GIS will issue regular updates on these incidents over the next three days, i.e. on Friday, Saturday and Sunday at 4:00 p.m. Any questions?" Motby concluded.

It was Cornelius Picket, Head of News at the privately owned Star News Corporation Inc. who was first.

"Prime Minister, with these two prisoners on the loose, can you assure Barbadians and visitors alike that they can continue to go about their business, day or night, in peace and safety? A follow-up too if I may…why were the deficiencies in the BPS – HMP Dodds in particular, not known about earlier and if they were known, by whom and why were they not fixed before this escape under your administration?"

"Mr Pickett! First in and on-the-ball as usual! Great questions, all of which I'm happy to answer for you, and the general public. I am assured by the Heads of our law enforcement and security agencies that…and I must emphasise this, the country is safe. There is no national security threat against the country, from inside or outside. These three incidents could have taken place together at any time of the year, or at separate times. It is unfortunate that they've occurred this week. But rest assure, prior to these incidents, we had set up an elaborate security system around the Test Match starting tomorrow and ending with the Commonwealth Sports Ministers meeting by the middle of next week. As a result, everyone here, Barbadians and visitors alike, should be aware that there is an extra level of protection for them over and above what they would normally experience.

"Now, as to your second question, I'll not prejudge what might or might not come out of the BPS review but again, please be assured that we will take its findings seriously and act on them promptly, even if it means my having to shift around some funds to satisfy elements emanating from the review in my forthcoming Budget."

"Prime Minister, can you give us a Budget date at this time please?" The questioner was Barbara Jarvis, Head of News at the Government-run Barbados News Corporation.

"Sorry, Mrs Jarvis. I've not decided that yet, but it is possible that the review's recommendations might prompt me to delay my timing a little, but not by much. Remember, I've not delivered any of my thirteen Budgets any later than the end of June. Okay?"

There were three other questions from local journalists, but none of them connected to the incidents mentioned by Motby. Then Oswald King from Sky Sports asked the Tourism, International Transport and Sport Minister a question.

"Tell me, Minister Grant…why should UK tourists come to Barbados in the future rather than go to other Caribbean islands? Your Prime Minister says safety is not a concern now, even with these three incidents, but what about the future? People back home want to be comforted before they come all this way and during their visit. What advice do you give to encourage them to come here?"

"Thanks, Mr King. As the Prime Minister has just intimated, and as I told you yesterday morning during our interview, Barbados is one of the safest places in the world to live, work, visit and play. We also have a lot of foreign investors and expatriates who run some of those businesses who not only enjoy living here, but the special working, business, social and recreational environment we offer here in Barbados. Visitors, certainly a lot of Brits, are already in for the start of tomorrow's Test Match. I've met some for example at the British High Commissioner's reception last night. They've told me how much they are enjoying their stay, the accommodation, the food, the sea, local entertainment and of course, to being at the cricketing tip of the world, that is New Kensington Oval, to see some great cricket. My advice, to answer your question directly, is for visitors to take the same precautions in Barbados that they would normally take when they are back home, wherever they come from. It is what I do when I'm away from Barbados."

With that answer, Motby brought the media conference to an end. The attending media appeared to be satisfied. He felt confident that he and his fellow Ministers had given a good account of themselves. It was always best to be open with the media…provide them with as complete answers to their questions wherever possible, as opposed to being evasive with (and certainly not lying to) them. His team had just accomplished that.

Being as open as he could be at most times was one of the secrets for his longevity and survival as a leader and as the Prime Minister of Barbados for the past thirteen years.

***

Around two hours after the meeting at the British High Commissioner's residence had started, it ended.

A 'verbal understanding' was now in place between the Heads of Barbados' security and a sub-regional one, plus the Head of one of Britain's most durable security agencies. Only time would tell if the understanding reached would become a formal written policy, protocol or agreement between the politicians on both sides of the Atlantic Ocean. They would have to consider the merits of and all aspects of implementing such an eventual agreement before full cooperation, collaboration and implementation could take place.

What the action timeline for this would be was yet to be decided. Given the speed at which these formal agreements usually took to be finalised, realistically it was unlikely to be completed before the end of 2018. In the meanwhile, a softer, informal working relationship might be implemented between the two sides once the 'reporting' was done back to the UK and Barbados governments by Sir Thadeus and Colonel Burke respectively.

***

After exiting *Ben Mar*, but still on the compound of the High Commissioner's residence, Superintendent Innis received a call from his secretary, Melba Bodie.

She was upset, because she'd just discovered that the original papers regarding Wednesday's PR had gone missing. She assured him that she'd secured them in the usual way on Tuesday before leaving work. The only other persons who had access to the filing cabinet where PR records were retained were himself and George Telford, HMP Dodds' Deputy Superintendent. Furthermore, Telford had apparently left the compound shortly after Superintendent Innis' departure to go to the British High Commissioner's residence. Telford had given no reason for leaving, stated where he was going or indicated if he would be returning to the compound. This was the normal protocol and practice when either of the compound's two senior members of staff left that facility during a regular work-day.

Innis thanked Bodie for informing him. *Seriously? George Telford!* Why would he break established protocol?

Then a thought started to come to Innis. *Could...?* He stopped himself in mid-thought. Yes, someone on the inside of HMP Dodds had 'sold them out' by providing details of Wednesday's PR to persons on the outside which enabled the daring prisoner hijack and escape to occur.

He became uncomfortable as things started to become clearer.

***

Colonel Burke returned to BIB HQ around 5:30 p.m. He found JJ, Mohammed, Jayne, Fred and Joe in the conference room just as his mobile phone rang. He put up a hand to stop JJ from speaking.

"Colonel Burke."

"Innis here, Trevor. Just got news from my secretary that my second man, George Telford, left HMP Dodds just after me this afternoon."

"Not normal...but why are you telling me this, Simon?" asked Colonel Burke.

"Because I'm beginning to think that Telford might have given up details of Wednesday's PR," answered Superintendent Innis.

"Oh really? Well, you better find him quickly and establish that for a fact," said Colonel Burke coldly.

"I've been trying to reach him ever since I heard the news. I'll keep trying. Once I get him, I'll provide you with a readout on what he says..."

"Yes. Please keep me posted." Colonel Burke ended the call.

"News?" asked JJ.

"Maybe. Just that Innis feels Telford might have been the person at HMP Dodds who sold out yesterday's PR. Apparently Telford left the compound this afternoon after him and during normal work hours without telling anyone where he was going. He's not reported in or returned. Innis is trying to track him down."

"Ah...alright. Let's focus on what we have again, just in case we've overlooked something," said JJ.

"Why not indeed," said Joe.

This time, more slowly, Jayne told them what had happened from her viewpoint.

"I recall seeing a masked man limping as fast as he could towards the getaway car before it screeched off. His right leg was hampering him as he ran. Three or four gunshots were fired from the car as it sped away."

Mohammed then did likewise, reiterating what he had seen. It was not dissimilar to Jayne's version.

"Once we arrived at the scene, we drew our weapons but did not fire them. The last person to enter the getaway car carried a limp. Everything happened quickly. The getaway car wasted no time in leaving –"

Colonel Burke interjected, "Why didn't any of you try to shoot out its tyres?"

"In the melee, we could have hit one of the prisoners. They were in close proximity to where the getaway car had stopped to collect Power. Once it had its passengers on board, including Power and the limping man it took off," answered JJ.

"Chief, I also reiterate my observation at the time that the getaway car used was a dark blue Mitsubishi Lancer Evolution 6 saloon," said Mohammed.

No one doubted him. Mohammed had been a fireman prior to joining BIB and had attended two crashes on the ABC highway where similar vehicles were involved.

Mohammed's observations were subsequently proved correct after a similar car had been spotted at the bottom of a shallow gully by a visiting hiker. He had reported his discovery to a passing police vehicle on patrol once he was back on the main road. A wrecker had been summoned to pull the car from the gully. The Barbados Licence Authority (BLA) subsequently confirmed that the bent-up number pates found on the car were false. The car's engine and chassis numbers matched those of a car that had been reported stolen to the RBPF two nights earlier.

The getaway car could now be checked for fingerprints and DNA evidence.

***

The established custom remained alive and well.

Promptly at 7:00 p.m., members of both squads commenced dinner with non-alcoholic drinks in different parts of the south coast hotel where they were both staying. Around the dinner table sat members of each teams' full squad. The eleven members of each squad chosen to represent the West Indies and England in the Test Match at New Kensington Oval from tomorrow and over a five-day period knew who they were. It was over dinner that final match tactics for the game would be conveyed to the players by their coaching staff.

Of course, it was recognised that tactics would need to be adjusted, if not changed completely, from day-to-day, session-to-session (three per day) or even more than once within a session, as the game progressed. One side might gain the upper hand over the other at any particular time. The beauty of Test Match cricket could happen over a sustained period or quite quickly, even within a single over. The first tactical decision would be taken after the toss of a coin was won or lost. Does your team bat or bowl first?

Having seen the pitch that afternoon and bearing in mind the fine weather conditions expected over the next few days, both sides were inclined to bat first. Whichever team did so would want to do well in their first innings at the crease to 'set up' the game for themselves, hopefully enabling their spinners to keep the opposition under pressure during their second innings. On the other hand, should they manage to bat better and score a lot more runs than your team did in its first innings, then your team might be in trouble and end up losing the match.

Aside from the batting, how a team bowled – hopefully to get wickets and if not, to stem any flow of runs, was equally as important. Here's where your coaching staff, a captain's skill and leadership ability, along with the 'buy-in' and commitment of all squad members and the support staff came in.

Both sides knew what they wanted to do at the start of Day 1, but everything would depend to start with, on which team won the toss.

***

JJ's Gold team, plus Fred and Joe spent another hour in BIB's conference room, going over everything that had happened during yesterday's prisoners escape, for what seemed like a tenth time. They came up with nothing new.

As Colonel Burke had left them to return to his office to finish off some paperwork before going home, JJ spoke to his fellow operators.

"Okay folks, let's save some energy for tomorrow, eh? If we all go home now, get something to eat and some sleep, we can meet back here early in the morning before we start playing our respective parts in the EEC security project. Makes sense?" he asked.

The others nodded.

They knew JJ was right. Tomorrow might see them in a better place to be able to find something to work with to get them closer to finding the two escaped prisoners and those responsible for making it happen. The angle that someone on the inside, in the BPS, specifically at HMP Dodds or even from the RBPF, had been involved in the whole mess, was now uppermost in their minds.

They would start by speaking with George Telford once he got to work in the morning.

***

The unexpected convergence of these three events, were all suspicious and prompted three diplomats from the Mexican Embassy, USA Embassy and British High Commission to meet with their opposite number from the Chinese Embassy, at the latter's rustic St. Thomas residence that night. The house, specially chosen for its isolated location, was an ideal venue for their clandestine meeting.

As with their earlier appearance in Independence Square, Jose Jesus Sanchez, Amarouse Busbee and Zoe Markowitz would ensure that they were not easily followed to Xui Kung Pei's residence. They had arrived there by complicated and roundabout routes. They'd certainly not travelled there from their own residences 'as the crow flies', i.e. as directly as they could have done. Anyone seeking to follow any of these three persons to their destination would surely have been spotted. Their *rare meeting* protocol was such that, should any of them feel that they were being followed at any time during their journey to the venue, they would divert away from their destination and return home.

Tonight, they had been no problems and everyone had arrived safely and covertly.

In true diplomat style, they shared some fine wine and a meal together. It was Chinese of course which had earlier been purchased from a Maxwell Road, Christ Church Chinese restaurant. That done, they settled down to conduct their collaborative business that was at hand. Their recent reading of the situation as of late-Tuesday afternoon, had changed…and not for the best.

Were the three events over the past thirty-six hours coincidental? Who were the players behind them? Were they local, regional or international? How had none of Barbados' security agencies (at least their contacts within these organisations) known about them in advance? How might they follow up tomorrow and which agency would lead the response on each event? Was there anything to suggest that any of the security agencies or the political directorate might have had a hand in creating these scenarios?

Sanchez spoke up. "In answer to your question, Zoe, it's been known that in other small countries with a struggling Government, it might want from time to time, to provide a 'distraction' from what might recently have been happening at home. But this clearly is not the case here in Barbados."

"I agree," said a mischievous looking Markowitz. "So, given our recent findings which we transmitted by respective dispatches to our capitals on Tuesday night, was our analysis flawed? If so, what did we miss?"

Busbee answered. "None, I'm sure we were accurate. Listen up. The prisoner rescue was obviously planned. The disappearance, let's call it that for now as we've no evidence to date of it being a kidnapping and as for the robbery? These things happen all over the world and at any time. That's just bad luck. Petty crime."

"Then, my friends, let's look at the other questions we've raised," said Pei. It was a command, not a request.

One by one, they examined and answered the questions they had asked themselves during the evening. Determined to be thorough, they next turned their attention to new developments they had picked up from their local 'scribes', persons known to dabble or operate in Barbados' small but active criminal underworld.

Was there a connection locally to the underworld activities happening in neighbouring countries?

***

The two men who had met the previous night in an Anglican parish church's car park, met again at 8:15 p.m. for their second night at a different venue agreed on earlier that afternoon. The location? Another Anglican church's compound, this time in the eastern part of Barbados.

They parked their vehicles side by side, but the visitor exited his vehicle and joined the Barbadian in his.

The Barbadian understood the purpose behind this second meeting. It was to enable them to finalise discussions on and set in-train appropriate arrangements for a future ongoing relationship between himself and the visitor's organisation.

The visitor, on the other hand and unknown to the Barbadian, intended a vastly different outcome for tonight's meeting.

"Good night," said the visitor.

"You too, man. How you doing?" asked the Barbadian.

"Fine. You?"

"I'm cool…had a trying day, you know, because of yesterday's incident."

"Problems? You're under pressure?" asked the visitor.

"Not really. Nothing I'm not used to or can't handle. Look, why you chose to meet here, man? I've never been comfortable in or around churches or cemeteries," stated the Barbadian who was growing more restless.

"Nor me. It's a good place for us to have our final discussion –"

"And for you to hand over the rest of my money!"

"Of course," responded the visitor.

"Let's finish up our business so I can get away from here and you can grab yourself a nice hotel dinner," said the Barbadian looking over his right shoulder.

When he turned around to face the passenger sitting in the front seat of his vehicle, he was shocked to see a handgun being pointed at him.

"Hey, take it easy man! What's that for? I thought we were here to finalise our future relationship, not play games. I'm not the snitching or telling type," rambled on the Barbadian, certain that his life was in danger. He realised that this was no longer just about gaining a few extra dollars on the side to help set him up for his old age.

"Here's the rest of your payment," said the visitor, slipping another white envelope into the driver's lap as he opened the front passenger door and exited the vehicle. "Drive over there…under that tree."

"Why? Just leave me alone man. Here, take back your money. I want out of our arrangement, right now okay. I'm leaving this place," said the Barbadian as he turned on the vehicle's engine.

"Too late. Drive over there slowly and don't look around," the visitor commanded, gun pointing at the Barbadian's head from outside the vehicle.

Terrified, the Barbadian reluctantly did as he was told. He stopped under the tree. He did not know where the man who had sat in the passenger seat of his vehicle a minutes earlier was.

Where's he gone? Perhaps he's changed his mind and won't hurt me, the Barbadian was thinking.

Regaining a little composure but still nervous as hell and fearing for his life, the Barbadian decided to exit his vehicle, intent on making e a run for it. As he opened the driver's door, he heard the visitor's voice.

"Stay in the vehicle…and close that door," the visitor ordered.

The Barbadian slapped his head. "Idiot," he said softly. Had he been thinking he would have driven away the vehicle as fast as he could.

He'd heard the visitor's voice but could not establish his location. Only the driver's window was open. Was the visitor somewhere to his right or near the rear of the vehicle? As he wondered what might happen next, he sensed a movement in the darkness and comprehended something bright – a flash.

Everything around him went dark.

The Barbadian never realised that after exiting his vehicle, the visitor had applied a silencer to the gun he was holding before calmly firing a shot that had caressed the cool night air on its way through the opened driver's side window before residing in the right side of the Barbadian's temple.

His phone rang a few seconds later. He did not hear it. Nor would he ever answer his phone again.

***

Mrs Alanya Telford wondered why her husband had not answered his phone. It was long past the time when he would normally have arrived home from HMP Dodds. His boss, Superintendent Innis had called home asking to speak with George on a couple of occasions, first around 5:40 p.m. and then a couple of hours later, but all she could tell him on both occasions was that George had not gotten home yet.

Mrs Telford decided to sit on their front patio and await his arrival. There had to be a reason why George had not even called home. He was known for lying to her, so his explanation would be interesting whenever he got home.

***

The visitor calmly removed the silencer from the Glock model 17 Gen 4.9mm handgun before placing both into his jacket pocket. He then opened the driver's door to re-enter the vehicle. He wound up the driver's side window, leaving enough space for some air to come in. He then reached over and similarly cracked the passenger's front window before carefully proceeding to professionally wipe down the vehicle. Anyone watching would think he must have done this before because he was so smooth in carrying out this exercise. They would have been right (and thankfully, no one was watching).

The visitor then set the deceased Barbadian to look as comfortable as possible, not that it mattered anymore. Finally, he withdrew the handgun from his pocket with a gloved hand and placed its handle in the Barbadian's lifeless right hand. As expected, the gun fell out of his hand, coming to rest just under the driver's seat and so out of immediate sight of any peering eyes. Using a bright penlight held in his other gloved hand, the visitor and former front seat passenger retrieved the shell from the fired bullet that was lying on the ground beside the vehicle and dropped it by at the Barbadian's feet inside the vehicle who now appeared to be asleep.

Sharp law enforcement officers would subsequently investigate the incident and question what appeared to have been a deliberate effort to make it look as if the driver had taken his own life in this quiet, almost secluded spot on a country church's compound. Would they be able to prove that this was the case?

Luckily for the visitor, no one had entered the immediate area around the church's compound since he and the Barbadian had arrived. Given its location, discovery of the parked vehicle and the man inside of it was unlikely until the following morning.

Before returning to his hired vehicle, the visitor placed three further $100 bills into the white envelope. He then lodged it beside the Barbadian's phone in the driver's side door pocket. This sought to set up the Barbadian in a particular way once he was found.

Or so the visitor thought! Despite his cover-up efforts, he made one simple but careless mistake.

When he had first bent over to position the driver's body, the visitor did not realise that one of his two *south coast hotel* room keys had fallen out of his wallet and lodged under the driver's seat. He had received two of these on his arrival at the hotel after checking in. As was his custom when travelling, he had placed his room keys in his wallet before leaving his hotel room. He would only realise that one of them was missing later when he returned to his room.

Having reached their conclusions, the four diplomats built a hypothesis through which each of them had parts to prove or disprove by 4:00 p.m. the following day. They departed for their respective homes contented, having agreed to meet again the next night in the above car park behind the Welches, Christ Church shopping complex thirty minutes after its 9:00 p.m. closing time. It was a public place but would not be busy at that time of night. They would be able to discuss their findings in peace. Then, if further work on their leads was still required to confirm their findings, they could use some of the weekend for this. In any event, transmission of their respective up-graded reports to their capitals would then take place at mid-day on Monday.

They would watch with interest to see if Barbados' security agencies could resolve these matters by then.

***

Given what Castille had learnt late that afternoon, tomorrow would see him intensify his search for Power. Finding Power ASAP would enable him to accomplish the task that he had been set by *The Organisation*. Failure was never an option for him – he would get that scumbag, although it would now be more difficult than before. He'd find the rock under which Power had disappeared. Securing the funds owed to *The Organisation* was imperative.

As he sought to enter his room, Castille realised that one of his room keys was missing. *Damn*, he thought. Once inside, he made a detailed search and realised that it was not there. He had lost it. There was nothing he could do about that now, so he would report its loss when he was checking out. He wondered, but did not think that his lost room key could be traced back to him until after he had left Barbados in another two or three days.

Having earlier pre-ordered a late room service delivery to his room, Castille tipped the waiter generously and sat down to enjoy his meal. His earlier action that evening did not hamper his appetite.

***

It was around 10:20 p.m. when the occupants of three vehicles left Pei's house, satisfied that they had a renewed handle on all that was now in play across Barbados' criminal underworld. Their counterparts in other capitals would be invited to comment on any recent significant criminal activities undertaken by gangs in their areas which mentioned or even suggested further contact with their Caribbean associates. This would form part of their ongoing work over the next year or two.

But one of the three persons driving away was unhappy. Zoe Markowitz, Consular officer at the British High Commission, had to do her 'day job' tomorrow at the Test Match, in case any consular-related incidents cropped up with any of the four thousand British supporters, media or officials who would be at or around New Kensington Oval for Day 1 of the game. As the originator and lead-player at the High Commission for its consular event response plan (CERP), Markowitz was expected to be present. As for her 'other' role, that of being the High Commission's MI6 officer, a fact only known to High Commissioner Tullock, getting out of what she had just agreed to do tomorrow was going to be tricky. She decided to call on her Consular assistant, Barbadian Barbara Lane, to cover for her during the Day 1's pre-lunch session. Markowitz would feign slight illness between 8:00 a.m. and 12:30 p.m. but would go to the office nonetheless to follow-through on her task.

Markowitz was a cricketing enthusiast and was very much looking forward to watching as much of the five days of the Test Match as she could. She had met both sets of players at the High Commissioner's reception the previous night so now wanted to see them in action. But as she had more important work to do, her hopes for the Test Match were not all going to be fulfilled. Would the two English players she had spoken to at length be able to play the game as well as they had been at chatting her up?

***

The WhatsApp exchange was unexpected but timely. It came from Barbados and was received in Miami, USA.

"Change of plan. Can't make your town, so come to mine."

"Okay. Same time?"

"Can't work. Have to attend a European conference then."

"Suggestion?"

"In Sunday. Out Monday."

"Deal. Will u collect."

"No…but look out for a very tall, dark and handsome figure."

"All American pizza-man."

"The one + only."

"Agreed."

The WhatsApp exchange ended. To the uninitiated, the above conversation made no sense. It was probably two old friends cryptically jive-talking. The communicators sex was unknown and unimportant.

To people in their line of work, the exchange was clear and understood by both of its participants. Once things went as planned, a twenty-four-hour visit to Barbados from Sunday afternoon to Monday afternoon should cement the proposed relationship between their USA-based and Barbados-based Caribbean entities. The absolute necessity for the meeting to take place now, rather than in another fortnight in Miami as earlier agreed, had nothing to do with Power's escape from the clutches of Barbadian law enforcement agencies. Rather, it was about the 'bigger fish' they were preparing to fry.

Pilessar would be in and out quickly, being accommodated at the home of her Barbadian host located on the east coast, where their discussions and at least a preliminary agreement would be worked out.

***

Power kept himself pretty quiet and below deck during the overnight sea journey from Barbados. He was an excellent swimmer, so was comfortable at sea and not worried by the constant bobbing of the powerful ice boat he was on as it made its way across the Caribbean Sea. His 'sea legs' were on. Having grown up not far from the seaside, Power had been a frequent visitor to the beach from early childhood. At weekends, he'd go with his father and uncle on one or two-day trips from their Bridgetown Fishing Complex base in *Old Faithful*, the family's fishing boat. Though many people would have been afraid to be out on the open sea after nightfall, Power was comfortable. In fact, he felt somewhat emboldened, knowing that he had departed Barbados, having escaped its law enforcement agencies. A return to HMP Dodds was not on the cards and so he was looking forward to starting a new life in another country. Technology was good, but the way he envisaged setting himself up after laying low for a while, he'd felt certain that he would be difficult to find, once he kept himself away from direct engagement with any law enforcement agencies in the new country.

Power's decision that afternoon to grow his hair long (into locks eventually) and a beard in his new country made sense. Changing one's facial features by surgery was not a readily available option. As that would cost him a lot of money he did not have at this time. He'd heard that a semi-retired plastic surgeon spent six months of the year (November to April) on Mustique, but that doctor had returned to his Boston, Massachusetts home earlier this year, so that option was out anyway. Power doubted that his fellow underworld colleagues would spend money to change his appearance. Getting him away from Barbados was as much as he'd expected them to do for him.

So, he would eat heavily to put on as many pounds as quickly as possible and grow a beard and long hair. These would be the tools he could utilise to alter his appearance within a couple of months. This would not make him a different person from the man who had just left Barbados, but it would make him *feel* like a new person by the end of June.

Hopefully, the Miami-based outfit known as *The Organisation* would also forget about him. He knew that the Barbados law enforcement agencies would not. Because of this, he would have to be very careful where he was seen and what he did going forward.

***

213

Chapter Fifteen
Test Cricket ... and Back Channels

FRIDAY, 20 APRIL

New Kensington Oval's head groundsman, Orwell 'Orrie' Moore arrived at the stadium just as dawn was breaking. Shortly thereafter, his crew also arrived. They commenced making their final preparations for the Test Match over the next two hours before the ground would be opened to the public. An hour after the groundsmen had arrived, the caterers, security and media people started to do so. Television, radio and the print media including photographers arrived later.

The weather forecast for Friday and the next three days were all set to be fine – long days of sunshine, blue skies, twenty-nine degrees centigrade and above all...no rain. A few showers were predicted during the overnight hours of Sunday and Monday which might affect Days 4 and 5, but hopefully not much.

Punctually at 7:30 a.m. the gates of New Kensington Oval opened to supporters of both teams, all lovers of Test Cricket. The several lines of patrons at New Kensington Oval's various gates wrapped themselves around the stadium, suggesting a bumper crowd would be in attendance on Day 1.

***

Magnus Hunter GCM, was a retired former Head of the Barbados Public Service, Cabinet Secretary and Permanent Secretary in the Ministry of Defence & National Security. He had been trying to call Colonel Burke, once his protégée, at home since early that morning, without any success. Admittedly, he'd not called either Colonel Burke's personal or official mobile numbers, deliberately so.

Eventually, Hunter got hold of Diane Burke. She advised him that her husband had long left for the office. She'd been out for her daily constitutional (a forty-five-minute walk) when he'd called earlier. Hunter explained that he had to speak with Colonel Burke as soon as possible on an important matter. Could he come over to their house in a couple of hours? Also, could she get Colonel Burke to return home without letting him know why he was returning? Diane knew Hunter well enough to pick up that he must have something worthwhile to tell her husband. She agreed to play along, confident that Hunter would not ask her to do this unless it was absolutely necessary.

Colonel Burke and Hunter usually met once a month for old time's sake, usually over a meal at Colonel Burke's home in an effort to maintain their thirty-year-long friendship. When they deemed it necessary, they also met 'on demand' to discuss matters of interest to both of them. They called these back-channel meetings.

Why did Hunter want to speak to Colonel Burke? He had noticed the recent developments in the country with growing alarm. He'd also been made privy to some scraps of information from credible sources which he wanted to personally convey to Colonel Burke. Hunter's knowledge, insight into defence, national security and criminal matters remained as 'on point' as they were while he was a top public servant. If anything, his vast contacts base had grown following his retirement. Having more time on his hands and making use of available technology made this possible.

***

Hunter would have to miss the first ball on Day 1 of a Barbados Test Match. So convinced was he that what he had learned and needed to convey to Colonel Burke was important, that he was prepared to forego a practice he'd undertaken since his retirement. There were always the other days. Given the mood of the current West Indies cricket team which was again playing well and the strength of the England team, the game was expected to go well into the last day.

As a two-decade-long life member of the Barbados Cricket Association (BCA), Hunter's seat was secure at the New Kensington Ova, even if the ground was sold out, as it usually was once England was the visiting team. The Balmy

Army crew would have helped to ensure the ground being sold-out for at least the first three days. Hunter hoped that his meeting with Colonel Burke would help lead to the three situations being 'cleaned up' before the Test Match's scheduled end on Tuesday.

***

Chief Superintendent Vickers' had spent the first part of the morning seeking to reach Barbados' Ambassador to the United States of America, HE Meredith Carter. An old friend from primary school, he finally managed to speak with her around 9:30 a.m. She had been chairing a staff meeting to finalise arrangements for a high-level reception that evening at her official residence for Caribbean Ambassadors to meet with senior US officials from the State Department.

"Hi, Johnny, you called for me earlier?" asked the Barbados Ambassador.

"I did Ambassador. How you doing? Getting any warm weather yet up there in Washington D.C.?" asked Vickers.

"Come on Johnny, you know and have been to this place. We had a few warm days back in late-March, but its' since been cold like mid-winter. No snow though. Summer seems a long way off! What can I do for you, and what's all this Ambassador stuff? I'm plain old Meredith, remember?"

Indeed. Vickers remembered! They had once been an 'item', but her unwillingness to get married at the time, preferring to take an overseas posting to Brussels as a Foreign Services officer in the Ministry of Foreign Affairs & Foreign Trade (as it then was). This had up-ended their relationship. As Vickers was not willing to give up his police career to follow her around the world, they had unfortunately called it quits, but had remained good friends since.

"Just following protocol. My call's official. Guess you've heard that Dr Albert Lewis, Deputy Governor at our Central Bank, has gone missing."

"Of course. It was mentioned by my deputy in our just-concluded meeting. His old friends in Washington were surprised to learn of his disappearance."

"Well then, you'll know Dr Lewis lived in the US for many years before returning to Barbados in 2015 on two-year secondment from the World Bank to work with our CBOB. Thereafter, he was offered a two-year contract by CBOB which he accepted. I understand that there'll be an option for him to extend for a further two years and he's likely to accept. That was, until he went missing as of late-Tuesday afternoon," explained Vickers.

"Shame."

"Yes. Can you please enquire of your 'in-house' team, or your US sources how he was viewed during the time he spent at the World Bank, indeed over the two decades or so he spent in the USA? I'm trying hard to pull together and build up some background on him prior to his return to Barbados. May not be important – will probably come to nothing, but it *might* help with our current investigation."

"Who's leading the investigation there?" Ambassador Carter asked.

"I am," replied Vickers.

"Of course. I should have known! I'll ask around…and also put out some feelers to see what I get back. The in-house trawl might turn up something quickly but the US one might take me a while longer. I'll try to get back to you by day's-end. Good enough for you?"

"Guess so…if you get anything firm from your team, please advise me of your findings ASAP."

"Got it. Speak to you later."

"Roger that."

With that, Ambassador Carter hung up the phone and called in her secretary. Brief memories of the nice times she and Vickers had spent together flooded back, before she returned to the task immediately at hand. If she could help him from this distance, she would.

Vickers started to work on his next task for the morning. Once completed, he would make his way to RBPF HQ.

***

By 9:50 a.m., New Kensington Oval was indeed heaving. West Indies had won the toss and decided to bat. First blood to West Indies!

New Kensington Oval's capacity of twelve thousand spectators were there to see the two standing umpires, an Australian and a Sri Lankan, stride out from the Garfield Sobers Pavilion at 9:58 a.m. towards the centre of the cricket field. They were closely followed by the England team, led by Brent Norbury, their captain. He assembled his team for the customary huddle to give them some final words of inspiration before they ventured onto the field to take up their positions on the outfield. The two West Indies' opening batsmen followed them, crossing the boundary line on their way out to the 'middle'.

The five-day cricket match was about to start.

Promptly at 10:00 a.m., with the standing umpire having called 'Play', the first ball of the second Test Match between West Indies and England was bowled. Needless to say, the Balmy Army were in fine voice and full of energy. Ticket sales suggested around one third of the spectators present for Day 1 of this Test Match were English or rather British, as Scottish and Irish supporters were also 'in the house'.

Would the West Indian batsmen be able to quieten them down with a good start and throughout Day 1? If they did, they might just be at the start of their journey to go two-nil up in the three-match series, having won the first Test Match in Jamaica at Sabina Park earlier in the week.

***

Magnus Hunter was sitting in the rocking chair he always chose that was situated on the veranda of Colonel Burke's house. Diane had finally managed to get hold of her husband, insisting that he come home urgently to deal with a developing family issue. When Colonel Burke had asked her what the family issue was, Diane had refused to say, only urging that he came home as soon as he could get away.

Colonel Burke drove past the front of his house and proceeded to park his BIB vehicle in the double garage at the side of the house. Hunter saw Colonel Burke as he drove by – he thought to himself that his protégé and friend looked unusually concerned. On his entry, he rose to his feet to greet Colonel Burke who was barely able to mask his surprise at seeing Hunter at his home at this time of day. Was something wrong with Hunter? Was that why Diane had called him home urgently because to Colonel Burke, Hunter was family. But his mentor looked fine, his usual upbeat self so it could not be illness. He was sure of this because Diane was not fussing over Hunter.

"I've not known you not to be at New Kensington Oval to see the first ball of a Test Match since your retirement, Magnus," said Colonel Burke.

"You're right, Six out of six, Trevor. Six years, six Test Matches. Until today. The game's underway now, so let's get down to why I've come over to see you."

Colonel Burke was grateful that there was no urgent or developing family issue for him to attend to, and so they sat down on the veranda. Pleasantries over, he started to listen to why Hunter had gotten him summoned home.

Over the next hour or so, Colonel Burke heard Hunter out. The exercise proved yet again that his old boss still had 'it', the reach, the savviness of having once been the senior public servant to hold overall responsibility for national security issues in Barbados while also being aware of the main security issues facing neighbouring countries too. Colonel Burke gleaned three nuggets of information that could be of great importance to BIB's investigations. Hunter offered up the first two. Colonel Burke had to push him for the third.

First, Colonel Burke received word on what the better known locally-based foreign Embassies and High Commissions security personnel had recently been working on. It was news to him…he would need to get on top of that situation by speaking with Ryan Appleton at MFA to confirm that the persons he understood to be each facility's security officers had not changed. Then he would do some 'digging' on those persons.

Second, escaped prisoner Power had left Barbados for another country late yesterday by either a private speedboat or an ice fishing boat, most likely from somewhere on the west coast. The exact location was not yet verifiable, but might become clear by mid-afternoon after a few more calls.

"You're kidding me!" exclaimed Colonel Burke.

"I don't joke, Trevor. Have I ever been wrong?" asked Hunter.

"No –"

"Please allow me to continue. I got word early this morning that Power left yesterday between 5:30 p.m. and 7:00 p.m. His destination? Either St Vincent and the Grenadines or St Lucia, but more likely the former. My sources indicate that he was, get this, not so much escaping from our law enforcement agencies and the wonderfully hospitable HMP Dodds offers, but was running away from an overseas group that even I do not have much information on. Ever heard of *The Organisation*? Has its US-based headquarters in Florida – Miami to be precise. It has links, tentacles might be a better word, in North, Central and South America. The entity started out selling vehicle parts and accessories, but expanded a few years ago into computers and related '*merchandise*'. My sources say that's all mainly a cover for selling more serious stuff like drugs and guns. Recalibration of activities to engage with country-resident criminal groups, gangs etc. are also in-play, with some of these operating not only in Barbados, but in our closest neighbouring countries," stated Hunter.

"Which ones, Magnus?" asked Colonel Burke instinctively.

"St Lucia, Grenada and St Vincent and the Grenadines. Slightly further afield too, in Antigua and Barbuda."

"Funny you should list those four countries! I recently met someone who told me that there has been increased activity by criminal elements operating here, with international entities endeavouring to break into the region via partnerships in these same countries."

"Who'd you meet?" asked Hunter.

"Can't tell you, but something like that never happened in your time, at least I don't *think* it did. I'm sure you'll work it out, especially if the words 'Brits' and 'intelligence' are mentioned."

"Trevor, Barbados really is a small place. There's word's already out on the street that some 'top intelligence dog' is currently on-island under cover of being a tourist. Is his visit more than a holiday, my friend?" asked Hunter.

"Magnus, you know I can't confirm anything that you've just stated. Correction, have intimated, but as usual, your 'ear' about most things going on around here is pretty solid. You keep telling me that you've retired? No way! Perhaps you're an undercover BIB operative that even *I* don't know about."

"Trevor, retired for sure but dumb I am not...my ears still work and my contacts remain in sync. That's one thing I *can* confirm. I'm not BIB's thirteenth employee, undercover or otherwise. Simply call me your 'invisible' man."

"And that you are, Magnus, so I remain grateful. You've long been my mentor and very good friend. Is there anything else that you want to tell me before I get back to the office? The third nugget? There's a lot on my plate, as you probably suspect."

"Well, yes, and here it is. Two of the alleged biggest underworld kingpins in Barbados might have had something to do with the disappearance of Dr Lewis. I got this information directly as I was taking my daily walk at Miami Beach this morning."

"Really?"

"Look, Trevor, I'll be honest with you. I'm not even thirty percent sure about this last tip, but it's what I've been told, okay? So, let me be clear. Of the three pieces of information I've just given you, this last one is by far the least reliable. Use it carefully, if at all, just in case my source is completely wrong. Proceed with caution on that tip. Approaching the wrong person on this matter could get BIB, even you, hurt. Not necessarily physically, more career-wise. I wouldn't want to see you land yourself in hot water with people you and I would rather not meet or mess with in broad daylight, let alone at night."

"Gotcha! Have any names for me?"

"Here." Hunter pulled a small piece of paper from his pants pocket and placed it in Colonel Burke's hand.

"Thanks for the 'heads up', Magnus."

Nodding, Colonel Burke stood up. He shook Hunter's hand before giving him a bear hug.

"Thanks, BIB 13! See you again soon...after the Test Match of course. Can I make it up to you in any way?"

"Not necessary. Trevor, you know I'm always here for you, so no need to put yourself out. My doing this helps keep an old man's mind active. I'll go home now and watch the rest of Day 1 on television. I never go to the Oval after a Test Match day's play has started. I'll be in my usual seat bright and early tomorrow morning though for sure, right behind the bowler's arm."

"Of course. I understand –"

"Trevor on second thought, was your offer of 'making it up to me' real?"

"Yes, it was, that is if I can afford it," said Colonel Burke with a chuckle.

"Good. Then please invite Anna and me over for one of Diane's seafood dinners. We haven't had one of those since we celebrated my last birthday in January."

"That's a done deal. Let Diane know when you're both free to come over."

"Good man... I will. Now, you'd better get going..."

"Right. Later, old friend."

With a final nod, Colonel Burke left Hunter to find Diane. They spoke briefly and he kissed her on her forehead before leaving to return to BIB HQ. He knew that she would take good care of Hunter until he was ready to head home.

Before he set off on the return journey to BIB HQ, Colonel Burke unfolded the small piece of paper he'd been given by Hunter to see if he recognised either of the two names written there.

He didn't, at least not at first. Neither name had any criminal-like connection that immediately jumped out at him. Colonel Burke could not recall BIB having any evidence on either person, even of an anecdotal nature suggesting any involvement in criminality.

Once he got moving, Colonel Burke thought some more. While the two persons may not have been knowingly involved in any confirmed local, regional or international criminal activity, he vaguely recalled that both names had been mentioned during the margins of a *P.A.A.N.I.* meeting eighteen months earlier, around Barbados' celebration of its fiftieth anniversary of Independence. The talk back then had been whether or not consideration should be given to rewarding either person with any of the special national honours then available. They had not made it to the serious consideration stage because Jeremie had mentioned that they were on a list of 'other Barbadians' who had also been under consideration for one of the fifty Barbados Jubilee Honour awards, but were found to be involved in one or two *fishy* things, though nothing of a criminal nature. What these things were never got mentioned. One of the names listed had also surfaced again at the Christmas party he and Diane had hosted four months earlier.

Colonel Burke decided that, once back in his office, he would ask his SIR team to check out the two persons and anything on their known legal (or otherwise) activities over the past three years or so to see what, if anything was there that could be looked at more closely. So far, the ECC security project had not kept his two operatives in BIB's SIR, Dr Samuel Atkins (code number V70) and Margaret Pearson (code number A18) busy, so he knew that they had capacity to run the checks he needed. They both loved having a 'license to poke around' from their Director.

***

Chapter Sixteen

Suspension

While Magnus Hunter and Colonel Burke were having their discussion at the latter's home, a messenger arrived at BIB HQ in a Cabinet Office vehicle.

"Good day. I'm looking for Mr James Johnson," he said.

Riley Morris, BIB operative (code number C16) was on front desk duty that morning, so he called JJ down to BIB's reception area to see the messenger.

"Hello, I'm Johnson?"

"Mr James Johnson, senior team leader here at BIB?"

"Yes, I'm he."

Without answering, the Cabinet Office messenger presented him with an ON-SERVICE envelope and asked him to sign the book he was carrying to confirm delivery and receipt.

"My friend, what's this all about?" asked JJ.

"Not sure, sir. I'm just the messenger. Guess you'll know what's in there once you open it. Good day, sir."

The messenger also handed a second ON-SRVICE envelope to Riley, requesting that he also sign for and would pass that envelope onto the person to whom it was addressed as soon as possible.

With that, the messenger turned away and headed back to his vehicle.

Strange, JJ thought. He started to walk back down the corridor.

On reaching his work station, JJ opened the envelope.

What he read made him instantly sit down in the chair behind his desk. The contents completely surprised him, so much so that he had to read the letter's contents a second time.

Is this some kind of a joke? he thought.

Fred, passing by on his way back from the conference room to his work station which was across from JJ, noticed JJ's posture and stopped in his tracks.

"What's up, buddy?" he asked softly.

JJ looked up and showed him the letter he had just received.

While Fred was reading, JJ made a quick phone call to Vanessa. In a low but calm voice, he told her to come and pick him up from BIB HQ as quickly as she could.

Before she could ask him why, or what was wrong, JJ had hung up the phone.

Something was wrong. She did not know what it was, but would find out shortly. This was not normal.

***

Vanessa Johnson had returned from the supermarket fifteen minutes earlier with the week's shopping. It was more convenient to shop for the family's needs before the afternoon rush.

So, she was alarmed by JJ's call. Nevertheless, she moved quickly having already put away most of the food items. Leaving the rest of the groceries on the kitchen countertops, Vanessa grabbed her car and house keys before re-setting the alarm to the house so as to go and collect JJ as he'd requested her to do.

Vanessa did what she did when tense…hum her favourite church song as she manoeuvred her car out of the driveway. JJ was just ten minutes away, Friday afternoon traffic permitting.

***

Fred's mouth fell open.

This can't be right!

To ensure that he fully comprehended the significance of what he'd just read, Fred sat down in the chair next to JJ's desk and started to read the letter addressed to his colleague for a second time, slower this time.

Meanwhile, JJ had started to clean out the draws of his desk. He placed the few personal items he kept there into his backpack. He also removed what was a meaningful item that had sat on his desk for years, He left all other items that were the property of BIB where they lay. JJ studied the item he had removed for a moment before carefully placing it in his backpack. It was a wood carving that had been presented on his fortieth birthday to him by Mark Egwell, his best friend outside of BIB.

It was a Bible verse which read: **'The Lord your God will be with you wherever you go…' (Joshua 1: 9).**

Given the kind of work that JJ had done for BIB in recent years, along with his immediate circumstances, he found that these words offered him some immediate comfort at this trying time in his life.

Fred, who had now looked up from reading the letter sent to JJ, noticed JJ's last action and instantly recalled the words on the carving. Having read them many times before but never pondered their full meaning, he now found himself doing so…

Just then, JJ spoke to him.

"I'm out of here, Fred. I'll take that if I may."

JJ stood up and gently took the letter from Fred. He also picked up the envelope the letter had come in which was still lying on his desk and began to leave the room, heading in the direction of the stairs.

Fred looked around to see if any other BIB operatives had seen all that had just taken place. Luckily, only Mohammed and Jayne were at their work stations and neither were looking in their direction, nor had heard their short and soft exchanges.

Fred decided to speak with Joe. She was somewhere in BIB HQ and not immediately in sight. Nor did he know where to start looking for her. His luck was in, because a minute later Joe reappeared, coming from the direction of the ladies' bathroom. Fred rushed over to her before she could reach her work station and insisted that he speak with her urgently and in private.

"About what, Fred? I'm starving and about to eat lunch. Can't it wait till I'm finished?"

"No, it can't," said Fred sternly, firmly grabbing her hand. Joe knew only too well what that grip meant. Trouble was about.

"Right. Coming," she responded.

With that, Fred let go of her and strode purposefully away, heading towards the conference room. Joe followed him quickly, unsure of what to make of Fred's urgency.

"*Well?*" she asked somewhat irritated once she'd closed the door behind her. No one else was in BIB's conference room.

Fred wasted no time in telling her about the contents of the correspondence JJ had just shared with him. He also told Joe what JJ's and his reaction to it had been. Joe was in disbelief. She, like Fred, was shocked at this development. They deciding that Fred should go off in search of JJ to speak further with him before Vanessa arrived at BIB HQ to collect and take him away. They did not want JJ to do anything stupid as a result of having received that letter.

They also decided that Joe would speak with Colonel Burke upon his return to BIB HQ to inform him of what had earlier transpired. Joe hoped that, with some luck, Colonel Burke would not be unduly delayed and would be back shortly, even if it was to be after JJ had left BIB HQ's compound.

Her thoughts of lunch had disappeared. She was very worried about the apparent injustice that had been done to her good friend and colleague JJ.

***

Meanwhile, Fred caught up with JJ in BIB's basement where he had just completed emptying the contents of his locker into a plastics bag.

"Hold on, JJ! What *the hell* is going on man? I don't understand. Don't do this…they *can't* be serious, I mean, they can't do this! *Can they*?"

JJ looked directly at Fred. "Yes, they can…and they *have* Fred. Look, Vanessa should be here any minute to pick me up. I have all that I need from this place, including my clothes and exercise gear, so I only need to grab my personal stuff from the BIB vehicle and I'll be gone."

"JJ, wait up –"

JJ cut across him. "Fred, there's nothing for me to wait up or around for. I'm out. Plain and simple. Come with me. I'll pass you my BIB equipment – vehicle keys, communications equipment, weapon, badge, etc. Give them to the chief once he's back."

Fred followed JJ out in to BIB's section of the car park before speaking.

"JJ, this isn't right man. Let's at least wait till the chief comes back. I'm sure he'll be able to sort this out with one phone call. There's obviously been a big mistake," Fred pleaded.

"No. What's done is done, Fred. Just let me get out my personal items," said JJ, opening the boot of the BIB vehicle he'd used as his own for the past eighteen months. He removed all BIB equipment and handed them to Fred. After closing the boot, JJ opened the front passenger car door and removed his personal belongings from the cubbyhole before also placing these into his backpack. He then closed the vehicle's door and locked it before handing the keys to Fred.

"All yours," JJ said with finality.

JJ was surprised that he'd been able to keep quite dispassionate since receipt of the correspondence from HOPS. He did not (yet) feel any pangs of embarrassment at what had just happened to him, only sadness and disappointment. Was he in denial? Maybe! Perhaps he'd feel differently and be upset in a few days' time once the full meaning of the letter's contents had sunk in. Anger might even follow.

He expected there to be an opportunity to clear his name. He would fight for that, alone if necessary.

Fred, once a fast-talking 'ladies' man', did not know what to say to his very good friend and work colleague. Damn, he knew that something was not right here! He felt, no *believed* that once Colonel Burke was made aware of this situation, he would 'make this all go away', if not on his return to BIB HQ, soon thereafter through phone calls he would make. One of those might even be to the country's leader.

"Hey, JJ, what if I get Joe to drop me home later to pick up my personal ride which I then lend you?" asked Fred.

"Thanks, Fred, but I don't think I'll have any place to go today once I'm back home."

There was silence between them. Feeling that he had hurt Fred's feelings, JJ changed his mind.

"Ah, what the hell, maybe I'll take you up on your offer tomorrow. I really don't want to inconvenience Vanessa from her usual routine by having to borrow her vehicle. Your car might come in handy after all," responded JJ.

"No problem," said a relieved Fred.

Five minutes later, Vanessa drove JJ away from BIB HQ. It was not often that JJ sat in the front seat of Vanessa's vehicle. Unkindly, as they left the compound, Craig David's *Walking Away* was being played on the radio station Vanessa was tuned to. JJ recognised the song's poignancy given his situation. Vanessa did not.

Fred and JJ did not say their goodbyes before JJ's departure either. Somehow, in each of their minds, both knew that their work association would continue unaffected by this incident, a mistake…a potentially bad and debilitating one for JJ and possibly BIB.

Fifteen minutes after JJ's departure, Colonel Burke arrived back at BIB HQ. Riley Morris handed him the ON-SERVICE envelope addressed to 'Colonel Trevor Burke, Director, Barbados Intelligence Bureau'. It was also marked 'Private and Confidential'. In the lower right-hand corner on the front of the envelope was stamped Cabinet Office, over which showed hand-written initials he instantly recognised.

"Strange, I've never gotten one of these before. It must either be a promotion or my dismissal," he said to Riley Morris with a smile as he started to leave the reception area.

"Surely to be the former, sir," responded Riley.

"If so, will you pay the additional taxes on the few extra dollars I might get?"

"No sir, but I'd certainly come along for the free drinks you'll host for your BIB operatives at your promotion party!"

"Good answer! I'd expect nothing less, young man," said Colonel Burke with a laugh as he headed up to his office.

Joe, who had by now eaten her fish cutter, green salad and drank her juice, was waiting for Colonel Burke. She started to approach him as soon as she saw him.

"Sir, can I please speak urgently with you? It's about…"

"Alright, Joe, just give me a couple of minutes please. I need a cup of coffee and to make a couple of telephone calls. Then, I promise, I'll come right out to you."

"Right sir…but I think you're *really* going to want to hear what I have to tell you," she persisted.

"*Okay,* Joe. I promise to get to you as quickly as I can, but give me five please," said Colonel Burke while continuing on into his office.

Joe nodded in submission. She also noticed that Colonel Burke had an envelope in his hand. She wondered if he knew what she so badly and urgently wanted to tell him. Perhaps he was already in the process of doing something about JJ?

***

Colonel Burke sat down in the chair behind his desk. He placed the envelope he had been given onto it and poured out the full mug of coffee he'd promised himself, before switching on his computer. After taking a couple of mouthfuls of coffee, he looked up the telephone number of a longstanding Caribbean friend from their days together at City University in London. Colonel Burke also wanted to speak with someone in Barbados he knew well to ask them a big favour.

Out of curiosity, before he made either call, Colonel Burke decided to open the letter he had been given while his computer continued to go through its warming and security procedures. He put down the mug and started to open the letter, but stopped. He had *sensed* that something was not quite right outside of his office on his way in, but it had only now hit him. Besides Joe, none of his operatives were at their work stations. Why was that? It was an unusual occurrence to see the BIB operations centre almost bare of human beings. That, plus Joe's demeanour signalled something was up. But what? *Strange.* He would find out after making his two calls.

Colonel Burke decided to examine this one piece of correspondence and finish his coffee before going to hear what Joe wanted to tell him. He would also establish where and what his missing operatives were up to. He knew that three of them were 'out in the field' at New Kensington Oval as part of the ECC security project. Another two were in BIB's SIR doing specific ECC-related work, which meant that seven operatives (himself, Joe and five others – well six if you excluded Riley Morris who was on reception duty), should be somewhere close-by.

Colonel Burke finished opening the envelope before taking a mouthful of coffee and starting to read its contents. What he saw caused him to involuntarily drop the mug, resulting in him spilling coffee everywhere – down the front of his trousers, on the envelope, the desk itself and the floor. He was shocked. No, Colonel Burke was mad with himself for spilling the mug of coffee all over the place, but more so, at the letter's contents and the person who had written it.

This is what Joe must have wanted to speak to me about. How did she know about this?

Anger was an emotion Colonel Burke seldom showed and had long learnt to control from his days as a senior BDF officer and through subsequent senior leadership courses and Special Forces-type training that he had undertaken overseas. So, while he did not swear because of this discipline, his throat was dry and he only eventually said incredulously, "What the devil is all this? Are they pulling my chain?"

The letter stated:

Cabinet Office,

Government Headquarters,

Bay Street,

St Michael

Friday, 20 April 2018

Mr James Johnson,

Senior Team Leader,

Barbados Intelligence Bureau,

Welches,

Christ Church.

Dear Mr Johnson,

RE: PRISON RUN (PR) ESCAPE, BARBADOS

I have decided to suspend you from all duties at BIB with immediate effect for three working days in the first instance.

Investigations are ongoing to establish what role you, or your 'Gold Team' might have played in, or failed to undertake (i.e. follow the correct procedures) during the PR of Wednesday, 18th April 2018 from HMP Dodds, St Philip to District 'A' Magistrate Court, St Michael during which there was an attempted escape of five prisoners' where BPS and RBPF officers were injured as a result. Two of the prisoners remain at-large, with one of them being rated as a major danger to society.

Your Director has been copied in on this correspondence. I will advise you of further developments as the investigation develops or its outcome.

Yours sincerely,

Winston P. Smith

Dr Winston Peter Smith GCM, Cabinet Secretary / Head of the Barbados Public Service (HOPS)

cc: Colonel T. Burke, Director, BIB

After attempting to wipe himself, the envelope and his desk down (and not making a good job of any of these tasks), Colonel Burke hurried out of his office.

Still no BIB operatives were visible. He made his way to the conference room where he found seven of them, including Joe. Samuel and Margaret had come up from the SIR, as had Riley from BIB's reception desk to join their other operatives. With Colonel Burke's attendance, there were now eight BIB operatives in the conference room. There was of course no JJ.

The operatives stopped speaking as their Director entered the room.

Fred did not give Colonel Burke a chance to speak.

"Glad you're back, chief. What's all this crap about JJ? This is bullshit, if I may say so, and with all due respect to you. I believe, speaking on behalf of everyone in this room…that we're *not* happy. This seems very, very unfair and unjustified and…*unwarranted*. What can we do about this?"

Colonel Burke knew his operatives well, his three team leaders best of all. Fred was not someone who often spoke first or loudest, unless asked or he was particularly peeved about something. As this had rarely ever taken place in public, this was unusual. Colonel Burke knew that Fred was JJ's closest friend in BIB…they had gone through a lot together since Fred had joined the agency.

Colonel Burke therefore forgave the outburst. He recognised Fred's anger once he started to speak and referred to himself in the third person. Colonel Burke also realised that JJ had either shown the letter he had received or at least told Fred about its contents. Fred in turn, must have told their fellow BIB operatives who were in HQ. Operatives who were closest to JJ were sorely upset at what had happened. Others were too, for he was widely admired for his leadership qualities across the BIB family.

Colonel Burke observed that his assembled operatives looked angry and yes, also confused. If he could do a 'Beam me up Scotty' routine, he'd instantly transfer all of them into BIB's gym, for he was sure they all wanted to be hitting something. The punching bags in the boxing area of the gym would come in handy right now for sure.

It occurred to Colonel Burke that HOPS had stirred up a hornet's nest here, unnecessarily so.

Undaunted, Fred continued to speak before Colonel Burke could explain himself. "Unless you were consulted on this action against JJ and did nothing to inform him that this was or might be coming down the pipe…"

"Enough! All of you. Let me make it clear that I don't appreciate being addressed by any of you in this way, now or at any time…even under such trying circumstances as these. I can also see that Fred – indeed all of you, are very upset by this development. Let me assure you that I knew nothing about this, in fact, it appears that I've only found out about it after all of you! Let me speak with JJ and the person who issued this directive. Can I suggest we re-assemble again in say, an hour from now? I promise to give you an update on this unfortunate situation then. For now, let's get back to work folks, we have not only the ECC project to support, but other matters that we're aware of, to deal with as well. By the way, where's JJ?"

"He's left the building. He called Vanessa and asked her to collect him, so I guess he's home, or nearly there. His desk, locker and BIB vehicle have been cleared of all his personal belongings. He gave all his official BIB equipment to Fred who will pass it all over to you shortly. JJ's BIB vehicle is also in the car park," said Joe.

"How long ago did he leave?" asked Colonel Burke.

"Half an hour, no more like forty minutes ago," stated Fred.

"Damn it! Okay. As I said, you all get back to whatever you were doing. Fred and Joe please come to my office in…another fifteen minutes. Mohammed and Jayne too."

With that, he left the conference room and headed back to his office to make some calls. Six to be precise.

***

The first call had been made to a VIP in a neighbouring Caribbean country to ask a favour. The second was to a fellow *P.A.A.N.I.* Head where another favour was also requested. The first two calls made by Colonel Burke saw him secure consideration, understanding and agreement to his requests.

***

The third call was more difficult, but Colonel Burke had to make it, and a point.

The person who had written, signed and dispatched JJ's letter was none other than Dr Winston Peter Smith GCM, Cabinet Secretary and Head of the Barbados Public Service (HOPS). As HOPS, Dr Smith was the most powerful public servant in Barbados. Administratively, he was required to provided Colonel

Burke, as JJ's Head of Department, with a copy of the letter that had been hand-delivered to JJ.

Dr Smith did not duck from taking Colonel Burke's call. In fact, he had expected to hear from Colonel Burke before day's end, just not this soon!

This was the one time that the usual pleasantries were not exchanged. There was an abruptness about their conversation, so much so that Dr Smith felt the need to explain why he had taken the action he had against JJ. It was based on the interim reports he had received and reviewed from the Superintendent of Prisons and the lead RBPF and BPS officers and BIB operative from the PR. These documents had led Dr Smith to an interim conclusion and the action he had then taken.

Colonel Burke told Dr Smith that he did not buy the reasons being presented for JJ's interim suspension. JJ and his Gold team had done what had been necessary in extraordinary circumstances. They had played things by the book. Why therefore had no one else, e.g. Lt. Colonel Simon Innis, Head of BPS/ Superintendent of HMP Dodds, been also handed a similar suspension?

"No comment," was Dr Smith's response.

The conversation was not going well. Colonel Burke had not expected it to. Dr Smith did not ask Colonel Burke if he had spoken to or met with JJ since his letter had been sent and delivered as they both knew was required. Nor did Colonel Burke volunteer this information, reflecting to himself that it was a question best not asked by Dr Smith or answered by himself at this time. Colonel Burke recognised that as this had not been done, JJ's interim suspension could not take effect until Monday.

Colonel Burke decided to end the conversation. The situation did not make any sense to him. JJ was an excellent, reliable and hard-working BIB operative. His best and most senior operative, no less. He would do all that he could to help JJ out of this situation, just as he would have done for any BIB operative where he felt they had acted in the correct way while responding to any dangerous situation.

You're entitled to your opinion and to pass judgment on what you see as the facts, but not to what the facts are, he thought, hanging up the phone.

***

As he replaced the phone, Dr Smith smiled uncomfortably. He'd only done his job – everything by the book and rules.

He knew Colonel Burke, and James Johnson would also do theirs. Here was an opportunity for BIB to help correct a mistake before things got really out of hand. There was a need to recapture the two escaped prisoners quickly – particularly Power. A successful outcome would repair the damage done to BIB's esteemed reputation as Barbados' best security agency suited to assisting the RBPF and BPS in achieving this recapture quickly.

Dr Smith would never acknowledge that the call he'd received at home early the previous morning had influenced in any way the actions he had taken since entering his office yesterday.

But it had. He was in a bind, but only he knew it.

***

By the time the four BIB operatives tried to join him in his office, Colonel Burke had made the first three of his six calls and was about to start his fourth. He asked his operatives to give him another ten minutes before returning.

The fourth he made was to Magnus Hunter.

"Can we meet again urgently, this time at the Barbados Museum in say, another hour and a half?"

"Yes, if you insist, Trevor," was the prompt response he had anticipated and now heard from Hunter.

***

Colonel Burke's fifth call was to his two operatives who had returned to the secure intelligence room (SIR) in BIB HQ. He said he would come and see them in about thirty minutes. They agreed to stay put and await his arrival.

In the meanwhile, Colonel Burke gave them the two names that had been presented to him by Hunter, requesting that they start looking for anything BIB had or could otherwise find on either person.

Anything at all.

***

The sixth and final call Colonel Burke made was to JJ.

He had considered calling JJ first after his meeting with his operatives, but had decided to gather as much new information as possible from a variety of sources before doing so. There was no need for him to speak with Superintendent Innis, as he had recently spoken with him on his way back into the office following his meeting at home with Hunter. By speaking with others, Colonel Burke felt he would have a better idea of how best to set up what he was thinking of asking JJ to do overnight. It would allow JJ the opportunity to play a potentially major role in retrieving the prisoner escape situation – and, given present circumstances, revive his own position.

Colonel Burke intended to tell JJ that he'd also received a copy of Dr Smith's letter, was sorry it had been written, and that the interim suspension was only that, *temporary*. He also had something for JJ to do.

***

Back at the Johnson's residence, JJ sat with Vanessa in their kitchen at the breakfast table. Vanessa had prepared lunch – flying fish, mash potatoes and green salad before she had gone to the supermarket. JJ had barely touched his and was quiet for a while. She checked her phone, not wanting to break in on whatever it was he was thinking about.

"*Shit*," he suddenly said, pushing away his plate and standing up.

"What is it, JJ?" Vanessa asked alarmed. She was wondering if the suspension letter he had received made him realise, perhaps belatedly, how grave his situation might be going forward. She had given no thought to how they would explain JJ's situation to family and friends.

Though it was three days later, JJ now not only remembered, but felt confident that he had recognised the well-dressed man who had sat on his own in P's Disco at table #6 on the previous Tuesday night. JJ had not noticed when the man had left, but surmised that he must have done so around 10:00 p.m.

"It's okay, V. I'm in control. Just had a light bulb moment, as Samuel at the office often says. I need to follow through on it," said JJ.

"Honey, everyone's going to be there for you. We're sure what happened Wednesday wasn't your fault. The powers that be on Bay Street have rushed to judgment, gotten it all wrong –"

"No, V! I don't mean that. Yes, I'm disappointed about the suspension, but that's not what's on my mind right now."

"What is then?" asked Vanessa.

"Well, I'm pretty sure I saw Dr Lewis on Tuesday night at P's Disco."

"JJ, you mean the Deputy Central Bank Governor who's missing? The news says that the man has not been seen since leaving his office late on Tuesday afternoon. You sure you saw him, or just someone looking *like* him? If you're right, you're probably one of the last people to have seen him on Tuesday. What would he be doing in P's Disco anyway?" Vanessa asked.

"To hear good music, grab a meal and a couple of drinks? Why not? It was still early. Perhaps he'd heard that I played at P's Disco twice a week and wanted to catch my set," was JJ's quick response.

Vanessa punched him softly on the arm. At lease her husband had not totally lost his sense of humour.

"Yeah. The great JJ, the DJ of Dr Lewis' dreams! He wanted to hear you play –"

"And why not? I'm not that bad you know. Or so the patrons tell me. Seriously V, the guy could simply be someone who loves back in time (BIT) music, and so came to relax for a while before going home."

"Do you recall seeing him in the club before Tuesday night?"

"No."

"JJ, are you sure about this?"

"Look V, there's only one way for me to be one hundred per cent certain that it was him. Please call Pierre and ask him to meet me at the club in say…thirty minutes. It's very important that I review the club's CCTV tapes of that night's patrons for the first couple of hours," JJ stated.

"Finish your meal before you go?"

"Sorry V, not really in the mood to eat. I've got one or two things on my mind."

"Yes, but –"

Just then, the landline rang, stopping their conversation dead in its tracks. Vanessa answered it.

"Hello," said a slightly exasperated Vanessa.

"It's Colonel Burke, Vanessa. Please may I speak with JJ?"

Vanessa passed JJ the phone, mouthing Colonel Burke before quickly leaving the room to give him some privacy.

"JJ. Can we talk? I've read a copy of the letter you got from HOPS. I'm so sorry –"

JJ cut him off.

"Chief, you know this is all –"

"Easy, JJ. I've just finished speaking with HOPS. He said that, having read the four initial reports submitted by relevant parties, including yourself, he decided to issue an interim suspension of you as only he has the authority to do. It's for three working days in the first instance, starting from today, as the letter states. If, by the end of this period, intervening investigations suggest that additional action needs to be taken against you or others in authority who might be held responsible, in part or whole, for the prisoner escape incident he would initiate such action after consulting with the PM and the Public Sector Oversight Committee (PSOC) Chair. The matter could then be referred to the full PSOC Board at its next monthly meeting that's set for mid-May.

"My understanding is that if, and only *if*, it gets to such a meeting, a hearing would then follow at which you would be entitled to have a representative accompany you, a family member, work colleague or lawyer when you appear. A Q & A session would form part of that process. Following that meeting, a decision would be taken by the PSOC on what action should follow – a lengthy suspension, dismissal or clearing your name of any formal charges brought. Of course, you may not…correction, I cannot see you being alone in such a situation if it even got so far as a PSOC meeting. But I promise you, JJ, I'll do my best to make this all go away well before then," stated Colonel Burke optimistically.

"Hell! Well, I never. Are you sure of this process? I, well my Gold team, have done nothing wrong here. After all that I've done for BIB? This incident wasn't of my team's making. Truth be told, without us being on scene, more persons could have gotten hurt and more prisoners escaped, 'cause none of our partner organisations were in any state to help themselves, let alone stop anything else from happening, what with their busted-up vehicles and all. Yes, as Leader of BIB's Gold team, I accept responsibility for the fact that the prisoners did not get to court for their appearances on Wednesday, but without us being on scene, we might be looking for all five and not two escaped prisoners," said an annoyed JJ.

"I know all of that, JJ…and I agree with you. Your Gold team did well from where I sit and all that I've since heard and seen written about the incident from others. I told HOPS so when we had our first conversation yesterday and again just now. I don't think he accepts that his decision may have been hasty or unfair, for in his eyes, and I gather from some of those at yesterday's Cabinet meeting, somebody has to carry the can, for now at least –"

JJ cut in. "You're telling me that I've drawn the short straw as it were?" he asked.

"I guess so. Look, I've learnt in this business that it's easy to do negative things, harder to do positive ones," was Colonel Burke's careful answer.

"Well, well," was all JJ could say.

"Listen, JJ. There's a view, indeed a clear expectation that these incidents will all be solved by Monday morning. In the circumstances, the 'can carrier' has to be somebody in a leadership role and unfortunately, you're that person. I've been assured that nothing about your suspension will be placed in the public domain until after the weekend. Experience tells me that eventually, the person who will take the hit will be Innis. Believe you me, he's in greater 'do-do' than you. Two reasons he's not been shut down yet. First, HOPS must know that a lack of organisational resources contributed to the incident. Second, one of Innis' closest, most trusted subordinates must have leaked the PR route. I understand that he's been given two working days, effectively until 4:00 p.m. Monday, to establish who that person is and collect the evidence on when, how and why they sold out. Hopefully by then, the missing pieces will all have been put back into the bottle."

"Great, so I'm the patsy being hung out to dry…the fall guy for Innis. Lucky old me," said JJ.

"I guess but look, I have a task for you. Complete it before the end of Monday and all will be well. Please meet me at 'Everglades' at 6.00 p.m. today. Bring along your *wet gear*. You're going on a trip for two or three days so will need your equipment. You'll have to apologise in advance to Vanessa for me…tell her you should be back home to her and the kids by Tuesday latest. You'll not be able to tell her or anyone else where you're going. I'll provide more details when we meet."

"Gotcha chief."

"One more thing. I told HOPS though I'd received his correspondence to you, you'd already left the office before I could meet with or discuss the contents with you. Therefore, according to PSOC Regulation 7 Part 2 (iii), the three-working days' suspension cannot become effective until we've held our formal face-to-face meeting on Government premises on a normal day of the week. Our session later this evening won't count, meaning that your suspension hasn't formally started yet. I'll return your BIB equipment when I see you. The mission you will undertake later will thus be official and legitimate," said Colonel Burke.

"Fine by me," responded JJ.

"Good. Six o clock."

There was a *click* as the call was ended.

JJ wasted no time finding Vanessa. She was in the sitting room fixing the flowers she had earlier bought outside of the supermarket into a vase.

***

Chapter Seventeen
Rising Tension

The discovery just before 2:00 p.m. in an Anglican church compound cemetery's car park in the eastern parish of St. John of a man wearing a blue T-shirt and a pair of jeans in a S-registered vehicle merited attention.

The cemetery workers who had stumbled on the gruesome discovery had arrived to work on the three burials they expected that afternoon. Given the ongoing ECC security project and search for the two escaped prisoners, RBPF patrol cars had been seen regularly in the area, but none of the workers had known the patrol cars to visit the cemetery's car park. So, one of the workers made a call to the police hotline and reported the incident, while another worker headed out to the main road to catch any patrol car that might be passing by. They were in luck, for a patrol car from District 'C' police station in St Philip soon came around the corner and was directed to the cemetery's car park.

What the two RBPF officers and one BDF soldier found was not pleasant. The senior RBPF officer in charge of the three-person patrol team, quickly analysed the scene before circling the parked vehicle. He made a decision and spoke directly to his junior RBPF colleague.

"We must alert the station. Tell them to send a doctor, detectives and a forensics team to this location. The undertaker boys too, as soon as possible. We have a deceased male in a parked vehicle at what looks like a suicide, but may be something else."

"Will do," said his colleague moving away to make the call.

The third member of the patrol team looked on, rifle in hand as if he was standing guard over the area.

***

JJ told Vanessa, "The chief told me that he has my back on this one, no matter how it looks at present. He has a job for me to do for him, so I'll be gone later this evening for a day or two, maybe three."

"What's that all about JJ? I'm confused. What should I tell the kids, given what's already happened today?" asked Vanessa.

JJ could not answer her first question.

"I'll find out more when I meet him. Why not take the kids by your parents to spend the weekend? That way they'll not be many questions to answer. It'll just be that I've had to go away for a couple of days. Oh…did you call Pierre for me?"

"Yes – he'll meet you at the club around 3:15 p.m."

"Thanks. No need to rush off then. After I've visited the club, I'll come back here to see the kids once you've brought them home from school. We can all have an early supper together before I leave… I'll need to be gone by 5:45 p.m."

"Right but, JJ, I'm worried about you and for our family."

"V, don't! I'm good. We'll all be fine, trust me. I'll go and try to eat what you've prepared for me before going off to meet Pierre. I'll have to be warm it up though."

Vanessa nodded and picked up her phone to call her parents to ask if the kids could come over and spend the weekend with them. Vanessa anticipated that they would enthusiastically say yes. However, on the spur of the moment, she decided against calling. Knowing that JJ would now be away for a few days, she did not want to be alone and so the children would be good company for her.

She found JJ in the kitchen and told him of her decision. He smiled. Though Vanessa's parents doted on both of their only grandkids and Vanessa and JJ liked it that way, keeping his family together in his absence was probably best on reflection. Angela and Andrew loved visiting their grandparents in the country or when Granma and Granddad visited them. But this weekend was not now going to be one of those occasions.

JJ decided to finish his meal and wait until Vanessa had left to collect the children from school before he would retrieve his *wet gear* from its special place underneath the stairs in an area apart from where she stored the family's Christmas decorations.

***

Colonel Burke spoke with Fred, Joe, Mohammed and Jayne following his discussion with JJ. He had in fact kept them waiting another ten minutes beyond that which he had asked them to return to his office. The four operatives knew that in the time since his meeting with all available BIB operatives in the conference room that Colonel Burke must have been working on something, but they did not know what.

"Right folks. This, in my view has gone way past *Houston we have a problem*. I've taken some action that should start to alleviate the problem over the next few days, but I cannot tell you what I'm doing yet. So, you'll have to trust me on this for now. I've spoken with JJ. Both he and Vanessa are okay, both understandably stunned at today's rapid developments."

"This is all crap, sir. Sorry, I mean unfair."

"I know, Fred, but we must keep it together –"

"Look, is JJ really off the job, sir?" asked Joe.

"That's what my copy of JJ's letter says, for the next few days at least. But you all know that a lot can happen quickly in this business, so don't rule me or JJ out just yet. BIB must quickly help find the two missing escaped prisoners and also assist with investigating the disappearance of Dr Lewis, on top of the ECC security project. Fred, I'm tasking you and Jayne with relating to someone I think you may know who is working on the RBPF team seeking the two prisoners' recapture, Sergeant Billy Browne. Remember, he's still part of Special Branch's Visitors CPU unit and is at New Kensington Oval for the Test Match, but is otherwise also working on the prisoners' escape investigation."

"And what about Mohammed and me, sir?" It was Joe, asking another question.

"I haven't forgotten you two. Check in with Johnny Vickers, your old boss. He's leading the investigation on Dr Lewis' disappearance. The PM's promised the country that his security agencies will be able to resolve all of these recent incidents by this weekend, so all hands-on-deck. Commissioner Jeremie is working the St Lawrence Gap incident directly, so hopefully, between us all, we can make the Prime Minister a happier bunny than he is right now if we're able to wrap up these incidents. Once we do so, we can all start getting some sleep again! Now, if you'll excuse me, I have a couple of people to visit."

Nobody smiled as the four operatives left Colonel Burke's office to contact their respective RBPF colleagues. Their ongoing ECC security project duties remained in tack and would hopefully continue running smoothly, enabling them to also complete these additional duties.

Fred and Joe did not forget that they also had a personal assignment to complete for a friend and colleague.

Meanwhile, although they were not listening, it appeared from the radio and television coverage of the Test Match that the West Indies team, in the post-lunch session, was beginning to claw its way into a position of strength. Only time would tell if that would continue.

***

Once the doctor, detectives and forensics team had arrived, the patrol car team were able to take a closer look at but did not touch the vehicle or body. Cash was found in the car. A phone, along with a wallet was also in the driver's door pocket which contained a Barbados I.D. HMP Dodds I.D.'s and a driver's license.

"They all carry the name George Telford. Hey, I know this guy, he's the second man at Dodds," said the lead detective.

"You sure?" asked the senior RBPF officer who had arrived earlier in the patrol car.

"Yeah, it's him alright! I went to school with his sister. We also played cricket together for a St James side a few years back. God, what a mess this is." It was the BDF soldier speaking.

Before any further conversation, the phone in the door pocket rang.

"Don't answer that," said the lead detective. "The forensic crew will need to attend to that later."

Everyone did as he said. The phone rang six times before cutting out. The phone could be a useful tool to help explain this situation. The detective realised that being a prison official, and a senior one at that, meant that this incident might have a bearing on the prisoners' escape from two days before.

The lead detective was asking himself three questions. *Why had George Telford killed himself? Or, if he had been murdered as was possible, then by whom? Lastly, what was his death connected to?*

Dr Samuel Atkins, ICT lead and Head of SIR and Margaret Pearson his assistant who was his collaborator, were working diligently on the specific tasks that had been allocated to them related to the nine-day ECC security project. This involved monitoring and co-ordinating (if and where necessary) any special communications requested by any of Barbados' law enforcement and security agencies during the short 'sunset life' of that project.

Nothing unusual had taken place between the EEC security project's Tuesday evening launch and this afternoon – at least not from a BIB perspective. There had been no need for them to respond to requests from BIB's sister law enforcement or security agencies to date, meaning that they were not exactly *busy*. Wednesday's prisoners escape, the CBOB Deputy Governor's disappearance and Thursday's early morning St Lawrence Gap attempted robbery and shooting incident, were not related to their role in the EEC security project or BIB's other routine work.

Samuel and Margaret loved their BIB jobs. They worked in a world of technology where they loved to test their skills – often against each other. Which was the quickest, cleanest (and meanest) was a game they often played among themselves. They knew that they were at their best when they co-operated and collaborated on set tasks. Their recent ICT work in the SIR had been nothing short of spectacular, helping BIB to achieve greater success by reaching higher targets that would not have been possible without the infusion of funds BIB had secured in the past year.

Colonel Burke's arrival in their SIR 'den' to specify the unusual task he wanted them to undertake, in addition to the ECC security project work they had been tasked with, was both exciting and extraordinary.

Once Samuel and Margaret comprehended Colonel Burke's 'ask', they agreed it would be fun. The ask enabled them to do something they had indicated a year before could be done, but had never undertaken.

Their task was Mission Impossible-like but right up their street. They were to 'poke around' to try and identify anything through the country's CCTV camera system that might assist BIB in resolving any of the three recent major incidents that had taken place in the country over the past forty-eight to seventy-two hours. The prisoners' escape should take precedence. Any lead generated that was related to this matter were to be reported to Colonel Burke immediately and in person. In addition, anything on either of the missing CBOB Deputy Governor or about the two robbers, would be nice bonuses.

With broad smiles, Samuel and Margaret stated in unison, "Yes, boss, we're onto it."

"Very well," said Colonel Burke before leaving them to meet with Hunter.

***

Over in St Vincent, Power ate the late lunch provided to him having had a rest. He knew that for his own safely, he needed to continue laying low in his first few days of freedom in St Vincent.

His host, Astor 'Brotherman' Delaney, was a man in his mid-thirties. He was the leader of a Rastafarian community group and had been instructed by a 'friend' to pick up a man from a Barbadian ice fishing boat just off the St Vincent coast earlier that Friday morning and to "look after him for the next few days". The arrangement called for Power to be initially hidden by Delaney and others in his Rastafarian group.

"How long before I finally get to settle down somewhere?" asked Power.

"Depends," answered Brotherman Delaney.

"Oh? On what?" persisted Power.

"My brother, when my Rastafarian brothers and sisters are told that it is safe to move you. I expect your police friends in Barbados will by now be aware that you've left the country and could be in a near-by one, possibly SVG. That means that we'll have to be even more careful about how we keep you 'under wraps.' Friends of mine can only get me so far with those in authority here after which, we're on our own man. Get me?"

"Sort of…if you say so. But I thought I'd be good for at least a few weeks with you guys, months even? I expect your support would translate into not being interfered with by the local authorities, no? If I'm wrong, please get me to another island."

"Take it easy, Baje. We got you covered. Things will work out, don't worry. My people are good. Very good. You're pretty safe with us."

"I damn well hope so, Brotherman," said Power.

For the first time since Power left Barbados on the fishing boat, now nearly twenty-four hours ago, he wondered if he'd done the right thing coming to St Vincent.

"Too late to turn back now," he murmured.

"What ya say, Baje?" asked Delaney.

"Nothing."

"Right. Let's get you to your first safe spot, Baje," said Delaney. He rose to leave the converted container they were sitting in, just as the Land Rover he had earlier ridden in drew up with two persons inside.

"Time to go, Baje. In another hour few persons except me, a couple of my people and my main man, will know where you are for the next two days. Even if our police boys and girls work out that you're in Vincie country, they won't be able to track you down within this period. Thereafter it could get more awkward but for now man, you'll be safe here with my group."

"I hear you! You really sure 'bout this, right?" asked Power uncertainly.

"Yep…as I am that Jah is looking over and protecting us all right now and forever," responded Delaney.

"Great, then I'm all ready to go. Lead the way," said Power.

Power started walking to the Land Rover, but Delaney did not follow.

Power stopped and looked back.

"Baje, my people will take you. I'll see you again in a couple of days…on Sunday. Your ride will take you a few miles and you'll then have to do some walking. You up for that?"

"Yes. Two days, you say?"

"Yep."

The driver opened the rear door for Power to enter the Land Rover, before getting behind the wheel. Just before they set off, a second person who had earlier been there, returned to the front passenger seat. They did not speak.

As the Land Rover rolled forward, Power wondered what the next couple of days would be like for him. How would he get through them? He was not used to being in such a rural area, He wasn't a reader, nor did he expect to have the comforts of a television. So, what would he do for two whole days? Perhaps someone would have a powerful radio which would enable him to hear what was going on in the world.

Power spent the forty-five-minute journey between dozing and looking out of his side window as they went deeper and deeper into the Vincentian countryside. When the vehicle finally stopped, he was invited to get out. "This is as far as I go. You and my friend will walk the rest of the way to your destination," said the driver pointing up into the hills.

Power did as he was told. Two rucksacks had been placed on the back seat next to him before the start of the journey. These were removed by the driver. "Take one."

Power obliged. The driver passed the second backpack to the front-seat passenger who had by this time alighted from the Land Rover.

Returning to it, the driver shifted the vehicle into gear and turned it around to head back towards Kingstown. He waved, shouting to his two passengers, "See you in two days. Don't worry Baje, you're in good hands. Sister Jas knows where to go," before he sped off.

Power was flummoxed. He had failed to observe that it was a woman who had sat in the vehicle's front passenger seat. As there had not been any conversation during their journey, he had gotten no inkling that the other passenger wasn't another man.

His mood instantly improved when he looked over at her and saw how attractive the female Rasta was. *This should be an interesting experience*, though Power, reflecting that it would be she and not him who would be in control of their situation for the next couple of days.

"My name is Jasmine Huey. My people call me 'Sister Jas'."

"Jasper Power. Good to know you."

"Likewise. Come on, we better get moving. I hope you can climb," Huey said setting off up the rugged path ahead at a good clip, rucksack on her back.

Power followed her without a word. The second rucksack was now also on his back, but he was thinking. *Maybe, just maybe, this woman will be good to me as we'll be together for a whole forty-eight hours.*

They walked for another fifty yards before starting up into the hills. After ten minutes, Power was puffing but he observed that Huey wasn't. He accepted that she was one strong, no-nonsense woman. It was therefore unlikely that he would get what he wanted from her.

I won't even try, was his final thought as he laboured after Huey.

***

Once in his vehicle, Colonel Burke remembered that following his meeting with Hunter, he had promised himself to call Ryan Appleton at the Ministry of Foreign Affairs and Culture. He needed Appleton to quickly e-mail him a list of the accredited diplomats in Barbados-based Embassies and High Commissions known (or thought) to be responsible for undertaking security (i.e. intelligence) work.

He made the call to Appleton once he was away from BIB HQ. Appleton agreed to respond right away. *Strange, that's the second senior Government person today to request such information, so something's cooking*, he thought.

"What's up, Colonel Burke?" Appleton asked.

"No particular reason, Ryan, but thanks. I owe you."

"No problem. Anytime."

Appleton hung up, knowing that if Colonel Burke asked for information, there was a reason. He was just not being told what it was, like he had not been the first time around either.

***

Forty minutes had passed since Huey and Power had been dropped off when the Land Rover arrived back at the converted container's location. Brotherman Delaney was waiting outside, having already closed up the container and so joined the driver inside the vehicle.

"All's well?" he asked.

"Job done," was the driver's response.

Twenty minutes later, they had made the fifteen-minute journey to Delaney's residence near Kingstown. The first thing Delaney did after going to his bedroom was to call someone he knew well, not as a friend but more as a collaborator.

"Hello," answered a male voice.

"Task completed."

"Thank you. Any problems?"

"None."

"Good. Let's speak again after church on Sunday."

"Fine, I'm always here."

***

In a prestigious Cane Garden residence overlooking Kingstown, there was silence. The recipient of Delaney's call was satisfied. He'd accommodated a requested favour from his Barbadian associate.

They now owed him a favour in return.

***

Samuel and Margaret knew they could not break any of BIB's stipulated rules, regulations or any of Barbados laws in pursuance of their task. They would use the 'free hand' Colonel Burke had extended to them to accomplish their three-fold task as soon as possible. He trusted their judgment. They decided to follow where their ICT noses led them, but first agreed on the systems and methods by which they would operate to achieve the goals they had set for themselves. These included a review and final *are-we-sure* process before any significant findings would be taken to Colonel Burke.

Truth be told, the ECC security project had to date not stretched them. Given the limited traffic they had seen to date, they did not anticipate anything sexy coming their way over the next five days of the project.

Colonel Burke's ask was going to be a challenge, so they got stuck into it.

***

Just after Vanessa set off to collect their two children from school, JJ saw Fred and Joe drive up in separate vehicles, Joe in her BIB vehicle and Fred in his private vehicle. Their arrival would lead to JJ being late for his meeting with Pilgrim at P's Disco.

Fred parked his private vehicle in JJ's driveway, keeping his earlier promise to lend it to him. The usual pleasantries between them over, JJ thanked Fred again for his kindness, friendship and support. As they were about to leave, Fred and Joe indicated that they might call JJ later that evening. JJ did not let on that he would not be there to take their call.

Fred, having joined Joe in her BIB vehicle, waved to JJ before speeding off down the road on their way back to their BIB HQ.

"Don't like how JJ looked, Fred," said Joe with a frown.

"You're kidding me, right? He may be upset, hurt, but JJ's a pro. He'll find a way to deal with this stupid situation. A few days off will probably do him good anyway as he's already worked pretty hard for the year. I expect the chief will have this matter sorted out for him…by the middle of next week, latest."

"Okay prophet, wise guy. I hope you're right. Here's a chance to prove how good your predictions are."

"No problem, Joe. Test me anytime. You know that I'm seldom wrong with my predictions…"

"Yeah, right!"

"But I'm still mad about this because I'm convinced somebody's doing a 'dirty' on BIB – on JJ in particular."

"Who could that be and why?"

"To cover their asses or distract us from something. Time longer than rope. We'll get to the bottom of whatever it is, and soon," Fred said.

"I'm with you on that if what you say is right," responded Joe.

They continued their banter. Joe soon dropped Fred off at BIB HQ before heading on down to New Kensington Oval for her two-hour BIB management stint at the game.

***

JJ was happy to be in the company of his fellow BIB team leaders, but truth be told, he was glad to see the back of them today. They recognised his unwillingness to 'small-talk' and need to have some JJ-time for himself. They were right. He did, but not for the reasons they may have thought.

JJ examined Fred's vehicle. *Nice wheels*! Though this was not the latest model of car as it was now five years old, Fred's personal vehicle had been kept in excellent condition. JJ knew he would not be driving Fred's vehicle much over the next few days, given the unknown nature of the assignment (whatever it was) Colonel Burke had for him to undertake, but he would use it to get to his meeting with Pilgrim.

Before then, he also needed to visit that special place in his home under the stairs to retrieve elements of his *wet gear*. Though JJ had not used this equipment in a while, he knew that, due to his experience and its tried, tested and proven nature, the items he selected were all in excellent working order and most reliable. His *wet gear* equipment reminded him of a life before BIB, Vanessa and his two kids…

After spending a few minutes ensuring that his chosen pieces of equipment were appropriate, JJ secured them in a special backpack. *Ready for action*, he thought as he placed the special backpack into the trunk of Fred's vehicle, before returning to the house to set the alarm.

Leaving his house for a second time, JJ pointed Fred's vehicle in the direction of P's Disco.

***

Pilgrim had waited for JJ to arrival before switching off the building's alarm and opening up P's Disco's staff entrance.

"Thanks a lot for breaking up my afternoon routine, JJ. What's this all about?" asked Pilgrim.

"Sorry, Double P, for having to drag you out this afternoon. BIB business. I need to review your CCTV images for Tuesday night, from opening at 8:00 p.m. till 10:00 p.m.," answered JJ.

"Are you looking for anything in particular?" asked Pilgrim.

"Yes, CBOB's Deputy Governor has been missing since Tuesday night and I'm sure I saw him in here then. I don't remember seeing him here before and I don't think we did anything to him while he was in the club. I just need to be double-sure that it was him I saw. I'd like to see who he interacted with that night, it might give law enforcement agencies leads to follow up on and help in the search for him."

"Fine. I'll set things up for you in my outer office so you can view the CCTV tapes. While you do that, I'll continue working on my tax returns as I was doing at home. I'd like to pass everything to my accountants tomorrow to check behind me. I'd like my returns to be submitted to BRA by the middle of next week. I think BRA will have a refund for me. Again."

"Thanks," said JJ ignoring Pilgrim's tax comments.

"How long will you be?" asked Pilgrim.

"Oh, no more than thirty minutes, an hour at most if I have to look at anything for a second time," responded JJ.

"That suits me, because I'd still like to get some rest before coming back here this evening. With the Test Match on, I expect some extra patrons to visit the club over the next few nights. After what happened on Wednesday night, I don't want to take any chances with my security, know what I mean?"

"Yeah."

"Here goes. The discs from Tuesday night, all of them. Each tape runs for 90 minutes, so I've given you the first of two for that night that will take you up to 11:00 a.m. You fast-forward everything to get through quicker," stated Pilgrim.

"Gotcha," responded JJ.

***

Samuel and Margaret were not looking for anything specific. They would look at everything they felt might be relevant. What a hand to hold in a complex card game.

They pulled up what CCTV footage was available from locations – more specifically the most likely relevant times around when each of the three incidents had or might have taken place. First, for the prisoners rescue they would check available CCTV footage from Six Roads to Bridgetown between 8:00 a.m. and 4:00 p.m. on Wednesday. Second, for Dr Lewis' disappearance, they would examine footage for the Bridgetown area alone from 3:00 p.m. to 7:00 p.m. on Tuesday afternoon. That timeline would cater to times when Dr Lewis was said to have departed from the CBOB and his disappearance (they might get lucky and establish if and how he might have fallen ill, gotten kidnapped or God forbid, committed suicide at a location during the past seventy-two hours). Third, they would look at the St Lawrence Gap incident last as it was the easiest case and shortest timeline to track (that is the 1:00 a.m. to 3:00 a.m. window in which the attempted robbery and shooting were said to have taken place). In each case, they would extend the times and days of their searches as necessary.

Samuel and Margaret would use matching facial recognition system technology (FRST) to help them. Images would be inserted into the system for Jasper Power, Warren Field and Dr Albert Lewis. Amalgamated descriptions by witnesses of the two robbers/shooters from St Lawrence Gap had been placed into various Government data systems. They had found no matches in the RBPF or Immigration Departments, Barbados Licencing Authority (BLA) or the Electoral and Boundaries Commission (EBC) electronic databases of a photographic nature. But hand drawings by RBPF officers of the alleged robbers based on the descriptions given by eye-witnesses early on Thursday morning would later also be scanned into BIB's ICT systems in the SIR to help Samuel and Margaret's efforts at identification of the two culprits.

Throughout this repeat process, they hoped to pick up red notices and if not, at least amber ones. Since seeing a renowned American bass play perform at a London jazz club two years ago, Samuel had grown to love his playing style.

Something he'd read about the bassist in the evening's programme had also stuck with and even grown on him, given Samuel's profession. It was *repetition begets success.*

Samuel and Margaret believed that the processes they would use throughout the rest of the day, night and into the following day if necessary, would bear dividends. If all else failed, they would try to make use of collaborative response graphics (CRG). This allowed law enforcement agencies, particularly the RBPF to view 3-D images off buildings in hostage situations. Perhaps CRG could help them convert the hand drawings into usable photographs which, once inserted into BIB's SIR, might help identify and lead to the capture of both robbers.

***

Superintendent Innis' visit to the crime scene where his now former Deputy had been found dead in his car, was unexpected and painful.

"Good God, who needed to do this to George and why?" was all he could say before quickly moving away from the scene as his stomach started to heave.

"Take it easy, sir," said one of the RBPF officers on the scene.

"Just give me a minute and I'll be alright," said Innis.

Ten minutes later, after notifying his boss, Hon. Sebastian Smith QC MP, Attorney General and Minister of Residential Affairs, he made the heart-breaking call to Mrs Telford to break the news of her husband's untimely and unfortunate passing. He felt it was his duty to call her, even though a RBPF team had been dispatched to the Telford's home which bordered the parishes of St James and Peter.

The circumstances of Telford's demise – the location, why now, the method used and any real or likely potential reasons for it even taking place, would be carefully and fully investigated before any findings would be determined and made known in due course. Even at this point, there was every suggestion that Telford's death might have had something to do with Wednesday's attack on the convoy which was transporting prisoners to court which resulted in the escape of two prisoners, one a very dangerous man.

***

Motby received news of the death of Telford through a telephone call from his Attorney General just after he came out of a meeting with Dr Smith. They'd discussed the latest aspect of the new pay rise for public servants which had to be factored into the next Budget he wanted to present to Parliament by June.

Motby took the news calmly. The questions he asked of his Attorney General could not be answered immediately, but these were promised within the hour.

***

Samuel and Margaret also knew that the installed CCTV cameras had an additional (but hitherto unused) special feature. Their goal was to utilise this feature from their BIB location. Once they were able to get it to work properly, they knew it should enable them to gain access to the conversations involving persons 'in the shot', as it were. That would give them something extra to play with. Through their CCTV camera sweep reviews, BIB's ICT team might secure something relevant to and have a bearing on one, two or all three of the ongoing investigations they were now engaged in.

It turned out that the two CCTV cameras on the old National Insurance building on Fairchild Street were not working. No surprise there! An all but abandoned Government building, so why bother to maintain the CCTV cameras affixed to it? Luckily, there was a CCTV camera on the roof of the neighbouring Government-run Fairchild Street bus stand which directly overlooked Independence Square, specifically the bandstand and Errol Barrow statue's location.

This CCTV camera captured the three 'tourists' who had assembled for their 5:00 p.m. meeting on Tuesday. Also, a private CCTV camera located on top of the commercial bank building at the corner of Fairchild Street also captured a tall Chinese man on the outskirts of Independence Square. He was looking directly at the three individuals while they met. He had then followed them away from Independence Square as they had left.

Samuel and Margaret's discovery of these and other images during Friday night would ultimately help local law enforcement and security agency personnel with their identification. The two tech wizzes were also able to enhance and clarify some of what had been said through this feature of the CCTV cameras at these locations.

254

Scraps of their interactive conversations about local criminal/gang activity would later give Colonel Burke an idea he would employ when he met with the US Ambassador three days later, all courtesy of Samuel and Margaret's technical skill.

***

The Attorney General's second call an hour later to the Prime Minister did not provide the answers to the questions that had been asked of him.

Though annoyed, Motby calmly responded. "No problem, Sebastian. Just let me know when you *have* the answers to my questions please."

"Yes, Prime Minister."

***

Superintendent Innis was puzzled. How had Telford managed to shoot himself in the right side of his temple. To do so, he would surely have used his right hand. But Telford was left-handed, in which case it would have been natural for him to have shot himself on the left side of his temple.

Innis' *eureka* moment.

Telford did not commit suicide. Someone had killed him and tried to make it look like he had killed himself. Innis would personally pass this information onto Commissioner Jeremie forthwith. It changed the nature and would surely broaden the focus of the investigation into Telford's death.

Murder had been committed! Without knowing it, he was thinking like the lead detective on the scene.

What Innis did not know was that a room key card had already been found inside Telford's car by the forensic RBPF crew. It had been collected and so the lead detective was aware of it. The card bore references to a south coast hotel. Once checked out, it could turn out to be a significant factor in helping to identify who might have done or been behind Telford's death.

***

Wharton received a call from Castille.

"Hello?"

255

"Any update on Power's whereabouts?"

"My brother…how you doing, man? Sorry, nothing yet. I'm still check with my sources though."

"Keep me posted on developments."

"Right. Be jolly now."

"Shit." Having ended the call, Castille swore softly in his hotel room. How could this have happened. Perhaps he should have stayed with Power throughout Wednesday night and all of Thursday while he supposedly worked to collect the funds owed to *The Organisation*. No point crying about spilt milk.

So Castille made three decisions. First, he would go for a swim later that afternoon, not in the pool, but in the sea. The experience might help him to think more clearly about what he must do next. He knew he would not be able to return to Miami as early as he had planned. Second, he would call his boss in Miami and report what was currently an unsatisfactory situation regarding their customer. Castille did not really care how his boss responded to his news, or what she now thought of him. She'd expect him to work something out. He would do so by establishing Power's location and then find a way of catching up to him and securing *The Organisation* outstanding funds. This remained his mission.

Third, Castille gave himself another forty-eight (seventy-two hours at most) to achieve his goal. He wanted to be back in the USA by Monday night at the latest, as his plans for the coming week were already being disrupted by his potential overstay in Barbados.

***

From Wharton's perspective, having just taken the third call that day from Castille, he was getting tired of the man. "He's persistent, that's for sure," he mumbled to himself.

Just then, '*Breaking News*' on the radio kicked in… "a body has been found in a vehicle in a St John church cemetery's car park with a gunshot to the head. Suicide is the suspected cause of death. Reporters are here on the scene with police investigators. A funeral home recovery crew is waiting to take away the body. The person is said to have been in their late forties." The reporter did not tell if the person was a man or woman as the body was covered over and police officials were not saying either way.

A suicide...in St John? Which church? Who was the person? Wharton decided to call his mother as she tended to know everything that happened in the parish of St John through her plethora of friends.

She had no news for him. Wharton did not know then who the perpetrator of that crime was, or that the package he had presented to an acquaintance he barely knew some forty-eight hours earlier had been used, or that the death was not a suicide, but was in fact a murder.

***

Hunter's meeting with Colonel Burke took place as they walked around the exhibits of the Barbados Museum, located next door to the Historic Garrison Savannah a couple of miles outside of Bridgetown.

"Sorry to drag you away from your TV, Magnus, but I couldn't speak with you about this on any phone."

"We meet face-to-face twice in one day. What's gotten into you, Trevor?" asked Hunter.

"Well, I have a slight problem. My main man, James Johnson...you know JJ, has just been suspended by HOPS over his team's role in Wednesday's prisoner escape. My team did nothing wrong. Bad call as far as I'm concerned. A hasty decision. Superintendent Innis has gotten off free, at least for now. I've spoken with Dr Smith and given him a piece of my mind. Is he really such a 'by the book' sort of guy?"

"I know Smith only too well! He worked as my Senior Administrative Officer for a spell...possibly twelve years ago on his way up the ladder. He's clever and a very efficient fellow. Yes, he likes to go by the book. I thought back then that he would go far in the service. If he's decided to take action against JJ, he must believe he has good reason for doing so, though I agree with you that his action, if it is as you've outlined, is indeed hasty, bordering on reflex – perhaps given the publicly around the known circumstances of the escape. Do you think this was for show? Has his actions gotten the PM's backing?"

"I've no way of knowing either, but I very much doubt the latter, Magnus. Not spoken with the PM about HOPS action against JJ...yet."

"Will you?"

"Maybe – perhaps later."

"Very well. Now tell me the real reason why I had to leave the comfort of my Berbice chair and wide-screen TV, a retirement gift which you contributed to I might add, to meet you here?"

"Don't miss a beat, do you?"

"I'm getting old, but not dead, Trevor! Oh, and by the way, there's something I should probably mention about Winston. It's what I was never able to quite put my finger on –"

"What's that, Magnus?"

"Well, I don't suppose you've ever had cause to look carefully into his background. Winston didn't come up wealthy – far from. In fact, he was brought up by a one-parent mum who had him young. He only met his father after he grew up. Still looks after his mum. She'd worked two, sometimes three jobs to support herself and her son. Winston's never forgotten that –"

"You're telling me that, like most of us born poor but having ability and by working hard, we manage to succeed at what we do?" Colonel Buke interrupted.

"Let me finish what I'm trying to say, Trevor. Smith won scholarships in his youth. After UWI, he went on to gain his Doctorate in Politics and Sociology from one of the UK universities up north. He now lives comfortably I'd say, with his mum in a big house in Frere Pilgrim. He has no wife or kids as far as I know. Drives a nice vehicle, an Audi if I recall correctly which I must say he is entitled to do. He even part-owns a couple of race horses, one of which you'll recall won the Gold Cup horse-race a couple of years back. Smith seems to be a straight guy. He probably saved up hard in the earlier part of his professional career and now that he's reached the top of the pile, is enjoying himself. No problem with that! They say you can't carry it with you when you pass."

"Very well, Magnus, but you have something else you want to tell me?"

"Still sharp as a razor blade, I see! Yes, I'll confess there was always something that bugged me about Smith, but I still can't put my finger on it. Just a feeling. Could just be my imagination gone awry."

"I hear you, Magnus. Anyway, I wanted to speak with you in person because I'm arranging for JJ to go over to St Vincent to hopefully recapture and return this Power guy. Do you from your past knowledge or current sources know any of the people over there who might have been asked to put up Power? I mean, someone there who might need or want to do Power (or someone here he works for) a favour?"

"Let me think a minute. Yes, there might be a couple no, *three* persons that spring to mind. I'd suggest you follow-up on with your Vincie colleagues on them. Got a piece of paper?"

"Of course, but why don't you just tell me their names?"

"Not my style. Remember this morning? I've always found that the written word is more powerful than the spoken word," said Hunter.

Colonel Burke passed Hunter a small covered notepad.

After a few seconds, Hunter returned the notepad. Lifting the cover, Colonel Burke saw nothing on the first three pages, but on the fourth page were three names of businessmen.

"You sure that these persons are still in these positions?"

"Yes, or at least they were there up to three months ago. I haven't heard that any of them have died, retired, been fired or sold out. The Vincie papers and the internet would have carried it had any of those things happened. My info should be good for your use."

"Then that's fine by me. I'll pass this information to JJ. He'll be able to ask his opposite number to look into their recent dealings. We may get lucky and be able to connect one of them to this Power thing. JJ should have something to give our Vincie cousins at the start of his sojourn."

"Right. I'd now like to return home and get back to my TV please. And don't call me tomorrow while I'm at the game."

"Yes, sir. Thanks again. Appreciate your time."

"My pleasure, Trevor. Wish JJ good luck for me."

***

Chapter Eighteen

Significant Discoveries

Fifteen minutes later, on his way to P's Disco, JJ wondered if things might somehow have been different had he made it his business to speak with Dr Lewis on Tuesday night. But he hadn't.

How important that might turn out to be in helping local law enforcement agencies track down Dr Lewis was as yet unknown. It never dawned on him that Dr Lewis' disappearance *might* or *could*, in some small but important way, be connected to the couple of missing prisoners, Field and Power.

***

It was around this same time that Field, accompanied by his mother and an attorney-at-law, presented themselves to the RBPF officer working the Incident Desk at Oistins police station in Christ Church.

"Hello, may I help you?" asked the RBPF officer, not looking up from the Incident Book he was reviewing.

"Yes please. I'm Jenson Clarke, attorney-at-law. I'm here to present and return my client, Mr Warren Field, to police custody. Your people are looking for him after his escape from legal custody last Wednesday."

Constable Roosvelt Dryer had by now looked up at the three persons standing before him. He recognised Field immediately, even before his lawyer had finished explaining why they were there.

"Uh…yes, of course, you are. Please take a seat. Excuse me a minute," he said.

Reaching for the black telephone that was located on the second tier of the Incident Desk, Constable Dryer dialled four numbers. He spoke softly to Station Sergeant Donald Avery who was the officer in charge of Oistins police station. Less than a minute later, Station Sergeant Avery had moved from his office at the back of the station to the Incident Desk. He was accompanied by two burly RBPF officers. They went directly to Field.

Station Sergeant Avery spoke first with Clarke. Next, he spoke directly to Field before reading him his rights and arresting him in front of his mother and Clarke. There was no fuss as Field was taken into custody.

A few minutes later, Field's recapture was communicated to Jeremie and Innis. Within another half hour, Field would find himself handcuffed to a RBPF officer in the back of a darkened vehicle and on his way back to HMP Dodds. The vehicle he was travelling in was preceded by a RBPF motorcycle outrider. He knew he would eventually find himself back in court, this time facing additional escape charges.

***

Back at P's Disco, JJ was able to confirm that it was indeed Dr Albert Lewis who had been captured by the CCTV footage as he had entered and left the club during the early part of the previous Tuesday night.

"There! I knew I'd seen him that night," exclaimed JJ.

"Found something, JJ?" asked Pilgrim, hearing JJ's excited exclamation.

"Yes. Come, let me show you."

Pilgrim exited his inner office and came to sit down next to JJ, who played back the images, lasting for just over an hour which showed Deputy Governor of the CBOB Dr Albert Lewis' approach and entry to P's Disco at 8:15 p.m. until he left at 9:55 p.m. During that time, he was on his own, appeared to order a couple of drinks and a meal while appearing to enjoy the music. He had seemingly coughed a few times and interfaced with one person, P's Disco waitress Zelda Hughes.

"Double P, can you get me a still, a screen shot of Dr Lewis sitting at the table eating his meal, showing the time? Actually, can I also get ones of his arrival and departure? A copy of the video for the hour or so while he was here would also be helpful please."

"Sure, won't take long. I'll send a copy of everything to your phone and put a set on a disc so you can pass it on to whoever you want, okay?"

"Yes, thanks a million, Double P."

"No problem, anything to help you out. Does this make me some sort of detective, JJ?" asked Pilgrim mischievously.

"I guess so, Double P..." answered JJ, satisfied that his hunch had paid off.

As JJ was about to stop viewing the footage and close down the replay machine, he noticed someone he had not seen for a while in the background just outside of P's Disco.

Miles 'Sugar' Roberts!

JJ didn't expect to see Sugar Roberts in this video – at least not this early in the night. He recalled that Roberts did not normally get to P's Disco before midnight. So why was he in the area so early, at 10:17 p.m. to be precise? Here was a new lead for someone, if not JJ, then someone else at BIB or preferably the RBPF to pursue. Surely, they would need to establish why Roberts had been there, this early, on this Tuesday night. Who knows, Roberts might have knowledge of something that could be handy to the people investigating the Deputy Governor's disappearance, the subsequent prisoners escape or even the attempted robbery and shooting incident several hours later. JJ would mention Roberts to Colonel Burke when he saw him later. He would also hand over the copy of the DVD that Pierre was preparing on Dr Lewis' exit from P's Disco to allow Colonel Burke to do whatever he wanted to with it. Perhaps he would share it with Jeremie and Vickers who was the lead RBPF investigator on Dr Lewis' case.

Another reason why Roberts might also be a good person to track down about these three incidents, was that a $20,000 reward had been offered by a private citizen for information that would lead to the recapture of Power, the most dangerous of the two escaped prisoners. JJ knew Roberts. A sum like that dangled before Roberts might help him 'remember' or provide something that would aid the situation.

JJ would later pass this information to Colonel Burke when they met.

***

Around 3:40 p.m., Castille used one of the mobile phones he possessed to call his boss.

"Yes."

"Trouble. Our pretzel's gone AWOL. Funds remain unsecured. I'm tracking. Locals not being as helpful as I had expected. Return delayed. Unsure of new departure date. Sunday unlikely so possibly Monday night or Tuesday afternoon latest."

"Let's meet Tuesday night. Same time, usual place?"

"Fine."

"Deal."

***

Meanwhile, Pilessar's coded WhatsApp exchange from the previous night with her proposed Barbados-based Caribbean counterpart was not conveyed to Castille. There was no reason for him to know of her imminent visit to Barbados. They certainly would not be meeting up while in country. Their visits to Barbados were for completely different reasons, so would remain compartmentalised. Ideally, Castille's return to Miami would not clash with her own proposed return on Monday afternoon, unless something further went wrong with his assignment.

Speaking with him reminded her that she had not finalised her travel arrangements to and from Barbados for Sunday and Monday respectively. She called in her assistant and directed her to correct this oversight.

Five minutes later, her assistant entered her office. Did Pilessar want to arrive in Barbados on the morning or afternoon flight, given that there are two daily flights between Barbados and Miami? Pilessar recalled with amusement the 'All American Pizza Man' phrase she had used in her WhatsApp exchange. It meant AA (airline) and PM (afternoon).

"What time does each flight leave Miami and arrive in Barbados?"

Her assistant told her.

"Let's go with the earlier option out and late option back," Pilessar said.

"Very well."

***

263

Ambassador Carter returned the call to Vickers as she had promised to do before the end of her working day.

"Chief Superintendent Vickers. May I help you?"

"My, my Johnny, so official. Are you trying to impress me?"

"Hi Meredith. I don't think so, at least not any longer. That's the way I always answer my office phone. You'll have to call my private mobile to hear me answer differently."

"Really! You'd better let me have that number some time so that I can hear the less official you. Hey, I'm back in Bim in another three weeks for a week. Perhaps we can meet up while I'm in town?"

"Sure, no problem."

"Good. Now to why you called me. My team reported nothing negative about Dr Lewis. Our WB contacts also spoke highly of Dr Lewis as an employee, colleague and person. In short, no red flags. All clear."

"That's good to know. Appreciate your call, Meredith."

"Anytime, Johnny. Have a good weekend. Keep Barbados safe and…see you in a few weeks then?"

"You bet! Thanks again. Enjoy your weekend too. Bye."

"Bye, Johnny."

That's all good news, thought Vickers. *Now, how will I handle Meredith when she comes home?*

***

Just after 4:00 p.m., Barbados' newest, smallest but arguably fastest and most powerful Coast Guard vessel, HMB Shark, was seen quietly leaving HMBS Pelican, the Coast Guard HQ located next door to the Bridgetown Port alongside the Spring Garden highway in St Michael.

HMB Shark, nicknamed 'Fifty' because it had been commissioned in December 2016 shortly after Barbados' fiftieth anniversary celebrations of independence from Great Britain, carried its usual Captain and four-person crew. Officially, Fifty was being taken for its third standard six-month service at its customary west coast boat repair facility a little early because a navigation instrument was mal-functioning and required fixing. Fifty was still under the three-year warranty provided by its overseas manufacturers, so the work required would be undertaken without cost to the Government of Barbados within a forty-eight-hour period by the licensed boat repair facility on island.

Not many of HMBS Pelican's personnel noticed Fifty's departure. Just before it left, a couple of senior Coast Guard officers were told not to be concerned about Fifty's absence for a couple of days. There was nothing seriously wrong with Fifty but it was required for an exercise, hence the vessel's repair 'cover story'. Similar things had happened before, so the senior Coast Guard officers noted the story and carried on with their normal duties for the rest of that day.

Once at the boat repair facility, Fifty's Captain and crew members were met by Commander Ted Madley and given forty-eight hours leave to coincide with their vessel's inability to fully function operationally over the period. There was no need for the Coast Guard or BDF HQ to issue a public statement on Fifty.

It's late-afternoon relocation had earlier been orchestrated by Madley on the specific instructions of Tenton. The faulty navigation instrument which allegedly required fixing had been used by Madley who claimed to have recognised some dysfunctional attributes in Fifty's navigational system the previous day when he had accompanied the vessel's crew on one of their routine patrols down Barbados' west coast. After being summoned to BDF HQ for a one-to-one meeting with Tenton at BDF HQ in St Ann's Fort, Madley had returned to HMBS Pelican and written-up his previous day's 'findings' for completeness and the record. He shared his navigational 'issue' about Fifty with his two immediate subordinate officers. They accepted what he told them without question. The word was issued to Fifty's Captain and crew to take their ship to be checked out at the west coast boat repair facility.

Besides Tenton and Madley, no one else within the BDF and Coast Guard family knew of the exact assignment being proposed for Fifty after it had left HMBS Pelican.

An hour earlier, Madley had therefore invited two of the most reliable seamen he could trust into his office for a 'chat'.

"Do you fancy an overnight sea journey with me?" he asked. Both men accepted his offer.

With that sorted, Madley had headed home to his kitchen to prepare some food for the journey.

***

It was just after 5:20 p.m. when JJ kissed Angela, Andrew and Vanessa before leaving his home in Fred's personal vehicle. With Andrew set to write the eleven-plus exam in another three weeks, this was a crucial time for him. Nevertheless, Andrew, precocious Andrew, would welcome the chance to be the 'man of the house' for the next couple of days. Angela would miss her dad more being a 'daddy's girl', but Vanessa would make a fuss over her to keep her upbeat in JJ's absence.

Having earlier packed his *wet gear* and supporting equipment in his special backpack in the trunk of Fred's personal vehicle, JJ drove away from his home a worried man. Not so much for himself, more-so about Vanessa. Her concern for his situation was palpable to him but thank God, she'd managed to hide her concern from their children. His *wet gear* and other equipment should enable him to cover any eventualities he encountered in the field, whatever his task might be and wherever his destination was going to be. It was clear to JJ that it would not be a cold one, so the equipment that had served him well before he had joined BIB, would again do so now, but in BIB colours, as it were.

***

The close of play score on Day 1: West Indies 325 for three. None of the English bowler's figures were that great. The off spinner was nearing his century after a torrid afternoon but had managed to capture two wickets. A run out had accounted for the third wicket, which meant that both of England's opening bowlers and first change medium pacer had not broken through in any way during the day. With one West Indian batsman, the number three being well over a century and now close to one hundred and fifty in fact, he was sure to sleep well tonight. He had a reputation for compiling high scores once he got past a hundred. England's bowlers planned to get a lot of rest overnight as tomorrow looked like being another tough day. West Indies might collapse in a heap during Day 2's morning session, but that seemed to be something that the team has cured by their recent performances.

Day 2 would see how quickly the West Indies would be able to push on. Despite the game's situation at the end of Day 1, another capacity crowd was expected at New Kensington Oval on Day 2 England's Balmy Army would again be in full voice, hopefully being none the worse for drink and after getting a good night's rest.

But a Friday night in Barbados was available to the visiting cricket lovers to explore and enjoy, members of the Balmy Army included!

***

JJ arrived at Colonel Burke's home at 5:45 p.m. for their 6:00 p.m. meeting. Colonel Burke was not yet there, so Diane greeted and kept him company with some small-talk until he arrived around 6:25 p.m.

Colonel Burke apologised for being late. JJ simply waved off the apology. He knew Colonel Burke could be late sometimes, but there was always a good reason for it. Colonel Burke waited until Diane had left them in private before he told JJ what was going on and specifically, what his assignment was to be.

***

The 'chance' early evening meeting (that later proved to have lasted for ten minutes) between a middle-aged man and a female of a similar age, took place in Oistins, Christ Church. It looked normal enough. The two were simply conversing, doing nothing wrong. They were certainly not broking any laws.

***

Word had come down during the late-afternoon from Dr Ronald 'Ron' Hayes, Chief of Surgery at Queen Elizabeth Hospital (QEH) to Rickson that he would be discharged that evening. This news was shared with and welcomed by his two friends, McPiers and Aitkin who had left before the end of Day 1 of the Test Match to look him up.

***

Colonel Burke explained to JJ what the assignment he wanted him to undertake was. As usual, he outlined the *SNARL Cycle (Situation; Normal – or not; Action required; Result achieved; Lessons learnt)* around the *Operation 'Fishhook'* assignment. JJ agreed to play his part, though he had a question.

"Makes sense, but why not fly me in? It would save us all some time. Memory tells me that LIAT has a last flight from here to St Vincent at 10:00 p.m. three nights a week. Friday is one of them."

267

"You're right. But we don't want to go commercial. Also, one of the BDF's planes is down. The second one, along with the RSS aircraft, are on assignment as I speak. Their pilots will be beyond their duty time by the time they get back, in another hour and by 8:30 p.m. respectfully. In any event, we *can't* give the game away by flying you in. That might signal to all and sundry that we're onto Power, enabling those who've looked after him here and may be doing so over there. We're therefore going to move you in quietly and clandestinely by sea, under the cloak of darkness."

"Oh my…" JJ started to respond. He loved taking a regular sea bath, but had never been keen to be out in or on the water for too long a period although he'd done so years ago when on secret BDF missions.

"I know what you're thinking JJ. I admit that the journey will be uncomfortable for you, but it is essential that we do it this way for the stealth of the mission at hand. Our RBPF and BDF Heads are aware of your assignment. You'll be pleased to know that your return journey will be by air and therefore more pleasant, once we've recaptured Power –"

"What? Am I to bring back Power on LIAT?" interrupted JJ.

"Good God, no. We'll use one of the BDF planes to come and get you and Power. You'll have active RBPF, BDF and BIB support for that part of the assignment…but only after we've grabbed Power. JJ, we need to get this guy back here, ideally by Monday night. The PM's expecting it, so no mistakes."

"Yes, chief, I may need some luck to meet your deadline, but I'll give it my best shot as always," stated JJ.

"I appreciate that. Oh, and by the way as I had promised earlier, here's your stuff back."

Colonel Burke handed back JJ his BIB equipment.

JJ took the items, but soon returned most of them to Colonel Burke. He retained his BIB ID badge and also took the secure BIB mini-computer that BIB operatives used on overseas assignments.

"Can you please keep the rest of these items until my return," said JJ.

"No problem. Time to get going. You'll leave from Marsh's Cove in St James, that's the Coast Guard's licensed boat repair facility's location. It's at the end of Gibson's Road," said Colonel Burke.

"I know it."

"Good. I'll call ahead to say you're on your way over."

"Thank you. See you in a few days," said JJ, rising from the chair, picking up his special backpack before fitting in the two items he had been given.

"One more thing, JJ. Here's a list of three possible persons who might be involved in keeping Power under wraps in Vincie land." Colonel Burke slipped JJ a piece of paper which he now carefully secured.

"That info came from a good friend of mine. Pass it over to Chief Inspector Terry 'TG' Gomez, Head of the Royal St Vincent and the Grenadines Police Force's (RSVGPF) Response Task Force (RTF). He'll decide what they do with that information as it's no longer of any concern to us. Remember, your objective is a simple one. With Vincie help, recapture Power. Once you advise me that's been done, I'll get trans-p over there for you and Power pronto," stated Colonel Burke.

"Got it," answered JJ.

Seeing JJ to the door, Colonel Burke said, "I noticed that you're using Fred's personal vehicle. I'll have Riley Morris pick it up tomorrow morning and return it to Fred at his place."

"You sure? I'd prefer Riley to drop it back at my home instead as I'll need it once I return…"

"No, you won't. I'll have your BIB vehicle waiting for you at the airport when you get back."

"Fine, but won't Fred wonder how it got back there?"

"No worries. I'll explain what's taken place to Fred when I see him at HQ tomorrow."

"Okay chief. Oh, and by the way I also have something for you on the Deputy Governor." JJ passed Colonel Burke the DVD he'd had Pilgrim prepare for him.

"I'm certain Samuel and Margaret can find something on that to enable them to help the police boys in their search for Dr Lewis. They are good at finding needles in a haystack, so their review is necessary. The DVD is from P's Disco last Tuesday night. I've looked it over. Miles Sugar Roberts, remember him from when the PM was shot? He was seen just outside P's Disco. That in itself was not surprising as that's his nightly hangout, but I could not help but notice that he was in that part of St Lawrence Gap unusually early that night. Might be worth one of our people having a word with Roberts, sooner rather than later."

"Gotcha, JJ. Great thinking. Best of luck with the trip, and JJ, be safe."

"As always, chief."

"Please tell Commander Madley I also wish him and his crew well with their overnight assignment."

"I shall."

***

By 7.00 p.m., all was set for Rickson's release. They were greeted by two special persons who had come to see him off and wish him well for the rest of his stay in Barbados. Liz Brathwaite presented Rickson with a bouquet of flowers and a green envelope containing three sets of tickets for him and his two friends to join her in the Barbados Tourism Hospitality Inc's box for the remaining four days of the Test Match at New Kensington Oval. This would be a sort of make-up, compensation to them for the early morning trauma they had suffered in St Lawrence Gap.

The second person was Keith Henderson, QEH's CEO. He informed Rickson that the medical cost for his stay at QEH had been waived. In addition, he should return to QEH's outpatients department for treatment on the gunshot wound at 10:00 a.m. on Thursday, the day before his scheduled return to Britain. At that time, Rickson would also be given correspondence about his injury to take back to his private doctor where his treatment could be continued. Finally, a taxi was waiting outside to take Rickson and his two friends to their south coast hotel. This taxi would also be available to collect them from their hotel and take them to and from New Kensington Oval for the remainder of the Test Match. It would also collect Rickson on Thursday at his hotel for the return journey to and from the hospital. There would be no cost to Rickson for these journeys.

Rickson thanked Brathwaite and Henderson for taking such good care of him over the past couple of days that he was in the QEH's care and for the Box seat tickets provided for the following days. Originally, they all had Test Match tickets in the Hall & Griffith (Upper) stand for all five days of the game. They could now sell those tikets for the remaining days of the Test match.

Rickson, McPiers and Aitken left the QEH in fine fettle, as the English say.

***

JJ left Colonel Burke's home in Fred's personal vehicle for the west coast boat repair location. He understood that the intention was to set off on the

270

overnight journey to a neighbouring Caribbean island at 8:00 p.m., with the intention of arriving at their destination sometime between 3:00 a.m. and 4:00 a.m. pre-dawn Saturday morning.

JJ hoped for a smooth journey but did not anticipate having a comfortable boat ride that night.

**

Oistins Bay Gardens had rapidly filled up by 7:15 p.m. with locals and visitors to Barbados alike. Other night spots across the island were also coming to life. This was *Friday night in Barbados*. Rum shops stood ready to accommodate their weekend karaoke sessions, while church youth groups were assembling to spend a few hours of gamesmanship, prayer and other forms of spiritual fellowship.

For Barbados' security services, their efforts continued in seeking to locate Dr Albert Lewis and the two culprits from the St Lawrence Gap attempted robbery/shooting incident. Of course, efforts to recapture the now sole remaining escaped prisoner, track down those responsible for the escape itself and the fallout related from the death of the former Deputy Superintendent of Prison, were also in focus.

**

Thirty minutes after leaving Colonel Burke's house, JJ arrived in Gibson's Road. He parked Fred's personal vehicle carefully in the small parking lot before making his way to and entering the boat repair complex. He was met by Madley.

"Hi, JJ, ready for a sea ride?"

"Guess so! How you doing, Commander?"

"Good. Boat's fuelled up, food's onboard and now that you're here, we'll be ready to go shortly."

"Sounds great. By the way, Colonel Burke sends his best wishes for a successful mission."

"I'll thank him on my return. Let's do this thing."

**

Fred called JJ's home around 7:30 p.m. As he was used to calling JJ on his BIB phone, knowing that he no longer had it, Fred had to look up the Johnson's landline in the telecommunications directory.

Vanessa Johnson answered the phone.

"Good night, Johnson's residence."

"Hi, Vanessa. Fred here. Can I speak to JJ?"

"He's not here."

"Oh! It's not like him to be out on a Friday night, away from you and the kids. You've no idea where he is?"

"No."

"Okay, Vanessa. Sorry if I'm being too nosy."

"That's okay, Fred. You're not. We're all fine. JJ is too, I'm sure. He's doing something for Colonel Burke. What, I do not know. Why don't you call him to find out what it is?"

"I might just do that, Vanessa."

"Good. Thanks for calling, Fred. Goodnight."

"Bye."

With that, Vanessa Johnson hung up the telephone.

Fred was concerned.

So, JJ is off doing a job for the Director and I have no idea what it's about, he thought.

Fred decided to call Joe in case she knew something he did not. She might be able to shed some light on what had transpired and what JJ might now be up to with Colonel Burke.

Fred and Joe had earlier agreed to both check in on JJ and his family first thing the following morning to see how they were doing before going into BIB HQ. Fred knew better than to call Colonel Burke at home on a Friday evening. Once he was not at work, Colonel Burke's Friday evenings were sacrosanct for having dinner at home with Diane. This was paramount and he would not appreciate being disturbed during his evening meal. To call after dinner on a Friday evening, even about JJ's 'assignment', would be pushing it, so Fred decided to speak with Colonel Burke in the morning.

The call to Joe was not helpful as she had no idea what JJ might be up to. Neither JJ nor Colonel Burke had placed her in their 'loop' of Friday night activity, though she too was now keen to learn what JJ was up to on Colonel Burke's behalf. They decided that they would ask Colonel Burke what was happening with JJ when they met with him at BIB HQ the following morning, after of course first checking in with Vanessa.

Tonight, Fred was the senior BIB operative on call until 12:00 a.m. for the ECC security project (just in case BIB was required in any related emergency). The BIB roster showed that JJ was to be the senior BIB operative on call for Saturday night, with Joe leading on Sunday night. However, given JJ's unavailability, Fred suspected that Colonel Burke would fill the void himself, as he had been known to do before.

Dinner with Charlee was next on Fred's agenda. She'd come off duty from the Queen Elizabeth Hospital a few hours earlier, gone shopping on the way home and on arrival at their now shared apartment, had showered before starting to prepare their evening meal.

Fred had not mentioned what had transpired with JJ, but once they sat down to eat, Charlee had innocently asked him, "How's JJ?"

Fred had responded, "He's fine, I'm hoping to see him in the morning to help him sort some stuff out."

"Good, let's eat," said Charlee.

Fred tucked in. "This lasagne taste's great. Can we save some for tomorrow evening?"

"No fear, there's plenty there, enough for an army," was Charlee's response.

***

Operation 'Fishhook' was a sensitive and important assignment, with Fifty required to transport a BIB operative to a neighbouring Caribbean country. With Madley as Fifty's captain, he had as his crew two of the best seamen in the Coast Guard whom he'd carefully chosen because he could trust them to undertake this type of mission. They were not normally part of any Fifty's crew.

Fifty's cargo was JJ Johnson, and *Operation 'Fishhook'* got underway. There was a lot at stake.

JJ loved taking regular sea-baths with his family or on his own after exercising on the beach. But boy, being out on the open sea in the dead of night, had never been his thing. The Caribbean trip he was undertaking in pursuit of Power was only going ahead with Colonel Burke having secured Tenton's co-operation. This was the second part of this assignment and it could not have gotten off the ground had the first part not been secured by gaining permission for JJ's visit to St Vincent and the Grenadines. That had been done through an old and dear friendship between two Caribbean pals.

The result? JJ now found himself making his way, not exactly comfortably, across the Caribbean Sea. Once his assignment was ultimately successful, JJ anticipated being officially restored to the BIB fold.

***

Friday nights, year-round in and around the south coast seaside town of Oistins, Christ Church was always busy. This Friday night was set to be busier than normal, with several thousand extra visitors being in Barbados for the ongoing Test Match, Saturday's international football game and Sunday night's big concert. Though everything had been shaken up by news of Wednesday's prisoners' escape and Thursday morning's attempted robbery and shooting in St Lawrence Gap, the usual Friday night activity in Oistins was set to go ahead unchanged. This would enable local and visiting patrons to interact with resident venders offering food, drink, souvenirs and entertainment to go on unhindered.

Included in tonight's attending patrons were visiting cricket lovers, their partners and families. The majority of them were British supporters who'd either attended or had watched at least part of the Test Match on television. Their intention was to have a great time sampling the local food, particularly the varieties of fish, sampling the drinks on offer and ultimately dancing to the local music that was always on tap from the Resident DJ, live band or individual stalls who also enjoyed competing with each other to see which could play music the loudest or be most amusing on the night.

Yes, this night would be memorable for many of Oistins visiting patrons.

***

Colonel Burke finished his evening meal with Diane. He checked his watch. JJ should be underway by now.

He called Fred, who by now had also finished his meal with Charlee and was in the process of washing up the plates, cutlery and utensils used to prepare their meal.

"Goodnight." It was Charlee who answered the phone.

"Oh, good night, Miss Piggott. Colonel Burke here. May I please speak with Fred?"

"Sure. Just a minute."

"Thank you," said Colonel Burke.

Charlee took the phone to Fred and whispered, with her hand over the mouthpiece.

"It's the Director."

What's up now, Fred thought. *News about JJ? Or has one of the cricketers or a VIP gotten themselves into trouble with drugs, have troubled a young lady or whatever. It's surely early for any of this to have happened already on a Friday night…*

Fred took the phone from Charlee apprehensively, but someone not knowing him would never know what his true disposition was when he spoke.

"Goodnight, chief. How may I help you?"

"Hello, Fred! I trust all's well at home?"

"Sure is, we've just had a lovely dinner. I'm now tackling the washing and drying up."

"Been there and done that. Fred, you remember Miles Sugar Roberts? He's the guy who hangs out mainly in Christ Church, St Lawrence Gap in particular. I need you to go find him later and ask a few questions. I'll send you a note shortly on what I want you to ask him. We need to follow up a lead from JJ that might be connected to Dr Lewis' disappearance."

"Good. Two questions. I didn't know that JJ is working on that case. When I spoke earlier with Vanessa, she mentioned that he's doing something for you. Can you fill me in on what he's doing please, and can I help him?"

"No to both of your questions, Fred! Just find this Roberts guy for me. I'm aware that you're BIB's team leader for tonight's duty related to the ECC security project, so you'll need to be available till midnight, just in case something crops up on that front. But I need you to find Roberts after your shift is over."

"Alright. Do you want me to report back to you tonight once I have found him, or can I do so when we meet at HQ in the morning?"

"Morning's fine. Nine o'clock as agreed. I'll e-mail the questions for Roberts before I turn in."

"I'll find this guy, chief. Should I detain him at BIB overnight or just get answers to the questions you're sending?"

"The latter. Goodnight to you and Miss Piggott."

"Right. Night, chief."

Charlee looked at Fred expectedly.

She'd heard his side of the conversation but was unsure what it all meant. Fred had not told her about JJ's situation, but on her arrival home she had observed that Fred's private car was not parked in its usual place. Charlee knew that Fred occasionally lent his car to his sister, but whenever he'd done so he had told her how long the car would be with her. It was strange that so far, Fred hadn't said anything at all about one of his most prized possession. Perhaps he would mention it later.

"What's that about?" Charlee asked.

"Oh, just Colonel Burke…being Colonel Burke. He needs me to find, and speak with someone later tonight. He'll send me what he wants me to ask them. It's all confidential, so he couldn't tell me the specifics over the phone. It shouldn't take me long to find and speak with the man, but I can't do anything until after midnight when my EEC shift ends. Once I get going, I fully expect to be back home no later than 2:00 a.m."

"All right, guess you have to obey the Director. That still leaves us a lot of time before midnight for each other, know what I mean?" said Charlee as she approached him with a big smile.

"Sure do. I just need a few minutes to finish up here and I'll join you in the lounge."

"I'd prefer the bedroom…"

"I get it, Charlee, the bedroom it is."

Fred turned his attention to finishing off his kitchen chores. What he would do after would be more fun with Charlee's cooperation.

***

For Madley and his two-member crew, *Operation 'Fishhook'* was a routine assignment. They were experienced and professional sea dogs, so were accustomed to being at sea under such conditions, even if not in this part of the Caribbean Sea. Fifty's mission, though sanctioned by their Barbadian superiors, would never appear officially 'on the books', i.e. it would never be recorded as having even taken place.

Fifty was the Coast Guard's newest and fastest Coast Guard vessel. The one hundred and ten-mile sea journey from Barbados to St Vincent was not expected to be smooth all the way. And it wasn't, as the sea had been choppy from early that Friday morning, and would continue that way for most of their journey.

***

The four casually dressed diplomats promptly met at 9:30 p.m. as arranged in the top car park at the back of the shopping complex in Welches, Christ Church.

Surprisingly, their day's endeavours had thrown up nothing new of value to their cause. Not being persons to waste their (or other people's time), they quickly agreed to continue their efforts and work their sources over the weekend. If such efforts also drew a blank, they decided that they would each then send off their second dispatches on Barbados' criminal situation to their respective HQs' by mid-day Monday as earlier agreed.

***

Colonel Burke had met Barbados' Ambassador to Washington D.C., United States of America on a couple of occasions since her appointment eighteen months earlier. As a matter of fact, she had been a guest at his 2017 Christmas party when she was last back home. She'd received an invitation from Diane and himself after High Commissioner Tullock had asked if he could bring her along with himself and his wife Andrea.

Colonel Burke had readily acceded to the High Commissioner's request. He later found out that Tullock and Ambassador Carter had met while he was working back at the FCO in London while she was serving there as First Secretary at the Barbados High Commission. They had become firm friends during that period and had maintained contact with each other ever since as they had undertaken various postings around the world.

Colonel Burke's decision to call Ambassador Carter at her official residence on a Friday night was not unprecedented. She was pleasantly surprised to hear from him, and a little taken aback by what he'd then asked her to try and establish from either her US high-level sources or her Deputy's security contacts.

Before making the request, they switched to their officially secure Government phones for that sensitive part of their conversation. Ambassador Carter had agreed to his request and would try to get some answers back to him by the end of the weekend, by 9:00 a.m. on Monday at the latest.

Wow, thought Ambassador Carter. She mused that sometimes she didn't hear from any officials in Barbados for a few days at a time but today, suddenly she'd received two calls from different agencies. *Some things, not all good, were taking place back home.*

Ambassador Carter called her Deputy Ambassador/First Secretary. Could they meet her at the Ambassador's Residence at 10:00 a.m. tomorrow? They agreed to do so. Their discussion would revolve around how best to carry out the request that had been made of them by Colonel Burke. Some of the persons with security connections that had been invited to their Embassy's last Independence reception at end-November were going to receive a call asking if they could meet up for a drink over the weekend.

"So much for my restful weekend in Washington DC. I can't wait to get down to Bim for a real break…" she murmured as she set herself up with a drink and some popcorn to watch her favourite TV show.

At least she did not have any official engagements to attend to over this weekend. She hoped to still be able to 'sleep in a little bit' on Sunday morning.

***

Also, around that time Pilessar sent a WhatsApp message to her budding Barbadian business partner.

"Confirm, All American Pizza Man 1:30."

An hour later, there was a response.

"Noted."

***

While some members of the England and West Indies cricket teams, support staff or management teams planned to have a quiet dinner at their hotel before getting a good night's rest, some members from both sides were more adventurous. Team curfews of 11:00 p.m. and midnight respectively were in place, so this allowed those keen to explore Barbados' nightlife the opportunity to visit St Lawrence Gap, Oistins or any of the popular south and west coast eating establishments during the course of the evening.

**

The two men on bicycles had been watching the activity at this gas service station on the outskirts of St Michael off and on for a few nights now. It was shift change time, and no vehicles were in place wanting gas. Strangely enough, neither were they any customers in the service station's convenience store. Only the male shift manager, two female gas attendants and two female shop assistants, one of whom was on cashier duty, were around.

This was the two men's moment to act and they seized their chance.

Without a word between them, they rode up to the door of the store, dropped their bikes and pulled the masks that were already around their necks up over their faces. They entered the store and made plain to the startled cashier that they wanted all the cash in her register. She screamed. The other shop assistant cowered on the ground. The shift manager rushed out from his small office to see what was going on and was hit on the back of the head by the second robber who was waiting for him behind a stack of bread, biscuits and snacks. He fell to the floor and appeared to be unconscious.

"Open it, now," said the first robber.

The cashier did as she was told. The robber pulled a bag from his pants pocket and threw it at the cashier.

"Fill it," he ordered.

Fumbling, the crying cashier did as she was told.

Just as the two robbers turned for the door, a couple entered the shop. The second robber had seen them enter and, hand shaking, had fired off a shot in the couple's direction. The man pushed the woman with him to the floor, ducking at the same time.

Grabbing the bag of cash, the first robber headed for the door. Everyone else in the shop stayed where they were, petrified and so watching as the two robbers tried to make their escape through the exit. The first robber made it, but the second robber's route to the door was more treacherous. The two pep-bottle drinks his wild shot had hit had spilled onto the floor. This caused him to slip and fall over. His mask fell off, revealing his face to the security CCTV cameras covering the store's entrance/exit point.

Though the second robber quickly scrambled to his feet and was able to make his escape through the door, his image had been captured. His bicycle ride away from the scene was not an enjoyable one, for he knew that the law would at some point, catch up with him.

That captured image subsequently gave RBPF officers something to work with. Once forwarded to Samuel and Margaret in the SIR at BIB HQ, identification of the second robber would be done by FRST. This would eventually lead to him giving up to RBPF officers details of his night's accomplice. As Samuel and Margaret were now aware of all recently attempted or successful robberies by two persons, especially from the St Michael and Christ Church parishes, with CRG drawings and Ziegler's description of the robbers (size, height, etc.) being cross-referenced and matched to CCTV images, capture was always inevitable.

***

Fred enjoyed a session of passionate lovemaking with Charlee and was pleased that his phone had not rung during that special time with her, even though he was still 'on duty' for the EEC security project.

After showering and dressing casually, Fred left his home at 11:55 p.m. and drove to the Worthing police station where he parked his BIB vehicle. He popped his head inside the reception area to speak with the RBPF officer standing behind the Incident Desk.

"Good night, officer. Fred George, BIB. I've parked in your car park. I'm in the Gap for an hour or two."

"Fine by me, sir," responded the RBPF officer waving Fred away. He knew who Fred was. His mind seemed to be elsewhere. *Clearly night shifts don't appeal to you, my friend*, thought Fred.

Nodding, Fred left the station. He crossed highway 7 and entered St Lawrence Gap. It was 12:20 a.m. and time to start his search for Sugar Roberts.

***

Chapter Nineteen

Out to Sea

SATURDAY, 21 APRIL

Halfway through their journey to St Vincent, Madley invited his two-man crew and JJ to share a meal with him. Offered were corn beef and biscuits, baked chicken, split pea rice and salad, washed down by as many cups of black coffee as they wanted. The meal had been prepared on the previous afternoon by Madley at his home.

After eating, JJ was encouraged to get some rest. That was not the easiest thing to do, given the bumpiness of the ride to date, but he eventually got off and grabbed a couple of hours sleep before he rose again to someone shaking him.

It was Madley.

"We're about two hours out, JJ. Thought you might want to collect your thoughts ahead of arrival. Care to join me on Fifty's bridge?" he asked.

"Thanks. I've nothing better to do, Anyway, I want to firm up SVG's geography in my head," JJ answered while rubbing his eyes.

Ten minutes later, they sat on retractable stools, at times awkwardly, on Fifty's bridge. JJ had by now reached into the special backpack he had brought with him containing his waterproof pouch in which were a couple of papers, photographs of Power and maps of St Vincent and each of the Grenadine islands. The backpack contained one of BIB's newer operational mini-laptops JJ would use during the mission to communicate with Colonel Burke.

"You really need the map, JJ? I've a good idea that you already have all you need to know sorted in your head, plus where you might want to go when we deliver you on shore to link you up with your Vincie buddies," opined Madley.

JJ nodded in agreement before adding, "You're right, but I always like to be prepared. There's never any harm in being so."

JJ poured over the map of St Vincent, aware that finding Power would not be easy, but had to done.

***

Fred found Sugar Roberts inside P's Disco, one of his usual hang outs, though he was not in either of his favourite spots in the club, propping up the bar or sitting at a table in the far corner of the dining area. In either place, Roberts normally managed to get someone to buy him a drink or a meal, often both and sometimes more than once.

Tonight, Fred found Roberts on the dancefloor. It was why he had not spotted Roberts sooner after arriving at P's Disco.

Fred headed to the bar and ordered himself a grapefruit juice, keeping his eyes on Roberts. Of course, Roberts did not know Fred wanted to speak with him. Fred remembered that Roberts liked a strong rum and coke, so ordered one for him and took both this and his own drink before going to sit at a recently vacated table. All the while he kept sight of Roberts, in case he left the club suddenly for some reason.

DJ Price had worked the crowd into a Calypso/Soca frenzy with the best up-tempo Trinidad and Tobago's 2018 Carnival tunes, so much so that when he decided to lower the tempo, he did so with the classic and raunchy Club version of Ralph MacDonald *You Need More Calypso*. The dance floor gradually started to clear of exhausted party people, enabling him to signal his twelve to fifteen-minute 'mellow mood' session's start so as to allow the 'lovers in the house' an opportunity to hold each other tight.

As Roberts headed to the bar, Fred cut him off and invited him over to his table. Roberts came, reluctantly at first, but on reaching the table asked, "That for me?" to which Fred answered, "Yes."

"Can I have something to eat too please?"

"Be my guest. Choose what you want from the menu."

"Thanks, man. You having anything?"

"Maybe, but let's get your order in and have a chat."

"Right, a large cheeseburger with chips will do nicely."

Fred caught the eye of one of the club's waitresses who came over to take Robert's order. Fred ordered a fish-cutter with salad so as not to look too out of place when Roberts' food order came.

Fifty minutes later, Fred paid the bill in cash for their food orders and Roberts' three drinks. Answers to the questions asked by Colonel Burke were in and would be presented to him in a few hours.

Fred wanted to get back home to Charlee. She would be fast asleep, but he believed that once he woke her to let her know that he was back home, then round three of their lovemaking might start. Luckily, neither of them had too early a start in the morning. His meeting was not until 9.00 a.m. and Charlee did not have to be on duty until noon.

***

An hour later, one of Fifty's two crew members joined Madley and JJ on the bridge. He said to JJ, "Time for you to get into this, sir," handing JJ a waterproof suit.

"Not sure how close we'll be able to get you to the shore, so you'll probably have to do some swimming, at least some wading, in which case this will help."

"Thanks, sailor," responded JJ.

He took the waterproof suit and threw it over his shoulder, before folding up the map and returning it to the waterproof pouch which was then placed in special backpack he had brought along. It would accompany JJ ashore and its contents would become important as his assignment developed.

***

Colonel Burke had long realised the importance of having 'friends from across the water'. Leading up to JJ's sea journey, he was able to confirm the importance of this adage.

He and Rt. Hon. Algernon 'Toby' Walker MP, Prime Minister of St. Vincent and The Grenadines had known each other since they were in their mid-twenties. They had met while studying together at City University in London. Once they had graduated with master's degrees and before returning to their respective Caribbean countries, they'd become firm friends.

Now, nearly three decades later, that friendship remained firmly in tack.

283

With the prior permission of Motby, Colonel Burke had called Prime Minister Walker to request that his Royal St Vincent and the Grenadines Police Force (RSVGPF) provide appropriate assistance to his most senior BIB operative who needed to quietly visit St. Vincent and the Grenadines within the next twenty-four hours. There was a need to pursue and recapture a most dangerous Barbadian criminal.

Walker had readily agreed to the request. To ensure that the Heads of Government were on the same page, Motby had later spoken with Walker on their secure telephone lines to officially sign off on JJ's visit.

Walker had then spoken with Commissioner Aubrey Gaynor of the RSVGPF. He in turn planned to brief and instruct Chief Inspector Terry 'TG' Gomez, Head of RSVGPF's nine-member RTF Respose Task Force to make himself and his unit available to support JJ's visit. If necessary, Gomez was authorised to also call on a small detachment of the St Vincent and the Grenadines Defence Force (SVGDF) to support any rural search that might be necessary to help apprehend the Barbadian criminal. The Vincentian Government did not want to have the Barbadian criminal loose on their turf for too long.

It was two hours into JJ's sea journey when Commissioner Gaynor had briefed Gomez about JJ's pending visit. They were to collect, transport, house, feed and generally support JJ in tracking down and recapturing Power. Once Power was caught, Vincentian authorities would inform their Barbadian equivalents. A RBPF officer would quickly but quietly be flown over to St Vincent (on either one of the BDF's available C26 aircraft) to collect and return Power to Barbados to face justice. JJ would of course return to Barbados with Power and the RBPF officer.

***

Madley reduced Fifty's speed to better navigate the supposedly shallow waters. The rocks in the water were picked out by Fifty's spotlights. Madley wanted to get JJ as close to the shoreline as he could without damaging Fifty. Satisfied that he had gotten as close as he could, JJ was advised that he would have to wade the final twenty yards or so to the beach. Meanwhile, the vessel was manoeuvred to enable either of its two crewmen to pick out what they were looking for, a flashing fluorescent light onshore.

There.

"Time to go, JJ," Madley ordered on seeing the light.

JJ knew what that meant. He said goodbye and thanked Madley and his two-man crew for bringing him safely to St Vincent. JJ had already placed his special backpack containing his *wet gear* under his waterproof suit, so now slipped overboard on Fifty's starboard side. He swam then waded ashore in relatively calm water towards Layou Bay. Out of the semi-darkness, two burly men appeared and approached him. JJ was not alarmed, for they were his Vincie reception team. They helped JJ out of the water.

Madley waited until he was certain JJ was on firm land. He did not need to know who the two men were as he was aware that JJ would be met on his arrival and so there was no reason for him to hang around. The fluorescent light, again flashing from onshore, confirmed that all was well.

It was the signal Madley wanted to see. He immediately swung Fifty back towards the open Caribbean Sea and gradually opened the vessel's throttles to start the return journey to Barbados. As he did so, he instructed one of his crew members to go below and radio back to BDF HQ that they had 'delivered the package'.

The seaman did as he was told.

"Roger that. Safe return," came the immediate response. The communication link was then severed.

There would be no further radio communication as Fifty made its way back to Barbados. *Operation 'Fishhook'* was fully up and running. The sea journey from Barbados to St Vincent was completed (Phase 1), and so the effort to locate, apprehend and recapture Power (Phase Two) was underway. Fifty's return to Barbados (Phase Three) was also underway. Power's subsequent return journey to Barbados (Phase Four) should see him end up in the safe and welcoming arms of HMP Dodds.

***

The person acknowledging the seaman's report was Tenton.

He turned to face the other two men sitting with him around the small table in BDF HQ and gave them the thumbs up sign. "Your man's in position," he said.

"Many thanks…great job," responded Colonel Burke.

"Mike, I concur with Trevor. Let's hope we can capture and retrieve Power quickly before he disappears into the Vincie underworld or one of their islands," said Jeremie.

"True. We know he was helped getting away, right?" asked Tenton.

"Yeah…we've got a couple of leads going about who might have arranged it, but we've not been able to nail anything down yet. Later today we should be closer to identifying that person or persons. The method used to get him away from here was almost surely by sea, unlikely a yacht so most likely via a fishing boat. Get the fisherman or crew who operated it and we'll be able to make some progress. Also, and most importantly, who made the arrangements and paid for Power's escape might take us slightly longer, but we'll also establish that. I've already asked the Comptroller of Customs and the Chief Fisheries Officer to run checks on outgoing yachts and fishing vessels to see which of the main ports of entry and fish landing areas recorded vessel movements between Thursday morning and last evening. Floyd and Jimmy have promised me their reports by noon today, if not earlier," stated Jeremie.

"That's great, Will," said Colonel Burke.

"Right. Where you guys off to now?" asked Tenton

"I'm off home for some breakfast, then hitting the office…there's a lot happening. Later, I'd like to pop down to the Oval to check how things are going, perhaps during the post-lunch session," said Jeremie.

"Well, I'm off to BIB HQ, an hour in the gym before using some of the stuff I ordered in from Rita's Kitchen last night for breakfast. That way I can get an early drop on my team who are due in at 9:00 a.m.," said Colonel Burke.

"What about you, Mike?"

"I've got some paperwork to complete here, recommendations for promotions and the like. Then I think a sea bath beckons after which I'll go home for a late breakfast and a rest! Saturdays don't mean what they used to mean to me anymore, not since I got this gig, know what I mean fellas?"

Jeremie and Colonel Burke nodded in complete understanding. Similar thoughts had also occurred to them related to their weekends.

**

Chapter Twenty
Vincie Country

JJ was led to a small portable cubicle where he was encouraged to change into some dry and more comfortable clothes. As he did so, he glanced around towards the sea and noticed that Fifty was quickly disappearing back out to sea in the pre-dawn light. He could see the bay's churned up surf in the wake of Fifty's powerful engines.

JJ was not surprised to find that the clothes provided fitted him comfortably, to a T in fact. There was a good reason for that. There were his own from a previous assignment. Once dressed, he exited the cubicle and again looked out to sea. It was again calm and Fifty had long since disappeared.

JJ was directed by one of the men, now also in dry clothing to an unmarked four-wheeled drive vehicle which had just pulled up close to the cubicle on the secluded beach. It had obviously come to collect him. In the driver's seat sat a heavy-set man with a broad grin and an outstretched hand by way of greeting.

"Terry 'TG' Gomez, Head of RTF, RSVGPF I presume," JJ said warmly.

"Welcome to Vincie-proper country, JJ. How was your journey across the water? Not too rough, I hope? Anyway, it's great to see you again my old friend," said Gomez.

JJ shook Gomez's hand to return the greeting with his own smile. They leaned over to embrace each other before settling down in the driver and front passenger seat respectively.

"It wasn't smooth, TG, but I survived it! Good to see you man. Thanks for the welcoming party, for collecting me and being willing to help recapture our escaped prisoner."

"No problem. Pleasure's all mine. Least I could do once we heard from our big chief through my Com. We'll do our best to help you while you're on our patch. Let's get you something to eat, then we get down to business."

Gomez started to drive away.

"Aren't you forgetting something?"

Gomez braked sharply.

"What you mean?"

"Your two men," said JJ.

"No. They are big boys. Seriously, a vehicle in our unit will pick them up shortly," replied Gomez.

With that, Gomez pulled the vehicle away from the beach and headed off in the general direction of Kingstown.

JJ and Gomez small-talked during their fifteen-minute journey there. "Is BIB involved with the forthcoming Royal Visit Programme to Bim?" asked Gomez.

"No. Correction – we are aware of it, but are not directly involved but let me guess, your RTF unit is?" asked JJ.

"Yes, we are. We were asked to join the RSVGPF team working that visit. We saw the two people during their recce from Wednesday through yesterday…they are serious people, a Major Moorhouse and Inspector Swetland," said Gomez.

"Well, good luck with that. I'm focussed on the job at hand," stated JJ.

"Course you are. Don't worry. Me too. We'll get you your man," responded Gomez.

BIB and RTF were lucky, as JJ and Gomez knew one another and got along quite well. They had worked closely together in the Grenadines six months earlier as part of a Caribbean-wide law enforcement team on Phase One of a human trafficking operation. Renewing their acquaintance now was not going to be difficult. The RTF unit was the closest thing St Vincent and the Grenadines had to Barbados' BIB, but the RTF had not yet been developed into a separate organisation for intelligence work like BIB had.

***

Fifteen minutes after JJ's arrival in SVG, Jeremie and Colonel Burke left Tenton at BDF HQ in separate vehicles, heading for their respective offices. During the next few hours, they would be checking to see what the latest stages of their organisations' respective pursuit of those behind the prisoner escape were. If they used their network of local contacts wisely and decided to engage the help of international entities, progress should be quickly made in this case. Additionally, there would be ongoing efforts to locate the missing CBOB Deputy Governor and find the two robbers/shooters from St Lawrence Gap.

***

There was an interim report from Samuel and Margaret that had been passed under Colonel Burke's door around 5:00 a.m.

On arrival, he'd read it before going to the gym to exercise as he'd earlier promised himself to do. After showering and getting into some clean clothes, Colonel Burke ate some food from Rita Goodridge, owner/proprietor of Rita's Kitchen's in Oistins Bay Gardens and got down to catching up on some paperwork that he had not been able to get to over the past few days.

***

The two cricket teams left their south coast hotel for the New Kensington Oval at 7:45 a.m. under police escort. The seventeen-minute journey was relatively quick, given the distance they had to travel from their hotel to the ground.

By 8:30 a.m., the team's coaches had all members of their squads in the outfield undergoing their warm up exercises. Twenty minutes later, they had split out into different groups, some undergoing fielding practice, others catching practice, others still were in the excellent nets at the ground for some batting and bowling practice.

***

It was only after Joe had poked her head in Colonel Burke's office around 9:10 a.m. that he remembered he had been scheduled to meet with several of his BIB operatives ten minutes earlier.

"Jesus, is it that time already? I'm sorry Joe! Be with you guys in a tick," he'd stated.

289

It was another five minutes before Colonel Burke finally appeared in BIB's conference room. There he found Fred, Joe, Mohammed and Riley waiting for him.

"My apologies again, folks. Fred, what did you get from Roberts?" he asked.

"Surprisingly, quite a lot after I'd fed and watered him. It's all in my report – here are copies."

Fred passed around his one-page report.

"Alright. Let's see what you have," said Colonel Burke starting to peruse the document.

Meeting with Mr Miles 'Sugar' Roberts: Saturday, 21 April 2018

As requested by the Director. I sought out and met Mr Roberts at P's Disco in St Lawrence Gap, Christ Church. He requested a meal and drinks which were provided. I posed the questions directed. His comments were as follows:

Robbery: Roberts left P's Disco on Thursday morning, 18th April, prior to the attempted robbery and shooting of the English visitors and so did not know who either of the robbers were. Nor was any information circulating on the street about who they were. Roberts' feeling, from what he has heard about their reported approach to the visitors, was that they were probably a couple of local boys simply seeking to take advantage of a group of drunken visitors who might have had money on them. Roberts thought the robbery went wrong, and in their nervousness had accidentally fired their weapon(s). Such persons would probably rob again in his view.

Power: He had heard nothing about Power's likely whereabouts, including if he was still in Barbados. 'Street vibes' on Power's escape suggested that his escape would have had to be well-funded, with the escape being pulled off by locals "who had real guts to even attempt the rescue". Roberts mentioned no names or groups that might have done the job. However, early last night he had heard that someone from overseas had arrived in Barbados following Power's escape. Why they were here Roberts did not know. He did not have a name to share with me but promised to keep his ear to the ground. Roberts has my number.

CBOB's Deputy Governor: Roberts has heard two rumours: (a) that the man was not well, but no one knew what his condition was (I put that down to pure Bajan gossip); (b) the man was probably dead already having committed suicide. Roberts dismissed this second rumour because he had heard that story from a well-known drunkard who was not close to being sober at the time of telling Roberts the story around 1:00 p.m. on Friday afternoon.

Conclusion: Justifiable interview. Follow-up necessary? Yes – during Monday, 23 April.

Signed: *Alfred George*. [Saturday, 21 April 2018]

Colonel Burke let out a long breath, placing his copy of Fred's report on the conference table.

"Thanks Fred. I'm glad you were able to tap into this guy! He may be a road rat, but sometimes he has better informed than us and most of the RBPF boys put together. Maybe not on this occasion though. Okay, what should be our plan going forward? How about we take the robbery/shooting and Deputy Governor strands and see where they lead? Use your contacts to see what they know or might have heard. We meet here again at say, 4:00 p.m. today to report what we've each come up with. Then we can pursue or discard further leads that we've developed as the case may be. Happy?"

Almost in unison, the other BIB operatives in the room nodded and started to rise from their chairs.

"Chief, where's JJ?" Fred asked.

"He's on assignment. Sorry, I'm not at liberty to say any more or where."

"Can you tell us in connection with what, sir?" persisted Fred.

"I could, but I'm not going to. However, if and when I think JJ requires support, I'll be sure to find you."

"Yes, sir," said Fred. He wasn't convinced but as usual, he trusted Colonel Burke who hadn't mentioned Power, so Fred suspected that JJ was somehow on that case, in Barbados or elsewhere.

Probably the latter, thought Fred.

***

Bang on 9:45 a.m., Magnus Hunter took his sea, No. 53, Row 6, Section 203 in the Worrell, Weekes and Walcott (better known to local cricket lovers as the Three W's) stand at New Kensington Oval before the start of Day 2 of the Test Match.

As a Life Member of the Barbados Cricket Association (BCA), it was the seat he had booked in the Members area of the Three W's stand for the past four years. It was directly behind the middle wicket on the square's bowler's arm, looking from the Joel Garner-end of the ground.

The West Indies would start from being 325 for three overnight after Day 1. This was a healthy position. Hunter was looking forward to seeing how Day 2 of the Test Match would pan out during the day. He would, as usual be discussing all this with his recently acquired cricket-watching partner, Charles 'Corey' Miller who had retired as Chief Medical Officer in the Ministry of Health just a year earlier.

Just then, Hunter heard, "Good morning, Magnus, you missed a great day's play yesterday. Our boys did good in your absence. Where were you?" It was Miller.

"Good morning, Chief Corey. Yes, I'm sorry I did. Had some personal business to attend to. Trust you're well this good morning?"

"I'm fine. Seen today's papers yet?" asked Miller.

"No, waiting to see yours!"

"Typical! Ah well, all hell seems to have broken loose in Bim since that attempted prisoner breakout on Wednesday morning. Two of them got away and, as far as the public's concerned, are still on the run. Not in the papers yet but I hear that the repeat child-support offender handed himself in yesterday afternoon at a police station. He only wanted to see his youngest kid."

"Which police station, Corey?"

"Can't say – I'd get my family into trouble…you know how it is."

"Alright, so the gun running drug dealer and British drug dealer are still on the loose, you say?" asked Hunter conversationally but focussed on a section of the English supporters.

"Yes… I mean no. The Brit never ran away. This Power guy is now the only prisoner on the run. Also, the CBOB's Deputy Governor remains missing too. Do you think there's *any* connection between the prisoners escape and the disappearance of the Deputy Governor?"

"Corey, your guess is as good as mine, but I doubt it," Hunter responded uncommittedly.

"Come on, Magnus, I know you well enough to pick up when you're holding back something from me, as usual! Am I not correct?" asked Miller.

Hunter ignored the question.

Just then the bell rang, signalling that Day 2 of the Test Match would commence in another five minutes. Soon the two umpires, having come down the steps of the Garfield Sobers Pavilion, crossed the boundary rope and started their walk out to the centre of New Kensington Oval. The West Indian and English supporters inside the ground cheered and clapped as the English fielders followed the umpires onto the field of play. In turn, the two overnight West Indian batsmen followed.

"Here's to a great day's play," said Hunter.

"Too right! I'll just get myself in the mood…" responded Bourne, diving into his well-stocked lunch and snack bag to resurface with a pep bottle containing some brandy.

"Want some?"

"Later, man – I want to focus on the game now. Lunchtime's good?"

"Fine by me," said Miller, dropping a couple of ice cubes into a plastic glass followed by a dash of brandy. He was ready for his day's cricket.

The first ball of Day 2 was sent down. It passed harmlessly wide of the off stump, landing in the wicketkeeper's gloves with a thud. The second new ball had been taken at last.

***

It was just after 1:30 p.m. when Fred and Joe popped down to the SIR to see how Samuel and Margaret were doing. They had nothing additionally substantive that they wanted to report as yet, though they indicated that they had made steady progress in the special tasks they had been given by Colonel Burke.

***

An hour later, Samuel and Margaret hit the mini-jackpot! Twice. Not about the escaped prisoner Power, but about Dr Albert Lewis and the St Lawrence Gap robbery.

Regarding Dr Lewis, in addition to the CCTV footage from P's Disco that had been presented to them earlier that morning, they now had further and clear evidence that Dr Lewis had not disappeared of his own volition.

It was CCTV camera footage from Speightstown, St Peter, dated Wednesday, 18th April (four days earlier). It showed Dr Lewis being moved by what appeared to be two men from one car to another in a car park identified as being just off the Speightstown by-pass road. Samuel and Margaret nearly missed the transfer as the camera located on the civic building panned from side to side as it had been set up to do. Neither car's registration number, front or back, were clearly visible, but the general make of both vehicles was established. Also, what could be termed the recipient vehicle, had a couple of distinguishable features about it. A large 'Garfield' hung from the rear-view mirror. Also, a school tie hung from what looked like the coat hook by the rear right-hand side of the car. The tie fluttered outside of the car window in the wind as Dr Lewis was helped, *forced* might be a better word, into the back seat. The door closed, with most of the tie being outside of the window. Noticing this, one of the occupants wound down the window, pulled the tie inside before winding back up the window.

Given that the CCTV camera only provided black and white film, it was left to those watching the images to 'colourise' the tie with a view to establishing which school tie it might be. It probably belonged to a former student who was now a parent of a school they loved and respected.

If somewhere in the near-nationwide CCTV system they could also now find a similar image of a light-coloured Subaru Impreza saloon with the Garfield and school tie, and where a registration number at either front or back could be deciphered on the vehicle, then they could start tracking down the vehicle's owner and address. Ultimately, who the men seen moving Dr Lewis were would be established.

Samuel took matters a step further by calling Jackson Bright, Director of the Barbados Licensing Authority (BLA). He provided Bright with what little information was available on the 2009 Subaru Impreza and requested a printout of all such vehicles that had been imported into Barbados and registered with the BLA.

How did he know it was a 2009 model? Simple. Samuel's father owned this make and model of car, so he was familiar with it and so easily recognised such a vehicle.

Regarding the St. Lawrence Gap robbery, one of the two culprits had now been identified. The use of facial recognition system technology (FRST) had been helpful, particularly the clear image of the second robber who had lost his mask in his effort to escape from the gas station. RBPF and BIB teams identified the twenty-two-year-old man from their electronic databases. It turned out that the image of the second robber matched that of one of the culprits from the St

Lawrence Gap incident three nights earlier. His name was Kenrick Hyman and his last known address was 'Rocky Bottom', Silver Sands, Christ Church.

Samuel and Margaret called Colonel Burke. They explained what they had found on Dr Lewis' disappearance and the St Lawrence Gap robbery and shooting. After listening carefully, Colonel Burke thanked his two ICT operatives, urging them to get back to work on Dr Lewis' case. They duly obliged.

Colonel Burke then called Jeremie to advise him on his team's findings in both cases, promising additional updates as they came to hand.

Jeremie instructed Vickers and Moss to arrange with Station Sergeant David Avery at Oistins police station to secure a backup team of three RBPF officers and two BDF soldiers to accompany Vickers and Moss on a visit to Hyman's address with a view to picking him up for questioning. If Hyman was not there, then an APB would immediately be issued for his arrest.

Vickers promptly complied with Jeremie's instruction by calling Avery.

***

Chapter Twenty-One
Balls – Big and Small

Colonel Burke's subsequent 4:00 p.m. meeting with his BIB operatives was productive. Not only had they received new information from Samuel and Margaret's investigations, but other prisoner related enquiries had also borne some fruit.

One such lead was an aged but distinctive looking open-back vehicle with unusual markings on both sides. This had been noticed by the eagle-eyed Samuel back in BIB HQ's SIR late on Friday night, or was it early Saturday morning? Samuel and Margaret had since been able to find and match an image captured from CCTV camera footage of that, or a very similar looking vehicle approaching the Six Cross Roads, St Philip roundabout at 8:31 a.m. on 18th April, the previous Wednesday morning.

The fact that the CCTV camera had captured the vehicle's driver appearing to have limped throughout the process of collecting and placing the large item, possibly a television set into the cargo bed, rang a bell with Samuel and Margaret. Mohammed from JJ's Gold team had mentioned "someone with a limp" running away from the six-wheeled truck towards the getaway car carrying Power.

They needed to establish who the owner of that vehicle was. If that person was incapacitated by a bad leg, then they would know they were onto something.

***

On his way to Hyman's home, having earlier secured a signed search warrant from a Justice of the Peace, Vickers received a call from Caroline Lewis-

Greenidge. She had arrived in Barbados late the previous night after a day-long flight trek from Texas (via Miami). Her brother had briefed her of their father's situation, but Lewis-Greenidge had been keen to speak directly with Vickers to introduce herself and maintain the pressure on him and the RBPF's efforts to locate her missing father.

Vickers was patient and polite but did not provide Lewis-Greenidge with any new information. He promised to call the family and update them around noon on Sunday, the following day.

Though the CCTV footage found by Samuel and Margaret had been passed on to Vickers by Colonel Burke, Vickers did not alert Lewis-Greenidge about it. The car's image (if not a licence plate) was sufficient to get the BLA started. Within a few hours, law enforcement agencies would start tracking down the owner of the 2009 Subaru Impreza and gain an address for them. Once secured, other dominoes were likely to fall into place, of that Vickers was *certain*. He began to feel greater confidence that Dr Lewis would soon be found, enabling them perhaps to close-out the Lewis case sometime Sunday night.

Something else had also found its way to Vickers' during the day. It was what looked like a room key found under the driver's seat of Telford's car. He would give this to Moss to run to ground. Which south coast hotel might this have come from? Once known, were there any fingerprints or DNA on the room key card or other markings that might give a clue as to who might have dropped it in Telford's car. Could that person be Telford's murderer and if so, were they from Barbados or overseas?

Vickers knew that once these questions were answered, the tracking down of who might have murdered Telford could commence in earnest. Given that Telford worked at HMP Dodds, his untimely ending might have had something to do with Wednesday's arrogant prisoners escape.

Vickers decided to set Moss on that part of the investigation in the morning. Other officers were also looking into other aspects of Telford's death.

***

Day 2 of the second Test Match had ended with the West Indies team in a commanding position, suggesting that a win for the home side might be on the cards. Over the next couple of days, if things went their way, the home team's push for victory on Day 5 should materialise. West Indies had declared half an hour before the end of session two (between the lunch and tea intervals) at 525 for seven. In the four overs before tea, three of pace and one of spin, England lost one wicket. Following the tea break and some free scoring by England's top order batsmen in response to some short and at times wayward bowling by the West Indians, England then lost four additional wickets before play ended, leaving them at 100 for 5. So, West Indies' day!

Sir Thadeus Thomas had enjoyed his first experience of New Kensington Oval, but was disappointed with the England team's overall performance. He was not alone, as the English media's reporting of what had transpired on Day 2 was not flattering for international internet cricket enthusiasts who read the day's reports overnight, or those reading national English newspapers' sports pages the following morning.

Liz Brathwaite had arranged for Rickson, McPiers and Aitken to view Day 2 of the Test Match from BTHI's hospitality box. Her guests had thoroughly enjoyed themselves – the view, food and drinks (well, not Rickson, but he *did* discover coconut water). BTHI's hospitality had helped them all to start the mental recovery process after their unfortunate St Lawrence Gap ordeal. Three more days of this treatment at the Test Match was going to be very nice. Rhonda Ziegler was unable to join them, as she was required to work in the media complex and report on each day's play for her British newspaper.

As for the thousands of 'Balmy Army' and other English supporters who had been at the game, they were disappointed with what they had seen. Following Day 2's play, some had drowned their sorrows at several of the road-side bars available to them along the roads leading to and from New Kensington Oval before heading back to hotels, guest houses or the residences of relatives and friends.

The visiting English cricket supporters had something else to attract them that evening. Everyone knows that the English are great attendees at major soccer matches. Soccer is, after all, England's number one national sport. No surprise then to find that a few hundred of those who were at New Kensington Oval would venture to the National Stadium that evening to watch a soccer match between Barbados and the USA. Though this would be a friendly international game, persons attending anticipated that it would be a competitive, perhaps somewhat feisty encounter. English supporters' interest in the match was further piqued by the fact that England and the USA were both in Group D at the forthcoming 2018

FIFA World Cup in Russia. This was the so called 'Group of Death' because within Group D were also Argentina, host-county Russia and Australia.

***

Hyman found himself in a cell at Oistins police station. After questioning, he admitted his part in both robberies. He was read his rights before being arrested on two charges of robbery in Christ Church and St Michael on the specified dates. In addition, he was charged with being in possession of an unlicensed firearm, discharging three rounds of ammunition from such in St Lawrence Gap, Christ Church on a specific date. Scared, Hyman quickly gave up his robbery partner in both instances.

***

Castille was frustrated. His original plan to have concluded his business in Barbados and of returning to Miami on AA's late afternoon flight today would not now transpire. A Sunday afternoon departure was also now unlikely. Reluctantly he had accepted that he would be leaving Barbados on Monday afternoon or even Tuesday morning. Whether successful or not in his efforts at recovering *The Organisation*'s outstanding funds from Power who had escaped his clutches (for now), Castille knew this made him look stupid to Pilessar and others within *The Organisation*. It may not cost him his Number Three position or job within *The Organisation* but it would cause him to lose face with his colleagues because of this failure.

As there was nothing more Castille could do tonight to solve his problem, he wondered how he would spend the evening? He was not one to go out drinking, attend shows or pick up women he did not know for a one-night stand. Then Castille remembered that at breakfast he had read about a friendly soccer match between Barbados and the USA that night. He decided that, rather than eat his dinner in the boringly stifling dining room he would spend a fourth night running in his room, this time watching the game on local television.

***

299

Colonel Burke and Diane dined at home. They had decided earlier that they could watch tonight's football game together. It was being broadcast live on both local and one of the USA's ESPN sports channels. Colonel Burke hoped for a Barbados win, but warned Diane not to be surprised if the game ended in an exciting draw.

This was to be a break for him, for once the match was over, he would be working again to see how else his fellow BIB operatives could help the country to overcome its current security challenges.

***

The newly refurbished and expanded National Stadium at Waterford, St Michael had stands all around the facility. It was a fine venue, one of the best in the country for a variety of international sports.

Barbados had gotten the closest they ever had been to reaching a FIFA World Cup Soccer Finals. A 1-0 defeat in their final qualifying match by Costa Rica at this very stadium four weeks earlier had sadly put paid to their quest.

That had been a sad night for Barbadians. It would have meant that two Caribbean teams would have been at the 2018 World Cup Finals. As it was, Trinidad and Tobago was the sole Caribbean team at the world's biggest sporting event, bar the Olympic Games. Caribbean people were now hoping that Trinidad and Tobago's team would, this time around, get beyond the group stage to the knockout stage of the tournament.

The game started at 8:00 p.m. Barbados scored the first goal from a corner midway through the first half. The USA team equalised just before half-time to make it one-one.

The half-time break was extended to accommodate a special presentation of Barbadian culture (stilt men and tuk band performance complete with two Mother Sally's, dancing and performing men and women).

***

Surprisingly, thirty-year-old Virgil Procter of Belle View, St Michael was at home and in bed when a team of armed RBPF officers and BDF soldiers descended upon his house.

Without looking outside, Procter had answered the knock on his door. Officers found an old firearm and six rounds of ammunition under his bed. Earlier contact with the RBPF officer allocated to that district (the 'resident beat-cop') had confirmed that Procter lived alone. He did not resist arrest. Hyman's earlier revelation to RBPF officers suggested that Procter was the one who had provided and fired the two firearms used in the attempted St Lawrence Gap robbery. It was Procter who had fired the shots at the taxi, one of which had hit the British visitor. This was *a case of criminals turning on each other*, thought Vickers. He wondered if Procter's interrogation would be as enlightening about Hyman once they reached the Black Rock police station.

***

The second half of the soccer match re-started and quickly saw the USA take the lead through a free kick. USA supporters in the crowd went wild and the Barbadians became as quiet as a door mouse. The USA team played some attractive football for most of the second half, but appeared to tire around the seventy-fifth minute, showing particular weakness down the right side of their defence. Selwyn Gay, the Barbados senior team's coach, noticed this and made some tactical changes, including a triple substitution in the eightieth minute. The equaliser for Barbados followed through a headed goal by one of the substitutes.

In the four minutes of injury time played, neither team was able to get a winner. Two-two. It was a famous draw for Barbados against a more experienced, well-drilled and funded USA team. Once the final whistle had been blown, Ambassador Rowley and Minister Grant shook hands and congratulated each other. It had been a good game, a fine evening overall. There had been no security breaches, invasions or other kind of confusion to mention leading up to or during the game. The game's aftermath was also free of trouble.

***

In St Vincent, JJ looked back on his day and was satisfied. He had made good progress. Having been keen to get down to work shortly after his arrival despite his long overnight journey with little sleep, he had readily joined Gomez and the rest of his RTF unit when they had carefully narrowed down to half dozen potential geographical locations in St Vincent where they thought Power might be being hidden. The RTF unit had sensibly established that Power's on-island suitors would not have risked moving him to any of the neighbouring Grenadine Islands of Mustique, Bequia, Canouan, or Palm Island so soon after his reported arrival on St Vincent. The RTF unit's members had therefore primarily focussed their efforts on the outlying parishes in the more rural areas of St Vincent where Power could be stashed. They had also considered popular inner-city areas around Kingstown where he might have been more able to *fit in*. Early tomorrow, they would decide on the agreed areas they would start searching for Power.

Thanks to RSVGPF Commissioner Aubrey Gaynor, who had taken the trouble to visit Gomez and meet with JJ late that afternoon, an arrangement had now been reached to allow the RTF unit to be supplemented for tomorrow's searches by a twelve-member detachment of soldiers from the SVGDF. The day had also been rewarding for Gomez's RTF unit. Tomorrow could see Power's recapture.

Following dinner with Gomez, JJ took a hot shower. Before turning in, he sent a short message to Colonel Burke on his secure BIB mini-computer. "Rapid progress being made. Tomorrow should be a good day with searches set to take place. SVGDF help confirmed. Optimistic on capture."

The reply received from Colonel Burke was one-worded. "Understood." Though it was still relatively early, JJ decided to turn in. He thought it prudent to get a good night's rest after last night and today's activities. He expected tomorrow to be another challenging day.

***

The Operational Commander and lead RBPF officer in charge of security for the international football match was Superintendent Barry Walford and he was quietly relieved. His next major task would be to repeat his Operational Commander role at tomorrow night's concert in the Garfield Sobers Sports Complex in Wildey, St Michael.

Given all that was happening security wise across Barbados, Walford had also carefully planned for tomorrow night's concert to come off as smoothly as the soccer match had. Rather than dealing with an outdoor, on-field sporting activity and surrounded by 3,500 spectators, Walford now had to deal with the opposite – an indoor event on a comparatively smaller stage with 8,000 paying patrons comprised equally of locals and tourists. The decibels would be consistently louder in the Garfield Sobers Sports Complex tomorrow night than they were at the National Stadium. The performance at the former venue would also be longer (close to four hours overall) compared to the two and a half hours of football and related activities which had just concluded at the National Stadium.

Walford decided to get a good night's rest. Tomorrow, he would visit the complex between 12:00 noon and 2:00 p.m., with his event security blueprint, just as he had done earlier today at the National Stadium. He would oversee the dress rehearsal performances of not only the Canadian pop star, but the four local artists (two bands, one instrumentalist and a comedian) who were also set to perform opening acts ahead of the main performance. This way, Walford would gain a true *feel* of the night's activity in advance.

***

Chapter Twenty-Two

Caribbean Support

SUNDAY, 22 APRIL

Power was awoken by what felt like something crawling on his back. As someone who preferred to sleep on his stomach, he decided not to move immediately. He hoped it was not a centipede that had crawled into the hammock and luckily had not bitten him yet.

As his scrambled senses became more acute and his eyes adjusted to the darkness, he realised that nothing was crawling on his back. It was a human hand that was doing a gentle dance there.

Power started to turn, but a voice said quietly but firmly, "Don't move."

He realised that this was not a dream. This was actually happening. Power wondered if the police had found him, or if this was an intended robbery of some kind at this sparsely furnished hut up in the hills in the middle of nowhere in St Vincent.

"Relax," said a friendly voice. *No police and not a robbery – something much better*, he comprehended.

Power recognised the now familiar female's voice that had been with him over the past thirty-six hours. He had heard her voice barely a couple hours earlier when she'd wished him, "Good night, sleep well." His head was now clear and he was enjoying the sensations generated by the tip-toeing fingers up and down his back so he reached out and touched her leg.

Huey jumped back slightly at his touch, resulting in her stopping what she was doing. As she moved away, Power took the opportunity to sit up and swing his legs out of the hammock where they could touch the floor. There was no light in the hut, but Power could not miss Huey's scent standing very close to him in the darkened confines of the hut.

"Don't be afraid," said Huey.

"I'm not," responded Power.

"I couldn't sleep. The night's chilly up in these hills, so I'm looking for something, *someone*, to warm me up..." she was explaining.

"Well, girl, you've found it. I'm available ..."

Nestling closer to him, Huey answered, "I can tell that you are," as she reached out for his body. Power knew from her slightly quivering voice and her increased breathing that she was not going to stand on any ceremony. Her aroma filled his nostrils. Clearly Huey was ready for sex. Power reached out to touch her and found that she was naked.

"Good. Let's do this. We have a few hours until morning..."

Huey took Power's hand and led him from the hammock to the single bed where she'd earlier slept.

They then made long and passionate love once, twice and then for a third time coming onto morning.

Six o'clock found them fast asleep, totally spent and entangled in each other.

***

JJ's phone alarm woke him at 6:30 a.m. He showered, shaved and dressed in order to meet Gomez in the hotel lobby just after 7.00 a.m. They made the short journey to RTF unit's operation centre at SVGPF HQ where a cooked breakfast and fresh fruit was waiting for them and the rest of the RTF unit.

***

Following breakfast, Gomez's RTF unit reviewed the information and conclusions they had come to the previous night. This led them to reduce the number of areas they would concentrate on that day. Four specific areas were chosen, two in the countryside and two villages closer to Kingstown. They considered tackling the Kingstown villages after dark that evening but felt that though it would give them an element of surprise, darkness might also work against them.

305

Hence their decision to visit all areas during daylight. Today's actions might help to 'flush out' Power into a more open and vulnerable space where it would be easier to recapture him. These three zonal areas selected were where serious Vincentian gang activity had historically been known to take place. RTF unit members believed shielding Power from Vincentian law enforcement officials after his escape from Barbados would fall into this category. Whoever was running the show had probably employed a known gang to operate the Power 'safe house' routine.

***

After showering, Motby and Jackie had taken a late breakfast before dressing for their official morning engagement. They left Ilaro Court at 9:10 a.m. to attend a special BDF anniversary service at St Matthias Anglican church at 9:30 a.m.

***

Back in St Vincent, RTF's overnight review had shown up no recent (past forty-eight hours) unusual or heightened uptick in local gang activity. Had RTF unit members missed a red flag? They did not think so. None of their informants had mentioned anything specific, although there was a vague report that a well-known Rastafarian leader had been seen coming down from one of the hillier sides of the island in an old black vehicle late on Thursday afternoon.

Gomez's RTF unit and JJ made a few more deductions before Gomez broke them up into three search teams. Two teams would visit out-lying country areas, while the third team would visit the two villages lying just outside of Kingstown.

***

Inspector Byron Moss wasn't quite sure what to make of the call he'd just received from Vickers this Sunday morning. Not one for church, he'd laid in bed and watched his wife Pearle get dressed and head off to the local church in St James that she'd been a member of since childhood and where they had also gotten married three years earlier.

Moss just wasn't a church-going person. Weddings, funerals, christenings (he was a god-father but not yet a dad) he could do and oh yes, Christmas and

Easter mornings. Otherwise, count him out. It wasn't that he didn't believe in God, he just could not get into the habit of going to the same place every Sunday, to hear practically the same thing and see the same people. When he'd explained this to Pearle a couple of years earlier, she'd reminded him that he went to work five and sometimes six days a week in the same place at RBPF HQ. Moss had two counters. First, he got paid for going to work, whereas he had to pay when he went to church. Second, because of the nature of work he now did, he was seldom in the same place every day and if so, he was seldom there for as long as any of her two-and-a-half-hour church services. Since then, Pearle had given up trying to reason with him about attending church with her.

Moss hadn't long nodded back off after Pearle's departure when his official phone rang.

"Hello?"

"It's Vickers."

"Good morning, sir, you're early!"

"Do you know what time it is? I've got a job for you Byron. I need you to run down something for me. Can you meet me at HQ in thirty?"

"I'll try sir, but it'll be more like forty-five. I'm still in bed!"

"I thought so! You're a lucky boy. I thought Pearle had broken you out of that habit and was getting you out to church more often, especially on Sunday mornings?"

"She's tried, sir, believe me but I've resisted."

"Well you can't resist me today! See you in forty-five. Bye."

"Alright."

Moss wondered if something had cracked on the Deputy Governor's case. He knew Vickers was getting some pressure on this case from all round.

In forty minutes, after a quick shower but no breakfast, Moss arrived at RBPF HQ and went in search of Vickers in his office to see what was so important for him to have to work on this Sunday.

Vickers confirmed that there was indeed a new lead on Dr Lewis, but it was not why Vickers wanted him at work. He explained to Moss about the room key card that had been found in the former Deputy Superintendent of HMP Dodds' vehicle. Vickers presented the card to Moss. No DNA but a smudged fingerprint had been found on it. The lab had not yet come up with who it belonged to, so neither had been of much help to RBPF investigators. Moss' task was to identify the hotel that the card belonged to and then visit it and look through the guest registry to see if anything jumped out at him. Also, he might just pick up if any guest had made any recent connection with George Telford.

Moss went to his desk and picked up a Barbados telecommunications directory. He would make a list of all the south coast hotels from Bridgetown right up to the St Christopher/Silver Sands districts in Christ Church. He estimated these numbered around thirty hotels of all classes and ten guest houses of varying sizes along or close to that coastline. He decided not to look at rented apartments just yet – that would be done if he drew a blank with the hotels and guest houses.

There goes all of my Sunday, thought Moss. Vickers had instructed him to work on this until he found 'something'. Moss knew what that meant. He would need to put in a very long day, hell maybe an a near all-nighter too if he had to visit all of these properties.

Moss hoped Pearle would understand. He'd sent her a WhatsApp message on leaving home, explaining why he'd not be home when she returned and that he couldn't start the Sunday cooking as he had to get cracking on a new assignment.

***

Jackson Bright, BLA Director had compiled the information requested by Samuel late on Saturday night, but had not bothered to forward it to Samuel until mid-way through Sunday morning.

Samuel did not arrive at BIB HQ until 10:35 a.m. He saw Bright's submission and immediately started to review the information received. There were 259 Subaru Impreza cars registered, with 203 of them being saloons. Of this latter number, seventy-five were either black, dark blue, red, green or brown, leaving 128 that could be white, light grey or silver grey. As the Subaru Impreza captured by the CCTV camera in Speightstown was clearly not dark in colour, this narrowed down the cars that he would need to start looking for to 128.

Margaret soon joined him. Samuel showed her Bright's information. She agreed with Samuel's analysis. They dug deeper to see which of the remaining 128 cars had a X or M letter that the CCTV cameras had been able to capture when Dr Lewis was being transferred.

Ten minutes later, Samuel and Margaret had narrowed down the search to persons, companies and organisations with addresses in the parishes of Christ

Church (X) and St Michael (M). These totalled 67, with 28 being registered in Christ Church, and 39 in St Michael. After deleting the six and fifteen cars from the final list because they were registered to companies or organisations, 22 and 24 cars respectively were left to be tracked down.

It was the 22 and 24 persons in the parishes of Christ Church and St Michael respectively whose details Samuel later passed to Commissioner Jeremie for his RBPF officers to start checking on. Did any of these Subaru Imprezas have a Garfield hanging from its rear-view mirror and a school tie hanging from the coat hook by the car's right-hand side's back seat?

Of course, Samuel duly alerted Colonel Burke prior to taking his proposed action and gained approval.

"Thanks, sounds good. I agree. RBPF have enough vehicles on patrol that should be able to get these checks done within three or four hours without too much trouble. But there could be a problem in that not all the cars will be at the addresses they are registered at, so it might be wise to request Commissioner Jeremie to also issue an APB to all patrolling vehicles to look out for the specific features you've identified on any relevant parked cars at picnic spots, beaches, churches, at the airport, seaport and of course, around Kensington. Keeping a *sharp* eye out will be the key," said Colonel Burke.

"That's true but gosh, doesn't that make the exercise a lot more difficult?" asked Samuel.

"Not really. Look, just pass on what I've suggested to the Commissioner. Do you have his mobile number?"

"Yes, I have it here somewhere on my wall," answered Samuel.

"Fine. Good luck and thanks again, Samuel," said Colonel Burke signing off.

"You're welcome, sir."

Colonel Burke did not hear him.

Samuel shook his head. Margaret found the number and he made the call.

***

Following the service, Motby had taken the obligatory salute during the march-pass of soldiers. Two days earlier Motby had advised Tenton that he would not be able to attend the traditional lunch that followed at BDF HQ, citing the need to attend to urgent matters of state over the weekend which he knew he'd not be able to get to before mid-day Sunday.

Tenton was disappointed, but understood there was nothing he could do to change Motby's mind.

***

Chapter Twenty-Three
Pursuit

Gomez acknowledged that access to the first of the two country areas he had chosen had a rough road which extended well up into the hillside, where a few overnight huts were known to be. That might have been the area where the vehicle had reportedly been spotted coming from, but his unit member had been unable to reach his informant the night before to clarify this. A six-member SVGDF detachment allocated to the RTF unit for Sunday was therefore dispatched by Gomez to see what (if anything) suggested that there had been some recent human activity in the area. This would include signs of recent tyre tracks, foot prints, or evidence of empty food or snack containers that would suggest persons had visited within the past forty-eight to seventy-two hours.

The other country area and two near-Kingstown villages would be visited at the same time, with the intention being to meet back at RTF's operational centre by 3:30 p.m.

Throughout the various morning discussions, JJ had chosen to observe. Gomez had noticed this and so, just before the three search teams had departed for their targeted areas, he'd invited JJ to speak to them. After all, Power was JJ's to recapture and return to Barbados, with their help.

"Thanks, Terry. Gentlemen, Jasper Power nicknamed 'Stabs', is a longstanding and dangerous criminal. He's been in trouble with the law since he was seventeen (at school in sixth form when he was caught selling drugs). He's served two relatively short custodial sentences in the past, back in February 2002 and January 2013. Once we recapture him, I anticipate the courts will ensure that he serves a lengthy sentence this time around. His crimes over time have been for selling a variety of drugs, importing and selling firearms and ammunition, and beating up people. He once shot his girlfriend but no one would come forward to press charges."

JJ could see that those he was addressing were getting the message.

"How did he get the nickname 'Stabs'?" asked Corporal Mitch Papos, a SVGDF soldier.

"In Power's early years of criminal activity, he tended to stab up people. Those he did not like, who disagreed with him or had something that he wanted that they would not give up when asked to do so. Possessions and women generally. His stabbings usually took place in night clubs or at private parties. Power got away with many of these attacks because the persons hurt never pressed charges against him.

"If given the chance, he'll not think twice about harming you. He'll probably kill to escape arrest. So, be careful out there. If you come across this man, have backup with or close to you," concluded JJ.

Gomez backed up JJ on this warning, being careful to remind his fellow Vincentians that their intention should be to recapture Power in the first instance, not kill him.

"Like Mr Johnson has stated, if it's a choice between you and him and you feel that you are in mortal danger, save yourself. I'll back you up," Gomez concluded.

JJ had no problem with Gomez's assessment or the instructions he had given to members of the three search teams.

"We hear you, sir," said Sergeant Casper Arnold, Gomez's second-in-command in the RTF unit and leader of search team #1.

Search team #2 would be led by Corporal Montgomery 'Monty' Conway, third-in-command of the RTF who was being supported by a second batch of six SVGDF soldiers. Gomez would lead search team #3, comprised of JJ and the remaining members of his RTF team.

Just as the search teams left the compound in a variety of four-wheeled drive vehicles, Gomez spoke to them on the radio.

"Okay, boys and girls. Remember to stay on your toes at all times. Good hunting and try not to make any mistakes. I want to see everyone back here at our operational centre in one piece."

It was clear that if any of the three search teams contacted the Barbadian criminal and his Vincentian protectors, fireworks could result. That was why the leader of each search group was a RSVGPF officer. They would take legal charge of any incident, including Power's recapture and arrest. The soldiers were there to help with securing the escaped Barbadian criminal. Everyone involved knew that on their own the soldiers had no legal authority to arrest and detain Power.

***

Search team #3 were first to arrive at one of their designated areas. The first village was only a ten-minute drive from central Kingstown. The team would spread out around the village with pictures of Power, asking if anyone had seen him and conduct searches for him if necessary.

Residents resented being picked on and raided by armed RSVGPF officers and SVGDF soldiers. Most shook their heads to indicate that they had not seen or even heard of Power. This was the second raid by Vincentian law enforcement personnel of their village within a four-week period, so communication was never going to be great. Finding drugs had been the target back then, but none had been found in the six homes searched.

Returning this morning to this village was not welcomed, even though the reason for the authorities' visit on this occasion was completely different. Residents did not see it that way. One elderly man spoke with Gomez after being shown Power's picture.

"No, I've not seen that man." He quickly added, "Nor are there any drugs in this community. Why can't you people just leave us alone? We're a God-fearing and peace-loving people around here so please stop harassing us," was his plea.

A young woman in her twenties who was standing close by added, "The old man's right. Most of us are tax-payers and law-abiding citizens, so why don't you stop persecuting us and go look *elsewhere* for what you're searching for, as you're never going to find any strangers or contraband here."

JJ waited in Gomez's vehicle, watching and thinking as the questioning went on. Somewhat surprised, he observed that not one person – man, woman or child, had acted suspiciously. They had spoken with Gomez or other members of search team #3 who were in JJ's view. They appeared to be just a group of people who were frustrated at being turned over by the law. JJ was at the time unaware that the local authorities had visited this community a few weeks earlier.

He also observed that for a Sunday morning, most of the persons were not dressed as if they were going to or had already been to church. Their actions

313

appeared to be of innocence, certainly not trying to protect a known criminal from Barbados who was hiding in their midst.

After an hour, JJ was not surprised to see Gomez gather his team together. There was no trace of Power. Speaking with JJ, who had now exited Gomez's vehicle to stretch his legs and had even heard a couple of the more 'salty' and foul-mouthed language responses from residents, he could only nod and agree with Gomez about concluding the search team's visit.

"Sorry you all had to cop that, JJ. Consider yourself lucky that it is Sunday morning," said Gomez.

"Don't worry! Back home, our police might have received a similar cussing out, especially if they had to leave without finding what or who they went into the district for with no arrests being made. Don't think police are exactly the most-loved breed of persons across the Caribbean, no matter how good they are at what they do," JJ said consolingly to Gomez.

"That, unfortunately is true, my friend. Some of these searches you get right, others you don't. Let's move onto our second village," lamented Gomez. "It's in another part of outer-Kingstown not far away."

"Fine by me. Heard anything from search team #1 or #2 yet?" asked JJ.

"Not yet," said Gomez as search team #3 set off for its second village destination.

***

Superintendent Barry Walford arrived at the Garfield Sobers Sports Complex around 11:40 a.m. He walked the entire outer area of the complex, taking note of the barricades that had been delivered overnight and were now appropriately placed in anticipation of patrons' arrival well ahead of 6:00 p.m. when the doors would be opened to them. Now inside the complex, Walford walked around the facility to ensure that his security blueprint for the event was in place before settling himself into the seat he would occupy later that evening.

***

Huey had prepared a late and filling breakfast for Power and herself. Once they had eaten, they showered and dressed before proceeding to clean up the hut. They gathered up the items they wanted to take with them, placing these into their backpacks. They burnt anything they could that was left in a small metal bucket to destroy any evidence of them having been there over the past forty-eight hours.

They then relaxed for a short while by listening to the radio Huey had brought with her before departing the hut.

***

It had taken search team #1 close to one hour and fifteen minutes from their departing point at RTF HQ in Kingstown to reach its countryside destination. It was expected that search team #2 would have reached its destination around the same time.

***

Once back at Ilaro Court, Motby and Jackie had gone their separate ways. Jackie focussed on completing preparations for Sunday lunch in the kitchen, while Motby worked in his study on the paperwork he wanted to complete. Later that afternoon, Motby was scheduled to address his constituency's monthly branch meeting. His intention was to wrap up that session by 6:30 p.m. before accompanying Jackie, Kimberley and Anton to the Leamore 'LP' Phillips concert. LP was the popular Canadian chart-topping pop, jazz, rhythm and blues recording artist/actress visiting Barbados, and performing later that evening.

***

Backpacks on, Power and Huey had headed down the hillside they had ascended, intent on being early for their pre-arranged 1:45 p.m. rendezvous. The pick-up point was deliberately different from where they had been dropped off nearly two days earlier. The Land Rover should be waiting for them.

Their projected fifty-minute downhill trek to their rendezvous took them longer than they had expected. It was made more treacherous due to a heavy downpour of rain that has taken place just before noon. Luckily, they had meet no one during their descent. The Land Rover was there. They were also fortunate not to meet any other vehicles on the minor roads until they re-joined the main highway leading them to a neighbourhood outside of Kingstown.

***

As it transpired, the scheduled 12:00 noon to 2:00 p.m. dress rehearsal performances for LP and her 'warm-up' acts, had gotten off to a late start. Walford had to wait until 1:00 p.m. before the dress rehearsals got underway because the various sound and instrument checks took much longer to perfect than was anticipated.

***

Having reached the designated area and after spending just over an hour searching for any signs of activity, search team #1 found nothing to suggest that anyone had been there recently. The heavy shower during the search of their designated countryside location had not been kind to them. It meant that the range of evidence they were seeking were no longer easy to identify and might not come into play.

Sergeant Arnold had started to report this to Gomez on his radio. Summing up search team #1's position he stated, "Unfortunately, sir, our efforts have drawn a blank..."

He suddenly stopped speaking before continuing.

"Hello, what have we here? Hang on a minute, sir."

Gomez waited. Not the most patient of men, he asked, "Casper, what's happening? Talk to me, man."

"Sir, we've just observed a washcloth. It's not something I'd expect to see out here in this wilderness Perhaps someone or persons have been here recently after all. We'll collect it and bring it back."

While Arnold was speaking, Corporal Mitch Papos reached down to carefully pick up the washcloth on the end of his army-issued rifle. Right away he recognised the washcloth's odour.

"I know this smell, Sergeant. It's from a popular perfume I bought for my girlfriend three months ago," said Papos.

"What's happening, Casper?" again asked an impatient Gomez on his radio.

"Sir, I'm being told that the washcloth found has an identifiable female perfume smell. Even its recent soaking by rain has not removed the smell. We may have something, though I'm not quite sure what it amounts to."

316

Papos flicked the washcloth over and motioned to Arnold. "Sir, the washcloth has the initials JH stitched into it. No other distinctive marks or stains that we can see. Looks pretty new too. We'll bring it back with us to HQ and the lab people can try to get something more from it…" Arnold trailed off.

"I agree, Casper. What you have is better than drawing a complete blank. See you back at HQ."

"Yes, sir," responded Arnold.

Papos placed the washcloth into a clear plastic bag provided by Arnold from his pants pocket. He then took possession of the plastic bag. Once back in the vehicle, he removed a label from the cubbyhole of the vehicle and stuck it onto the plastic bag, marking it 'Power case washcloth'. He also placed the location and date before signing his name, enabling search team #1 to commence its return journey to Kingstown.

***

Pilessar's arrival in Barbados that afternoon went unnoticed.

She was just one of the many US nationals who arrived from the USA that afternoon for any of the following reasons: three days of work with their company's local agent; attending that night's Leamore 'LP' Phillips' concert; watching the final days the intriguing Test Match; visiting to simply relax for a week in a different environment.

On her Barbados Immigration/Customs form, Pilessar had ticked the *vacation* box.

A friendly Immigration officer asked her, "What's the purpose of your visit to Barbados, ma'am?"

Pilessar responded, "The big LP concert tonight."

"How long will you be staying in our country?"

"Just one night."

"Well, I'll see you there perhaps," the immigration officer responded with a smile, before returning her documents to her.

"Enjoy your stay, ma'am."

"I certainly will."

Pilessar could have filled in any of the other more appropriate boxes shown on the Immigration/Customs form e.g. *Business*, *Visiting Friends/Relatives*, *Meeting*, but she did not. Had she done so, she feared that an Immigration officer might have asked her further, more searching or different questions that she might have struggled to answer convincingly. Why take the chance that an officer might do so and have to tell a series of lies to cover up her real reason for visiting Barbados?

Damn right! Tell a good and simple lie, get officialdom to accept it, get in, complete your business and get out, especially if it could all be done within a twenty-four-hour period. This was how Pilessar intended to complete the business she'd come to Barbados for. By this time tomorrow, she expected to be checking in at the airport to leave Barbados on the outgoing AA flight back to Miami.

Pilessar had also indicated that she would be staying at a *Private Home* on her Immigration/Customs form (she had inserted a fictitious friend and address in Plum Grove, Christ Church). She knew Immigration departments did not normally follow-up to check – she had learnt that much from her years of travelling around the world. *The Caribbean would surely not be any different*, she had thought and was right.

Once out of the Customs hall and GAIA's Arrival terminal itself, Pilessar saw the 'very tall, dark and handsome figure' her host had told her to look for.

They exchanged courtesies before he took her pull-along. "My name is Benedict Shepherd. Did you have a good flight ma'am?" he enquired.

"Yes. Smooth. Uneventful," was Pilessar's response.

She accompanied Shepherd to the ticket machine where he paid the parking fee for his vehicle's stay in the airport car park. He then led Pilessar to the vehicle where he placed her pull-along in the trunk before opening the front passenger door for her. Once she was inside, Shepherd walked around and sat down in the driver's seat before turning on the engine and the air conditioning.

He spoke to her again. "I love welcoming visitors to Barbados ma'am. You will enjoy your stay here. I'll get you to your host who's about a forty-minute ride away, so please sit back, relax and enjoy the scenic journey."

With that, Shepherd drove his vehicle towards the bank of airport car park exit booths. He inserted his parking card into the machine which gobbled it up as the barrier rose, allowing him to depart from the airport compound on a journey to the east coast of Barbados.

Pilessar appreciated that Shepherd did not say much during their journey. She was thinking about her forthcoming first face-to-face meeting with her budding Caribbean counterpart in crime. To Shepherd, Pilessar appeared to be enjoying the scenery as he drove.

On arrival at her destination, Pilessar hoped to have a late lunch, a good pina colada and an hour's rest. Then, after a shower, she'd hope to thrash out most of the parameters around a future collaborative arrangement between their two organisations with her host which might even be initialled tonight. As she planned to depart tomorrow afternoon, Pilessar hoped to be able to see some more of this supposedly beautiful island before returning to the USA. The formal signing of the contract between their organisations could then wait for signature in Miami whenever her host could get there inconspicuously, most likely on their next professional visit.

***

Surprisingly, rehearsals ended earlier than Walford had expected at 2:30 p.m. The reason for this was that Phillips had abruptly decided to shorten her rehearsal in order to get a few extra hours' sleep prior to taking the stage that evening.

Walford left the gymnasium complex thirty minutes later. He felt comfortable with the finalised security arrangements and reported this to Jeremie. The fact several VIPs were scheduled to attend tonight's concert had made the lunchtime news broadcasts was of no concern to him. For security reasons, the attendance of the Prime Minister and his party of three was, up to this time only known to Jeremie, Walford, his deputy Incident Commander and Motby's CPU team.

Walford planned to return to the complex by 5:45 p.m. Everything was set for tonight's concert.

***

The news from Sergeant Arnold's search party simultaneously disappointed and raised expectations. Getting anything from the washcloth would be a longshot, as the lab would be unavailable to them until tomorrow morning.

It turned out that search team #2, led by Corporal Conway, had drawn a blank from the countryside area it had visited. Gomez also instructed them to return to RTF HQ. As his search team #3 had also had no success from its visit to the two

319

villages on the outskirts of Kingstown, he decided that it was also time for his team to return to RTF HQ.

Each search team's expedition had been disappointing overall. Perhaps a good meal and a joint discussion by all three teams' members would inspire some new thinking on how best to pursue, capture and repatriate Power to Barbados.

So, *back to the drawing board,* thought Gomez.

***

It took RBPF patrols longer than expected to find the vehicle decorated with a Garfield and a relevant school tie. It was parked down on Brandon's, St Michael beach. Spotted by a uniformed RBPF patrol team, the reported sighting led to an unmarked RBPF vehicle quickly appearing on the scene to monitor who would return to the vehicle.

Meanwhile, a check with the BLA confirmed that the Subaru Impreza belonged to Mick and Lorburn Wayne of Scarsville, Christ Church. Were these Dr Lewis' kidnappers and if so, where had they stashed him? What was his condition? If they were not, then they might be able to advise who such persons were.

***

The *Live* Sky Sports television interview with Hon. Preston Grant MP took place during the tea interval on Day 3 of the Test Match. It went off surprisingly well, without a hitch in fact. Perhaps this was due to the West Indies being in such a good position to win the match that Oswald King did not feel inclined to press Minister Grant too hard on anything, certainly not about the current state of the game.

Grant had been prepared and was determined to pivot away from any hard or contentious questions about the country's security situation, or the missing CBOB Deputy Governor. His 'go-to' talking points were put across about the country's forthcoming Tourism and Sporting Policy initiatives and to giving a 'shout out' on the forthcoming Commonwealth Sports Minister's two-day conference which would start on Tuesday morning. The conference would be preceded by a reception on Monday evening. At the end of the interview, Grant reminded King that he and his visiting Sky Sports unit were invited to the

320

reception. He'd be happy to speak with them again on camera then if they wanted.

***

Brotherman Delaney welcomed Power to his new interim location. Huey had exited the Land Rover and disappeared without saying a word to Power who would not see her again for another few hours.

"I hope Sister Jas managed to keep you out of harm's way these past forty-eight hours?"

"She kept her and my head down alright. Now when can I move on to someplace more homely?"

"Glad to hear that. She's a good girl. Now, we'll take you to your new place soon, probably tomorrow night. You'll then be there for a few days. It'll not be as quiet as it was up in the hills, but you'll be very comfortable. Just keep your head on, start to grow a beard or something so as to start altering your features. We're close to figuring out where your final location will be," Delaney said.

"Guess I'm in your hands," responded Power.

"Yup. That bag of clothing is yours to use for the next couple of days. I'll get you something to eat in a while and then, if I were you, I'd get some sleep... I've long known that an early night works wonders around here. Tomorrow you could spend the day relaxing and then we'll get you a ride across town in the evening, probably near the end of rush hour. There'll be a lot going on so no one will take notice of us moving then. That room there is yours while you're here. In it is a solid bed and there's a bathroom at the back."

"Thank you, Brotherman."

"No problem, Baje."

***

An hour-long stakeout by RBPF officers in an unmarked vehicle finally bore fruit when two men, one looking slightly the worse for wear, approached the Subaru and were quickly approached by officers. They were startled by their approach.

"Mr Lorburn Wayne? Mr Mick Wayne? Can we have a word with both of you please?" asked an officer now standing close to the Subaru vehicle.

321

"Hey, who are you guys?" asked Mick Wayne.

"I'm Detective Philbert Fontain of the Royal Barbados Police Force and this is Detective Flynn Rice. Can we have a few words with both of you please?"

Hearing that, Lorburn Wayne took off, surprisingly heading back towards the beach and beyond that, the Caribbean Sea.

Detective Rice followed him. A former Barbados sprinter and still in his twenties, he easily caught up with the more-portly of the two Wayne brothers despite his attire and the heavy sand underfoot. Rice rugby-tackled Wayne, causing him to crash into the sand with a soft thud, bursting his bottom lip on impact.

"Why you running, sir? Now you gone and made me all sandy. These are clean clothes I put on today man and so my wife's not going to be pleased with me. You're in trouble with her and my superiors, know what I mean Mr Wayne?" asked an annoyed Rice.

"Bloody police! You caused me to burst my lip," mumbled a frustrated Wayne, rubbing his bloodied mouth while spitting out some sand. "Anyway, I don't know what you guys want to talk with me and Mick about. Tell your wife I'm sorry 'bout your clothes if you like," he concluded angrily.

"That's right Lorbee. Tell him nothing," shouted Mick Wayne to his brother as Rice brought Lorburn Wayne to his feet.

"Nothing to tell, bro," was Lorburn's fighting response.

Mick Wayne turned and spoke directly to Fontain. "You've got something to say to me too, officer?" he asked.

"Yes. We're taking both of you in for questioning at Central police station. I think you know very well what this is about," he said authoritatively.

"What about our vehicle?" asked Mick Wayne.

"We'll have someone stay with it until it can be collected by our people who will take it to Police HQ. Give us the key for the vehicle please," answered Fontain.

"Man, you guys for real?" asked Lorburn Wayne.

"Mr Wayne, your vehicle keys please," said Fontain for a second time.

"Come on fellas. Hand the keys over," pleaded Rice.

The Wayne brothers glanced at each other before Mick Wayne duly handed over their vehicle keys. It was only then they comprehended being almost encircled by several additional men who they immediately presumed to also be RBPF personnel. They wondered, *Where did they come from all of a sudden*?

"Hold still while we put these on you guys," said Fontain as he and a third officer shaped to place handcuffs on each brother.

That task completed, Rice said, "Okay fellas, let's roll out of here," marshalling the portly Lorburn Wayne off to one of the unmarked RBPF vehicles. A third officer did likewise to Mick Wayne and pointed him towards a second similarly unmarked vehicle.

"We didn't mean to hurt nobody," said Lorburn Wayne on reaching the RBPF vehicle.

"I told you to shut up," said Mick Wayne to his brother.

"That may be true, but you'll get a chance to tell your story to our boss at the station shortly and to the courts after that," said Fontain following the Wayne brothers' exchange.

Five minutes later a convoy of four unmarked RBPF vehicles made their way from Brandon's beach towards Central police station. There was no need to put on sirens.

Two officers stayed behind to watch over the Wayne brothers' Subaru vehicle until it could be collected.

**

Day 3 of the Test Match ended with England having fought back somewhat, forcing West Indies to bat again. There was still some work to be done if the West Indies wanted to win the Test Match before the end of Day 5. Scores: West Indies 525 for seven declared; England 270 all out thirty minutes after lunch. West Indies, batting a second time, had not scored quickly but were still in a good position. They ended Day 3 on 218 for nine, an overall lead of 473 runs which most people knew was already *more* than enough runs to win the Test Match, weather permitting of course. Supporters of both teams and the media wondered why the West Indies hadn't already declared. It was beyond them.

The two sets of supporters left New Kensington Oval in different moods, Sir Thadeus amongst them. For the third day running, West Indian supporters felt good overall after a day's play, although they did not understand their team's reluctance to go in for the 'kill'. The English supporters and UK cricket correspondents, on the other hand, were again unhappy. Yes, they had seen some fight from their boys in the post-tea session, but basic errors had continued to plague them while fielding. Three catches had been put down and a stumping opportunity missed. There was also some uncertain captaincy. These errors had allowed the West Indies to get away and had surely hindered England's efforts to save the game. They would have to bat extremely well in their second innings on Days 4 and 5 and hope that the heavy overnight rainfall promised by the local weather office for Monday night and early Tuesday morning), would combine to ultimately help save them from defeat. If these things came to pass, then the three-match Test series would remain alive with one Test Match to be played.

A big ask indeed! Nevertheless, both sets of supporters would return to New Kensington Oval tomorrow, determined to have some more fun at Day 4 of the Test Match.

**

It was 6:15 p.m. Castille knew and was annoyed that he had spent another unproductive day. Wharton had not been very helpful – in fact he had not provided Castille with any reliable information on the current whereabouts of Power. The rumour Castille had heard about Power having left Barbados, possibly on Thursday night or early Friday, had not yet been substantiated by Wharton. Local, regional or internet media reports he'd trawled had been equally un-helpful.

Room service and a quiet night beckoned before he would try to get some sleep. He knew that his hotel did not have on any entertainment tonight. *Damn. A fifth lonely night in paradise,* thought Castille.

"I must have come to the wrong Barbados," he said quietly to himself.

Just then, the phone rang in his room. He was tempted to answer it by saying, "Mr Wharton, I presume," but thought better of it.

"Hello!"

"Is that Mr Rice?" asked the caller.

"Wrong room," answered an annoyed Castille.

"I'm so sorry, sir." The caller hung up. Castille made a decision. He would order his evening meal from the room service menu forthwith. After eating his meal, he would take a walk on the beach and come up with a plan of attack for the next day. He recalled Wharton mentioning during one of their conversations that he ran a shop. Its location was unknown to him but he would establish its location and pay Wharton a visit first thing in the morning if he did not hear from him during this evening.

Castille picked up the house phone and dialled the room service number.

"Good evening. Room service. Sam speaking."

"Hello. Mr Castille in room 310. Please send me over meal number 14 on your room service menu, a pina colada and a pot of black coffee."

"Number fourteen, a pina colada and a pot of black coffee to room 310. Be about fifteen minutes, sir."

"That's okay." Castille hung up the house phone and switched on the television to see if he could find something interesting to watch. *I wish I was back in Miami*, he thought.

***

The second telephone call to Brotherman Delaney came around 7:15 p.m. from the soft-spoken Vincentian whom Delaney had spoken with earlier in the day. It was unexpected.

The earlier call Delaney had received around noon had confirmed that the original arrangements for their guest would remain in place. Now, this second call, its nature and timing, changed things radically. It was clear that the soft-spoken Vincentian man who had often given Delaney's gang 'projects' to complete for him, had received information warning that if he was in anyway involved with keeping the escaped Barbadian safe and away from local law enforcement, he should move his guest from wherever he was currently located to a more secure one – sooner rather than later.

The soft-spoken Vincentian had indeed been tipped off by a Government official who was now one of his best friends, having helped fund the official's daughter's completion of her master's degree overseas a couple of years ago.

"Brotherman, shift the package to the agreed back-up location Do it later tonight, ideally before 10:00 p.m."

"You sure about this? What's changed?"

"Don't ask! Just make the move."

"Fine. I'll have it taken care of. You've called ahead?"

"Yes."

"I'm onto it. Call you once it's done?"

"If you wish."

Following this latest conversation, Delaney stroked his long dreadlocks in wonder. He'd do as he was instructed. He knew that payment for his gang's services was assured. He treasured his long-standing relationship with the Vincentian caller. Delaney hoped for and expected that their 'business' relationships would continue for a good while yet.

***

"Wake up, Baje. Time to get moving," urged Delaney.

Rubbing his eyes, Power wondered what was happening.

"Get moving? What's up, Brotherman?" he asked.

"You're being shifted early. Instructions. I'll give you ten minutes to get ready to move out."

"Why? Are your police onto me?"

"Look man. I don't know. I've got my instructions, so am just following them. Get yourself together. You want to survive in Vincie country or not?"

"All right," said a worried Power.

I might have to make a break for myself because these people who should be looking out for me don't seem to know what they are doing or what's going on, he was thinking.

"Here, move with this just in case."

"You're expecting trouble, aren't you?"

"No, but just in case we ah, run into any of our law enforcement friends along the way, although I don't expect to."

With that, Delaney handed Power a bag with a few items. Power felt inside the bag and clasped the barrel of some kind of a firearm. He pulled it out and examined it briefly. The look he gave Delaney suggested that he was not convinced that the firearm would work if he was forced to use it. *It's better than nothing.*, thought Power.

Seeing the look Power had given him, Delaney spoke. "Trust me, it works! I've used it myself a couple of times."

"I can tell that it's loaded. Got any extra shells?" asked Power.

"Yes, in the bag," answered Delaney. Power felt inside the bag and found them before nodding as Delaney left him. Power went into the bathroom to wash his face and relieve himself. There was no time to do much else. Once out of the bathroom, Power put on his training shoes and went outside to join Delaney for the journey with the bag he had been given.

He hoped Delaney was not in the process of selling him out.

***

Chapter Twenty-Four
Found

Wharton received a frantic call at 7:25 p.m. from Norbert 'Nobby' Kirton. He had noticed up to four security service (police and army) vehicles moving around in his Pigeon's Nest, St Michael village from late afternoon. They appeared to be looking for something, or someone.

Given his involvement in the prisoner's escape on Wednesday, what should he do? Kirton was not someone who panicked easily. Effectively Wharton's closest associate in the Pressure Group gang, they had been friends since primary school. Their gang had been up and running now for close to four years, both having effectively 'graduated from similar units' as they liked to call them from around Barbados. As a result, Wharton and Kirton tended to see things – situations and opportunities, more clearly that the other two members of their gang. Any concern of Kirton would also be such to Wharton.

"Sit tight but be ready to move out if things start going south."

"I hear you," said Kirton.

"No reason to think that we're blown, but let's meet up in half an hour."

"Usual place?"

"Yes."

"Right. I'll call the others."

"Good. Be jolly now."

***

Members of the RTF unit were still at its HQ running down their sources for any information that may have been out there on Power's whereabouts. However, no serious leads had shown up. Unit members had even considered lucky ways they might be able to apprehending Power, but none were practical or reliable.

JJ, desperate to help, was thinking hard about how Power might be located. *What if Gomez tried something that had worked in Barbados following a hit and run incident which had enabled RBPF and BIB to quickly track down the responsible culprits? It would involve diligence, hard work and Gomez's agreement to use all members of his RTF unit and if just one of them got lucky, who knows what might result?*

He touched Gomez and moved away from the group. Gomez followed him into a corner of the room.

Speaking softly, JJ said, "TG, I've an idea. How about if we ask your RSVGPF colleagues on the move and at stations to inform you of any reported major traffic accidents or traffic infringements over the past 24 hours, or of any that might occur between now and tomorrow morning. Once we're aware of such and the people involved, the locations, etc., we might get lucky and find someone connected to Power. We might then be able to track him down in some way. Remember, we're pretty sure that Vincentians are helping Power to hide out," JJ concluded.

"Man, they are some long shots that you're trying to make me play, but I've nothing to lose. Let's try what you say," responded Gomez.

"Since you're in, can we go a bit further –" started JJ.

"Hey, I think I have your train of thought. You'd also like me to secure reports of any patients who might have attended hospital A & E's, clinics or doctor's offices for unusual treatment like from a road accident, fights, domestic dispute etc., right?"

"Well, yes. Given Power's violent history, we might also be on the lookout for patients with stab or gunshot wounds as a result of robberies too over the past few days," said JJ optimistically.

Gomez smiled. "Genius! I'll get my boys onto it. I'll only ask for reports from mainland St Vincent initially though, so would expect to start getting information within a couple of hours," responded Gomez.

"TG, I don't mean to order you to do this. I'm just trying to help out," said JJ.

"JJ, we've known and worked with each other over time. No sweat. We're going to catch your guy. When we do, we'll want you and your people to get him out of SVG and back behind bars in good old Barbados," said Gomez.

Gomez excused himself and went over to speak with Arnold and Conway. Their task was to get the word out to the specified Vincentian entities. Gomez also instructed that any responses with relevant information be related to him immediately, no matter what time of night it was as he planned to spend the night at the RTF's HQ compound.

***

It was 8:15 p.m. when Commissioner Jeremie received word from Vickers that Dr Albert Lewis, Deputy Governor, CBOB had been found and was alive and well, though he was hungry and dehydrated. He was being taken to the country's main medical facility, Queen Elizabeth Hospital (QEH).

"Thank God for that," said Jeremie.

"Sir, will you call the Prime Minister and Governor Edwards, and can I notify the family?"

Jeremie agreed to Vickers' three suggested actions, adding, "Good job, Johnny."

"Thank you, sir. Have a good evening."

Vickers' looked up the Lewis' number from the 'Contacts' section in his phone. He called and spoke with Bertram Lewis. Vickers passed on the good news that Dr Lewis had been found and was safe following a rescue intervention by an RBPF team. He was being taken to QEH to be medically checked over. Vickers encouraged Lewis to inform the rest of the Lewis family and suggested that they make their way to QEH in another half-an-hour or so to see their husband and father.

***

Jeremie made the promised calls. The Prime Minister's phone was not answered, so after half a dozen rings Jeremie sent him a brief WhatsApp message: "Lewis found alive and well. He's now at QEH being medially checked-out. Please call me at your convenience for further update. Com J."

It was only then that Jeremie remembered that Motby was attending the LP concert at the Garfield Sobers Sports Complex. That explained Motby's unusual behaviour of not answering his phone. It made no sense Jeremie calling Walford to ask him to ask Motby to take the call either, as this was *not* a national emergency, though important. Jeremie did not want to disturb Motby on one of the few nights (no, hours) that he was taking away from Government business, except for when he was asleep. They would undoubtedly speak later, and this would give Jeremie more time to gather additional information on what had transpired with Dr Lewis over the past five days he had been missing.

Next, he called Governor Edwards who was over the moon on hearing the news.

"I'm much relieved…and grateful to you, Commissioner. I'm available to make my way over to see Albert shortly if that's advised. Otherwise I'll catch up with him tomorrow, at home I presume. I take it his family has also been advised?"

"They are being informed by Chief Superintendent Vickers as I speak with you, Governor."

"I thank you and members of your Force for their excellence work on this. I'll speak with you again soon and write formally to express my and the Bank's appreciation for everything," said Edwards.

"No problem Governor. That's what we're here for. Goodnight."

Jeremie also decided to make a third call. Colonel Burke received the information calmly and stated that he would alert his operatives who had been working on the case accordingly.

***

Bertram Lewis, having taken the brief call from Vickers, informed his sister and mum that Dad had been found alive and well. Mrs Lewis started to sob, not in pain but from pure relief. Caroline Lewis-Greenidge wanted to know more. Was her dad really okay? Where was he found? How soon could they see him? When would he be able to come home?

Lewis held up his hand.

"Hold on, sis. Let me tell you what little Chief Superintendent Vickers told me…"

After relaying what he'd been told by Vickers, Lewis suggested they all get dressed to go to QEH. Fifteen minutes later they were set to get underway. Everyone was relieved that Dr Lewis had been found and was apparently in a good condition. What had happened to him over the past five days could be established later. Mrs Lewis sat in the back seat of the car. She was still crying, but in a happy way. Lewis-Greenidge sat beside her mother. Having always been close to her dad and often said to be 'the apple of his eye' by other family members, she was staring out of the window while holding her mother's hand, remembering more fun times she'd spent with her dad.

Ava Prescod sat in the front seat beside Lewis. She had spent Sunday with the Lewis family and when asked by Mrs Lewis to accompany them to QEH, had willingly agreed to do so. Dr Lewis was a good man to work for and he'd never been known to leave her out of any major family celebrations. She guessed this was another such occasion, going to see that he was fine along with the rest of his delighted family.

***

Moss had worked his way through most of the properties (eight of the ten guesthouses, twenty-five of the thirty hotels) on the south coast by 8:30 p.m. He'd only taken a break once during the day to grab a cup of coffee and eat a double slice of pizza. Not his usual Bajan Sunday lunch at all!

He was therefore 'running out of gas' when the call had come through from Vickers for him to urgently make his way to QEH. The call had surprised him, given the mandate he had earlier been given by Vickers to try and complete the task that he had been set by the evening. Moss had already sent home the two rookie police constables that Vickers had provided to help Moss from mid-afternoon in an attempt to complete the exercise that night. Vickers' call effectively changed the outcome of that objective.

***

Coming up to 8:45 p.m. on this Sunday night, SBB&G was quiet. There was no big crowd in SBB&G. On his arrival and as was usual for a Sunday, Wharton decided there and then to close up early, no later than 10:30 p.m. Even the English cricket fans who had patronised the bar in great numbers since their arrival in Barbados from the previous Tuesday afternoon, were very few in number. He suspected that some of them were attending the LP concert and once that was over, they would either head for the nearest bar or return to their hotel for some overnight rest before attending Day 4 of the Test Match.

Nobby Kirton had called the other two members of their Pressure Group to SBB&G, so they were all waiting for Wharton. Once in the back room (his office), Wharton asked a staffer to bring in four Banks beers and not to disturb him afterwards.

A couple of minutes later, each with a beer in hand, Pressure Group members discussed Power's last known potential location. Word on the street had reached them on Friday night that Power was no longer in Barbados, possibly in either St Lucia or St Vincent. Wharton had notified them late on Thursday afternoon that Power had left his house in Bathsheba, but where he had gone was unknown. News that Power might have left Barbados, possibly that same Thursday night, had not shocked them.

There had been no further updates, so they still did not know for sure where Power was tonight. Nor did Castille, Wharton told his fellow gang members.

Also, for law enforcement officers to visit this St Michael district where Power was known to have intermittently resided within the last ten years was not a surprise. The exact address was a house just two streets away from where Kirton lived. In fact, Power's mother still lived there.

Once Kirton had left home, he had received a call from his neighbour that the police had been following up on a lead in their search for the missing CBOB Deputy Governor, now unaccounted for since the previous Tuesday night. The caller did not know if they had found him.

As it was now clear to Pressure Group members that the visit by law enforcement members to Kirton's St Michael district had been nothing to do with him or their Wednesday morning 'rescue' of Power, Kirton felt the need to apologise to his gang colleagues for over-reacting. They understood and accepted his apology. Potential threat to themselves over, Pressure Group members now wanted to get away from SBB&G to get on with whatever plans they had for the remainder of their Sunday night.

Before they left, Wharton felt it necessary to remind them of his earlier admonition that they should continue as normal with their daily routines, he running SBB&G and Kirton as a self-employed tiler.

As for the other two gang members, Keith Lee (a handyman at a Bridgetown mall and relief/ part-time watchman at a private school on Thursday and Saturday nights) and Arnold Rowe (a former but now unemployed lorry driver with a major construction firm), they were to follow their usual routines of working (or not in Rowe's case) each day. Wharton urged them, above all, not to 'splash the cash' that they had gained from Power's rescue around. Everyone nodded. No mass spending would take place. Pressure Group members then left and went their separate ways, satisfied that they were all safe.

***

Castille was glad that he'd taken that walk after his meal. He had not heard from jolly man Wharton so would go and find him in the morning. There *had to be something new and specific* on Power's whereabouts by then. If it was true that Power had gone to a neighbouring island, he'd expected Wharton to be able to confirm this and pinpoint which island he was on. Then he could book a flight, travel there, find Power and extract *The Organisation's* funds from him. If the only way to solve the problem for *The Organisation* was to finish Power off, then he'd do that too. He needed to complete his assignment.

Castille eventually fell into a deep sleep, unaware that Moss was closing in on establishing that the room key card found inside Telford's vehicle was from the south coast where Castille was staying at, and that it would be traced back to him by the RBPF.

***

Unknown to three members of the Pressure Group, one amongst them had not been exactly honest with his colleagues that evening. That member had already broken their agreement, though in his view, he hadn't been on any mass spending spree. He'd only bought himself something that was much needed at home. Yes, he'd made a cash purchase, but who would know that? At SBB&G that night, this gang member had therefore maintained his silence, even after Wharton's second request of them. Who was it that said 'honesty among thieves, gang members or persons operating anywhere on the cusp of illegality, was guaranteed'? That person was wrong.

Looking back, that sojourn to Bridgetown and then Fontabelle three days earlier on Thursday, would be the tip that led law enforcement agencies to identify the first Pressure Group member. Once you had him, who were the other members of the gang and how soon could one get to them?

***

In St Vincent, Power's departure from Delaney was delayed. Why was not explained to him.

They had already passed through central Kingstown safely and were heading to the other side of the city when the accident happened. Power was sitting in the back of the enclosed van as it travelled up the hill on Murray Road. Two motorcyclists were racing each other, travelling in the opposite direction to the van. They either did not see or could not make the adjustment to avoid hitting the van.

Both cycles smashed into the van head on which caused the van to careen out of control off the road, breaking through the concrete barrier and down a steep precipice. The van rolled repeatedly until it came to rest, twenty-five feet below the side of the road. One of the mangled motorcycles and its injured rider were also catapulted on an unexpected journey in a similar direction to the van. The second motorcyclist fared slightly better as he'd only been thrown on impact with the van from his motorcycle and now laid in a heap in the middle of the road. His broken motorbike was close by.

It was still early in St Vincent at 9:05 p.m. Vehicles following the van had witnessed the accident take place. Drivers stopped and rushed to try and lend assistance to those who had been hurt. These potential rescuers realised that safely getting down the steep precipice was going to be tricky.

As luck would have it, a St Vincent and the Grenadines Fire & Rescue Service (SVGFRS) vehicle on its way back to its central Kingstown base after putting out a fire at Villa, came along five minutes after the accident. It stopped and its occupants immediately proceeded to assist the Good Samaritan Vincentians who had stopped their vehicles to do their best to assist the unconscious motorcyclist in the road. His fellow motorcyclist was not visible.

As for those in the van, whoever they were, no one had yet reached them. SVGFRS to the rescue?

Walford enjoyed the first half of the LP-headlined concert. The 'warm-up' Barbadian artists had delighted the large crowd with their performances. *No security issues so far*, he thought gratefully.

Following a twenty-minute interval when the stage was re-set for Leamore 'LP' Phillips', Canada's most popular international singing star and actress, the house lights dimmed as an off-stage announcer spoke from the darkened stage to introduce Phillips' ninety-minute performance.

The audience went wild, screaming, shouting and clapping as LP came on stage. Phillips was handed a microphone as she greeted the crowd. Her band kicked in and Phillips launched into her latest worldwide hit from six months earlier called 'Let's Ride'.

***

Having worked his way down to the area where the badly damaged van now stood, Leading Fire Officer Maxwell Ferogie, officer-in-charge of the SVGFRS unit, found two persons.

One, a female was strapped into the front passenger's seat of the van. Her seatbelt had kept her in position. A man, most likely the driver, lay a few yards from where the van had come to a rest. Ferogie surmised that the man might not have been wearing his seatbelt at the time of the collision and had therefore been thrown through the van's windshield on one of its impacts with the ground. Ferogie felt for a pulse. There was none.

Jasmine Sister Jas Huey was the female passenger. Forty-five minutes after the accident had taken place, she had been recovered and was on her way to the Kingstown General Hospital. She was in bad shape, with a broken right leg, broken right arm, at least two broken ribs, a busted jaw and had lost her front teeth. She was in great pain, slipping into and out of consciousness and so understandably had not been able to answer any questions about the accident or who else may have also been in the van besides the herself and the driver.

Ferogie's quick search of the vehicle found a bag of clothes, men's clothing. He also found a note in the glove compartment. Both items suggested that there had at least been one other person in the van at some time during its journey. Had this person been in the van when it had gone off the road?

The piece of plain white paper had an address written on it and a message…
"JP to ask for Cedric on arrival."

Ferogie wondered who JP was? Might this note have any significance to the crash?

His instinct told him that it did, but he could not immediately work out how it might have. The address was familiar to him. It was thought to be a safe place, a 'recovery house' where recent Vincentian drug addicts could go to for help. The facility was run by one of the island's charities and was located within sight of the old Arnos Vale airport. Ferogie knew the charity to do good work because it had assisted his nephew a couple of years ago when he had gone there a few times for psychological treatment as part of his efforts to beat his drug habit. The initials on the paper meant nothing to Ferogie. Why should they?

***

Power had watched as the rescue effort commenced and then intensified.

He knew that he'd been lucky to survive the crash. He had been wearing his seatbelt and was sitting in one of the back seats in the van. When the motorcycles had crashed into the van, the back door had been flung open. The fall down the precipice was quick. Along with the impacts as the van rolled over on its way to the bottom of the drop, the impact on each occasion seemed harder and harder but Power had managed to remain calm. Once the van came to a complete stop, he'd disengage himself from his seatbelt (it still worked, despite the several jolts it had received) and quickly crawled away. The van's contents had been thrown around. Indeed, Power had felt during the fall like he was in a tumble dryer machine. He could still see the crash location from his hiding spot. Huey remained strapped in the van's front passenger's seat, but he could not see the van's driver. He assumed that he had been thrown through the windscreen at some point during the fall down the precipice. Trying to help either of his fellow passengers would only get him recaptured, something he could not afford, hence his focus remained purely on escaping.

***

Dr Lewis looked up when the door of one of the examination rooms in the inner sanctum of the Accident & Emergency wing of QEH opened, ushering in a junior doctor, his wife, son, daughter and Prescod to set eyes on him for the first time in six days. Vickers, Moss, Dr Ronald 'Ron' Hayes, QEH's Chief of Surgery and a nurse were already with Dr Lewis.

"Hi folks. What are you two kids doing in Barbados?" asked Dr Albert Lewis, trying hard to smile.

"Dad, it's good to see you. You went AWOL so had Mum and the two of us very worried. How come we couldn't find you for the past few days?"

Surprisingly, it was not Lewis-Greenidge who was speaking, but Lewis.

Mrs Lewis jumped in with her own questions before Dr Lewis could answer his son. "How you doing, Al? Have you been eating? How do you feel right now?"

"Look, let me again apologise up-front for the mis-steps which have resulted in my absence from you in recent days. I did a stupid thing after leaving work early on Tuesday afternoon. As I've already told the RBPF officers here, I returned to a doctor that afternoon to get something further for the bad cough Mum knows I'd had for a few days prior. That in itself was not a stupid thing to do. What I did next was though. On leaving the doctor, I felt like taking a drive up the west coast."

"Dad, I don't understand why you didn't just go straight home." It was Lewis-Greenidge being her usual blunt self.

"I ah…wanted a drive up the west coast. I also felt the need to have a stiff drink and so stopped off at a bar for one. It felt good to do so at the time, but I soon realised that I shouldn't have had done that, given the medication I had been taking earlier."

Lewis-Greenidge jumped in again. "Dad, that's not like you. Surely –"

"I know Caroline. It *was* stupid of me all around. Anyway, can I finish telling you what happened? Please?"

Everyone watched him but no one answered, so Dr Lewis continued his intentional monologue.

"Right. As I was saying I felt sleepy after the drink, so went to the car to sleep it off. A couple of hours must have passed before I woke up and caught myself –"

"What happened then?" asked Lewis impatiently.

"I was hungry. I also had an urge to listen to some music. You all know what I like, the back in time stuff. I'd heard about a club in St Lawrence Gap where that kind of music is played on Monday and Tuesday nights, so I went in search

338

of it. There was no place to park though it was still early in the evening, but one of the craft vendors directed me to a spot and pointed out the club. I went in, had a meal and a soft drink before leaving around minutes to ten to come home. The music played was good. As I approached my car, I noticed that I had a flat tyre. A couple of guys offered to help me put on the spare. I thanked them. They asked me to drop them in Kendall Hill. I didn't object since they'd helped me and it was all on my way home."

"Dad, why were you so trusting? I'd never do that in the States," injected Lewis-Greenidge.

"Yes. You're right. Anyway, I was told where to drop them off. As I did so, I felt a blow to the back of my head. I blacked out. When I came to, I realised that I was in the boot of my own vehicle, going where I did not know. I was subsequently moved around in different vehicles and from house to house until the police found me… I still don't know where my vehicle is."

"I can confirm that the Force has not found Dr Lewis' vehicle to date, but will continue looking for it," stated Vickers.

"That's some story, Dad. We wondered if someone had kidnapped you for money, but never called us with a ransom demand," said Lewis.

"Trust me, those two guys wanted more than a ride home. Robbing me was probably their goal all along, but as they did not get much money from me that night, I suspect they got confused and ended up kidnapping me. As that wasn't planned, they obviously forgot to demand a ransom. Stranger things have happened, eh? How a criminal's mind works I'll never know. The guys never failed to feed me, nor did they do me any harm. They even gave me ice to put on the bump on my head from Tuesday night through Wednesday. Yes, my dignity's been hurt. I've embarrassed the Bank, my family. Overall, I realise I've been stupid and can only sincerely apologise to everyone for my behaviour," concluded Dr Lewis.

Dr Hayes chimed in, seeking to break up this confession story. He needed to get home after a long day.

"I don't want to spoil this reunion Dr Lewis, but I want your family to know that we've checked you over. Except for having the back-end of a bad cold, you're physically well and mentally alert. The swelling from the bump you indicated you'd received to the back of your head has disappeared. There's nothing more that we can do for you tonight. I recommend plenty of rest and generous intakes of liquid over the next seventy-two hours. A full recovery is projected for you sir. I've prescribed some medication for you to help clear up the remnants of your cold and to help speed your recovery. You'll be free to return to work thereafter."

"Thanks, Doctor," said Mrs Lewis.

"Prior to your arrival, we'd arranged a private bed for you to stay overnight for observation, but since we've now determined otherwise, I'll authorise your release in care of your wife on my way out. Dr Lewis, here's my card if you or your wife need to contact me for anything further," said Dr Hayes.

He handed Mrs Lewis one of his business cards, nodded at Vickers and Moss and headed for the door to leave the room. "Night, folks," were Dr Hayes' parting words. The nurse followed him.

"I'd better be going too. I still have a few more visits to make tonight," said Moss.

"Byron, can you fit them all in tonight?" asked Vickers.

"I doubt it, sir. I plan to work up to 11:00 p.m. and then make an early start tomorrow. All being equal, I expect to be done by 9:00 a.m.," responded Moss.

"Fine. Good luck, but call me once you've knocked off tonight."

"I'll do that, sir. Bye everyone."

With that, Moss also departed, leaving the Lewis family alone with Vickers in the A&E room.

"Last week's all behind us now dear. We're all so glad to have you back with us," said Mrs Lewis, unabashedly hugging her husband before kissing him on both sides of his face.

"I'll call home to tell Jack and the kids that you are safe, Dad. Excuse me for a few minutes please," said Lewis-Greenidge, hustling out of the room as an orderly arrived with a wheelchair to help Dr Lewis with leaving QEH's premises.

"We've brought some clean clothes for you. Do you want to change before we leave this place?" asked Lewis.

"No, Bertie. Let's just get out of here," was Mrs Lewis prompt response.

***

Ferogie spoke with his two colleagues who had joined him at the crash location where the van now rested. They started to search for a third person who might have also been thrown from the van and could be lying around, badly injured. They might have missed he or she in their rush to get to those in the van in the originally poorly-lit area. Using the lights on their helmets, they searched more carefully. No one else was there, lying around or otherwise.

Later, in their search of the van before the wrecker truck that had been summoned was making its preparations to recover the vehicle, Ferogie took another look inside the van. He hadn't noticed it before, but there was fresh blood on the inside of the vehicle, confirming without doubt that someone else besides the driver and the front seat female passenger had also been there and may also have been hurt. Whoever the person was, they had managed, for whatever reason to make a quick (and he suspected a painful) escape from the scene.

Ferogie then remembered receiving an alert on his unit's way to the Villa fire requesting that all emergency services should report any traffic accidents to RSVGPF's RTF unit and any persons involved therein. He surmised there was the possibility that the missing person might be someone the local police were looking for, so he decided to contact Gomez, an old friend from secondary school directly.

***

Lewis was an experienced criminal lawyer. He knew there were a lot of holes in his dad's story. What they had been told by his dad did not add up. But what the hell, once his dad stuck to his story, Lewis and the rest of their family would have to accept it and move on, unless the police officers did not. To challenge his dad's version of his absence minus any evidence to the contrary would be futile and unnecessary. Anyway, his reason for coming home had been achieved.

He and his sister had their dad back and a wife had her husband home again. He wanted to leave it at that.

***

Chief Superintendent Vickers had not shared with Mrs Lewis or her children what had been discussed in his earlier private discussion with Dr Lewis about the mislabelled, erroneous laboratory results. Dr Dawson had not been at fault. The results shared had *not* been Dr Lewis', because of the mix-up at the laboratory where a mislabelling of samples and erroneous results had been provided. The results attached to the confidential medical records were therefore all incorrect for that unfortunate day. Such should never have happened, but it had. The laboratory could expect to be prosecuted by the affected doctors and individuals for its incompetence at some future time. The laboratory's future would certainly be under a cloud.

Dr Lewis had fallen victim to what, the successful candidate in the US Presidential election of November 2016 had coined as '*fake news*'.

Once Vickers told Dr Lewis that he had insisted that Dr Dawson reveal the (erroneous) blood test results that had been given to him at the Dawson Clinic on that Tuesday afternoon, Dr Lewis admitted that the news from Dr Dawson had indeed 'set me off'.

"How could I go home and tell Betty whom I've been faithful to for all of the thirty-five years we've been married that I was HIV positive which would lead to my having the AIDS virus?" was his question.

Dr Lewis explained that he had felt the need to calm himself down and to think on his own after receiving the alarming news. He wanted to work out what and how he would tell his wife. His intention was to tell her the very Tuesday night. Shocked, embarrassed and frightened for his own well-being, he had stupidly decided to go for a drive up the west coast to think how this situation could have come to pass. Yes, he had even thought of taking his life, but as his life-long philosophy was to give everything time and that most issues eventually resolve themselves, usually in a positive way, he had dismissed that option.

Dr Lewis was now extremely glad he had *not pulled that trigger*, so to speak.

He had also explained to Vickers why he thought the blood test results *might* have been correct. He had given blood a few months earlier at a mobile blood collection facility to help a fellow Central Bank employee who had been involved in a car accident. In his ignorance, he wondered whether that process could have been faulty, e.g. if a contaminated needle had been used in the process and as a result, he had been infected in that way? Not being a medical doctor, his fears and imagination had run amok. These had led him to make bad decisions at the wrong time about the wrong thing last Tuesday night. He and his family had paid the price for those errors. He would forever chastise himself for not directly going home from Dr Dawson in the first instance! He was not thinking clearly at all back then.

The bright side of the situation was that he did not tell his wife a harrowing story. Thank God he had not. Now, in the calm, loving and comfortable arms of his family inside QEH, Dr Lewis was greatly relieved. Had the laboratory error not been made and passed onto him, none of what had transpired would ever have taken place. Six days and nights of uncertainty were over.

***

Power wondered why the van he was moving in have to get into an accident on a quiet Sunday night? As he was only hiding behind a two-foot hedge from which he was sure he would be discovered in any search of the immediate accident area, Power had decided to move further away once he could find a safer hiding place. Power knew rescuers would shortly come looking to assist the van's injured passengers. Limping gingerly and keeping low, he started to move away from the hedge just as a small dog appeared and started to bark. Though the dog did not attack him, it continued to bark shrilly. This caused his already throbbing head, banged about during the van's fall, to pound even more furiously. He looked around for a stick to defend himself from the dog in case it attacked him, but found none. His left hand was by now also hurting from the cut he'd gotten from broken glass inside the van when he'd made his escape.

Power decided to keep his eyes on the dog while continuing to move towards a wall that was no more than five feet tall just a few yards ahead of him. Once he got there, Power knew that he would find a way to get over the wall, leaving both the barking dog and his potential local rescuers behind. Power did not wish to meet anymore Vincentians tonight because he knew this would mean his having to tell Vincentian law enforcement officials what he knew about the accident. This in turn, by his voice alone, would give him away, showing up who he was. Power knew what that would mean, a speedy return for him to Barbados where a country facility named HMP Dodds, his least favourite place on the planet, would gladly welcome and accommodate him for a very long time to come.

The dog came closer. Power stopped in his tracks. How to shut up and distract this dog to reach and scale the wall was his next challenge. Typical for him, he quickly found a solution. He'd often heard that dogs will eat most things once it's nicely presented to them. He would try to prove this belief.

Brotherman Delaney had given Power a third item as he had entered the van, a pack of thin but meaty sandwiches to eat on arrival at his destination. They were still in the waist pouch that he had strapped around his waist on leaving Delaney's home.

343

"These will keep you till morning."

Power was not going to use the gun Delaney had given him on this small dog. It was time to use his common sense. He quickly realised that giving the dog a couple of the meaty sandwiches to eat would stop his barking for a while and distract it from paying attention to him, allowing him sufficient time to cover the short distance required to reach and climb over the wall. The cuts on his forehead and left hand were hurting like hell, but had not hindered his thinking. Power was still focussed on achieving his ultimate goal of escape.

Power put his simple plan into action. He withdrew a couple of sandwiches from his pouch and threw them on the ground a few feet away from where he was standing. The dog continued to bark but did not move for a few seconds. Nor did Power. Then, tongue hanging out, the dog went for the sandwiches. As he did so, Power took the three steps he needed to reach the wall. Once there, he hopped onto an oil can about two feet high that stood beside the wall. Power hoped it was sturdy enough to support him. It was. He pulled himself up and over the remaining height of the wall. He did not know what was on the other side. Another dog, cactus plants? Lucky for him, he landed quietly on firm grass.

Twenty minutes after the accident, Power found himself walking down a secondary road heading back in the direction, he thought, of central Kingstown, away from the crash location. It was surprisingly quiet. He encountered no one. Only the occasional vehicle passed him by.

Then Power had an idea.

***

Veronica Ash was returning home from an outdoor church revival meeting in central Kingstown when she saw something lying in the road. She was not sure what to make of what it was in the middle of the road. Her headlights picked up what she thought was an individual, was that a body? Her next thought was that this was probably the result of a hit and run accident. As Ash was close to her home, she slowed right down. Putting on her full beams, she thought *yes, that's someone hurt!* As a practicing Christian, she felt compelled to assist the unfortunate soul. Stopping her car, she turned off the engine but left the headlights on. Before exiting the car, she remembered that her husband had always told her never stop, especially at night to pick up or help anyone that she did not know. Nevertheless, the Good Samaritan in her took over and so she walked over to the person lying in the road.

As she approached, she noticed the person make a slight movement with their right hand and a moaning noise. Frightened, but convinced that she had to help and do the right thing, Ash moved closer. As she started to bend over them, the person – a man, reached up and grabbed her arm. This action caused her to fall to the ground. She screamed in pain from the hard yank and the blow to her knee as she hit the roadway.

"Give me your car keys," said the man in an unfamiliar accent. Later, she would recall that it sounded like a Barbadian. She knew this because one of her previous church pastors from fifteen years earlier had the same accent.

"In the car. Please don't hurt me anymore," said Ash.

"I won't lady. I only want your vehicle," responded Power.

With that, Power got into Ash's car and drove off.

Ash realised she had made a mistake. Her mobile phone was in the front seat, so she could not even call her husband. She'd observed that the man who had hijacked her car had a cut in the middle of his forehead and another one on his left hand.

Thankfully, Ash was just five minutes away from her home when she had been hijacked. Still in shock, she was able to make it home on foot. There, she reported what had happened to her alarmed husband, who in turn promptly reported the incident to the RSVGPF.

There were six important things her husband was able report to the RSVGPF about the incident. First, the approximate time it had taken place. Second, where the incident had occurred. Third, what the man had looked like. Fourth, that the man had a Barbadian accent. Fifth, he had cuts – in the centre of his forehead and on his left hand. Six, he provided the make of vehicle and its licence number. This would help the RSVGPF in locating the vehicle once they started their search for it and its temporary occupant.

***

Leading fire officer Ferogie had asked to speak with Gomez when he had called in the accident and his suspicions to the FTC unit. Gomez was happy to hear the details. Having known each other from school days, their paths had since crossed many a time given their respective occupations.

Gomez was able to clarify some of Ferogie's initial findings and suspicions. He had placed the call on speaker to enable both JJ and Sergeant Arnold to listen in on the conversation. All three men instantly grasped the substance of what Ferogie was suggesting about the possibility of a third person having been in the van at the time of the accident. The mention of the initials JP on the note found by Ferogie helped JJ to fix their thinking once this was thrown into the mix.

Less than an hour later, now having also seen the report on Ash's incident, it became clear to both Gomez, Arnold and JJ that the man who had hijacked and taken Ash's vehicle had almost certainly been Power. He was therefore not only dangerous, but also mobile. Thankfully, they had details of the vehicle and the general direction in which he had set off.

Central Kingstown.

Gomez decided that his RTF unit and supporting agencies needed to cut off Power at all points leading out of the Greater Kingstown area. Once they could do this quickly, their chances of capturing Power sometime tonight would be enhanced. Power might be on the move, but they were sure he had absolutely no idea where he was going. The three men agreed that given the circumstances, were any of them him, they would try to find someplace to hide out for the rest of the night and tomorrow, before trying to move on Monday night to somewhere far away from any built-up areas in the country.

Gomez badly wanted to recapture Power. He believed that this night was their best chance of doing so. He was also clear in his mind that Power's recapture was unlikely to come without a fight of some kind. JJ even anticipated that the people who had been looking after Power since his arrival in St Vincent would by now have provided him with a weapon of some kind to defend himself should he be cornered by law enforcement authorities.

***

JJ left Gomez's side, hoping to find a quiet room. There was none, so he found a vacant corner and typed out a brief but coded message to Colonel Burke on his secure BIB mini-computer about the almost certain sighting of Power. The reply he got was a seven-letter one. STABPWC.

JJ knew this meant… '*Seek to Apprehend but Proceed with Care*'.

JJ had always known that on this trip, his carefully secured and maintained 'old faithful' weapons might be needed. These were the Glock 19 and Sig-Sauer

P226 weapons now in his backpack. He had carried them on any major assignment he had undertaken for several years. They offered good and reliable protection if he ever found himself in a firefight situation where their use could be crucial to securing BIB's desired outcome in a particular situation.

Given that he was dealing with Power, the next few hours might require him having to use his weapons. Unless the Vincentians used theirs first!

***

Walford watched Phillips' encore from his comfortable Incident Commander's station high up in the Garfield Sobers Sports Complex.

From that vantage point, he had to admit that tonight's concert experience had been an enjoyable one, if only because it had been free of any security problems. It was only left now for the patrons to leave the complex safely. His traffic officers would try and see to that.

***

Having visited the QEH and seen that Dr Lewis was none the worse for wear despite his near week-long ordeal, Moss resumed his hotel assignment. He worked through another two hotels before deciding to call it quits for the night. He would make an early start in the morning by tackling the final cluster of three hotels to complete his task. They were larger properties but located quite close to each other. A couple of hours work at most. One of them was sure to have what he was looking for.

He made the promised call to Vickers on his way home to Pearle.

"Do you want another two men with you in the morning?"

"No, I can handle it. Night, sir."

"Good night, Byron."

***

Power had driven around slowly for over an hour without having much of an idea where he was going. His head had continued to throb from the blow he had taken to his forehead where blood from the cut was trickling. So too, was the blood from his left arm.

Power pulled into a darkened ally. This was a woman's car, so there had to be a first aid kit or some form of clothing or cloth somewhere in the vehicle that he could use to attempt to wipe away blood and stem the blood flow with. After a check of the back seat, Power found a skirt and a scarf. He also found a small first aid box under the front passenger's seat.

Ten minutes later, Power thought to himself, *That's better*. He had done his best to clean up the two wounds and stem the bleeding. Not knowing anyone that he could turn to for help in St Vincent besides Brotherman Delaney, he decided to use the woman's phone he'd found in the front seat of her car to call him.

There was no answer from Delaney.

Frustrated and not certain of what his next move should be, Power had at first decided to hunker down in the car simply to think.

Then, once he'd worked out his next move, he'd get moving again. But not in the woman's car. He realised that she would have reported the hijack to Vincentian police. Details of her car would have circulated, along with her description of him. He was sure these details would be all over the place soon, if they were not already.

Power knew he needed a new vehicle and fast. Thoughts of tiredness and sleep quickly disappeared as his survival instincts kicked in. He needed to get as far away as he could from St Vincent's capital city as soon as possible. He'd then try to find a place to lie low on his own tomorrow well before daylight arrived if he could not reach Delaney during the night.

He tried Delaney's number again. Still no answer.

***

Chapter Twenty-Five
Captured

MONDAY, 23 APRIL

Unknown to Power, Brotherman Delaney's practice was only to answer his phone if he recognised the number or person's name that showed up on his log. Delaney did not know anyone named Veronica, let alone a Veronica Ash. This was one of his most basic and sensible security default positions that he had implemented and followed for the past two years now.

Delaney did not answer his phone when Power had called the first time. Nor did he do so ten minutes later when Power had tried to reach him for a second time. Nor would he answer his phone the third and fourth time Power called.

Delaney *did* answer a call from a number he knew, that of the soft-spoken Vincentian who lived in Cane Garden.

Delaney was asked if he had heard about the accident that had occurred on Murray Road earlier that night. Delaney said he hadn't. When Delaney was told that it had involved a van which had left the road and was now lying at the bottom of a steep precipice and at least one of its passengers had died – a male, this made Delaney literally sit up in the bed. *What the hell had gone wrong? Was Power the dead male passenger?* Possibly, because Delaney knew that the other male in the van had been the driver.

Oh dear, he thought to himself. *There goes my reputation*. His people hadn't managed to safely deliver Power to the location after all. What a pity. Unfortunately, it was not something that he could now easily rectify. Delaney sincerely hoped that in time, the person who had just called would afford him another opportunity to come good by delivering on another project.

It bugged Delaney that the assignment he had masterminded had gone awry. He would eventually establish why. He liked Baje and so his death or recapture would damage his local reputation, but only short term he had reasoned. His life's experience to date suggested that, once given time, reputations could be rebuilt. He recalled his grandmother's words: "Worrying never helped anybody." She still held a special place in his heart as she had raised him following his parents' departure for the United States.

Delaney did not think about the two calls he had ignored earlier. When another two calls also came from Veronica Ash during the night, he wasn't even aware of them because he had turned off his phone and fallen back into a deep sleep after those initial few minutes of concern. He would deal with any repercussions that came from tonight's accident after a good night's rest. He could not change what had already happened. Tomorrow would be a day when he would establish what had gone wrong.

***

Power broke the driver's-side window of a taxi that was parked in a residential driveway before hot-wiring the vehicle.

Its owner was Jenson Parchmore who heard his taxi being started up. Instantly alarmed, because no one else had keys to his taxi, he'd run out of his house in his undershorts (against his wife's wishes). He saw his taxi being reversed out of their newly built driveway into the road before watching it disappear into the distance. There was no point in him shouting, or chasing after the driver of his taxi because he knew the driver was never going to stop.

Whoever it was, Parchmore hoped that they were only 'borrowing' his taxi to get home somewhere on the other side of the island. Perhaps the police would recover his taxi in the morning, hopefully with it being fully intact at best and at worse having only minor damage to its exterior and interior. A write-off would be most painful as his taxi was only six months old.

Once back inside, Parchmore called the RSVGPF to report that his taxi had been stolen from his driveway. His insurance company was notified next. Only then did he remember that he'd left his wallet underneath the driver's seat. *Idiot!* It contained the takings from his island tour from that day.

Ah well, if the thief searches and finds my wallet, there goes the money I had to pay the men for finishing off the last part of my driveway, thought Parchmore.

By 1:30 a.m., Power was driving around in the taxi he'd stolen, more uncertainly than before.

***

The blockade set up to catch Jasper Power on the assumption that he was somewhere inside the Greater Kingstown area, had been established relatively quickly. Gomez's teams at the main intersections around Kingstown would simply wait for a break.

Meanwhile, clinics, hospitals and police stations across St Vincent remained on high alert for any males entering their facilities looking remotely like Power or speaking with a Bajan accent. Such persons would be reported and held, with calls being made to Gomez and his RTF unit who would be expected to get to the location quickly to apprehend the person.

***

Gomez was ready to catch an alien criminal. From all he'd heard and read in recent days about Power, he did not think it would be easy. Gomez half-expected gunfire to be exchanged, preferably in an isolated area that was not too public a place.

Gomez pulled JJ aside. "I'm ordering my men to wear bullet-proof vests. Do you want one?"

"Yes please. I was going to recommend that move if you hadn't. I've brought two weapons with me that I hope not to have to use. Tell me, do your people have written permission from Commissioner Gaynor to shoot at Power if there's no choice but to do so?" asked JJ.

Gomez signalled to one of his RTF members to crack open the box of bullet-proof vests used when they were going out on dangerous assignments. Only then did he answer JJ.

"Not necessary, JJ. Our PM above him, gave his consent for us to assist you on your Government-sanctioned visit, so we have all the cover we'll ever need. I'm sure your PM would do the same for me if the tables were turned, although he hasn't yet had to do so.

"JJ, I don't want Power's apprehension to get nasty, as my style and preference is to do things fast, clean and quietly. My sense is that things will

351

come together during tonight and that by daylight, your man will either have been recaptured or he'll be dead. Greater Kingstown's now been locked down as if a major hurricane's coming. The only Vincentians you'll find on the road are the boldest of thieves, serious criminals or vagrants. Quite frankly, I'm doubtful we'll even see any of them now because since they have heard what we're up to, they'll keep the streets free. Their business is done for tonight," concluded Gomez.

"That means –"

"Yes, JJ, Power should be easier to find once he's still in that taxi," said Gomez.

"Well, let's hope you are right," said JJ as he adjusted the bullet-proof-vest he had now received from one of the RTF unit's members.

Gomez returned to monitoring the calls being filtered through to his RTF unit. The report that Parchmore's taxi had been stolen from his home was alarming but not surprising given the current circumstances. It provided Gomez and his unit with details of the current vehicle Power was now presumably travelling in – its make, license number along with the address from where the vehicle had been stolen. This suggested that they were now almost certain Power was still in the Greater Kingstown area.

JJ moved away from the crowd of RTF unit members, other RSVGPF officers and SVGDF soldiers to find a quiet area where he could safely check both of his weapons and ammunition.

Whenever the time came for him to move, he would be ready...

***

Back in Barbados, among the things the night RBPF/BDF patrol vehicles were keeping an eye out for was a distinctive looking open-backed vehicle with unusual markings on both sides of the vehicle.

One of them covering the parish of St Philip nearly missed it. After running the vehicle's license number through their on-board RBPF/Barbados Licensing Authority's traffic computer, they confirmed that the vehicle PZ612 was registered to Arnold Rowe of No. 2, Markville Development, St Philip. Reporting their 'find' back to RBPF HQ, they were asked to stay close to their location but to keep Rowe's vehicle in sight.

Back-up was on the way to them.

Around 2:20 a.m., Gomez received a call from Sergeant Rolf Boorman, officer-in-charge of the joint RSVGPF/SVDDF roadblock team that had been set up at the Leeward Highway/Cyrus Street junction close to Cemetery Hill. A white taxi, with the license number now known to belong to the taxi owned by Parchmore, had approached their roadblock but on being asked to stop, had quickly reversed before turning around and heading back towards Cemetery Hill. The driver obviously did not know where he was going, for he turned into a dead-end street in his bid to by-pass the roadblock.

Four RSVGPF officers and two SVGDF soldiers had made up the roadblock team. Half of them went in pursuit of the taxi. The team stopped at the top of the dead-end street, thus ensuring that the taxi could not escape the way it had gone in as it was effectively now cornered at the bottom of the street where it had stopped.

Boorman's team radioed him for instructions about what they, or rather Gomez wanted them to do, making it clear that they were willing to act immediately to try and apprehend the escapee.

Boorman spoke to Gomez.

"Members of my roadblock team have the taxi cornered at the bottom of a dead-end street, sir. They could go in, but want to know if they should wait for reinforcements before doing so?" asked Boorman.

"Is the taxi the only vehicle in that street?" asked Gomez.

"Hold on." Boorman checked with his team before confirming this was the case.

"It's dark in that area, but they see no other vehicles there so believe the taxi is isolated. If I was the taxi driver – this man Power, I'd anticipate being surrounded by law enforcement people sooner rather than later. I might even choose to leave the taxi and try to make a run for it if I felt threatened. Power's reputation alone suggests that he will make it difficult for us to secure him alive. There's been no exchanges of any kind to date between my team and Power, so we've no way of knowing whether he has a weapon inside the taxi or not," answered Boorman.

"Thanks, Rolf. I need your team to stay put. That way the taxi stays in that street. Under no circumstances allow it to get out. Take your second vehicle from the roadblock to the scene. I'm on my way to you. Be there in…seven or so minutes, maybe even five," Gomez ordered.

"Got it, sir. On my way. I'll wait for you at the Cyrus Street junction of the Highway. Perhaps you can send other people to cover the other approaches to the area, just in case the driver makes a run for it on foot," suggested Boorman.

"I'll get that covered right away Rolf. See you shortly," said Gomez.

"Roger and out."

Gomez looked at JJ. "You heard all that? Looks like we're got your man cornered, so we're in business."

JJ nodded. While Gomez raised his voice to give a variety of instructions to his team, JJ retreated from them. Retrieving the secure BIB mini-computer from his backpack, JJ typed another brief update to Colonel Burke.

"Believe we've located the package. Hoping to secure it incident-free."

The reply was instant. "GHBS," which JJ knew meant, '*Good Hunting, Be Safe*'.

While JJ was putting away his secure BIB mini-computer, but before Gomez's assembled team could move to the four-vehicle convoy lined up outside, Gomez gave a final warning to everyone.

"Remember, be careful once we're out there. Be ready for anything, in case this guy has local help somewhere nearby, though that's unlikely from what we know," he said.

JJ did not rush to be among the first persons to leave the room. In fact, he was near to being the last. A now familiar voice spoke from behind him, "After you, sir."

The person was none other than Corporal Monty Conway. Unknown to JJ, Gomez had assigned Conway to be JJ's 'protector' for tonight's exercise. No surprise then that Conway would be the last man to leave the room and was also expected to ride alongside JJ in Gomez's vehicle.

Halfway to their destination, two of the vehicles turned left while Gomez, with JJ beside him and the fourth vehicle continued on the main Leeward Highway towards their rendezvous with Sergeant Boorman at the junction of Cyrus Street.

***

It was five and a half minutes later when two RTF vehicles arrived on the scene. Sergeant Boorman met them and they began to take in the scene from the top of the dead-end street.

***

The fact there were roadblocks all over the place did not surprise Power. He would have been disappointed if there had not been any. Obviously, the authorities were onto him and were intent on re-capturing him. From their show of force, they wanted to achieve that goal tonight.

Power felt he was now between a rock and a hard place. *What should I do* he wondered to himself seeing no other roads off the street he'd entered...*Damn, this is a cul-de-sac, a dead-end street, would you believe it?*

This resulted from not knowing where you were going. He made some calculations. Escape would be tricky. The vehicle that had followed him had stopped at the entrance to the dead-end street. There were a few houses, a couple of which appeared to be old warehouses, and a lot of bush around. He'd noticed the sign at the top of the street as he had entered it. Cemetery Road. *Oh dear, not a good omen for me.*

Those who had followed him were obviously policemen but they had not pursued him, at least not as yet. Power was sure they would do so once others had joined them. In westerns, they formed a posse to go after a criminal. He expected the modern-day version was forming while he sat there.

Power decided to 'fight fire with fire', if it came to that. There was no way he wanted to end up back in Barbados. The key was to wait and see how the Vincie police boys would play the situation by making the first move. Power promised to himself there and then that he would 'give as good as he got'.

***

Sergeant Boorman spoke to Gomez once they were at the top of the dead-end street. "Your man is in the taxi at the bottom of this street," he said.

They got out and spoke to the two RSVGPF officers and SVGDF soldier who had first arrived on the scene for about twenty minutes now.

"Any movement?" asked Boorman.

"Nothing that we could detect from here. He turned off his headlights once he realised that we had parked our vehicle here to block any escape back this way he might have had in mind," said an officer.

"Does anyone live in these houses around here?" asked JJ.

"Yes, but not many. This area is pretty run down and is set for redevelopment by the Government. Most of the people who lived here have moved on, either gone overseas to join relatives or were shifted when other Government housing areas were developed around Kingstown. Little happens here now," responded the RSVGPF officer.

"Except that something will happen here tonight!" was Gomez's apt response.

Gomez worked the radio. His officers who had entered the area on foot from the other side of Cemetery Road were in position. On the way to Sergeant Boorman, Gomez had also asked for the two roadblock teams closest to their location to abandon what they were doing and to join him at the top of the dead-end street. Over the next ten minutes, four additional RSVGPF vehicles arrived with a mix of officers and soldiers.

Gomez assembled the twenty or so persons. Their plan to recapture the Barbadian convict was a simple one. Two of the quieter four-wheeled drive vehicles would approach the parked taxi vehicle located at the bottom of the dead-end street quietly, without any lights on. Once close to the taxi, they would announce their presence, call out Power's name and request that he surrenders quietly. Depending on his reaction, they would respond accordingly. Law enforcement personnel were ninety-five percent certain that Power was still in the taxi. There were few places for him to run to or hide from them without being seen.

Gomez waited a further ten minutes for the ten persons outside of the two approaching vehicles to get into place on either side of the street at fifteen feet intervals before starting the operation in the street. Though they hoped the surprise element would help them to catch Power without incident, everyone was prepared should Power have firepower and use it against them. They would match him shot for shot should there be any gunplay resistance.

The operation started at 3:05 a.m.

By 3:15 a.m., it was all over. Anti-climactic perhaps, but happily so. Mission accomplished without bloodshed. How did it all go down?

Power was unconscious. His injuries had caused him simply to pass out in the taxi.

***

Power had tried his best to keep himself alert, expecting the Vincie policemen and soldiers at the end of the street to come directly for him sooner rather than later. When they had not, he'd decided that their plan must be to wait, perhaps for the dawn light before moving in on him.

Power had re-developed his plan. He would escape out the back of the taxi into the tall bushes that were directly behind where he had parked the taxi.

He was not focussed on the fact that, as a result of his having broken into the taxi, the cut sustained around the wrist of his left hand had slowly continued to bleed. The cut had also gradually opened up and in the darkened confines of the taxi, Power did not notice this or comprehend the overall deterioration in the use of his left hand, indeed the impact this loss of blood was having on his overall body. Hence his passing out.

The tugging at the taxi's back doors caused Power to briefly stir but in his current state, he immediately relapsed into his unconscious state. Half-a-minute later, when the passenger-side window and the right rear seat window behind the driver were smashed, the noise caused Power to attempt for a second time to become alert and this was almost as sluggish as on the first occasion. Somehow remembering where he was, Power subconsciously started to reach for the bag containing the old Smith & Weston weapon Delaney had given to him at the start of his night's journey.

Two things happened at once. His right hand did not make the move he wanted it to make. Certainly not as quickly. Nor did his head feel right. *What's going on*, he thought.

"I wouldn't do that if I were you," said a voice to his left as Power's hand felt the last of the sandwiches instead of the weapon. Despite the warning, Power persisted with his effort to reach the gun.

It was then that Power felt a gun at the base of his head. He also recognised that men were now standing in a half circle around the front of the taxi he had driven into the dead-end street. They were all staring directly at him with guns drawn and pointed directly at him.

Then the person behind Power spoke.

"Give it up, Power, you're nabbed. I'm James Johnson of the Barbados Intelligence Bureau. My good friend to your left is Chief Inspector Trevor Gomez of the RSVGPF. The other people you see surrounding you are Vincentian policemen and soldiers. We ask that you come quietly with us. I've arranged a nice ride for you back home. We are keen to re-acquaint ourselves with you. You'll be read your legal rights by a member of our RBPF in due course. Do you understand me?" asked JJ.

Power wanted to react but decided against doing so in such fruitless circumstances. He nodded.

"Mr Power, I need a verbal response from you please. Do you understand what I've just told you?" asked JJ again.

"Yeah. I hear you, man," said Power, still groggy.

Power swore under his breath. Luckily for him, the Vincentian law enforcement personnel outside of the taxi did not hear what Power was saying. Just as well, for had they done so, it might have led them to drive some lashes into him to teach him some manners. He was not being kind to his Vincentian hosts.

Power was then removed from the taxi, handcuffed by a RSVGPF officer before being led to the first of the two four-wheeled drive RTF vehicles, and placed in the back seat to sit between two burly SVGDF soldiers. Conway slammed the vehicle's door shut.

"Job done again, JJ," said Gomez.

"Indeed, Terry. As always, a pleasure working with you in these parts, and I didn't need this thank God," responded JJ, holstering his Glock 19 weapon.

"I share your feeling. Now let's get our guy back to RTF HQ. You should be able to get him back home sometime during the day."

"I certainly hope so. I'll get word to my chief but first, please get one of your guys to check Power over. I don't like the look of his left hand," answered JJ.

"Okay, JJ. I'll see to it," said Gomez.

Walking away, JJ heard him say, "Conway, get our first aider over to look at our prisoner's left hand."

"Yes, sir," said Conway looking around to find the RFT officer with that skill and the first aid box of tricks.

***

It was very early morning in Barbados, but JJ knew that Colonel Burke was awaiting his further communication. He also knew that he would have gone into his study at home since JJ had sent the first message to him earlier in the night and that he'd stay there until JJ had accomplished his mission.

On nights like this, Diane simply closed their bedroom door.

***

JJ had left Gomez to go to the second four-wheeled drive RTF vehicle that had blocked the taxi.

On his own, JJ removed his secure BIB mini-computer and deftly sent his message to Colonel Burke. It stated: 'Package secured minus excitement. Send collection unit and usual baggage ASAP'.

***

Once JJ had sent his message, Colonel Burke's device whirred on its receipt. Although he anticipated the communication, he still jumped when his secure BIB mini-computer whirred into life.

Having read the message, he was satisfied and so sent an immediate response: 'Congrats P3. Will arrange as requested. Expect this to happen this AM. Surprised no fireworks.'

JJ responded: 'So were we, but grateful none realised.'

'Good. Well done again. WTS.'

That meant 'watch this space'. Colonel Burke's concluding message ended their on-line communication. He now had some arrangements to make and would start by waking up some people.

To set matters in motion, he called Brigadier Tenton.

***

Twenty-five minutes later, everyone was back at RTF HQ. The roadblocks around Greater Kingstown had been removed. While Power had continued to receive medical attention as a result of his involvement from the road accident, Gomez was on the phone reporting to Commissioner Gaynor what had happened

359

so far that night to enable him to fill in Prime Minister Toby Walker at their breakfast meeting.

Co-operation and collaboration between the two Caribbean countries had been successful. While all of this was going on, JJ had decided to take a nap on the sofa in Gomez's office. He'd asked Gomez to 'nudge' him no later than 6:00 a.m.

***

Meanwhile, back in Barbados, two support patrol vehicles carrying police and soldier personnel arrived quietly on scene. One of the RBPF officers knew the house Rowe lived at. The house was in darkness. After it was surrounded, the senior RBPF officer from the three patrol vehicles approached the front door and knocked. No response and so he knocked again, this time more loudly.

After a while, a light went on before a sleepy-eyed Rowe answered the door. "Yes? Man, you know what time of night it is? Who are you and why you breaking down my house?" he asked frustratingly.

The RBPF officer introduced himself before asking if he could come inside to ask Rowe a few questions about an incident involving his vehicle. Now unflustered, because Rowe knew this must all be a big mistake as there had been no incident involving his vehicle over the past year that he was aware of.

Rowe agreed to allow the officer to enter his home. "Just you though," was his condition.

Rowe led the way into the small living room, limping more than…in recent weeks he'd felt the need to limp more because of his leg injury from a car accident seven years earlier. As he got older, the injury had plagued him more and more but he'd accepted the need to just get on with what was left of his life. *It's better than being six feet under* he'd thought to himself a few weeks earlier.

Rowe certainly did not imagine that his Thursday lunchtime sojourn into Bridgetown and then Fontabelle to purchase his new television would result in this visit from a team of RBPF officers in the dead of night. The interview lasted only five minutes before the RBPF officer invited Rowe to accompany him to RBPF HQ to answer a few more questions about the alleged incident. Rowe started to protest, but then decided to go along. He went and spoke with Iris McCarthy, his girlfriend before dressing and leaving his house alongside the officer. No handcuffs were used.

It was only after Rowe was outside that he noticed several RBPF vehicles with officers and BDF soldiers close by. It became clear to him that there was more to the officer's visit than had been told to him. *Do they know that I was involved in the Power escape* was the questions in his head and if so, who or which of the other members of the Pressure Group gang had spilled the beans on him? Should he retaliate and do the same to them?

The garbage skip nearby was almost full, but lying near the top of it were the visible remnants of packaging and the protective moulding that was usually discarded after purchase of new electrical items, e.g. computers, DVDs and televisions. The packaging here had contained a large television, like the one that now sat in Rowe's living room. One of the observant soldiers noticed the packaging and mentioned it to the officer who was in charge of the initial RBPF patrol vehicle on the scene. In turn, this officer mentioned it to the officer in charge of the Rowe operation. Having just been inside Rowe's house prior to their departure for RBPF HQ, he put two and two together. It might be minor, but he would mention it to his superiors once back at RBPF HQ.

The RBPF officers and BDF soldiers in the three assembled patrol vehicles had all noticed Rowe's limp as he made his way from his house before entering one of their patrol vehicles. The right leg seemed to be giving Rowe some trouble.

***

Captain George Collins, Head of the BDF's Air Wing, was awakened at 3:55 a.m., approximately one hour ahead of his usual 5:00 a.m. wake-up time by Tenton who had just finished speaking with Colonel Burke.

"Good morning, Captain Collins. Sorry to wake you up extra early today, but I have a job for you. Please meet me at GAIA in an hour. You'll need your co-pilot, but not the rest of your normal crew. I've lined up three other people you know to keep the two of you company on an urgent assignment."

"Yes, sir. No problem, but with respect sir, what's this all about?" asked Collins.

"Look, George… I'll tell you everything you need to know when I see you. Right now, time to call your rostered co-pilot and then get going. See you both up the road shortly?"

"Very well, sir! I'm getting out of bed as I speak! I'll make the call, hit the shower and then the road."

"Good man! I'll have some eats and coffee waiting for everyone. Bye for now."

"Roger that."

Tenton then made a second, but similar 'wake-up' call to Commander Bruce Alleyne of the BDF's Special Task Force unit. Same instruction, but Tenton would pick him up from his home on his way to GAIA in another forty minutes, to arrive there by 5:00 a.m. He was not to wear any military attire. He should travel with his usual operational equipment though in case it was needed.

He got a crisp, "Yes, sir, see you in forty," from Alleyne in response to the orders he had just received.

Thirty minutes later, after taking a shower, dressing and collecting his equipment, Alleyne wrote and left a brief note for his wife before easing out of their Maxwell Coast Road, Christ Church home to await Tenton's arrival.

***

While Tenton was making his first call, Colonel Burke was calling a member of his RED team. Fred George was also to undertake the early-morning overseas assignment. Fred was instructed to get to GAIA as quickly as he could, by 5:00 a.m. latest. Colonel Burke would meet him there to provide briefing on the assignment that was ahead of him.

"Is this a solo operation?"

"No, it is not…but don't worry about that now. I'll fill you in when we meet up."

"Right. Want me to bring anything specific with me?"

"Just yourself…and your regular gear."

"Understood. See you shortly."

"Right."

***

Last, Colonel Burke called Commissioner Jeremie. Another early call, but this one was half-expected.

Colonel Burke requested the services of one of Jeremie's senior RBPF CPU unit officers for a maximum six-hour overseas assignment related to the matter that both their agencies, along with the BDF, had together initiated on Friday afternoon.

Jeremie readily complied. Just the previous afternoon, Colonel Burke had briefed him on the assignment's most recent development. He was therefore aware that there was a possibility that a 'recovery assignment' might be required at some time but to be honest, he hadn't expected it to come this quickly.

Having already identified the officer he would call on to respond should Colonel Burke request RBPF assistance, Jeremie immediately called Sergeant Billy Browne and instructed him to make his way to GAIA by 5:00 a.m.

Browne obeyed the instruction. Luckily for everyone, he lived in Gemswick Development, St Philip, one of the neighbourhoods located within ten minutes of the airport, so his getting to the airport for the required time was not going to be a problem, although he had a few questions for his Commissioner.

"Should I be in uniform, sir? Can I carry my sidearm? Oh yes, do I need to travel with any special pieces or correspondence from you related to this assignment?"

"All good questions, Billy. No, yes and yes. You'll get the last item from me just before you depart."

"Right sir, I'll get going. You'll bring the correspondence with you, sir?" asked Browne.

"I'm not coming, Billy, but I've sent it over to Colonel Burke. He'll deliver and explain a couple of things about your assignment before you depart. My authorising correspondence will be provided for your use," explained Jeremie.

"Very well, sir. I understand."

"Good. Bye. Have a good trip."

"Will do, sir."

***

Promptly at 5:00 a.m., Colonel Burke, with Tenton beside him, commenced the mission brief to the five assembled persons: Collins; first officer (FO) Annette Taitt, also of Air Wing, BDF; Alleyne, Special Task Force unit, BDF; Browne, CPO, RBPF; and Fred from BIB. Between them, they would complete the overseas portion of *Operation 'Fishhook'*.

There were no questions when he'd finished. All five persons knew the dangers that this escaped Barbadian prisoner posed. The fact that JJ now had his Power in his custody in St Vincent and was awaiting their arrival to bring him back to Barbados made them feel comfortable that things were under control and would remain so. Their task was to ensure that nothing went wrong after all of the hard work that had been put in by Barbadian and Vincentian security personnel. They needed to complete *Operation 'Fishhook'* by going to St Vincent, collecting and bringing Power back to Barbados to his nice, comfortable bed inside HMP Dodds. Should be simple enough. What could go wrong?

***

Following a good 'operational breakfast' in the hanger after Colonel Burke's briefing but before the team boarded the BDF1 aircraft, Colonel Burke pulled Browne aside and gave him two envelopes containing correspondence, one blue and the other red. He invited Browne to read the unsealed contents of the blue envelope as the red envelope was sealed.

DATE: Monday, 23 April 2018
FROM: Commissioner, Royal Barbados Police Force, Police Headquarters, Bridgetown, Barbados
TO: Mr Aubrey Gaynor, Commissioner, Royal St Vincent and the Grenadines Police Force, Police Headquarters, Kingstown, St Vincent

JASPER POWER, Barbadian prisoner #XFG18-215-07177-3 escaped legal custody on Wednesday, 18 April 2018. Sometime shortly thereafter, he is believed to have fled Barbados jurisdiction and entered St Vincent and the Grenadines where he has today been recaptured.

Under the established CARICOM Protocols where law enforcement and security agencies have committed to assist each other in cases where there is: (i) evidence of a crime having been committed; (ii) an arrest has been made; and or (iii) an arrest made against the said JASPER POWER in a CARICOM member state, I hereby request that JASPER POWER be handed over from the custody of a RSVGPF officer(s) to the custody of a RBPF officer(s) who will accept responsibility for his safe transportation and return to Barbados from the jurisdiction of St Vincent and The Grenadines.

Signed: *WP.Jeremie* COMMISSIONER, Royal Barbados Police Force

Correspondence Received / Prisoner Delivered by: -------------------------- ---------------- Royal St Vincent and the Grenadines Officer; Date: Monday, 23 April 2018

Correspondence Delivered /Prisoner Received by: -------------------------- --------------- Royal Barbados Police Force Officer; Date: Monday, Monday, 23 April 2018

Once Browne had read the correspondence, Colonel Burke gave him a specific instruction. "Give both envelopes to Inspector Gomez. He'll be at the airport with JJ and will hand Power over to you. Both you and Gomez must sign the two copies of the memo in the *blue* envelope, okay? He'll keep the original and you bring back the copy to us. Gomez will be responsible for passing the red envelope onto his Commissioner. Understood?"

"Got it, sir," responded Browne.

"Then off you go, son. Good luck."

***

The *red* envelope Browne held contained one copy of a memo of similar content to what was in the blue envelope, minus the last two items below Jeremie's signature. In reality, the correspondence in the red envelope had already been transmitted by secure e-mail directly to Gaynor from Jeremie's personal computer in the dead of night, but this was a hard copy with Jeremie's signature. This action would close the official loop, ensure the delivery of Power and enable his return to Barbados.

This arrangement was nothing new. It enabled smooth working between neighbouring East Caribbean country police forces and their Barbadian counterpart. But established and agreed protocols and procedures required that this bureaucratic chain of events had to take place whenever such criminal or similar exchanges formally took place shall we say, 'below the radar'.

This was something Caribbean Governments had learnt from the Brits. *Always dot your I's and cross your T's*, no matter what the circumstances were.

***

Prior to departure, the passengers had checked in their weapons with Collins. He locked them away in the special compartment built into the aircraft's cargo section for such items to ensure safety during the flight before BDF1 left Barbados at 5:55 a.m. for the forty-minute journey to St Vincent.

Once airborne, neither Fred, Alleyne or Browne spoke about the assignment before them. The flasks of piping hot coffee placed on board for their use remained untouched. Their assignment was expected to be a simple and straightforward one but their experience made them wary as one could never be 100 percent certain of any assignment's success until it was safely completed.

After ten minutes of non-chatter it got boring, so the three-men not in the cockpit started small-talking amongst themselves. Their discussion revolved around the best or most memorable films they had seen recently.

Fred mentioned *The November Man.* "It is about an ex-CIA assassin who is drawn out of retirement to help get a double agent out of Russia, but there is a lot more going on behind the scenes than the ex-agent is told. His efforts to get to the truth and clean up the mess gets complicated after his daughter is kidnapped. I found it to be a fascinating film and so recommend it to you both."

Neither Alleyne nor Browne had heard of the film, but expressed interest in seeing it sometime. Browne spoke about a comedy he had watched with his children the week before, but Alleyne had nothing to offer to their discussion.

Just prior to landing at Argyle International Airport, Fred shared something from the film he had mentioned which had registered with him ever since. "The ex-CIA assassin explained to his protégé what a single gunshot can do… '*a bullet travels at over four thousand feet per second, four times faster than the speed of sound. The effect of that velocity is absolute. You just…cease to exist.*' That frightened me man. I mean, we work with firearms almost every day but I'd never thought about the effect a fired bullet would have on the human body when it hits like that, at least not in the way described by that character. It sent chills down my spine hence I now wear a bulletproof vest whenever I undertake any outdoor assignment. That includes overseas ones like this."

"Makes sense," said Browne.

"Are you wearing one now?" asked Alleyne.

"You betcha," answered Fred emphatically to make his point.

They fell into further silence just as BDF1 touched down on St Vincent soil.

***

Rowe knew he was in big trouble. The game was up as far as he was concerned. Pressured for the names of all the others involved in Wednesday's 'grab' of Power from the prisoner transport vehicle, Rowe did not hold back. He provided names, nick-names, addresses, vehicle numbers, work places, named gangs and finally, relayed the when and where they had met to plan their 'mission'.

However, Castille's name was not mentioned, as Rowe had neither met nor spoken to him.

The evidence gleaned by Inspector Gray, Public Relations officer at RBPF HQ regarding Rowe was indisputable. She was amazed at how easy getting all of this information out of him had been. She called AC Smith to give him the good news. She would secure Rowe at RBPF HQ but suggested that Smith inform both Jeremie and Innis about these developments quickly. She knew once Jeremie was made aware of this development, he would in turn advise Colonel Burke.

Smith then instructed Gray to speak with Vickers about organising three 'visits' (she knew he meant raids) by mid-morning to apprehend the other members of the Pressure Group gang.

***

Castille woke earlier than he would normally have done back home in his Miami apartment. It was 6:00 a.m. He body felt rested and refreshed, yet his mind was uneasy and somehow out of sorts. His brain quickly told him why. He had not yet succeeded at the task assigned to him. Castille had to change that. "This Power situation has gotten out of hand," he murmured to himself, becoming more determined than ever to resolve this problem for *The Organisation* on this very day.

Finding Wharton's location was how he intended doing so. Wharton had to have something for him.

***

On his way back home, Colonel Burke called Superintendent Innis.

"Good morning, Superintendent. I'd like you to prepare HMP Dodds to receive our escaped prisoner. As part of those preparations, please make available one of your three special isolation cells to receive him."

"Good morning, Colonel Burke. Thanks. I'll start making those arrangements. By any particular time?" asked Innis.

"As soon as possible. Also, please make your way over to Harold Oliver, CEO at the airport no later than 9:00 a.m. Once there, he will provide you with a briefing on where we are and what is to happen next," Colonel Burke concluded.

***

Ambassador Madeline Carter had kept her word. Colonel Burke's secure phone rang at 6:30 a.m., just as he had started to drink the cup of tea Diane had made for him.

What she told him was both insightful and alarming. Colonel Burke wasn't sure from whom Ambassador Carter and her team at the Barbados Embassy in Washington had secured their information from, but she had been able to turn up much more than he'd ever imagined or expected might be possible. A 'big fish' from 'an up-and-coming' trading organisation (diplomatic speak meaning a commercial entity involved in serious criminal activity) was in Barbados on a one-day visit. The US Embassy in Barbados' security team was said to be aware of the visit but had no plans to engage the visiting individual, although US authorities were well-advanced in building their case against the entity and members of its leadership.

One of these was known only as 'The Principal' whose initials were thought to be any of RT, RC or RP. Further information on this person was likely to be gathered by the Barbados Embassy's security team before day's end. Meanwhile, details – a name and a picture of the alleged 'big fish' now in Barbados had just been sent to BIB HQ from her Embassy. Once Colonel Burke got to BIB, he would be able to access that information.

Carter also offered an opinion. If she was Colonel Burke, she would consider approaching the USA's Ambassador to Barbados, The Chief Immigration Officer and the Commissioner of Police to see how they might be able to help by providing any additional or related information. She hadn't known why

Colonel Burke had called her on Friday night, but suspected that something his BIB unit was working on was afoot which he could not share with her.

Of course, her suspicions were correct. Carter and her security team at Barbados' US Embassy had been happy to respond to Colonel Burke's request. She knew that she did not need to suggest that he should check with airlines carrying passengers between USA and Barbados to see a list of passengers with the initials RT, RC or RP who had travelled between the two countries in the past couple of days.

Colonel Burke thanked Carter stating, "I'm much obliged to you, Ambassador. You and your team have been a tremendous help to us. When you are next home, please let me know."

"No problem, Colonel Burke. As it happens, I'm back there in another three weeks, so happy for us to meet up for a chat then."

"I'd like that very much. Over a meal, I hope. Thanks again and have a good day."

"You too. Goodbye."

***

Chapter Twenty-Six
Diplomacy

Castille showered and dressed before calling Wharton to hear if the information that had been promised on Power's whereabouts was available. Power was thought to be in St Vincent, but where? Castille needed an area or a village or better still, an address. Once he had this, he planned to jump on a flight to St Vincent and get to work. Castille desperately wanted to complete his assignment, by fair means (collect payment) or foul (kill Power).

Most of all, he now wanted to return home to the USA, ideally later this afternoon but otherwise, being realistic by tomorrow night.

***

Soon Colonel Burke placed a call to Jeremie. "Will, can you meet me urgently at BIB HQ at 7:30 a.m.?"

"Yes," was the immediate response, before Jeremie added, "I'll have some good news to share when we meet."

"I'll be keen to hear it. Today looks like it's shaping up to be a special day for Barbados' law enforcement agencies. See you shortly, Will."

"Right you are, Trevor."

Next, Colonel Burke called USA Ambassador Rowley. After pleasantries were exchanged about the time of day, Colonel Burke asked if he and Commissioner Jeremie could call on the Ambassador at 9:00 a.m. at his Embassy on an urgent matter? Without hesitation, Ambassador Rowley agreed to receive them. Colonel Burke was surprised Rowley did not ask him what the urgent matter was.

From Rowley's perspective, he knew Colonel Burke to be a solid man. They had developed a strong professional working (though not personal) relationship since his arrival in Barbados three years earlier. Rowley surmised that there must be a very good reason why BIB's Director, accompanied by the RBPF's Commissioner wanted to see him urgently so early on a Monday morning.

Following Colonel Burke's call, Rowley spoke with Amarouse Busbee, his Cultural Secretary (also his CIA officer in post). Always one of the first to arrive at the Embassy each day, he asked her to think of any reason why Colonel Burke and Commissioner Jeremie might want to meet with him urgently that morning. No outstanding issues between the Embassy, BIB or RBPF immediately came to Busbee's mind and she told him so. Rowley was surprised at her response. Nevertheless, he invited Busbee to join him prior to and at the meeting from 8:45 a.m. when they would consider their approach at the meeting. He did not want them to be caught by surprise by any unexpected requests, especially if they were related to funding.

Colonel Burke's third call was to Alwin Greene, Chief Immigration Officer, Barbados Immigration Department. He requested an email with a list of all USA passengers with the initials RT, RC or RP who had travelled to Barbados within the past seventy-two hours, along with their pictures from the airport's CCTV system.

Greene asked for an hour to deliver the information.

"Thank you, Alwin," said Colonel Burke.

"Anytime, Trevor."

Colonel Burke made a final call to Motby. He asked for an item, just in case it was necessary. Once the basis of the request had been explained, it was granted to Colonel Burke.

"I'll have an officer hand deliver this to you Trevor – to HQ, I presume?"

"Yes please, Prime Minister. I'll be in my office by 7:30 a.m. Thank you."

"You're welcome."

By their proposed actions, Colonel Burke and Motby hoped to be able to 'nip' pending criminal activity in the bud. It was strange how things can come together if you played your hunches right.

***

BDF1 was now sat at the far end of the Argyle International Airport's parking apron. Due to the openness of the airport's layout, it was never going to be easy to hide BDF1's presence, but at least it was far enough away from the general public's view.

The Barbadian contingent had been met by Gomez. As neither Fred, Alleyne or Browne were in uniform, anyone looking on would not know who the three men walking alongside Gomez towards and then into the new airport's air-conditioned VIP room were. Once inside, they were met by JJ.

"Hello guys, thanks for coming over so quickly," he said.

"So, this is where you disappeared to?" asked Fred, hugging JJ with a broad smile.

Returning the hug and smile, JJ answered, "Yeah. When the chief calls, you move. I had a rough sea ride over. Almost sleepless nights too, but it was all worth it. The ride home should be more pleasant…and we have our guy."

"Buddy, you know you shouldn't keep secrets from me!"

"I only do as I'm told," responded JJ before turning to shake the hands of Alleyne and Browne whom he both knew.

"Good job, JJ. Where's the escaped prisoner?" asked Alleyne.

Gomez answered, "Somewhere very safe but not too far away from here. Not even a cockroach could get out from where he's been stashed."

"Fine. How soon can we get him and be on our way back to Bim?" asked Browne.

"Relax, guys – no need to be so anxious. We'll move your man shortly. We could not keep him at this place because it's insecure. We also did not want him to be on the move close to your arrival in SVG and were then ready to receive him. So, make yourselves comfy. My men and JJ will go for him, returning with an appropriate escort, just in case someone or one of his friends from a Vincie organisation have any thoughts of trying to spring him for what would be the second time in a week," said Gomez.

"How long do we have to wait before you and JJ come back with him, Inspector?" asked Alleyne.

"Hour…hour and a half max," responded Gomez.

"*That* long? Well, can we do anything to help you to speed up the process rather than our just sitting here twiddling our thumbs for the next couple of hours? I don't mean to appear harsh or rude, but with all due respect, I didn't expect we would have all this down time here this morning. You sure that your guys can't get him here any quicker, enabling us to get away sooner?" Again, it was Alleyne asking the searching questions.

"Look, friend, I've just told you what our realistic timelines are. The sooner we stop talking, JJ and I can get moving. We'll do our best to deliver your man as quickly as we can to allow you to depart our shores. Getting back to normal will be a real pleasure for my small unit. Now gentlemen, if you'll excuse us, JJ and I'll be on our way. Stay here. This place has no bookings for today, so no one will disturb you. My Commissioner has arranged with the Airport Manager to have his staff provide you with some refreshments, you know. Vincie hospitality. It should be here any minute," said Gomez, starting to make his way to the door.

Catching JJ's eye, Fred chirped in to help diffuse a potential tricky situation.

"Thank you, Chief Inspector. We'll sit tight. Can our two air-crew also join us?" asked Fred.

"Of course! I'll go and bring them over before I go. We've included them in our offering that's being delivered."

"Many thanks," said Fred.

With that, Gomez left the room, heading for the airport parking apron where BDF1's air crew had remained in BDF1.

JJ spoke. "Sorry about that, guys, but I think we all need to take a breath. Take it easy on this guy. Fred knows that I've worked with Gomez before. He's a good man to have on or by your side in any tight situation as I've found out in the past. He's been kind and accommodating to me since I arrived on Friday morning. So, lighten up guys. Remember, it's our prisoner that his team have recaptured. He escaped from us, yes?"

"We hear you, JJ. I'm just not used to hanging around," said Alleyne. He was not angry, just wanted to get on with the job that he'd come to do. His work often called for speed, accuracy and efficiency which were at a premium and always uppermost in his mind. The current standstill, as he saw it, was a tad sloppy and inefficient. Such situations worried him. However, he understood the need to keep the escaped prisoner in a safe and secure place. His experience told him that airports were never the safest or most secure and reliable place to keep dangerous people.

Five minutes later, Gomez returned to the VIP room with Collins and Taitt in tow. He motioned to JJ to follow him and together they exited the VIP's security door and headed towards Gomez's vehicle to start the journey back to where Power was being held.

Minutes later, two ladies rolled in a trolley on which were sumptuous breakfast items – fresh fruit, tea, banana bread and juice. There were also five small plates with bacon, sausage and scrambled eggs.

Before taking their leave of the five persons in the VIP room, one of the ladies turned on the large television nestled in the middle of a well-laden bookcase. She asked them which of the cable channels showing international news or morning magazine programmes they wanted to watch. Fox, MSNBC, ABC, CBS, CNN, NBC or the local station's 'SVG Today' programme. They chose the local station and thanked the two maids for delivering the goodies.

"The remote control is here in case you want to change…" were the parting words from the second lady as they departed, leaving the VIP room to their Barbadian visitors.

***

The news Castille received from Wharton during their phone call was at last good.

"He is either in St Lucia or St. Vincent, I think it's the latter, though his exact location remains unknown. Yesterday evening, I was promised confirmation by 8:00 a.m. today of his exact whereabouts from a Vincentian friend of mind living here whose ear is pretty close to the ground in Barbados' neighbouring countries You should consider booking a flight to where he is. There are several daily flights to both countries that leave between 11:30 a.m. and mid-day.

"Is your friend reliable?" asked Castille.

"Yes," was Wharton's instant response.

"Will you call me back with the country and an address, or should I come to you?"

"No. I'll meet you at the airport and put the information in your hand. How about 8:30 a.m.? Phones have ears, understand me?"

"Yes. Here is like the US. You can buy your airline ticket at the airport."

"How much?"

"How much what? You don't need to pay me anything for what I'll give you."

"Not going to. I mean how much are the flights to St Lucia or St Vincent?"

374

"Don't know, but I doubt it would be more than $500."

"You're kidding!"

"No, not US money, Barbados dollars…so US$250."

"Return to Barbados?"

"Unlikely. Probably a bit more."

"Thanks. Where to meet?"

"By the electronic departure notice board."

"Which one?"

"There is only one."

"Any specific place?"

"It's in the open area, across from the British Airways check-in area."

"'8:30 a.m.?"

"Yes," said Wharton.

"Got it. Bye," said Castille.

"Be jolly now," said Wharton.

Castille decided that the phone he had just used had outlived its usefulness and so should be disposed of. He would also skip breakfast and check out of his south coast hotel and head for the airport. He could pick up breakfast there before or after meeting Wharton and buying his ticket to either country. Checking himself in for the flight should be easy enough before clearing immigration.

Castille was feeling better. *Real progress at last*, he thought.

By 8:10 a.m., he was driving away from the hotel. His conversation with the car-hire company had confirmed that he could take the vehicle he'd hired to the main airport car park where they would meet him to retake possession of it.

***

Inspector Moss had come up empty at the first of the three remaining hotels. He now approached the second hotel's reception. Showing his RBPF identification, he asked to speak with the Manager on duty.

Desmond Alli quickly appeared. After introducing himself to Moss, he listened attentively before taking the room key card presented by Moss. Turning it over, he stated quickly, "Yep, this is one of ours."

"Are you sure?" asked Moss.

"Yes, Inspector. All hotels on Barbados' south coast carry the *south coast hotels* logo on their room keys," explained Alli. "Rather than promoting our hotels individually using separate business cards, we have collaborated while identifying each property operating on Barbados' south coast through specific property room keys which look like a business card."

Alli beckoned Moss to come closer to him before continuing.

"This is one of our room keys because of the code shown on the back. See it? In the bottom left hand corner is S/17. That's our property's code. It's actually built into the card itself. Each south coast property has its own code shown on the back of its *south coast hotels* room key. Once a guest checks in, we provide them with two room keys. If there are two guests in a room, then they receive four room keys. We no longer use old-fashioned door keys to enter rooms on our properties Inspector, and guests are required to return all room keys issued to them on their departure."

"I get it. Now, can you tell me the room number and the name or names of the guests to whom the room-key card was allocated? Also, are they still with you?"

"Just one moment please," said Alli going off to check the residence computer.

Less than a minute later, he returned to Moss.

"Room 310. Mr Rhohan Castille. He arrived last Wednesday afternoon and was originally set to leave on Saturday but had extended to Sunday and then did so again till today. Our system shows that Mr Castille has already checked out."

"Oh? When?"

"This morning – not long ago in fact."

"Thank you. Any idea where he was going…the airport perhaps?"

"No idea, Inspector."

"Okay. Can I see the room he occupied please?"

"Sure. The maid would not have gotten to it yet, but…is something wrong, Inspector?"

"Maybe. Tell me, when Mr Castille left this morning, did he hand back in both of the room keys that were issued to him on arrival?"

"Again, let me check on that for you Inspector."

Alli shuffled off to speak with one of the two receptionists on duty. The one closest to him was dealing with departing guests, while the second receptionist was working with an airline crew which had just arrived.

Alli decided to make the check himself before returning to Moss with a slight frown.

"Are you clairvoyant, Inspector?" he asked.

"Not that I know of, I prefer common sense and evidence. Now Mr Alli, what do you have for me?"

"Well, you're onto something here. Only one of the two room keys we issued for room 310 to Mr Castille was returned. Our record show that he claimed to have lost the second room key somewhere on our property. One in six guests misplace their issued room keys on our property, so his explanation would not have raised any eyebrows. It's obviously not the case here as you have it. May I ask where you found it please?"

"I'm sorry, but I'm not at liberty to say, Mr Alli. Before I see the room, I need to make a call, so excuse me for a minute please."

"Sure thing. I'll wait here for you, Inspector," said Alli.

Moss walked away from the reception area to call his boss.

"Chief Superintendent Vickers, may I help you?"

"It's me, Moss. Jackpot. Found the hotel, room and have identified the person allocated to it who had been given the room key you presented me with yesterday. It's the 'Rising Sun' in Rockley. Guest was a US citizen, a Mr Rhohan Castille. He checked out this morning. I'm planning to check the room which has not yet been cleaned by the hotel's maids. Wouldn't expect to find anything left behind, except for his fingerprints and DNA but on reflection, I think our forensic boys should come over and do their stuff."

"Excellent work, Byron. That thinking may make you Commissioner someday," said Vickers.

"That's unlikely but thank you, sir," said Moss before continuing.

"I'm speaking with the property's Duty Manager, a very helpful guy. I'll place the room 'off limits' and stay there until our boys arrive. You may want to consider alerting the Commissioner about issuing an APB for Mr Castille...a 'Stop Notice' too so as to stop him from leaving Barbados through any of our ports of entry. If you ask me where he's heading, I've no idea but suggest we first check the airport in case he plans to leave us today, if not for the US then a neighbouring island."

Moss realised that he was almost out of breath. "Just saying, sir," ended Moss.

"As you were speaking, I was thinking similarly. Yes, I'll get one of our forensic teams over to you ASAP. I know where to find the Commissioner so will contact him. Your discovery will give them more ammunition to help with whatever he and Colonel Burke are planning to discuss with the US Ambassador this morning. I'll put out the APB and a Stop Notice on Mr Castille. We sure don't want him leaving Barbados before we can speak with him. Can you get a screen shot of him from the hotel's CCTV system? It would have captured him on arrival, indeed whenever he passed through reception. Send it to me and I'll have the APB unit place his picture alongside the notice. Okay?"

"Yes, sir. Just that I could do with some more sleep and some TLC, but you can't help with either," answered Moss. Luckily, he and Vickers had a good rapport so he knew such comments were not out of line.

"Well, Byron, you can enjoy both of them when you get home tonight with Pearle. What's your answer to that?"

"I'll get working on your requests, sir."

"Thank you. Bye."

Moss looked at his phone before going back to Alli. Moss had to ensure that he got to Room 310 before the hotel's maids did so.

***

On hearing from Moss, Vickers had stopped his vehicle by the side of the road. He'd been heading in to RBPF HQ but now needed to make a few appropriate calls.

First, he called the Superintendent-in-charge of the RBPF's three forensic teams to request that one of them be urgently sent over to the Rising Sun property where Inspector Moss was waiting for them outside of Room 310. Moss would brief them on arrival. That was agreed.

Vickers' second call was to Jeremie on his secure phone. Jeremie had made Vickers aware that he would be meeting with Colonel Burke at BIB HQ early that same morning ahead of a potential meeting later that morning with the USA's Ambassador. Vickers felt sure that Moss's information on Castille might help them with whatever they were seeking to discuss with the Ambassador.

Third, Vickers called Operations Control at RBPF HQ. He instructed that an APB and a Stop Notice be issued for Rhohan Castille as soon as his picture was received from Moss.

These calls having been made, Vickers decided to turn his vehicle around and head for the airport. If Moss was right, Castille might already be on his way there.

Vickers' call to Jeremie was indeed timely and most welcome.

Colonel Burke and Jeremie were travelling in the former's BIB vehicle along Wildey Road about five minutes away from the US Embassy's compound. Jeremie had placed the call on speaker. The developments regarding a US passport holder named Rhohan Castille were interesting. Find him and some more problems could be solved.

Having earlier heard from AC Smith that RBPF now had the names of the individuals involved in Power's 'rescue', Jeremie and Colonel Burke believed the jigsaw puzzle related to Power's escape was falling into place. Those behind the escape would soon be caught. The RT, RC or RP mentioned by Ambassador Carter had led to Castille's identification. With regard Telford's death, Castille was now connected to it by a *south coast hotels* room key that had been issued to him but had not been returned to the hotel on his departure. Pilessar was the 'big fish' from the Miami-based, USA entity known as *The Organisation* and she was in Barbados. Power's overnight recapture in St Vincent and his imminent return to Barbados were also good.

Missing were other pieces of the puzzle that still needed to be fathomed. Who was Pilessar here to meet with? They needed this information ASAP. Time for Samuel and Margaret to push the boat out to establish who the person (or persons) were. The potential capture of both Castille and Pilessar during the day would be a very nice way to close off.

Colonel Burke nodded. Next, he and Jeremie had to tackle the USA's Ambassador. They arrived at the US Embassy's Wildey, St Michael compound at 8:50 a.m.

Innis had earlier made the appropriate arrangements on arrival at HMP Dodds that morning to receive the recaptured prisoner. Once everything was in place, he left HMP Dodds and headed for GAIA, ensuring that he was early for his meeting with Oliver. Innis had always disliked being late for any appointment or meeting, hence his tendency to be in place well before any agreed time.

Knocking on Oliver's secretary's doors, he had again achieved his wish. It was 8:55 a.m.

Castille and Wharton met as arranged at the airport by the electronic departure notice board at the airport, not at 8:30 a.m. as they had planned, but nearer to 8:50 a.m.

"You're late," said Castille.

"The call came through later than expected, hence I've only now got here," responded Wharton.

"Tell me," said an impatient Castille.

"I've written it down. Page ten," said Wharton passing Castille the day's local newspaper.

"Thanks. Now where's the airline counter…you said LIAT? Where do I buy my ticket?"

"Over yonder, near the top of the hall. LIAT counters are second in line," responded Wharton.

"Thanks. Bye."

"Be jolly now, my friend."

Wharton turned and left Castille. He headed to the ticket booth to pay for his airport parking ticket before going to his vehicle. He was keen to get to SBB&G as he would be opening up that morning.

***

Punctually at 9:00 a.m., Colonel Burke and Jeremie were shown into Ambassador Rowley's large office by his trusted secretary, Mona Fisher.

"Good morning, Ambassador. I hope you had an enjoyable weekend? Thanks for seeing us on such short notice. I trust your seeing us hasn't messed up your schedule too much at the start of a new week?" asked Colonel Burke.

"Good morning, gentlemen. No, not at all. I'm always happy to meet with any of my host Government's Ministers or senior officials…you both know Miss Busbee, my Cultural Secretary."

"Indeed. How are you, Miss Busbee?" asked Colonel Burke.

"I'm fine sir, thanks for asking," she answered with a quick smile.

"Gentlemen, let's get down to business. How might I or the USA Embassy be of assistance to you today?"

It was Jeremie who spoke. He came straight to the point.

"Ambassador, are you aware of a US outfit known as *The Organisation*? It's based in Miami, Florida."

Ambassador Rowley looked at Busbee. "No, Commissioner. What are they into? The mere fact that you as Commissioner is in my office asking about this entity suggests that they've done something wrong here, or are about to, no?"

"We've no clear evidence that it has done anything wrong in Barbados yet, but there are indications that they might be gearing up to do so, perhaps at this very moment."

"Okay…that being the case I'll have my people look into your claim and get back to you in due course. Do you have contact details for this entity, the people leading it, or related info you could leave with us?"

"As a matter of fact, we do." Colonel Burke passed over a sheet of paper with the requested information. He also handed over a picture of Pilessar.

"And who is this?" asked Rowley.

"That, Ambassador, is Miss Emma Pilessar of the Greater Americas' Corporation, a.k.a. *The Organisation*. We understand her to be its CEO. She arrived in Barbados yesterday afternoon and is scheduled to leave this afternoon. She did not go to the *Private Home* address in Christ Church that she listed as her temporary place of residence on her immigration document on arrival. No one there had ever heard of her, so where she is on the island is not clear at this time. We've therefore concluded that Miss Pilessar is here to meet with potential local business partners. Do you believe our thinking is way off base, sir?"

"Perhaps Colonel Burke, but there could be other reasons why all that you speak of is not the case, something that neither of you, Miss Busbee or I have even thought of," Rowley stated.

"What other reasons might there be for her visit, Ambassador?" asked Colonel Burke.

"Gentlemen, it's not my place to guess, but while she is in Barbados, can't she meet with whomever she pleases?"

"She can indeed Ambassador, but I promise you that we're close to finding out who she is meeting with (or has already met), along with the why before she departs," responded Jeremie.

"As I've indicated to both of you, all we can do here is examine your claim and get back to you. I promise to do so as soon as possible. Would tomorrow be soon enough for you? If that's acceptable and there is nothing else that I can do for you two goodly gentlemen –" stated Ambassador Rowley rising from his chair with a straight face. His gesture appeared to offer friendliness and co-operation but yet was a clear attempt to dismiss Jeremie and Colonel Burke.

"With all due respect, Ambassador. No and yes are our responses to your observations. Tomorrow is *not* good enough and there *is* something else that you can do for us," answered Colonel Burke firmly in response to Ambassador Rowley's comments. Jeremie knew from Colonel Burke's posture that he was determined for them not to be dismissed so easily by Ambassador Rowley.

"Tell me," was Rowley's response, his face showing the first signs of agitation. Or was it anger? He was not used to anyone coming into his embassy, *his office* and speaking to him in such tones.

"We'd respectfully like an answer before we leave your embassy. Also, we now make a formal request for your country's assistance related to the use of one of your drones to help us locate…not Miss Pilessar, but one of her employees. We'll be able to speak to her when she turns up at the airport for her flight. As far as we know, she is unaware that we're looking for her," stated Colonel Burke.

"My friends, where do you get your information from? Hollywood? Our embassy has no drones, drone facilities or even operational capabilities here. American media often carry stories about our Government taking out terrorists in far off places by the use of drones that are operated by our military personnel. Some of that may well be true but Embassies, certainly none that I know of in this hemisphere including the Caribbean, have any such facilities," said an unhappy-looking Rowley.

"We hear you loud and clear, Ambassador. While we have no reason to doubt you, the information available to us suggests that you have the capacity to facilitate our request," responded Colonel Burke.

"Pray tell me how so…and how would you know that, Colonel Burke?" requested Rowley.

"You forget that I've sat in with one or two of your security agencies and have completed courses put on by your military in the US not that long ago. I'm pretty sure that the US Frigate now anchored in the Bridgetown Port has at least two drones on board and with that, the appropriate operational capacity. Come on Mr Ambassador, give us some help here. We don't want your drone to blow up or kill anyone, just help to capture someone who has broken our laws. I'd be very surprised if your request to the ship's Captain, even your superiors somewhere in the State Department in DC, would not exceptionally facilitate my country's official request. If it was not of primary and crucial importance to us, we would not be asking you for this specific kind of assistance. Be assured that we're not about publicising such cooperation between our two countries."

"Well —" started Rowley.

"Look, I'm being honest with you."

With Ambassador Rowley looking clearly uncomfortable, Jeremie took over.

"We need this assistance as one of our senior Government officials was recently murdered. You follow the news, I believe. We're pretty sure that it took place as a direct result of actions taken by an employee of *The Organisation*, possibly on the direct instructions from its Head. We want to find that employee. We are endeavouring to secure him, and it is a him, before he leaves our jurisdiction. We must also speak with both Miss Pilessar, Head of *The Organisation* as well as her underling. Both are currently on our patch, not the US's. We can legally hold Miss Pilessar responsible for the senior Government official's death as an accessory, even if she was not at the murder scene."

"Gentlemen, are you being serious?" asked an incredulous Rowley.

"Yes, we are, sir. We're happy to step outside to allow you the time needed to make the requested arrangements. To help you, I have here and now present you with a formal letter of request that should help to smooth the way with and for your people. It specifies the assistance we are seeking. You'll see that this is all connected to the recent prisoner escape," said Colonel Burke imploringly.

Ambassador Rowley accepted and opened the envelope presented by Colonel Burke and read the letter inside. It was signed by Prime Minister Motby.

Ambassador Rowley shook his head. "You mean the Power guy? Very well, gentlemen. I'll pass on…up your request and ask that it receives urgent attention and consideration. I anticipate and warn you that the answer is likely to be negative. Also, I can't even promise a quick reply."

Colonel Burke and Jeremie had never seen Ambassador Rowley look so rattled.

"Miss Busbee, please show our two guests into our conference room and keep them company while I make some calls. On your way out, please send in Mona."

"Of course, Ambassador. Gentlemen, this way please," said Busbee, leading Colonel Burke and Jeremie out of the Ambassador's office.

"Thank you, Ambassador," said Colonel Burke as he and Jeremie followed Busbee.

***

JJ was in the unmarked windowless vehicle which brought Power from RSVGPF HQ in central Kingston to the back part of the Argyle International Airport. Rather than arrive as part of a heavy and visibly armed security convoy, the unmarked vehicle had made the forty-minute journey with minimum escort to its destination. This way, it attracted little attention to the general public.

The vehicle containing Power had been accompanied by two also unmarked RSVGPF vehicles containing several armed police officers and soldiers. The escorting vehicles had carefully interchanged during the journey.

***

It was around 9:35 a.m. when Castille's phone rang. He was finishing up a late breakfast in the airport restaurant, his purchased ticket and boarding pass for his scheduled 11:45 a.m. flight to St Vincent in his shirt pocket.

"Hello."

"Wharton. Big news! Cancel your trip to Vincie country. Your boy was captured early this morning by Vincie police. He's being brought back to Barbados later today. Don't yet know how or at what time."

"Really! You sure? When do the LIAT flights usually arrive from St Vincent?"

"Not certain…late afternoon and early evening. I can check for you."

"No worries. I can check that for myself up here. I'll not go to St Vincent now."

"Would make no sense man. Got to go. Be jolly now." Wharton hung up.

***

Castille looked at his phone. He shook his head. How might he (or someone he paid) get up to Power before he was returned to his jail cell? Realistically, he felt there would be no chance of doing that. Getting back *The Organisation's* outstanding money from Power was also now unlikely on this trip.

Castille reasoned that *The Organisation's* best option for recovering its debt from Power would have to be long-term. It would require awaiting Power's eventual release from prison, with him being charged interest of course. The other option available to *The Organisation* of harming Power while in HMP Dodds was there, but Castille did not believe that could easily be pursued. That way *The Organisation* would gain satisfaction, but no return on its investment in Power. After all, that's why *The Organisation* exists.

Castille made a decision to confirm his flight home to Miami that afternoon. Even if he received word from Wharton about Power's arrival in Barbados on one of the two afternoon LIAT flights, Castille knew Power would be transported back to the prison facility with a lot of security around him.

There was now one major task Castille had to complete before he attempted to clear airport security ahead of his departure from Barbados that afternoon. He knew how he would accomplish this, having done so two years earlier in a South American country. He needed to do some 'shopping' around in order to make disposal of pieces of the item he had to get rid of look natural.

He would face the repercussions of his failed Barbados intervention once back in the USA.

***

It was 9:45 a.m. when simultaneous swoops were made by three armed RBPF officer and BDF soldier teams, resulting in the capture of Demario 'Spend Big' Wharton, Norbert 'Nobby' Kirton and Keith Lee, at their known and main places of work, SBB&G, Kirton's home, and the Bridgetown mall respectively.

The swoop had been so clean and successful that Wharton did not have the chance to consult the Bible he kept at SBB&G. Had he gotten the opportunity, the outcome might have been different, for in that Bible was a pistol with which he would have stoutly resisted capture with. As a result, there was no blood-shed on this day, at least up until this point.

They were each taken to RBPF HQ in central Bridgetown. Once there, they were processed and charged with the legal terminology for four crimes: (a) aiding and abetting a lawful prisoner, Jasper Power (a.k.a. Stabs) with escaping legal custody from Barbados' law enforcement authorities; (b) owning an unlicensed firearm; (c) discharging a firearm without an appropriate licence; (d) wounding police and prison officers with intent to harm and maim.

They all wondered if none of the four of them had said or done anything to give themselves away on the roles they played in helping Power escape, how the hell did the RBPF get onto them?

Wharton, believing himself to be the brightest member of the Pressure Group gang, was thinking (wrongly) that it must have been Castille who had sold them out. *Despite all that I've done for him*! In his unwillingness to accept any other possibility, he decided to tell all that he knew about the US visitor.

Wharton had forgotten that Castille had only met him. Furthermore, he had not told or even intimated the names or descriptions of the other members of the Pressure Group gang to Castille.

***

Alone in his office, Ambassador Rowley attempted to recover his diplomatic composure.

How dare those two men come into my Embassy, my office and make demands of me – no, of the United States of America, he thought as he dropped down into his huge executive chair behind what was an oversized desk. To top it off, they even had the temerity to come with a letter signed by Barbados' Head of Government (one of the seven Eastern Caribbean countries to which he is accredited) and where he has resided for over two years.

Of course, Colonel Burke's understanding of the US's drone capability was correct.

A month earlier, Rowley had been advised by the US Ministry of Defence of a US ship's visit to Barbados for three days of R & R. He had received a 'soft' briefing from the State Department which mentioned in part that the ship would be carrying 'drone equipment with varying capabilities'. He was not sure what that fully entailed, but as the availability of such equipment on US ships was generally not revealed and anyway was not-ever going to be used in Barbados during the ship's short visit, he had not borne the notification any serious mind. His curiosity had however been peeked a week later when he had seen a film, *Eye In The Sky* on a US cable channel which featured US personnel using military drones to eliminate proven British and US terrorists somewhere in Africa. Collateral damage had been a concern throughout the film. If what transpired then was anything near to being correct, then military personnel, including those based in far-flung locations around the world, could be in the so-called 'kill chain' and so play roles in operating such drones. *Wow*!

Ambassador Rowley understood clearly that while the Barbadians did not want to use a US drone to eliminate anyone, there could be serious political ramifications nonetheless if such an operation was sanctioned, went wrong or God forbid ever became public knowledge. Rowley's fear, as a long-standing US Ambassador, had always been to avoid any major international incident occurring during his watch.

"It's time I found out what's involved here. I'll talk with both Major Rice and the ship's captain. I'll also speak with the State Department, no matter what Rice and the captain say, for assurance on how to respond to Prime Minister Motby's letter. If not satisfied, I'll go as high as our new Acting US Assistant Secretary of State for the hemisphere," said Rowley nervously speaking to himself.

That longstanding, popular Barbadian saying about talking to oneself sprung to mind – was his thinking 'a sign of brilliance or sheer madness'? Rowley knew he was neither brilliant nor mad! Reasonable, yes.

He picked up his internal phone to speak with Major Ashford Rice, his Defence Advisor just as his secretary Mona Fisher walked into his spacious office. Rowley halted his attempt to call Rice.

"You wanted to see me, sir?" she asked.

"Ah yes Mona. Please dig out the cell numbers for the captain of our ship that's in port. I also need the Acting Assistant Secretary of State for our Hemisphere at State's number – he's new," he said.

"What's his name, Ambassador?" Fisher asked.

"Sorry Mona, I can't recall. He's only been there a couple of days. I'd never heard of him until the President announced his name to the media and nation in the White House Briefing Room a week ago. I know that he's not the permanent appointee for the position, as it will take some time for the Senate to vet and approve the eventual permanent nominee once he or she is identified."

"I'm on it. Captain of the ship's cell number coming up," said Fisher, quickly heading back to her office.

Ambassador Rowley then called Major Rice. They agreed on three things. The Barbados Government's written request was unusual. Washington DC (their State Department superiors) had to be consulted urgently about the request before any – even a verbal response, could be given to the Barbadians. The ship's captain was unlikely to agree to any such action without direct US Department of Defence approval.

Two minutes later, having received the captain's cell number from Fisher, she went about finding both an office and a cell number for the Acting US Secretary of State for the Hemisphere.

***

After a fifteen-minute wait, Colonel Burke and Jeremie, accompanied by Busbee, were invited back into Ambassador Rowley's office by Mona Fisher who quickly left once they were all seated.

Rowley's cool composure had returned.

"Ah gentlemen. I'm sorry to have kept you waiting. I've duly consulted with my superiors as you'd requested me to do.

"Unfortunately, they have indicated an unwillingness to accede to your Government's request. Our Acting Assistant Secretary of State for the Hemisphere will formally respond shortly in writing on my Government's behalf to your Prime Minister's correspondence. I expect this to be here no later than 4:00 p.m. today. However, I can confirm one thing, that my Government and its agencies are aware of the Greater Americas' Corporation, *The Organisation* as you've referred to them. Its gradual uptick in activities back home and across Central and South America have been noticed and are of concern to us, but we have no evidence of *The Organisation* having undertaken any major business activity in a Caribbean country," stated Rowley smoothly.

Colonel Burke and Jeremie glanced at each other before returning their full attention to Rowley who continued his monologue.

"With regard to *The Organisation*'s employees, if you have evidence that any one of them while visiting Barbados *may* have committed a crime or crimes, then of course you are free to prosecute them for any such offences through your law courts. Citizens of the United States of America – the person you have mentioned by name and the as yet un-named person that you say is implicated in having done wrong, are entitled to Embassy's counsel. We will of course be duty-bound to pay attention to any potential action or processes that may be taken by Barbados against our citizens. We hope such persons would not be restrained from being speedily returned to the USA once they wish to do so," he concluded.

"Mr Ambassador, thank you for your courtesy, valuable time and for making the requested enquiry. We look forward to seeing what your Government's formal written response is to the Prime Minister's correspondence. We also respectfully advise that it remains our duty to continually enforce the Laws of Barbados against whoever may break them. Diplomats like yourself are different from the persons we are seeking to deal with. Our thanks also to you, Miss Busbee for keeping us company," said Colonel Burke.

"I'm sorry I could not be more positive and was unable to facilitate a happier outcome to our meeting today, gentlemen," said Rowley.

It was Jeremie's turn to speak up. "We are too, Mr Ambassador. Good morning to you both."

With that, the four persons in Ambassador Rowley's office rose and shook hands before the two Barbadian officials started to leave the room, leaving the two US diplomats alone. Colonel Burke and Jeremie were met at the door by Mona Fisher who escorted them back to the Embassy's main reception area where a security guard took them to Colonel Burke's vehicle.

The contentious fifty-minute meeting was over.

No winners. Despite that feeling, Colonel Burke and Jeremie felt they held the upper hand. Capture the two members of *The Organisation* today, and this meeting will have been worth it.

***

Back in Rowley's office, there was an uncomfortable silence.

"Do you think this will damage our relationship with Barbados, sir?" asked Busbee.

"Quite possible, my dear. To repair the damage, I might need you to talk to some people back home, wearing your other hat, of course, to get us out of this jam. *The Organisation* needs to be brought to heel, you know what I mean?" he said, looking directly at Busbee.

"I think I understand you, sir. I'll start discussions about making the appropriate arrangements," Busbee responded, rising to leave Rowley's office.

"That would be appreciated. Thank you."

After Busbee had left, Rowley pondered the action he presumed she would now initiate. No matter what the Barbadians had or subsequently did, the US-end of the growing monster known as *The Organisation* needed to be resolved. Busbee knew who to call. *The Organisation* would soon be no longer powerful. It should soon be something of the past, more-so than being of the present or heaven forbid, of the future.

***

At 9:57 a.m., Dr Rollerick Edwards strolled into CBOB's Boardroom for his 10:00 a.m. media conference. He was accompanied by Claire Parnell, Head of the Research Department who worked closely with Dr Albert Lewis. She was there because he was not.

Their task this morning was to formally discuss CBOB's just released First Quarter economic report. Dr Edwards' video presentation on the quarter's results had been recorded on Friday afternoon and uploaded at midnight last night to enable the media and public alike to review ahead of this morning's conference.

Once the CBOB's PR officer had introduced the Governor and Parnell, Dr Edwards explained that he would show his ten-minute video presentation first before making a further short statement to be followed by a Q and A session. Hard copies of the First Quarter economic report had been placed on each chair in the Board Room. Dr Edwards and Claire Parnell did not expect today's event to last for more than the usual forty-five minutes. But, before entering the Board room, they recognised that, due to the Deputy Governor's recent absence from work, there might be some questions about him, perhaps even more than there would be on the good figures contained in the First Quarter economic report. Therefore, they had allocated one hour in their respective calendars for this event.

As the video played, Parnell leaned over and whispered to Dr Edwards. "All's well, sir?"

He responded, "Yes, I'm fine Claire, thanks for asking. If there's something I say which you also want to expand on or clarity, do chime in."

"Very well."

As it turned out, following Dr Edwards' short statement, he was able to handle the media's questions on the economy's First Quarter performance with aplomb. His calm nature, obvious intellect and professionalism were soothing and polite, even engaging.

He had also prepared a stock answer to any questions that might have been asked about Dr Lewis. It was simple: "I have nothing further to report on that matter, so I refer you to the Royal Barbados Police Force which is handling it. Chief Superintendent Johnny Vickers, to be precise." Parnell was not required to speak, and did not do so.

***

The transfer on the Argyle International Airport tarmac from the van onto BDF1 had been done quickly. The increased activity around BDF1 fifteen minutes prior to the van's arrival could not have been missed by friends or family members who had been brave enough to go up onto the blustery viewing gallery to wave off departing passengers on the two mid-morning LIAT flights that had arrived and would soon take off heading for Trinidad and Barbados respectively.

Once Sergeant Browne and Chief Inspector Gomez had signed off on their documentation enabling Power to be passed from the custody of RSVGPF to RBPF, Power was secured on BDF1. Now, with the Barbadian security contingent all on board, BDF1's main exit door was closed following JJ having said a final word of thanks and a fond goodbye to Gomez. BDF1 was then authorised by the airport tower to taxi to the far end of the runway in preparation for its forty-minute return journey back to Barbados with its recaptured prisoner.

Power's time in St Vincent was at an end. The look on his face as he sat on BDF1 showed no emotion, but inside of him was seething with resentment at three sets of people: those who had caused the previous night's accident; caught him; and who now sat with him on this aircraft for the short journey back to Barbados.

How might I get out of this situation this time around, he was wondering to himself?

Whatever happened next, Power knew his luck had finally ran out. It was time to face up to what he had done, in reality many times over. He would have to pay a price for those actions. Shame!

***

Chapter Twenty-Seven
HQ Action

For a variety of reasons, BDF1's departure from St Vincent with Power on board had been further delayed, resulting in a slightly later departure time than what had been planned.

They eventually departed St Vincent at 10:15 a.m. The forty-minute journey back to Barbados would be swift and direct.

***

Harold Oliver had invited Superintendent Innis to accompany him to the hanger twenty-five minutes earlier. There, Oliver had provided the briefing promised by Colonel Burke to Innis. He was somewhat amazed to see BDF soldiers in the hanger but comprehended the nature of their involvement in this particular exercise. He was grateful for their support.

Innis called Colonel Burke at BIB HQ to confirm that he was in position and that all was set to receive the returning prisoner at the facility he ran.

"Very well, Superintendent. I'd like you to accompany the prisoner back to HMP Dodds. I'll have someone return your vehicle there later today, so please leave its keys with Oliver," said Colonel Burke.

"You got it, Colonel Burke."

With that, Innis separated his vehicle key from the bunch of personal office and house keys that hung from his belt. He passed his vehicle key to Oliver.

"He said to give you this. You'll get someone to drop off my vehicle at Dodds later?"

"Sure thing, no problem."

***

The overnight rain had delayed the 10:00 a.m. start to Day 4. If this was the old Kensington Oval, it would have been pretty certain that most, if not all of Day 4 would have been lost.

Fortunately, as a result of the West Indies having hosted ICC's Cricket World Cup 2007 (with New Kensington Oval hosting the Final between Australia and Sri Lanka), the entire stadium – ground and stands, had been completely rebuilt. Part of that process had involved a completely new drainage system for the ground. It was this system that enabled play to commence at 10:45 a.m. rather than the scheduled 10:00 a.m. It was time for one team to win a Test Match, or for the other to save it.

West Indies had declared at 218 for nine, their overnight score, just before play commenced. England therefore needed 473 to win. An unlikely winning target, even with nearly two days of the game to go, given that the highest and therefore world record score to win a Test Match in the fourth innings was 418 for seven, set by the West Indies against Australia in Antigua in 2003. So how would England do?

***

Captain Collins touched down BDF1 at Grantley Adams International Airport (GAIA) in Barbados at 10:50 a.m., five minutes earlier than scheduled. A couple of hours earlier, the hanger had been secured by one dozen members of Alleyne's BDF Special Task Force unit on Tenton's instructions, after consultation with Jeremie and Harold Oliver. Both had given formal approval for this national security operation to take place on the airport compound.

The aircraft followed Adams Tower's instructions, taxiing to a part of the tarmac usually reserved for private aircraft. BDF1 was directed to taxi into a hanger where seeing activity from the outside was near impossible. This was away from any prying eyes of passengers and almost all airport workers.

The Special Task Force unit knew they were there to receive a package – an individual from an incoming aircraft who they would take to a secure place. That individual's name and the place they were to take them was not provided to

393

members of the unit at first, although they soon worked out that their 'prey' was to be the escaped, now recaptured prisoner Power and his destination would be HMP Dodds.

As the aircraft's engines died down, Collins, turning around and spoke to those in the cabin.

"Gentlemen, our job's done here. All yours now. Good luck boys."

"Many thanks, captain," said Browne as Collins released the lock for the main cabin door.

"Yes, see you another time captain, hopefully under more pleasant circumstances," said JJ.

"Sure, whenever that happens. I'm always happy to accommodate you guys," said Collins.

"Good. Thanks again," said JJ.

"JJ, have a great and safe day now," responded Collins on behalf of himself and co-pilot Annette Taitt.

Alleyne, a long-time friend of Collins, simply added, "Well done, skipper. Thank you too, FO Taitt."

Smiling broadly, Alleyne gave Collins the thumbs up sign before he went back, along with Browne to focus on the imminent delivery and transfer of Power to the custody of Innis, who would now be responsible with the BDF's Special Task Force unit for Power's safe return to HMP Dodds.

Innis was surprised at first that none of his BPS officers had been asked to help with completing the recapture exercise, except for himself. But on reflection, given all that had taken place with Power's escape, the lack of BPS/HMP Dodds prisoner transport equipment and of course what was now being referred to as **'The Telford Incident'**, he wasn't entirely shocked.

In fact, he was secretly delighted and relieved that Barbados' other security agencies had taken on that responsibility today.

Innis had learnt his management lesson over the past few days. Always act promptly when any crisis threatens your organisation. *In future, I'll not wait until any situation gets out of control before initiating corrective action*, he was thinking to himself. He would take his *P.A.A.N.I.* colleagues more into his confidence going forward, that is, if he was kept on in his position and not transferred to another post in the Public Service. The prisoner transport situation (or at least the prisoner escape) might have been avoided had he spoken up. Innis had lost a deputy but then, from what he now knew, losing Telford was probably always going to happen, sooner or later. A pity.

***

The 'unlocking' of Power from his seat on BDF1 was a sight to behold. Once his restraints had been removed, Power was slowly eased up from his seat and moved with the help of Browne to the door of the aircraft, then down the aircraft's steps, across the few yards of concrete and into the back of a heavily fortified, windowless BDF vehicle.

Browne and Alleyne joined Power in the back of the vehicle before the door was slammed shut and locked from the outside. On his way into the BDF vehicle, Power noticed two men in civilian clothing who stood watching him. He recognised one of them. Innis, HMP Dodds' Superintendent.

Browne secured Power again to the BDF vehicle before starting to chat with Alleyne. The vehicle's engine purred into life. A dimmed light inside the vehicle came on, along with the air conditioning system which made breathing a lot easier. Power remained as quiet as a mouse. He realised that he was about to make the journey he had not anticipated having to make for a long time, if ever and certainly not within a week of his leaving a HMP Dodds prisoner transport vehicle. Power expected no rescue from this particular vehicle or scenario. *Only a dog returns to eat his vomit*, he thought. Recently, bad situations had followed him (being in prison, indebted to *The Organisation*, escaping from Castille, escaping from the prisoner transport vehicle, escaping with his life after the Vincie accident), and soon he was going to be right back where he had started – HMP Dodds. *God, what a mess!*

Of course, Browne and Alleyne's jobs would not be complete until they had accompanied and seen to it that Power was secured again in HMP Dodds.

The original letter of authority Browne had received via Colonel Burke from Commissioner Jeremie had been handed over to Gomez on arrival in St Vincent. He now held the signed copy of that document in his possession and would personally deliver it, not to Colonel Burke but to his Commissioner before the day was out. Various RBPF and BDF personnel had also been engaged to provide support elements across *Operation 'Fishhook'*, although BIB was ultimately responsible for and in control of the operation's execution from beginning to end.

The BDF vehicle exited the covered airport area and set off towards one of the restricted but lesser-used airport compound's gates at 11:25 p.m. It was a rapid fifteen-minute drive to HMP Dodds in St Phillip. The BDF vehicle was escorted by a heavy BDF and RBPF escort. Their convoy would not be stopped.

Fred noticed JJ's BIB vehicle was neatly parked at the back of the hanger. Colonel Burke's work!

JJ pulled a key for his vehicle from his backpack. "Want a ride to HQ, Fred?"

"No thanks, my vehicle is up here. Can you give me a ride to where it is and I'll meet you there?"

"Sure."

JJ found his BIB phone in the driver's seat of his vehicle.

"Excuse me Fred, but I must make a couple of calls."

"Go ahead boss."

JJ's first call was to Vanessa.

"Hi, V. I'm back in Barbados. All's well with you and the kids?" he asked.

"Happy to hear your voice JJ. Everything is well with me, the kids and at home. We're all looking forward to seeing you later today," she stated.

"Me too love. Gotta go now, so be good till I get home."

"Fine. Bye."

JJ's second call was to Colonel Burke.

"Hello chief, we're back in Barbados. I can confirm that I've brought Power back and he is on his way back to HMP Dodds."

"Thank you, JJ. Wonderful news. Look, we're having our *Operation 'Fishhook's* debrief at 12:30 p.m. here at HQ with Commissioner Jeremie and Brigadier Tenton. I'd like you, Fred, Mohammed and Jayne to join us."

"Okay. Fred and I are about to leave the airport for HQ, chief. We should be there in another…twelve minutes."

"That's great. Tell Fred to come in with you as I've had his BIB vehicle brought down to HQ. His personal vehicle leant to you is now also back at his house. Well done again boys. See both of you shortly," said Colonel Burke.

JJ told Fred what Colonel Burke had told him about his vehicle before turning on the vehicle's engine. Playing on the radio was a Trinidad calypso JJ had heard but did not own, Organiser *The Bandit*. What a fitting song, given the operation he had just completed.

During their twelve-minute journey to BIB HQ, the two operatives surprisingly did not say much to each other. Fred assumed that from JJ's standpoint, having conducted his two necessary conversations, he was probably still thinking about his suspension letter from HOPS. Fred hoped the successful *Operation 'Fishhook'* assignment would help turn that situation around in JJ's favour.

Unknown to Fred, JJ's mind was not on the suspension at all. He was simply tired after his ordeal over the past four days. He was looking forward to getting a good night's sleep in his own bed that night.

***

Vickers received an important call from Inspector Melanie Gray at RBPF HQ.

After listening for a minute, he responded, "That's interesting. That's another string to our bow. But are you sure Wharton understood what he was saying when he mentioned the firearm?"

"Yes sir. Our boys think he regretted mentioning it though," said Gray.

"Very well. Thanks very much. Great work. We're already looking to pick up this guy. Back-up's being arranged," Vickers said.

"Good luck with that, sir."

"Roger that."

***

Colonel Burke had waited to hear from JJ before calling Prime Minister Motby. He gave him a 'head's up' on *Operation 'Fishhook's* outcome. The basic facts about Power's recapture were then passed to Giles Archer, Communications Director in the Prime Minister's Office. These would form the basis for a short media release Archer would prepare and, after passing it through Colonel Burke for approval, release it through the Government Information Service (GIS). The media release would be withheld until 12:45 p.m. The GIS release indicated that Hon. Sebastian Smith QC MP, Attorney General and Minister of Residential Affairs, would hold a media conference at his Wildey, St Michael office at 4:00 p.m. that afternoon. He would be joined by Commissioner Jeremie from the RBPF (if available) and Superintendent Innis of the BPS.

Colonel Burke also decided to call Dr Winston Smith to advise him of Power's overnight recapture in St Vincent and return to Barbados this morning.

That way, Dr Smith would not be surprised when a GIS media release hit the airways in a couple of hours or so.

Colonel Burke deliberately did not report JJ's involvement in Power's recapture. That would come later.

***

By 11.50 a.m., the convoy carrying Power had arrived inside HMP Dodds. There, Power had been removed from the BDF vehicle and personally escorted by Browne, Alleyne, Innis and two BPS officers into the reception centre for new or returning inmates.

Browne and Alleyne had brought *Operation 'Fishhook'* to its conclusion. For them, mission accomplished.

Power was back behind bars in HMP Dodds. For him, the opposite. What a pity.

***

Castille had completed the major task he had earlier set himself to undertake. There had been no complications.

He did not hear from Wharton again. Castille was of course unaware that Wharton could no longer call him. Or that he would not be able to reach Wharton by phone even if he had tried, for Wharton, like the other three Pressure Group gang members, were all sitting somewhat uncomfortably in separate interview rooms at RBPF HQ in central Bridgetown.

Castille had sat quietly for well over half-an-hour on one of the airport benches. During that time, he watched persons checking-in at various airline counters before he headed for the AA check-in area to secure his boarding pass for the seat he had re-booked for the afternoon AA flight to Miami.

Castille decided to call his boss to report the failure of his Barbados mission. There was a prompt answer.

"Hello."

"It's me. Look, I've not gotten anywhere here. Our debtor's been caught overseas and should be brought back to Barbados later today. It will now be impossible to get close to Power to either collect or finish the job without causing an uproar, so I've decided to return home this pm. We'll need to find another way of resolving our issue. I suggest in slower time, eventually getting paid. Working from the inside is unlikely to work."

"I agree. Don't worry. Time longer than rope."

"Eh?"

"I'll explain when we meet…tonight?"

"Fine. Usual venue?"

"Yes. Goodbye."

The line went dead.

***

Pilessar was disappointed, but not unduly upset. Her session with her Barbados host had gone extremely well. Much better than she had expected in fact. As a result, she was relaxed about their future sub-regional collaborative relationship.

When Power got back to Barbados would not matter. Once he was in a secure environment, there could always be a way to get at him. This was one occasion where she and Castille were thinking differently on the way forward with a client. Power's not paying back what he owed *The Organisation* would be costly to him, if the prison in Barbados was anything like those in the US. She could arrange for someone to take Power out, accidentally of course. The option of waiting until his eventual release to effect recovery of his outstanding payment with interest, did not appeal to her. What was certain was that *The Organisation's* debt would not be written off. *Should word get out, it would send the wrong message to our clients, especially our new potential Caribbean ones*, thought Pilessar.

That would not be good in a new geographical business area. She would reflect further on the action she would need take regarding Power on her return to the USA.

***

Castille collected his boarding pass from the AA self-check-in machine and was leaving the AA area to head towards the airport security checkpoint and beyond that the Immigration departure area when he noticed several men watching, or were they waiting for him?

Keep cool, he thought, as a couple of serious-looking men now approached him. He felt no need to run – indeed there was no place for him to run to. No one to seek assistance from either. He had no weapon of any kind that might even have encouraged him to take someone in the immediate area as a hostage. With no options available to him, he kept his calm and limited his actions.

"Mr Rhohan Castille?" It was the man who appeared to be the most senior of the two that were now standing before him.

"Yes."

"Can you come with us please?"

"Why? Who are you? Airport security? Police? What have I done?"

"Mr Castille, please don't make a scene. I'm Chief Superintendent Johnny Vickers of the Royal Barbados Police Force and my colleague here is Inspector Byron Moss. We just want to ask you a few questions concerning your stay at the Rising Sun hotel…"

"Oh? What questions?"

"We'd prefer not to do this here in public, Mr Castille. It really would be better for everyone concerned if you came with us please," answered Vickers.

The few passengers standing at the AA self-check-in machines and assisting AA staffers looked over at them, concerned but not too alarmed. This was none of their business.

"Look…just give me a minute to put away my documents –"

"Please don't reach into your bag, sir. In fact, let me help you carry that –" said Moss.

"There's no need for –"

"No, but I must insist, sir," stated Moss as he took possession of Castille's pull-along.

Castille saw no point in resisting, so walked co-operatively with the two RBPF officers towards the Arrival hall area of the GAIA compound where inside, a couple of Customs back rooms were located. He had also noticed four other men close by who he felt sure were supporting the two officers.

***

The news that Vickers, Moss and a team of four other non-uniformed RBPF detectives had nabbed Castille, at GAIA and that he was now sitting in a Customs back room at that location reached Jeremie at BIB HQ around 12:15 p.m., just as he started to tuck into lunch ordered in by Colonel Burke from Rita's Kitchen.

If, as they all thought, it was indeed Castille who was responsible for the murder of George Telford, the former Deputy Superintendent of HMP Dodds and so a high-ranking public servant, then they had struck gold. Jeremie asked Colonel Burke if his officers could bring Castille to BIB HQ to conduct the interview there, rather than doing so at the less secure airport. There was no objection and so the order was given.

***

Operation 'Fishhook's debrief commenced in BIB HQ at 12:30 p.m. as planned. The *SNARL Cycle (Situation; Normal – or not; Action required; Result achieved; Lessons learnt)* was used to conduct an initial operational debrief of its success (or not) by the time Vickers, Moss and another RBPF officer arrived with Castille just after 1:10 p.m.

The first stage of the operational debrief was adjourned at that time. It had been decided to continue the debrief session at 3:00 p.m. when the persons required for the first stage of the debrief would all be back at BIB HQ. Then they would endeavour to preliminarily complete their review of *Operation 'Fishhook'* so as to enable Colonel Burke to provide a final written report to Prime Minister Motby for the record.

The adjournment also allowed for Joe and her three fellow BIB operatives – Riley Morris, Ivan Forde (code number Y50) and Steve Rogers (code number T30) to undertake another assignment which, as it turned out, was also connected to *Operational 'Fishhook'*.

What was it, where and why? To catch a 'big fish', as doing so should help tie up everything nicely.

***

The announced capture of Power, broadcast by media houses in *'Breaking News'* packages just after 12:45 p.m., caused the four diplomats to hold back on issuing their second dispatches. They knew from experience, that this action would result in a major government statement in the next few hours. Also, because of this development, other 'shoes might drop'. They did know and could not imagine what these might be so decided, following their round robin telephone call, to issue their second dispatches the following morning.

***

The basement of the BIB HQ building was not an unpleasant place to visit or operate in from an operative's perspective. But to BIB 'guests' (and other persons brought there by other law enforcement agencies), the basement could be viewed as and be made to feel lonely, uncomfortable, in-hospitable, daunting and so frightening. Deliberately being left alone to 'stew' in a locked, windowless room was definitely intimidating. But Castille was not someone who was easily intimidated.

He was the latest BIB guest to be placed in a locked, windowless room in BIB HQ's basement. He had been 'fed and watered' by BIB operatives before being left alone with his thoughts. Castille was unsure what would happen next as his interview had not yet taken place. If that went badly for him, how long might he end up having to spend in Barbados? Being cooped up like a bird in a cage or a dog in a kennel was not to Castille's liking. He was starting to feel some pressure, having worked out that his return to the USA that afternoon was now looking highly unlikely. That meant that his boss would not see him show up for their meeting that evening back in Miami. She would know that something was up, as it was not like him to miss any of their meetings.

What was meant to have been a quick and easy assignment in Barbados had obviously not panned out the way he or his boss had anticipated. *Where did he or it all go wrong?* Well, he had made a few errors since his arrival for sure, including being too patient with Power and Wharton perhaps? Castille's mind was working along negative lines, but he remained cool and started to ponder how he might still get out of this well-fortified place.

Be positive. There's always a way out of any jam, he was thinking to himself.

Castille's problem was that he knew of no one or organisation in Barbados (except the Embassy of the USA) that might be willing to pull a string or have some influence to work quickly to get him out of the predicament he was in. As this was unlikely, the realism that he could be stuck in Barbados for a while started to sink in.

***

Following her earlier discussion with Castille, Pilessar realised that he would now also be on the same afternoon AA flight to Miami as herself. She hoped they would not see each other during pre-flight, the flight itself or the post-flight period in Miami International Airport's Arrival hall. If they did bump into each other, they would ignore each other and simply keep moving. Explanations about why she'd visited Barbados at the same time as Castille could come later when they met in that down-town bar.

Pilessar placed Castille out of her mind as she was given a whistle-stop tour of Barbados' east and west coasts over the next two hours by Shepherd, the same 'very tall, dark and handsome figure' who had met her at the airport the previous afternoon. Pilessar enjoyed the experience – the sights of large and sprawling private homes, chattel houses, varied hotel and villa properties, and above all the spectacular views of the placid Caribbean Sea and more energetic Atlantic Ocean. She could understand why her host retreated daily to a place overlooking Barbados' quietest but most scenic coastline.

There wasn't time to see much more of Barbados on this brief visit. Anyhow, she did not want to venture anywhere near to the capital city of Bridgetown. Nor did she have the desire to visit shopping malls, supermarkets or the more public areas where she would surely have been captured on CCTV networks that were seemingly in place everywhere. Being inadvertently photographed by a local or visitor was also not on her 'bucket list' for this or any of her previous overseas business trips, given her line of work.

Shepherd dropped Pilessar off at GAIA at 1:25 p.m. After removing her pull-along from the trunk of the vehicle and placing it on the sidewalk, he wished her goodbye.

"Well, it's been nice having you here ma'am, short though it was. Come again. Safe flight home."

"Thank you for so safely moving me around, Benedict. Goodbye."

With that, Shepherd and Pilessar parted company. She did not respond to Shepherd's invitation about returning to Barbados, though she felt that she might well do so one day.

It was still a good couple of hours before her flight to Miami was scheduled to depart. She checked herself in at the AA first-class counter and secured her boarding pass before proceeding to the security officer. He checked her passport details against her boarding pass and directed her to the Immigration officer in the Departure hall. Soon, Pilessar's departure from Barbados was formalised by a young female officer who stamped her passport.

Once through inner security, Pilessar walked through into the Departure area and looked around the airport shops. In one of them, she purchased a large bottle of water. She had nobody to buy anything for. A few minutes later, she sat comfortably in the upstairs area of the Departure lounge, sipping her water reflectively. She felt she had completed the business she'd come to Barbados to do in the twenty-four hours she'd spent on the island. Her host had been gracious and friendlier than she'd ever expected. More professional too, which was not always the case in her experience of working for *The Organisation*.

The only thing Pilessar wanted to do now was to hear her flight being called, get through the four-hour journey to Miami without incident, spend the obligatory thirty minutes passing through US Immigration and Customs, before being picked up and driven to her down-town high-rise apartment.

Pilessar suddenly became conscious of three men approaching her. She looked around to notice other men who appeared to be trying to blend in with the departing passengers but she knew otherwise as they were also looking in her general direction.

That was when she heard her name being spoken.

It was the commanding voice of a woman who was standing beside her. "Miss Emma Pilessar?"

Looking up sharply, Pilessar wanted to see what the woman looked like.

"Excuse me...who are you and what have I done?" asked a puzzled Pilessar.

"I am Kylie Callendar of the Barbados Intelligence Bureau (BIB). With me are three fellow BIB operatives and two Royal Barbados Police Force officers. We'd like to ask you a few questions ma'am, so please come with me," said Joe, showing Pilessar her BIB badge.

Reluctantly, Pilessar rose slowly from her seat, hand bag in hand. She reached for her pull-along but realised that one of the officers had already picked it up.

"Miss Colinder –" started Pilessar.

Joe corrected her. "It's Callendar, ma'am. Please follow me," said Joe leading the way.

"If you insist, but you should know that my Embassy will hear about this, especially if you make me miss my flight. Your treatment of me will not do your country's reputation for tourism any good back in the USA."

"Perhaps not. This way please, Miss Pilessar," said Joe, descending the stairs from the upper area of the Departure lounge and heading towards one of the rooms in the airport's Immigration department area.

On arrival in the room, the senior Immigration officer in charge of the 8:00 a.m. to 3:00 p.m. shift at the airport held out a phone in her hand to Joe.

"Miss Callendar, for you."

Joe took the phone.

"Thanks. Hello, Callendar here."

"Colonel Burke. Please bring Miss Pilessar to BIB HQ as soon as you can," he ordered.

"On it chief, if that's what's required."

"It is. Goodbye."

Joe spoke to her fellow operatives. "Listen up fellas, we're to take her to BIB HQ."

Morris, Forde and Rogers nodded in acceptance of their changed duty. Turning to Pilessar, Joe explained. "A change of plan. We've been asked to take you to our headquarters office. It's not far away."

"Look, this *isn't* funny. You haven't told me why you are stopping me from getting on my flight. I've done nothing wrong since arriving in Barbados for what, twenty-four hours –"

"Miss Pilessar, all I can promise is that I'll do is my best to get you to our headquarters quickly. I'm unable to tell you how long you'll be there. That will depend on my boss and what he needs to discuss with you. Can we get moving, please?"

Unhappy and concerned, Pilessar turned around and started to follow Joe out of the door, with Morris, Forde and Rogers in tow. The two RBPF officers also tagged along behind them.

***

After consultation, it was unanimously agreed to push back the planned 3:00 p.m. re-convening of the *Operation 'Fishhook'* mission debrief. The tentative new time was set for 5:00 p.m. Jeremie had been particularly strong about a delayed start because he wanted to learn what Castille and Pilessar might say in their simultaneous but separate interviews that would hopefully shed light on

Power's escape, George Telford's murder and *The Organisation*'s activities, current and proposed, in Barbados and other Caribbean countries.

Colonel Burke had decided that, for completeness (some would say wickedness but hell, why not) that he would find a way for Castille and Pilessar to at least see each other, perhaps even get them to meet up once their separate interviews had been completed.

***

Castille was interviewed by Chief Superintendent Vickers, Inspector Moss and Fred in Interview Room 1 (IR1). His forty-five minutes interview had focussed primarily on what he had come to Barbados to do and why, plus the murder of George Telford. Castille kept his cool, speaking little. He never admitted hearing about or ever meeting anyone named Telford.

When Vickers asked, "How then do you explain your hotel room key being found inside Mr Telford's vehicle?" Castille simply shrugged his shoulders and stared directly ahead.

Moss followed up. "We know that you did not return one of your two room keys to the hotel's reception on checking out. Why was that sir?" Again, he did not speak, continuing to stare at one of the walls inside the room.

"Don't worry, Mr Castille. I expect our forensics boys will find some fingerprints on the room key. Who knows, as the last person allocated that key by the hotel, don't be surprised if yours appear on it," stated Vickers before ending the interview by formally charging Castille for Telford's murder.

Unknown to Castille, Wharton had earlier confessed at RBPF HQ to having been engaged by and meeting with him on more than one occasion in recent days, with their last meeting being that morning at the airport. Contacts had initially been about engaging Wharton's Pressure Group gang to undertake Power's escape from legal custody on 18th April. Wharton confirmed receipt of payment from Castille for that job and sharing such with fellow gang members. He also admitted that his Pressure Group had tried to assist Castille with finding out Power's location after he had left Barbados' jurisdiction.

Finally, Wharton had answered a seemingly innocent question. "Did Mr Castille request anything else from you in exchange for the payment you received?"

Wharton had quickly answered, "Yes, and I guess you want to know what it was?" before realising his mistake.

"I would indeed, Mr Wharton. Please tell me what 'it' was," quickly answered Inspector Gray.

He had then admitted to providing Castille with a firearm during their first Barbados meeting on the afternoon of 18th April. Wharton did not make the connection between his provision of that item to Castille and Telford's death up to that point, but Gray and her colleague RBPF interviewers did and had quickly passed that information onto Vickers and Moss.

Castille did not know that two of his interviewers now had this information prior to the interview's start. His plan was *not* to cooperate with his interviewers. He reasoned that his lost room key could have been found by anyone, and of course, it *would* have his fingerprints on it. *Tying me to Telford's murder was going to be difficult without real evidence (i.e. the weapon used)*, having earlier disposed of it in pieces in different parts of the airport after having received word of Power's recapture.

So Castille was not concerned about the murder charge. He remained confident that, somehow, he would eventually get himself out of this jam he was in.

***

Pilessar's interview commenced in Interview Room 6 (IR6) shortly after Castille's had commenced in Interview Room 1 (IR1) at the opposite end of the corridor. Her interviewers were Colonel Burke, Jeremie and Joe.

Pilessar's interview lasted thirty minutes. In response to questions about Power, Castille and *The Organisation's* general activities, particularly any activity taking place in Barbados, she was unsurprisingly bland and non-committal in her answers. It was as if she was speaking about matters which meant nothing to her.

Asked by Jeremie why she did not stay at the private home she had placed on her Immigration/Custom form on arrival, she'd shrugged her shoulders.

"Why did you make what amounts to an overnight visit to Barbados?" asked Colonel Burke.

"Tourism. I attended the LP concert last night," Pilessar stated.

"Have you any proof of your attendance?" asked Colonel Burke.

She did not answer so, on a whim, Joe asked Pilessar, "Where did the concert take place last night? Do you have your ticket stub?"

Again, Pilessar did not respond. Perhaps she did not know the venue or have her ticket stub.

Prior to the interview's end, and after more questions which got similar non-responses, Jeremie charged her as an accessory to murder.

That statement definitely got Pilessar's attention. She knew Castille was in Barbados but was unaware of everything he had gotten up to since his arrival. Having only been in the country from the previous afternoon, Pilessar was unaware of what had happened in Barbados in the previous days. During their conversation that morning, Castille had not mentioned any 'incidents' (code to them for a killing having been done). Pilessar wondered why Castille would not have told her of such if indeed it had taken place. *So that's where the accessory charge is coming from…these people aren't bluffing* was her line of thought.

A quick-thinking woman, Pilessar began to get an inkling as to what might have happened. This realisation caused her to slowly sit upright in her chair as the gravity of the charge hit home. Her facial expression also changed from 'can't touch me' to one of 'how the hell did I get myself involved in this'. She shook her head. *What specific evidence do they have to link me to Castille's actions?* she pondered but at this stage, did not know.

Neither Colonel Burke, Jeremie or Joe knew whether Pilessar's response was out of anger, fear or disappointment. They assumed that she might not have known who Telford was, or of his murder.

With both sets of interviews completed, it was time for Colonel Burke's engineered 'accidental sighting' of each other by the two interviewees. He wondered how that might play? Would sparks fly?

***

Mohammed Car and Jayne Bixley had been alerted to Colonel Burke's thinking and ploy and so were casually sitting around a table in the recreation room in the basement area awaiting the end of both interviews.

They looked up when one of the doors opened. Castille was brought out of Interview Room 1 (IR1) by Vickers, Moss and Fred. The plan was to take him upstairs where he would be transported to RBPF HQ for processing. Pilessar was also brought out from IR6 by Colonel Burke, Jeremie and Joe. Neither interviewee was handcuffed, that would be done once they were upstairs and prior to being placed into the RBPF vehicle that would take them on the twenty-minute journey to RBPF HQ where they would be formally charged and photographed. As they were US citizens, the US Embassy would be informed at that stage.

Castille was looking down, so did not see Pilessar. She, on the other hand, had her head up and was looking straight ahead. She was thinking about how she might get herself out of this predicament. Who in Barbados did she know beside her host and Shepherd? No one else. She certainly was not going to call her host. Having always been a positive person, Pilessar believed that as an US citizen, someone from the Embassy would have to be notified of her arrest and that should lead to her release. As easy as that.

It was then that a sharp message was transmitted from her eyes to her brain – one of the four persons ahead of her she recognised. Castille! No, it couldn't be.

What was he doing here? Though shocked, Pilessar had sufficient control not to shout his name or otherwise show any recognition of him. The first group of four persons stopped to speak with Mohammed and Jayne. It was only then that Castille casually looked around him and saw his boss, Emma Pilessar coming towards him in the midst of three other persons.

Castille and Pilessar's eyes met, but neither spoke.

Colonel Burke's group stopped just short of Vickers' group as Joe conversed with Mohammed and Jayne. Once their conversation had ended, Mohammed called someone on his phone. Speaking softly, he alerted his BIB colleagues that they were about to come upstairs with the two packages, so ask the driver of the police transport vehicle to be in place and to prepare the appropriate sets of restraints Shutting off his phone, Mohammed nodded to Colonel Burke who now moved forward towards the lift that would take his group with Castille up to the ground floor.

Though the lift could carry up to ten persons at a time, BIB In-house Protocol #15 had long established that no more than one 'package', along with their escorts (four in each case here) should be moved in the lift at a time. Therefore, it was Vickers, Moss, Fred and Castille, along with Jayne who used the lift first. Once the lift had returned to the basement of BIB HQ, Colonel Burke, Jeremie, Joe and Pilessar were joined by Mohammed for their ride up to the ground floor.

***

Giles Archer had duly organised the promised 4:00 p.m. media conference at Hon. Sebastian Smith QC MP, Attorney General and Minister of Residential Affairs' Wildey, St Michael office. Jeremie was not available, so had sent AC Smith as his representative. Superintendent Innis, Head of the BPS (including the HMP Dodds facility), was also there to support Attorney General Smith.

Once Smith had read an opening statement, the media were informed that little new information could be shared on Power at this time, except that he had been recaptured and was safely locked away in HMP Dodds. The other immediate security matters of concern to the country were resolved. Prime Minister Motby would be making a Ministerial Statement on the country's overall security and the recent security challenges to Parliament when it re-convened at 10:00 a.m. the next day.

Media houses got to ask questions, but accepted that with tomorrow's promised Ministerial Statement to Parliament by the Prime Minister, Smith would not be giving much away.

Hopefully, another (new) security issue would not pop up before then.

***

BIB In-house Protocol #3 had been in place from BIB's inception. No firearms were to be carried by or on the person of any BIB operative or visiting law enforcement personnel during an interview. Operatives and law enforcement visitors alike abided by this rule. There was therefore no opportunity for either Castille or Pilessar to gain access to any firearms during their time in these areas. This did not mean they were not on the lookout for *any* situation or alternative weaponry they might use to help aid escape from their current predicament. Should such an opportunity present itself, they knew they would use it.

Once out of the lift, there was a short walk to the main door at the back of BIB HQ where the RBPF transport vehicle was already lined up to take Castille and Pilessar to RBPF HQ. Bruce Jordan, BIB operative (code number X60) was standing by with two sets of handcuffs at the ready to secure them.

The uniformed RBPF officer allotted to drive Castille and Pilessar to RBPF HQ, entered the building to use the bathroom. His vehicle was visible just outside of the building's back entrance.

The on-duty security guard standing outside of the door entered the building after the RBPF officer, presumably to check for something he had left behind the security desk. His entry was unfortunate, for this presented the opportunity Castille was hoping for. In his rush to avoid tardiness for having started his shift some five minutes late, the guard had forgotten to properly snap his firearm into its holster.

Bruce had by now placed the handcuffs on Pilessar and was about to turn to do the same to Castille. Noticing the opportunity to fight for the security guard's firearm, Castille viciously elbowed Vickers and Moss simultaneously in their stomachs before making a lunge at the security guard. Caught unawares, the security guard was startled. He dropped the book he'd just collected. Castille thrust himself forward, knocking over the security guard before struggling with him in an effort to get hold of the firearm that was in his holster. As the guard fought back, the gun went off and he fell to the ground, still.

Castille now had the guard's gun in his hand. He pointed the weapon at the nearest group of persons standing not far from the lift in the small corridor, shouting, "*Everybody stand back.*"

The security guard groaned as he lay curled up in the foetal position on the ground in front of them.

"Let me help him," said Colonel Burke.

"Stay put. I don't plan to use this again, but I *will* if any of you make me," said Castille. It was clear that he was not joking. Colonel Burke knew Castille's type. He meant what he said.

To Pilessar, Castille urged, "Let's get out of here…no, wait. You," he said pointing at Bruce Jordan. "Unlock her. Quickly."

Jordan reluctantly complied with Castille's order from the set of keys he held.

"You won't get far," said Colonel Burke.

"Wanna bet?" asked Castille, making a step towards the door.

"I don't bet but am dead certain."

***

The security guard lying on the ground was in obvious pain but, being aware that it was his unprofessionalism that had made this situation possible, wanted to help retrieve the situation and not let it get completely out of control. Before

Castille got away, he grabbed Castille's left leg in an effort to pull him down so that he could not leave. A man in his early-60's, he was not strong enough to topple the much stronger Castille.

Now free of her handcuffs, Pilessar now stood alone and quickly moved to the security guard's location and kicked him in the face, screaming at Castille, "Let's go."

"Okay. Go and get the vehicle running. I'll be along," he responded.

Pilessar hesitated before moving off towards the automatic door and on reaching it, she turned back to mock Colonel Burke.

"You were saying?" she asked sarcastically.

***

Neither Pilessar or Castille had noticed the nod and a wink between Colonel Burke and one of his BIB operatives. Truth be told, Colonel Burke had not been speaking with Castille, but to Mohammed who was standing beside him. There was a pane of glass next to the lift containing three items: a bucket of sand, a fire hose, and an axe. These items were to be used in an emergency situation to either help put out a small fire or help to rescue someone possibly trapped inside a stuck or broken lift.

***

"Now," said Colonel Burke, appearing to talk to himself.

"What?" Castille asked hesitatingly, mystified and confused by Colonel Burke's order.

"Now, Carr," said Colonel Burke again, this time more forcefully.

Mohammed reacted. He broke the glass with his right shoe and as if he had eyes in the back of his head, reached for, got hold of and threw the axe that was there, seemingly all in one motion.

The thrown axe hit Mohammed's chosen target.

Rhohan Castille.

Still puzzled by Colonel Burke's two comments, he was turning towards the open door to make good his escape. He had a nanosecond to think *this man is all talk,* just as he felt something strike him deep into his back which sent him sprawling to the floor.

The gun was no longer in Castille's hand and he was experiencing a sharp pain in his back that was quickly radiating throughout his now almost prone body. Reaching back, he tried to feel what it was.

Where had it come from? He'd been shot before, admittedly not in his back but he'd never felt pain like this. A sweet yet horrible and distressing pain. *What's happening to me?* he was wondering. His mind re-confirmed that this was not a normal gunshot – anyway he hadn't heard an explosion. His left hand found the place where the pain was emanating from in his back.

What he felt surprised him. *Is that metal or wood?* he wondered. Then it dawned on Castille what had mortally wounded him as he started to lose consciousness. Blood was now pouring from the gaping wound in Castille's back. From his mouth too…and his nose, slowly at first then more steadily, forming a pool of red liquid which now spread beneath his body.

Mohammed had thrown the axe perfectly, catching Castille in the middle of his back. He hadn't lost any of his fireman's skills! One of these was making use of his training in the use of an axe in appropriate circumstances, usually to rescue people. Tonight, unfortunately or luckily, depending on which side of the fence you sat on, he had rescued not a person, but a situation.

"Oh my God!" screamed Pilessar, bringing up one of her hands to cover her mouth.

The security guard's firearm which Castille had been holding when he fell to the ground had bounced twice across the marble floor. Luckily, with the safety off, it had not self-fired and now lay just outside the bathroom door.

JJ, followed by a uniformed RBPF officer, had rushed out of the bathroom after hearing the gunshot. He was coming to see what was going on and to see if he could help. He saw the gun which was a foot away from him. Reacting quickly, he scooped it up.

"Stop her," ordered Vickers.

JJ pointed the gun at Pilessar, saying, "Stay right there and don't move an inch."

Seemingly transfixed, Pilessar did as she was told, continuing to stare down at the man who, until a minute ago, had been number three in *The Organisation*.

Meanwhile, the others in the immediate area slowly started to re-gather their composure.

***

As it turned out, England played quite well on Day 4. They ended the day at 255 for seven, 218 runs short of the 473-run target. With more rain due tonight and tomorrow, England might still, with luck, get a draw here. But the West Indies remained the firm, if not heavy favourites to win the Test Match.

***

Three hours later, the security guard, having undergone emergency surgery at QEH for the gunshot wound he had received, was resting comfortably. His doctors expected him to make a full recovery.

Castille had died of shock from his back wound. He was no great loss to mankind. Pilessar was about to learn that she should expect to spend several years in HMP Dodds in Barbados once the evidence on her connections to the late Castille and *The Organisation* were revealed. Extradition to the USA was a possibility (in due course) for her. Power was set to spend a lengthy period in HMP Dodds.

***

An hour after that, with the back entrance to BIB HQ now having been cleaned up, the *SNARL Cycle* session for the debrief of *Operation 'Fishhook* re-convened. It lasted another thirty minutes, with the meeting's participants having been fortified by food ordered in by Colonel Burke from Rita's Kitchen. So much had happened during this long day.

Once everyone had left BIB HQ, Colonel Burke verbally briefed Prime Minister Motby on '*Operation Fishhook*'s outcome. He then worked well into the night to finalise his written report based on the mission's debrief and provided additional comments for Motby's potential use in a Ministerial Statement Motby earlier announced that he would give to Parliament the following morning.

Having submitted both documents to Motby, Colonel Burke left BIB HQ for his home where Diane was waiting for him. It was close to 11:00 p.m. when he arrived. He was as pleased to see her as she was to see him. He used the cup of tea she had made for him but declined the meal, as the only thing he now wanted to do was to take a long shower and fall into his bed for a long sleep.

After all, he had scarcely slept since Friday night.

***

Chapter Twenty-Eight

Game Over

TUESDAY, 24 APRIL

JJ had also been glad to be able to get a full night's sleep in his own bed on Monday night. He'd slept so soundly that he'd missed the children's departure for school. When he finally woke up, he found a note from Vanessa on his nightstand and a fully-cooked breakfast downstairs.

Having taken Angela and Andrew to school, Vanessa returned home around 9:30 a.m. She and JJ decided to go for a sea bath at Enterprise Beach. Vanessa walked up and down a few times on the beautiful beach while JJ ran his usual twelve times up and down the beach before they spent twenty minutes in the clear, almost wave-less water.

***

As usual, Parliament's session commenced at 10:00 a.m. Following prayers and the suspension of a few Standing Orders, the Speaker recognised the Prime Minister. Motby had indicated to him late on the previous afternoon that he would be making a Ministerial Statement to Parliament at the start of the day's sitting regarding the recent security challenges the country had faced and overcame.

Motby's thirty-minute Ministerial Statement was quietly received by Parliamentarians and those sitting in the public gallery, media included. It was carried live on all local radio and television stations. Motby gave away no sources and or methods during his presentation which Colonel Burke and his fellow *P.A.A.N.I.* Heads were grateful for.

In short, the security challenges experienced in Barbados had all been resolved. Motby thanked the law enforcement and security services for their diligent efforts. He also thanked the neighbouring countries who had cooperated in the overall exercise. Following the security situations that had arisen would come an overall assessment of existing procedures. New funding streams would be established. Existing protocols would be examined and out of this review would come recommendations in a matter of weeks regarding changes, greater situation awareness and new procedures that would correct past errors and system deficiencies to benefit all Barbadians and visitors alike.

Motby concluded by saying, "We must never let a critical situation, some might even say a crisis, go to waste! Believe you me, crises prompt our creative juices to flow and result in new opportunities for improvements in the way we do things. As Barbadians, let us grow closer together, get better and be more agile at handling all kinds of situations that we may encounter, whatever their way, shape or form."

***

JJ and Vanessa arrived back home around 11:15 a.m., just in time to meet the postman. He handed over their mail. Among the collection of envelopes was a bank statement, a couple of utility bills, the same old stuff one gets from their postman all over the world.

Shortly after that, a car from the Cabinet Office drew up in their driveway. The messenger handed JJ an envelope which he quickly opened once the messenger had driven away.

To his surprise, it was a letter confirming his full reinstatement at BIB. The letter was signed by HOPS and had also been cc'd to Colonel Burke. Passing it to Vanessa, he punched the air and let out a scream of satisfaction in relief. She started to cry softly after reading what was a short, half-page document. He pulled her close and they embraced for a full minute. Vanessa knew how much his BIB work meant to him, especially as he was BIB's most senior operative after Colonel Burke.

JJ recognised that Colonel Burke, who yesterday had encouraged him to 'take a week off' to recover from his recent ordeal, had come through on his promise that all would soon be well again between JJ and BIB. Colonel Burke had also indicated that it might take a week or so for 'the powers that be' to correct their error and issue fresh correspondence to him that would replace the earlier inappropriate letter he had received.

Having accepted the week off that had been offered to him, JJ had decided how he would make use of this unexpected break. After his return from St Vincent yesterday morning, he'd thought again about his family. He was torn over whether he should to continue working for BIB, whatever subsequently transpired officially with his suspension case. He'd try to relax, get in some exercise, do some more reading particularly of **The Art of War** book, and of course, play some music that he had not for a while.

Now, with his reinstatement letter in hand, JJ was eminently relieved. Everything had come through much sooner than he could ever have expected. He felt in celebratory mood. What better a place to do so than at P's Disco tonight?

While Vanessa went off to start preparing some lunch for them, JJ allowed himself to focus on the material he would play later that evening. He decided that he would extend his usual hour-long *'Strut Ya Stuff'* segment at 9:45 p.m. by starting it fifteen minutes earlier. He'd make that segment a very special one, as it had already quickly become the favourite part of his show for P's Disco patrons. It was a period where JJ sought to encourage patrons, whoever they were, young or old, single or partnered, happy or sad, rich or poor, to 'let their hair down' on P's Disco's large dancefloor. JJ always tried to select exceptional tunes to ensure there was no excuse for patrons not to dance.

It was only when Vanessa called him, shouting "Lunch is ready. I was thinking we might watch a DVD together tonight once the kids have gone to bed…" that he caught himself.

JJ had forgotten that he hadn't played at P's Disco last night and had in fact advised Pilgrim that he would not be there tonight either for his ETT show because of work commitments. Pilgrim had understood. Though disappointed, he hoped JJ would be 'back in the saddle' at P's Disco for the following week. JJ made no further commitment to Pilgrim.

"I'm coming," JJ answered to Vanessa's summons. He would have to 'cool his heels' for another few days before he could return to P's Disco.

Once he reached Vanessa, he added, "Yes to the DVD tonight. Any particular one you have in mind to watch?"

"That book Colonel Burke gave you for Christmas. I stumbled across a film by that name on the internet that was made a few years ago. Why not watch it? The clips I saw looked good."

"Okay, once the kids have turned in," said a satisfied JJ. *I might learn something from it*, he thought.

***

Day 5 of the second Test Match between The West Indies and England started late. The morning's two-hour pre-lunch session had been washed out following heavy overnight and early morning rain around the Fontabelle, St Michael area but funnily enough, not in many other parts of Barbados. New Kensington Oval's excellent drainage system again worked perfectly to enable the heavy waters to drain away. Bright sunshine from late-morning and a brisk wind helped the drying-out process. Added to that was the tireless work by the Oval's efficient ground staff, the game was re-started at 1:40 p.m.

***

The weekly *P.A.A.N.I.* meeting at BIB HQ that afternoon commenced at the scheduled 2:00 p.m., although the Heads would have much preferred to watch the last part of the Test Match on television.

It did not last that long either. *P.A.A.N.I.* Heads agreed that the Prime Minister's Ministerial Statement to Parliament that morning had gone well. It had certainly been well-received. Their task now would be to develop new streams of work that would see their organisations more readily be-able to combat situations, particularly those where multiple scenarios cropped up in the future like those they had just experienced and overcome successfully.

P.A.A.N.I. Heads knew for sure, especially following their meeting with the Head of MI6 on the previous Thursday, that more international threats were out there and possibly on their way to the Caribbean region. They would not stop coming to small countries like Barbados or other small states around the world.

***

Surprise, surprise!

The Test Match was all over by 2:35 p.m. It took just seven overs of pace and three of spin for The West Indies cricket team to secure England's last three wickets for an additional sixty-eight runs and win the game. England all out then for 323, an improvement on their first innings score of 270. The margin of victory for the West Indies was 150 runs which was quite satisfying. Having won the much closer first Test Match in Jamaica one week earlier by just two wickets, this win at New Kensington Oval gave West Indies a winning and unassailable two-nil lead in the three-match series. It also meant that the West Indies would retain the Wisden Trophy, played for by the two Test teams since 1963, with a Test Match to spare.

"Just like old times," one noted West Indian commentator stated in his usual colourful way during the match summary. Magnus Hunter and Corey Miller were not opposed to this view, which was now being shared by West Indians living in the West Indies, by those who were part of the overseas diaspora and, ironically, by vanquished English supporters back home as well.

As for the visiting supporters who had come to see their England team, though disappointed with the result, they appeared pleased to have been in Barbados for the Test Match. Most of them still had three days of their ten-day cricketing holiday left, so all that was left for them to do was to enjoy Barbados' sun, sand, sea, sights, excellent rum, beer and the restaurants that were available to them. For most, these memories would last a lifetime.

The third Test Match was set to be played at the Queen's Park Oval in Port-of-Spain, Trinidad and Tobago from the coming Saturday.

***

The original plan had been to raid *The Organisation*'s Miami headquarters complex at 8:00 a.m. the following morning. However, once Prime Minister Motby's Ministerial Statement had been delivered to Parliament that morning, things changed. Though Motby had not mentioned *The Organisation* (or its full and correct name), those connected with or to it knew that it had been implicated and therefore exposed.

That prompted USA Embassy personnel in Barbados to encourage that urgent action be taken to finalise investigations pertaining to *The Organisation*. Raids of Pilessar, Castille and Thomas's apartments and on *The Organisation*'s Miami headquarters were to be brought forward to that night and end by dawn.

Ambassador Rowley was instrumental in this regard, working through Busbee and her 'people' back home. Once notified, Tom Huney in the FBI's Miami field office agreed to take action and the raids were organised for execution between 10:15 p.m. and 2:00 a.m. the following morning. The required search warrants had been secured from a District Judge to cover US Law enforcement's actions around 6:00 p.m. that afternoon.

**

Later that night in Miami, the repeated ringing of Royce Thomas' apartment doorbell was unexpected. It was late, close to 10:20 p.m.

People seldom came to his second-floor apartment after 10:00. p.m. Thomas looked out the large window to see if there was any unusual activity outside on the street below. It was quiet. There were no unusual vehicles parked or traffic movements. He assumed that the person ringing his doorbell must be a friend and not a foe. Given his kind of work, one could never be sure but this was his well-protected apartment, not *The Organisation*'s respectable office complex in down-town Miami.

Thomas therefore felt safe as he went towards his apartment's front door. Looking through the door's peephole, he saw what appeared to be a uniformed Miami police department (MPD) officer. He did not open the door but spoke through it.

"May I help you, officer?"

"Good evening, sir. There's been a recent break-in in a neighbouring apartment in this building."

"Really? Well, I'm fine, but if your officers are looking for a criminal, why don't I see any police vehicles outside…"

"We're doing this quietly, sir. The perpetrators may still be around."

"Very well. Thanks for stopping –"

Thomas did not finish the sentence. The window he had earlier looked out of had been opened. Thomas turned to see one, then a second masked person entering his apartment through his now opened apartment window.

"Miami PD. Hands up!" Thomas did as he was told. The gun-toting MPD officers looked serious. It quickly dawned on him what might be happening. He thought quickly. *Was there was no robbery in the building block after all? Was someone out to get him, or The Organisation he worked for. Who might they be? Local law enforcement?*

Thomas turned away from the two gun-toting MPD officers when he heard his apartment door being bashed in. It splintered before being broken down completely. Three more armed MPD officers flooded into his apartment. They approached him. He meekly put his hands further up in the air.

These people clearly knew who I am, probably everything about me, The Organisation, Emma and Rhohan too, he was thinking.

"Shit, who are you guys? What have I done? Miami PD don't break into people's apartments without warning or warrants. You guys have a search warrant?" Thomas asked as he was being handcuffed.

In walked a couple of men in dark suits. They flashed identity badges and what was a warrant of some kind was also shown to him. Having never seen a warrant up close before, Thomas didn't know what a warrant looked like and so if it was genuine.

"I'm Tom Huney, FBI Special Agent-in-Charge of Miami and Surrounding Districts. This is a warrant to search these premises. We're also taking you downtown to read you your rights and to ask you some questions about the business you're involved in, the people you work with. Do you understand me, Mr Thomas?"

"Be my guest."

"Right then team. Search every nook and crevice of this place. Be careful not to break anything. Log each and every piece of evidence you collect and be careful when removing it from Mr Thomas' apartment please," said Huney.

With that, Thomas knew that his day was done, so to speak. Given what he knew about *The Organisation*'s activities over the past seven years since he had joined it before quickly risen up its ranks, he started to anticipate having to spend a long time in a penitentiary somewhere in the USA. Facing that would be a real challenge for him, given what he'd heard often happened in such places.

As he was being taken out of the space where once his apartment door stood, he decided that no, he could not do any time. Dying might be better. This way he could not give away any of what he knew about *The Organisation's* activities and commitments.

And so, having made his choice, Thomas who not been handcuffed behind his back but in front of himself, swung and elbowed the MPD officer on his right sharply in the stomach before kicking out at the officer on his left. Thomas was able to get away from both officers and make a bound through the doorway in an effort to escape down the corridor outside of his apartment. Two more men in suites and several MPD officers were standing around, looking the opposite way.

Hearing shouts from inside of Thomas' apartment of "Stop him, STOP HIM," they turned around to see Thomas coming at them. Without hesitation one of the suited men un-holstered his weapon, shouting "Stop" to Thomas as he closed in on them. Thomas ignored the command and continued towards the standing MPD officers who had all now turned in Thomas' direction. One of the masked officers who had entered the apartment through the window had followed Thomas out of his apartment doorway and had fired his weapon at Thomas without hesitation, hitting him in his left leg and causing him to fall in great pain in a heap on the floor. Thomas, now crying out in pain from his gunshot wound, knew there was no getting away from US law enforcement personnel tonight, or any time soon for that matter.

Just before midnight, having received medical attention for his leg wound, Thomas was asked in the ambulance outside of his apartment about *The Organisation*'s activities. This took place while the search of his apartment was ongoing in earnest to see what documents or electronic files Thomas kept at home on his computer that was the property of *The Organisation*.

Thomas started to co-operate...

***

Chapter Twenty-Nine
Laying the Trap

TUESDAY, 1 MAY (ONE WEEK LATER)

On the previous Wednesday afternoon, JJ had called Pierre Pilgrim to confirm that he would return to P's Disco to play his twice weekly ETT set for the club's more mature patrons. Pilgrim was happy. JJ too, for he had missed doing his shows and felt guilty having let down those patrons who had regularly came to hear him play. Like the song by Chaka Khan *You Never Miss the Water (Till the Well Runs Dry,* JJ's need for P's Disco was back. Playing there twice a week was the water in his well.

JJ prepared hard and enthusiastically for his return to DJing duties on Monday, 30 April. Vanessa surprised him by accompanying him to P's Disco where she remained for all of his four-hour show, having arranged for her mum and dad to visit for the night to look after Angela and Andrew. They loved it all because they got a night with Granma and Granddad. They knew they would be 'spoiled rotten'.

This was Vanessa's way of visibly supporting JJ's return to doing something she knew he loved doing after the upheaval that had taken place in his life over the past couple of weeks. She made a few new friends that night, mainly patrons who loved what JJ played.

***

In Barbados, May 1 is annually celebrated as Labour Day, a public holiday. Prime Minister Motby was scheduled to attend and speak at the Barbados

Workers Union-organised and sponsored 'Labour Day Rally' at noon, so he had a few spare hours in the morning to relax while trying to further polish the remarks he planned to make.

The 8:00 a.m. telephone call he received from Colonel Burke requesting an urgent meeting with him at Ilaro Court was unexpected but was granted.

They agreed to meet at 9:00 a.m. Colonel Burke arrived ten minutes early and so was seated in the family room to wait for Motby. He was offered a hot beverage, cold drink or water by a butler. He chose water which was quickly brought to him.

"Good morning, Trevor. I'm intrigued…what makes you want to spend part of your public holiday with me, and so early in the morning? I'm hoping that what you have to share will not be another evolving national security situation but is something to make me laugh. I'm looking for a good joke to include in my speech today, ideally at the start. I'm struggling for the right opening line!"

"Good morning, Prime Minister. I'm not good at telling jokes, sir. I can seldom remember the punchline. Nor do I have any dire warning of an imminent national security situation. I do need to speak with you about someone you know well, have hitherto trusted and relied greatly upon."

"What are you talking about, Trevor?"

Colonel Burke removed the file that he had brought with him from his briefcase and presented it to Motby.

"Let's go into my study." Motby knew from Colonel Burke's demeanour that this had to be something serious as Colonel Burke was not one for jokes.

Colonel Burke followed Motby out of the family room down a corridor before they reached the Prime Minister's study. He closed the door behind them.

After reviewing the contents of the file, Motby looked up at Colonel Burke. The latter's quietly undertaken week-long investigation had been shared.

"My God Trevor! We've been, are being played! Clever bastard. You sure all of what's presented here is gospel?"

"*John 3:16*, sir. If it wasn't, it wouldn't be in my report, nor would I be here."

Motby nodded gravely before making his decision.

"Okay, I buy it. You must finish this, but in the correct and proper way. While my paws must *not* be all over this, I don't mind making it known that I'm happy with the action that you've suggested be taken. You've done fine work here. Let's bring this unfortunate situation to a quick and quiet end. As you know,

Parliament breaks up after tomorrow's sitting for a fortnight. Try to complete what needs to be done by then and I mean tomorrow, Trevor."

"Yes, Prime Minister."

"Tell me, would it help if I were to prepare an appropriate document for your use?"

A smile appeared on Colonel Burke's face. "That would be helpful, sir."

"Very well. How will you execute your task?"

"I have a plan, Prime Minister…"

"I'm not surprised, Trevor. Please advise me what it involves," said Motby invitingly.

Colonel Burke explained what he intended to do.

Motby listened carefully. Seeing no big holes in Colonel Burke's plan, he agreed to its implementation, timings and all. They anticipated little or no 'fallout' from the plan. The trap was laid for their prey. They hoped it would work. They had faith that it would.

Similar to a previous occasion, Motby turned on his computer. A few minutes later, he handed Colonel Burke a piece of paper and a plain white envelope. Colonel Burke read what was on the piece of paper.

"Thank you, Prime Minister."

"No problem. I must say that it is *not* a pleasure, Trevor. Now, don't forget. If you come up with any kind of joke between now and 11:30 a.m. that I might use, let me have it," said Motby with a half-smile.

"Don't bank on it, sir," said Colonel Burke.

"Then allow me to show you out and thank you again for coming over. Do try to enjoy what's left of your public holiday, and my regards to Diane."

"I'll try and will pass on your regards to her, Prime Minister."

As Colonel Burke drove away from Ilaro Court's gates, the vehicle's dashboard clock showed 9:45 a.m.

***

JJ's family had a lazy morning. After playing some family games, including Jenga at which both children excelled and had managed to beat JJ and Vanessa, they ate lunch. As Angela and Andrew were getting a little restless, so Vanessa offered to take them out for a drive and some ice cream at their favourite shop in Oistins.

Vanessa knew JJ would not be accompanying them because he'd earlier stated that he would use the afternoon to prepare his final playlist for the various segments of his show later that night at P's Disco. Last night had gone well, but JJ wanted to make tonight, his second night back at P's Disco, even more exciting and an extraordinarily good one.

Vanessa wished JJ good luck and warned that she would not rush back to give him all the time he needed to complete his task. She would stop by Carmen, one of her girlfriends she had not seen for a couple of weeks. JJ was happy for her to do that. This suited Vanessa perfectly. Being away from JJ for the next two or three hours would give her the time she needed to execute her plan for that evening. She believed she had most, if not all of JJ's friends' phone numbers. Those she did not have she knew Fred and Joe would provide to her.

After the drive and ice-cream stop, Vanessa headed for Carmen's house in Atlantic Shores, Christ Church. There, because she knew that Angela and Andrew got on 'like a house on fire' with Carmen's kids of a similar age, Vanessa could spend up to an hour making telephone calls.

The last person Vanessa called was Mindy Dane, the Johnson's older and reliable neighbours. Could she bring Angela and Andrew over to them around 8:30 p.m. that evening and could they spend the night with her? JJ would be working at P's Disco until midnight and she knew JJ's work friends were planning to surprise him with an award. She of course, had to be there to see JJ receive it, so by the time they returned home, it would be well after midnight, too late to wake and take home their kids. She and JJ would come for them early in the morning, clean them up, and provide breakfast before getting them ready for school.

Mindy spoke with her husband Roger. They said yes to a night of baby-sitting. Auntie Mindy and Uncle Roger loved the Johnson kids a lot, especially as they got on well with their own grand-children whenever they visited. Vanessa had one further request of Auntie Mindy and Uncle Roger. Should they see JJ during the afternoon, they shouldn't mention that Angela and Andrew would be sleeping over at them tonight. Again, Vanessa secured the Danes agreement. The Johnson children had overnighted with the Danes grandkids a couple of times before, so would be comfortable.

***

JJ focussed in earnest on his task. His theme for tonight's four-hour set was celebration, particularly after his reinstatement at BIB a week earlier. As usual, he would break his set up into his four hourly segments, namely H1C (the 'chillin' hour), H2G (the 'groovin' hour), H3F3 (the 'floor fillin' funk you good' hour) and H4FGD (the 'final get down' hour). He would play happy songs he genuinely loved and had a strong bond with. His selections would reflect his beliefs and love of his patrons.

After an hour's research and reflection on what his potential selections across these segments might be, JJ chose: Cloud One *Atmosphere Strutt*, Brass Construction *Changin'*, Archie Bell & The Drells *Strategy*, George Benson *Shiver*, Yvonne Gage *Lover Of My Dreams*, Raw Silk *Do It To The Music*, Temptations *Treat Her Like A Lady*, Brothers Johnson *Stomp*, Sylvia Striplin *Give Me Your Love*, S.O.S. Band *Take Your Time (Do It Right)*, The Whispers *And The Beat Goes On*, Yvonne Gage *Garden of Eve*, Bobby Thurston *You've Got What It Takes*, Gap Band *Burn Rubber On Me*, Nathan East *Daft Funk*, Quincy Jones *Razzamatazz*, KC & The Sunshine Band *Get Down Tonight*, Herbie Hancock *You Bet Your Love*. Excited by the selections he had made so far, JJ turned his mind to choosing a mini-mellow-mood segment that should cool the place down. He decided to set use a triple offering of Maxwell *Welcome/Something, Something/Ascension*. As usual, he would encourage patrons already on the dancefloor to stay there and cling to their partners. To those sitting down, he'd urge them to grab a friendly soul and cling to them on the dance floor. Other mellow tunes he identified to use, perhaps at the start of his H4FGD segment: The Whispers *No Pain, No Gain*, Johnny Gill *My, My, My* and Melba Moore *Falling*. Back up cuts were Bobby Brown *Rock Wit Cha*, Everette Harp *If I Had to Live My Life Without You*, and S.O.S. Band *The Finest*.

During his 11:00 p.m. ten-minute break, his mix of primarily instrumental and jazz/funk tunes would come down. He had prepared an hour-long CD the previous Sunday afternoon or himself, featuring Paul Hardcastle *Rain Forest*, Total Contrast *Sunshine*, S.O.S. Band *Groovin' (That's What We're Doin')*, The Temptations *Stay* and more During this break, he share the first four tracks from his CD while everyone in P's Disco, himself included, would have the chance to catch their breath, purchase a drink, make a bathroom stop, clear tables, order some food, chat up a fellow patron or pursue a mixture of the above before JJ would get the final segment of his set going around 11:10 p.m.

An experienced JJ loved to make the last hour of his ETT set special for patrons. Tonight, he wanted to make it *extra-special*, so he decided to spend another hour pulling together a great close out musical package for the night. Immediately, JJ was decided to get his final hour underway with Temptations *Stay* followed by BT Express *Give Up the Funk (Let's Dance)*. *Should be great fun*, JJ was thinking.

He also made up his mind to do something he had not done before after his set was finished. He would hang around the club for a while, perhaps for an hour or so. He'd not heard DJ Price play for a while, so would tell Vanessa of his plan to stay on at the club for an hour on her return home.

***

It was just after 4:00 p.m. when Colonel Burke, who had popped into BIB HQ for a few minutes, received a call from Sharon Evans, Motby's Executive Assistant. She was at Ilaro Court and had just been given an envelope marked 'Private and Confidential' addressed to Mr James Johnson at BIB from the Prime Minister. It was being sent to Colonel Burke via a Government courier and he was being asked by Motby to personally hand-deliver the envelope to Mr Johnson on his first day back at work, or earlier if Colonel Burke intended to see him before that time.

Excellent timing! Vanessa had just called him a few minutes earlier to invite Diane and himself to her surprise gathering for JJ at P's Disco that evening. Of course, Colonel Burke had agreed to attend, although he did think to himself… *Me, in a night club? Diane and I dancing the night away?*

Colonel Burke decided that, since he would not be going home for another hour or so, he would call Diane to alert her of their evening engagement. He knew she had nothing planned for that evening except dinner at home with him around 7:30 p.m. He was determined to complete the final draft of his latest *P.A.A.N.I.* SSB following what had been a longer than usual three-hour session the previous afternoon. It had reviewed all that had taken place over the past three weeks and would contain recommendations for implementation from *P.A.A.N.I.* Heads.

There was therefore a lot to report following that session. Some of what he was putting forward was not new, but most of it would be. It would be very important to get the recommendations that had been made by *P.A.A.N.I.* Heads down accurately because they had implications for the country's law enforcement and security agencies' operational rules and regulations. Motby and his Ministerial colleagues would have a lot to chew over at a forthcoming Cabinet meeting. Some of what was being recommended would, if approved by Cabinet, result in amendments to various pieces of legislation, all as a result of the recent security situations that had been experienced.

Much later than he had planned, Colonel Burke left BIB HQ around 5:40 p.m., having received the envelope for JJ. Not many operatives had been in office although for a public holiday, several BIB operatives were out in the field supporting various RBPF programmes. Colonel Burke placed JJ's envelope in his briefcase. In the morning, he would finalise the SSB before forwarding it to Motby. In view of the nature of what was being submitted, he had already been invited to attend a special 8:00 a.m. meeting at Government Headquarters on Thursday of that week with Motby and other *P.A.A.N.I.* Heads. This was to discuss their recommendations ahead of the day's 10:00 a.m. meeting when members of the Cabinet would receive their copy of the recommendations which would be discussed, one by one.

Once at home, Colonel Burke reminded Diane of their late-night engagement. Once upstairs, he noticed that she had laid out a couple of outfits she might wear on the bed in their bedroom. He removed JJ's envelope from his briefcase and placed it on the side-table at his side of the bed, with his wallet and vehicle keys. This way, he would not forget the envelope when he ventured out to P's Disco for JJ's event in another three hours. He took a shower before dinner and reflected on the BIB organisation he led that was trained, enlightened, and transformational (TET). He liked that.

***

Chapter Thirty

Surprise

At P's Disco, it was coming up to 10:00 p.m. and JJ had already decided that tonight, he would not take his customary ten-minute break at 11:00 p.m. JJ's set that night had gone down pretty much according to plan. Patrons were having a great time. He wanted that to continue and so was fully intent on 'rocking the house' with the tracks he'd chosen to play earlier that afternoon.

Having decided not to take his ten-minute break, he also discarded playing the instrumental and jazz/funk tunes usually heard at that time, launching straight into popular, long-loved 'floor-fillers. His playlist was to be: Luther Vandross *The Rush*; Atlantis *Keep On Movin' and Groovin'*, Eddie Grant *My Turn To Love You*, Oliver Cheatham *Get Down Saturday Night*, War *You Got The Power*, Shalamar *Take That To The Bank/Right In The Socket*, a mix of Patrice Rushen *Forget Me Nots*, Will Smith *Men In Black* and George Michael *Fast Love*, Cerrone featuring Adjana *Good Times I'm In Love,* Melba Moore *Love's Comin' At Ya*, Michael Jackson/Justin Timberlake *Love Never Felt So Good*, Thelma Houston – *You Used To Hold Me So Tight,* Fatback Band *Bus Stop (Are You Ready)*, Tata Vega *Get It Up for Love* and Positive Force *We've Got The Funk* before he would also slip in a few of Trinidad & Tobago's up-tempo 2018 Carnival hits from a couple of months earlier.

JJ usually finished the last segment of his four-hour set with what had become his signature close-out song, The Three Degrees *When Will I See You Again*. Near its end, he would as usual wish his patrons, "Peace and God's speed for a safe journey home." He'd encourage them to "visit P's Disco on Monday and Tuesday nights for more BIT music, eight thru twelve (ETT) with yours truly

JJ, De Ole Time General. Yes, the tunes we share on these nights are real. They'll keep you beautiful, alive and sane."

Tonight though, after his recent trials and tribulations JJ intended to provide P's Disco patrons with something different, more uplifting to show them everlasting love. There was no better track to end his set with tonight than Love Unlimited Orchestra *Loves' Theme*. His usual admonition would follow along with the usual ETT stuff just as DJ Price took over the DJ's booth for the next three hours.

Unknown to JJ, this Tuesday night would be different, a very special night for *him*. An appropriate track to mark what happened next could have been Shalamar *A Night to Remember*.

***

No way would JJ have expected Vanessa to return to P's Disco for a second successive night. In fact, she had already indicated to him before he left home that she might be in her bed early after being out late the previous night, but would listen out for his return home after his second night back at the club.

So, totally unaware of Vanessa's secret scheme, JJ was a very relaxed man. Vanessa had invited, more like strong-armed, many of JJ's friends including his BIB colleagues and their partners who were available. They totalled around forty persons. Those invited had readily agreed to participate in what Vanessa had termed as a 'Welcome Back JJ' event.

It was 10:59 a.m. by the clock in the DJ's booth at P's Disco when JJ thought he caught a brief sighting of Fred standing at the bar. But as the man's back was to JJ, he decided that it could not be Fred, for they'd spoken that afternoon and Fred had not mentioned that he might pop into the club later that night.

Focus on the task at hand, boy, JJ thought as the Luther Vandross floor filler faded into the Atlantis track. He was again raising the tempo on the dancefloor which had started to fill back up for the final hour of his four-hour set. For the next ten minutes, JJ continued to make clean mixes, frequently glancing up and around to see how his patrons were working themselves out on his dancefloor.

On one of those occasions, JJ also thought he caught a glimpse of someone, no, a *couple* of BIB colleagues and his best friend away from BIB, Mark Egwell. This time he was certain of whom he saw, Joe and Colonel Burke along with their better halves who were all standing by the bar.

"Hell…something's up if Colonel Burke's in here," he said softly to himself. He'd never known BIB's Director to visit any night spot, P's Disco included. The closest he might have gotten to such a place in recent years might have been while he was out to dinner at a restaurant and someone had turned the background music up.

Then JJ noticed Vanessa. She was standing beside Diane Burke and appeared to be in conversation with her and Egwell. Although the light in P's Disco was not bright, he knew his wife. The light reflection from the bar half-shone on her face. He thought she looked as beautiful as he could ever remember seeing her. She was also wearing what appeared to be a new outfit – he had not seen that dress before.

JJ felt a tap on his shoulder. He turned around to see DJ Price, P's Disco Resident disc jockey standing there. He was in the club a full thirty minutes before he usually appeared in P's Disco and almost a full hour before his set was to start tonight. JJ knew DJ Price enjoyed making an entrance at the club, usually around 11:30 p.m., so this was highly unusual.

JJ's operational BIB antennae had by now fully kicked in. Something was up, but he did not know what. Why were his wife, Director, best friend, DJ Price and people he worked with – he was now seeing Samuel, Margaret, Mohammed and his wife, Jayne, Billy Browne, Ted Madley, George Collins, Bruce Alleyne. What were they here and what were they up to? He suspected more colleagues were also in P's Disco, somewhere.

DJ Price spoke in JJ's ear just as he noticed Pierre Pilgrim signalling to him to come over to where he was now standing with Vanessa and Colonel Burke.

This makes no sense…

"Night JJ! I got you covered man, it's time for you to take a break – for the rest of the night. Some special people are here tonight to see you so relax, go and see Double P. Leave the booth to me and start enjoying the rest of your evening. I'm taking over from here."

"Look GP, I'm in the middle of the last hour of my set. It's stuff I badly want to play and –" JJ protested.

"Look, I know. I have your playlist in the computer. I'll do my best to honour *most* of it. They'll be one or two surprises along the way, but I'll not take over your segment completely. Vanessa also shared your set with me earlier this evening, so everything's cool. Go and enjoy yourself with your friends. Leave the night's work to me. Tonight's your night man, so go have some fun."

With that, DJ Price took control of the DJ station.

JJ removed his headphones and moved somewhat uncertainly towards Vanessa who had by this time started to cover the short distance between them. She took his hand and led him over to where his friends and colleagues were standing. There was applause and cheering from them that was heard over the music.

Pilgrim pointed to the assembled group standing with drinks in their hands. He understood their appreciation of JJ who was now back within the fabric of the BIB family. Though only his friends knew why JJ had been *out* of things for a few days, the obvious warmth of feeling being expressed towards him was refreshingly uniform. Many thought it was JJ's birthday and that this might have been a surprise party – sort of. But there was no cake or candles to be blown out.

JJ had been unfairly hung out to dry and badly treated by someone who should have known better. Colonel Burke was happy to be a part of tonight's activity which would help to facilitate JJ's full return to the BIB fold. This had all been Vanessa's doing. DJ Price's announcement prompted JJ to look around to see a banner that had now been unveiled over the bar. It read: *JJ, job well done and welcome back, though you've never been away from us, or us you.*

***

Colonel Burke had two tasks to complete in the next twelve hours. The first would be done tonight.

The second would be undertaken tomorrow, sometime before mid-day.

***

Colonel Burke moved towards JJ from the midst of the group perceived to be 'JJ's supporters' and presented him with a hand-written addressed envelope before leaning over to speak softly into his ear.

"Open this when you get home… I'm sure you've recognised the handwriting. Everything that needs to be said to you on behalf of our country has I suspect, been stated therein. I don't have a copy, but I've been asked to offer you lunch with the writer sometime next week. I recommend you accept the invitation."

Task number one was complete.

JJ nodded, unsure how to react. He knew who the hand-writing on the outside of the un-opened envelope belonged to, having received a similarly hand-written envelope after the attempted assassination of Prime Minister Motby. Receipt of a second hand-written note from Motby was flattering…exciting. But it wasn't necessary for after all, he'd only been doing his job.

DJ Price had obviously been briefed on what was to happen after 11:00 p.m. He invited JJ and Vanessa to take to the dancefloor as he played two special songs for them, Atlantic Star *Always* and The Deele *Two Occasions*. Near the end of the second song, DJ Price asked JJ's supporters to join the love-fest, playing that classic track by Dionne Warwick *That's What Friends Are For*. The response was incredible, with most patrons also wanting to get in on the act. This led DJ Price to push a twenty-minute, ten-cut 'love, family and friends' mix featuring Isley Brothers *One of a Kind*, Sade *Nothing Can Come Between Us (Remix)*, Phyllis Hyman *Under Your Spell*, Tina Moore *Never Gonna Let You Go*, Incognito *Every Day*, Pauline Henry *Happy*, Sister Sledge *We Are Family*, Shalamar *Friends*, Arrow *Long Time (We Ain't Fete Like This)* Cameo *Candy*.

DJ Price spoke intermittently to the patrons: "We all need good, kind and reliable friends, like those here for JJ tonight. JJ you're the man, with not only kind, but good, no *great* and reliable friends. We all appreciate and love you man. I suspect P's Disco would now not be the same without your Monday and Tuesday night sets."

JJ kissed Vanessa to thank her for arranging this night for him at the club. It had been very creative of her. He had never doubted that she, his friends and BIB colleagues were wonderful and reliable to boot. He knew they would be there for him in times of personal or professional difficulty. JJ did not need proof of this, but their support and actions over the past few days and especially tonight had re-affirmed his belief. JJ would be sure to be there should Vanessa or any of them ever require him to return the favour.

He would treasure and never forget this night. JJ also made a mental note to congratulate DJ Price on his musical selections since he had kicked JJ out of the DJ area. JJ did not know of DJ Price's deep knowledge of BIT tracks and so greatly appreciated the way he had mixed things up.

***

435

Just after midnight, JJ felt a gentle but firm hand on his shoulder. He looked around to see Colonel Burke facing him.

"Time for Diane and me to take our leave of you, Vanessa and your friends. Tonight's been great, but it's way past my usual bed time even if I didn't have work tomorrow, which I do! Remember, no need to come in tomorrow. I mean it."

"But…" JJ started.

Shaking his hand, Colonel Burke insisted.

"No JJ, Wednesday morning and not an hour sooner. Enjoy the rest of your, ah morning. I'll cut everyone some slack if they come in one or two hours later tomorrow morning. JJ, it will be good to have you around the place again as I've missed your dulcet tones inside BIB. Goodnight."

Colonel Burke slapped JJ on his back and waved farewell to Vanessa before heading for the exit where Diane stood waiting for him. She returned Vanessa's wave as they left the BIB crowd and growing group of younger P's Disco patrons.

It was only then that JJ became conscious that Colonel Burke had also slipped something into his shirt pocket during their farewell exchange. JJ retrieved the item. It was a small, flat and light ceramic object. Examining it, JJ saw that there were a few words written on it. He moved closer to the bar where the light in P's Disco was better in order to read them. *"Some people make the world more special, just by being in it!"* JJ passed the ceramic object to Vanessa, who had joined him. She smiled broadly before saying, "You're appreciated by your leader, my love."

DJ Price was making another announcement over his microphone which caused everyone to turn towards his area.

"Hey, people, listen up! I've got another song for our star boy tonight and his lovely lady. JJ and Vanessa, this one's from me to you, Patrice Rushen *Remind Me*. It's a song for the ages, a proper song, for a proper couple. Enjoy!"

DJ Price insisted that JJ and Vanessa re-take the dance floor. What with his introduction, how could they not do so? Other patrons allowed them the floor before joining them for DJ Price's follow-up mega-mix of KC and The Sunshine Band *That's The Way (I Like It)*, Kool & The Gang *Get Down on It/Fresh* and Daft Punk *Get Lucky*. He then morphed into 'doing his thing' to start satisfying the younger patrons who had entered P's Disco in the last forty minutes by playing more current tunes that were more to both of their liking and in keeping with his own modern playing style.

***

Chapter Thirty-One

Confession

Of BIB operatives, only Fred and Joe knew of Colonel Burke's intention to meet with Dr Smith sometime that morning. But when and how he would play out that meeting was known only to Colonel Burke.

***

It was 11:25 a.m. when the Very Reverend Dr Boyd Mercer parked his vehicle in the space reserved for 'Dean' just outside of the Cathedral building in central Bridgetown. As usual, Dean Mercer had arrived well before the weekly Wednesday mid-day church service would commence. The service catered to the Cathedral Church's congregation, workers in and around Bridgetown, and visitors alike.

His secretary, Mary Jones was speaking with a young lady as he entered the office's reception area.

"Good morning to you both," he said as he made his way on into his private office.

Jones didn't answer, but excused herself from the young lady and followed him into his office. She closed the door behind her, but was frowning.

Dean Mercer noticed that she was uncomfortable. He tried to relax her.

"Good morning again, Mary. What brings you in here so quickly after my arrival? Are you volunteering to preach in my place today? I'm happy to stand down…" he said with his usual broad smile.

With a serious face, Jones replied, "Good morning, Dean. Sorry, you don't get off that easy! You know that I'd only disappoint the congregation who come primarily to hear your sermon, so I don't think I'd want to do so today or ever to be honest with you. I came in straight away because I'm very worried about the young lady you saw me with as you came in. She was here when I arrived at 10:45 a.m. and I've since spent at least thirty minutes with her," said Jones.

"What's her problem?" asked Dean Mercer.

"Well, she's been crying…in between some cursing, telling me in a rambling sort of way about a bad relationship she's involved in with an older man than herself. It's gotten so bad, she says that she feels at her breaking point, close to doing something to harm herself before her boyfriend does the job for her. She says she's desperate, and as a last resort, came here to see how the Church can help her. She's asking for you."

"Phew! What's her name? Is she from the Cathedral parish?"

"Miss Betsy Hefton. She's from St Andrew. She doesn't go to church regularly anymore, but she was brought up as an Anglican, went to Sunday School until she was thirteen. She's now twenty-two, doesn't work, lives with the older guy who's in his forties. She has no children. Can you spend some time with her please before the service, perhaps counsel her, sort of pep her up? I've given her a box juice from the fridge and my sandwich lunch because she said she hasn't eaten since yesterday morning," said Jones.

"I've barely got time, Mary –"

"Please Dean –"

"Okay. That's a lot to chew on, Mary. Wheel her in, but give me a minute before you do. She'll have fifteen minutes max, before I'll need to go robe for the service. If Miss Hefton wants to wait until after the service to speak further, I'm open to that but will have to leave here by 2:30 p.m. to go to a 3:00 p.m. funeral at St Cyprian's.

"Do me a favour? Call the Chairman of our Home Aware Committee. Fill him in on Miss Hefton. The Welfare Department's Director too. Ask if and how they might best help her with a proper meal, overnight lodging, and other things that from what you've told me, she needs. Involve the resident beat RBPF officer too," said Dean Mercer, fixing his so-called dog collar into place.

"Thanks, Dean. I've already told her that she's come to the right place for help," said Jones.

"That's what we're here for. I'll try my best to help her build up faith and confidence in herself, our Church and the wider society. Putting a support structure around her should, I think be our goal."

"That's great. Take your minute," said Jones, leaving Dean Mercer alone.

As usual, Dean Mercer had prepared his sermon the night before. His practice of looking it over one final time before the service started was not going to happen today. The arrangements for the service had been agreed two nights earlier in a meeting with the second priest on the Cathedral staff who was also designated to attend today's service.

There was a knock on his door, followed by the appearance of Jones, accompanied by Hefton.

***

Colonel Burke's second task for completion from the previous night was about to be implemented. It was a meeting with Dr Winston Peter Smith GCM, Cabinet Secretary and Head of the Barbados Public Service (HOPS). Under normal circumstances, the request from Colonel Burke for a meeting with HOPS would not have been accommodated within twenty-four hours of the request being made. Dr Smith was after all, a very busy and important official who was constantly in high demand. Such meetings would also normally take place at Government Headquarters and in Dr Smith's office. However, at Colonel Burke's specific request, the urgent nature and venue for today's meeting was to be BIB HQ because of what Colonel Burke had indicated to Dr Smith was a 'highly confidential matter'. He'd indicated to him that what he had to share was indeed sensitive and could not be properly facilitated at Government Headquarters. Dr Smith bought the explanation. He expected to see and hear other materials at BIB HQ's secure facility.

Their meeting started at 11:55 a.m., twenty-five minutes later than agreed. Why? Dr Smith had been asked to go and see Motby at 11:00 a.m. ostensibly on a pay-related issue related to the forthcoming Budget. Motby's meeting had not lasted long, but it had delayed Dr Smith's arrival at BIB HQ.

On arrival, he was met in reception by Joe who introduced herself.

"Hello. Yes, I know who you are and this is my second time at BIB HQ," Dr Smith responded as they started the walk towards Colonel Burke's office.

"Do you like working here for BIB? I mean, it's still quite a young agency," Dr Smith said.

"I enjoy my work, sir. It's a fair place to work," Joe opined.

"I hear that regularly from the Prime Minister. He is very proud of the work you all do here, indeed the entire country is grateful to BIB's ongoing efforts," said Dr Smith conversationally.

"Thank you, sir," said a smiling Joe, knocking on Colonel Burke's door. It was, half-open as usual.

"Come on in. Thanks, Joe. Hello, Dr Smith. Welcome to BIB," said Colonel Burke.

"Nice to be here, Trevor. I was just telling your Miss Callendar how much I and the country, appreciate the work that your agency does. My apologies for being late, I got called in by the PM just as I was leaving."

"No problem, Dr Smith. We're tough on the outside, but easy going on the inside here at BIB. Joe, close the door on your way out please."

"Yes, chief." Joe exited Colonel Burke's office, closing the door softly behind her.

"Can I offer you something to drink? I'm having a coffee. You have a choice of soft drinks or something harder if you'd prefer."

"Water please."

A couple of minutes later, pleasantries over, they got down to the reason Dr Smith was at BIB HQ. He expected Colonel Burke to share sensitive information, perhaps some sort of restrictive briefing or a video on some new threat to the country? But that could not be it, because Jeremie, Tenton and Innis, the other security Heads in Barbados (the *P.A.A.N.I.* 'lot' as he privately referred to them) would also be here as would Holloway. What, therefore, was this all about? Perhaps it was to provide details of the proposed new security procedures that were being planned for implementation at the main air and sea ports in Barbados in another couple of months, once Cabinet had approved the procedures and after the existing law had been suitably amended in Parliament.

***

Colonel Burke wasted no time in getting down to business.

"Dr Smith, have you ever heard of Dr Sharon LeKasha Gladwell?"

441

"Who hasn't? But I've never met her, at least not that I can recall," Dr Smith added carefully.

"That's interesting, because the much publicly maligned and un-loved CCTV system suggests that you've met with Dr Gladwell not once or twice, but on three occasions in the past fortnight and at different locations around Barbados."

"What's your point, Trevor?" asked Dr Smith.

"You've just told me that you've never met Dr Gladwell."

"No, I didn't! I said that I could not recall meeting her. In my position, I obviously meet a lot of people in loads of places."

The two men stared at each other. Dr Smith did not believe Colonel Burke had anything on him. In fact, Dr Smith felt that if anything, it was the other way around. Though he'd always said the right things about BIB, he'd never been a fan of the agency, of Colonel Burke, *or* his leadership of it if he was honest. If Colonel Burke had nothing else to discuss or to show him, then he'd be on his way back to Government Headquarters where he still had a lot of work to do today. It was clear that he would remember this his second BIB HQ visit.

Colonel Burke knew he had Dr Smith thinking, so decided to push harder. Dr Smith was a clever and resourceful man. He was not going to be a walkover.

Colonel Burke unlocked the drawer on the right-hand side of his desk and withdrew a leather folder. He took out a few pictures from the folder and passed them across the desk to Dr Smith, and waited for his reaction. There was silence, which prompted Colonel Burke to ask, "You were saying, Dr Smith?"

More silence. Then, after an awkward moment, Dr Smith finally spoke.

"Look, I can explain this, the…these photos!" he stuttered.

"Go on then. Please, I'm listening," encouraged Colonel Burke.

"Well, a lot of Barbadians and visitors go to Oistins on Friday nights, other nights of the week too. I'm allowed to do so too. I didn't recall actually speaking with the woman shown in the photo on this occasion if it is Dr Gladwell."

Colonel Burke decided to pass the entire folder over to Dr Smith. He watched Dr Smith's reaction as he examined the various photographs of himself with Dr Gladwell. The first set of photographs featured Dr Smith in the large car park behind one of the fast food outlets in Oistins, on his own at first, then in seemingly animated conversation with a woman. The photographs were time and date-stamped (between 6:00 p.m. and 6:07 p.m. on Friday, 20 April). There was no doubt that the two persons shown were Dr Smith and Dr Gladwell. They obviously had not realised that they were standing directly across from a CCTV camera which had perfectly caught their profiles.

Dr Smith now grasped how his clandestine meetings with Dr Gladwell had been captured. He had always sought to hold their meetings under the cover of darkness and at different locations. The Oistins meeting had been the shortest of the lot, with thousands of people all around them. He had also taken the precaution of dressing in such a way that even his closest staffers at Government Headquarters would not normally recognise him, unless they heard him speak in his customary distinctive voice. The more recent photographs of Dr Smith's meetings with Dr Gladwell – greeting each other on the steps of her east coast home on Sunday evening, 22 April and just last night at a St James restaurant, all showed that they knew and were comfortable conversing with each other in different situations.

"So, what does this prove, Colonel Burke? That I lied? That I have indeed met with Dr Gladwell on more than one occasion recently. Yes, I've visited her home. Come on man, what does this all say? I meet and dine or visit with all sorts of people as part of my public duties. That's done for all sorts of reasons. It's all legitimate and above board," said Dr Smith.

"Granted. I'll not dispute your last point. But you can get away with most things with your staff, not with me, Dr Smith. Would you believe me if I told you that on each of the recent occasions that you've met with Dr Gladwell, I have a pretty good idea what you were both discussing, at least in part? It affects national security and in fact, might even border on treason," stated Colonel Burke.

"Rubbish. Prove it," was Dr Smith's arrogant response.

"You really want me to do so? Right this minute? BIB's equipment, when used in collaboration with our overseas friends, should convince you that I have all the evidence of what I speak. I can get additional evidence if I look carefully and long enough too. Your voice discussing –"

"You're bluffing, Colonel."

"I never bluff, Dr Smith. Let's cut to the chase. I am authorised by the Prime Minister to request your resignation with immediate effect. If you don't comply by end-of-day, you will be arrested and charged for breaking all sorts of public service rules. A good lawyer will surely add to the list of charges – collaboration with known criminals, treason too. Commissioner Jeremie will personally and *publicly* arrest you if you make us do so. We all know you well enough to understand that the latter would be more painful, not only for you, but for your mother and other relatives. If I were you, I'd think of the court appearances, newspaper coverage and infamy you'll have to endure. You won't get off in the courts with the amount of evidence I assure you that we have and are willing to produce to gain your conviction. We're continuing to dig through your past as I speak to see what else you've been up to over the years. You're a lucky boy in that we no longer hang people in Barbados, but you're assured of a lengthy prison sentence instead if you choose the court route. Even with good behaviour, you'll not get out before you're an old man. I'm sure HMP Dodds will prove to be a most hospitable home."

Colonel Burke's office was deadly quiet. For a black man, Dr Smith looked quite pale. He was contemplating his future, or lack thereof before conceding.

"*Jesus Christ*! Shit, shit, shit." He placed his head in his hands.

"Alright, you win, Colonel. Where do I place my x? I suppose you already have something prepared for me to sign?"

***

Colonel Burke recalled his earlier thought, *You are entitled to your opinion and to pass judgment on what you see as the facts, but not to what the facts are.* Now that he had his man where he wanted him, he turned that thought around. *The facts are clear and indisputable, so your opinion doesn't matter.*

Colonel Burke unlocked the drawer on the left-hand side of his desk. This time he pulled out an envelope. He passed it across the desk to Dr Smith. He also handed him one of the pens on his desk. Dr Smith opened the envelope. He withdrew and read *his* 'letter of resignation.' It had been prepared on his own official 'Head of the Barbados Public Service' letterhead and written in his style. The date was today, Wednesday, 2 May. Dr Smith read the letter for a second time before signing both the original and copy that was for his personal records. He pushed the original letter and envelope back across the desk to Colonel Burke.

"What about my pension rights and my gratuity? Are they protected? Will I get what's mine? Also, you're certain that my resignation will be the end of this thing?" he asked uncertainly, knowing that he had no leg to stand on because he'd been found out and defeated.

"Yes. I have been assured that both are the case. Whatever your entitlements are, you'll get now that you've signed that letter. The reason presented to the public for your 'early retirement' is yours to decide and state. You've been in the HOPS job for what, five years I believe. I can only imagine what the stresses in that job must be like and how difficult some situations were for you at times. You'll now have time to relax, travel or whatever. Going overseas to visit that cousin you have in South Africa for a while might not be a bad option –"

"Alright. I *get* it! One last thing. Do I get to clear out my office, or have you or someone else already done that for me? Also, can I say goodbye to my staff, if not this afternoon, when?" asked Dr Smith.

"You can clear your office yourself, but please do so this afternoon. Not doing so would raise suspicion about the real reason behind your departure. I've been authorised to facilitate assistance for you from a couple of Government Headquarters handymen who will help you. You can call your relatives now and announce your departure to staff on your return to Government Headquarters."

With that, their meeting was over.

Colonel Burke stood up and walked towards his office door. Opening it, he signalled to Joe to come for Dr Smith. By the time she arrived, Dr Smith had not only regained his composure but was standing beside Colonel Burke. They shook hands firmly and formally, but did not exchange goodbyes.

Joe duly escorted Dr Smith back down to BIB's reception area and to his vehicle. They did not speak along the way. Colonel Burke, having closed his office door, immediately made a call on his secure line.

"Hello."

"It's done, Prime Minister. I have it."

"Problems?"

"Thankfully no. Our bluff was not called."

"Thank you, Good job, Trevor."

"Thank you, Prime Minister."

Colonel Burke recalled that on more than one occasion he had told his twelve operatives that *BIB is an ordinary Government Department whose operatives regularly do extra-ordinary things.* That included himself. The belief and passion he had for his BIB operatives meshed nicely with the *Spurs* Motto.

To Dare Is to Do. BIB had successfully done so again.

***

The quiet arrest of Dr Sharon LeKasha Gladwell, prominent dentist and a latent top underworld figure at her dental surgery in St Michael later that

445

afternoon was efficiently completed by Vickers, Moss, Colonel Burke, Fred and Joe.

Dr Gladwell departed her office in police custody without any fuss, leaving her staff and patients somewhat dumbfounded. Two Bajan sayings or proverbs sprung to mind to Colonel Burke as she left. He was aware that Dr Gladwell's formerly latently-known underworld dealings and activities had been exposed. 'What you do in the dark will come out under light' or 'you can hide and buy land but you can't hide and work it'. Both sayings meant that you cannot hide all of your actions or activities forever – at some point they will become known.

RBPF officers asked Dr Gladwell's staff and patients to leave the premises immediately, taking only their personal belongings. Officers then collected and took away into custody files, papers, computers, phones, contact books and anything else connected to Dr Gladwell's office that might show up her widespread underworld and illegal business dealings, her otherwise 'above-board' dealings too. She was told that there was a simultaneous visit being paid to her residence on Barbados' east coast, which would see the collection of similar materials and equipment. It transpired that most of the items found there were taken from the windowless room. DVDs of her residence's archived CCTV surveillance cameras' footage for the past three months were also recovered.

The image of an attractive, shapely forty-two-year old brunette would later be found on those DVDs. Emma Pilessar.

**

The following day, Dr Gladwell's lawyers would be presented with a full list of all the items and materials that BIB operatives and RBPF officers had taken from her dental surgery, office building and her home. Her court case, whenever it came up in the future, would be a major event in Barbados.

**

As it turned out, Power, Pilessar, Waldron and his three fellow Pressure Group gang members of Kirton, Rowe and Lee, plus Dr Gladwell had all been hung out to dry. They were in police custody, had lost their jobs or positions – some of them prestigious and were facing court trials at the end of which was expected to see them serve long prison terms. Castille was dead and Dr Smith was no longer of importance.

It proved one thing for sure.

Crime does not pay.

In JJ's case, he had gotten himself out of a tricky position and had survived to tell the tale. He was now reintegrated into BIB. His family was reinvigorated by his presence. He also knew where his future lie and had no need to be looking over his shoulder. Better days were ahead for him and BIB.

***

In other Caribbean countries, in North America, Europe and beyond, whoever had underground connections with Dr Gladwell were concerned (worried might be a better word) about what Barbados' law enforcement authorities had secured from her properties, and might share with their indigenous law enforcement agencies. Fear was in the ear. How soon before there were similar knocks at their various workplaces, clubs, and homes was unknown, but those knocks and raids were coming. They were inevitable. Some would commence in a couple of days.

***

Given all that happened to *The Organisation*, its overseas clients who were lucky enough to have received but not paid for its materials, felt they were off the hook for payment.

But that was far from the case, for unknown to them or law enforcement authorities, a shadow entity known only to Emma Pilessar already existed and was set to continue *The Organisation*'s work. Her brainchild, she had established *The Agency* six months earlier while on a private visit to Brazil. Its purpose? To be a continuum in case something ever went wrong with *The Organisation*.

Now sitting in HMP Dodds in Barbados, Pilessar was already contemplating how she would get out of her situation and start her next project? The savings she had stashed away in *The Agency* for a 'rainy day' would come in handy once she got out of Barbados. She would then have to identify another Castille-like character to be her number two once she got it going.

***

THE END

***

BIB operatives will return in…

'12 PRESENTS'

The Characters

Rt. Hon. Jeffrey Zachariah Motby QC MP, Prime Minister and Minister of Finance, Economic Affairs and National Security; Political Leader, Barbados United Party (B.U.P., a.k.a. BUP) / CARICOM Chairman

Mr Joseph Medbin, Permanent Secretary, Prime Minister's Office (PMO)

Mrs Sharon Evans, Executive Assistant to the Prime Minister, PMO

Mrs Elizabeth Burkett, Executive Secretary, PMO

Miss Debra Adams, Diary Secretary, PMO

Mr Giles Archer, Communications Director, PMO

Mr Delaney Prescod, Executive Officer, PMO

Miss Jessica Bean, Clerical Officer, PMO

Dr Winston Peter Smith GCM, Cabinet Secretary and Head of the Barbados Public Service (HOPS)

Mr Elvis Springer, Permanent Secretary, Ministry of Finance and Economic Affairs (MFEA)

Mrs Valerie Holloway, Permanent Secretary, Ministry of National Security (MNS)

Mrs Petra Carmichael, Barbados High Commissioner-designate to the United Kingdom (former Permanent Secretary, PMO)

Mr Roger Carmichael, Petra Carmichael's husband

Hon. Sebastian Smith QC MP, Attorney General & Minister of Residential Affairs

Hon. Byron Drew MP, Minister of Trade, Commerce and Investment

Hon. Walter Thompson MP, Minister of Foreign Affairs and Culture (MFAC)

Mr Justin Ian May, Permanent Secretary, MFAC

Mr Ryan Appleton, Chief of Protocol, MFAC

HE Meredith Carter, Barbados Ambassador to the United States of America – Washington

Hon. Preston Grant MP, Minister of Tourism, International Transport & Sport (MTITS)

Miss Eunice Atwell, Minister Grant's secretary, MTITS

Mrs Rosalyn Dalrymple, Permanent Secretary, MTITS

Miss Elizabeth 'Liz' Brathwaite, CEO, Barbados Tourism Hospitality Inc. (BTHI)

Sen. The Hon. Leroy Finch, Minister of Public Works and Energy (MPWE); former Barbados High Commissioner to the United Kingdom)

Mr Alwin Greene, Chief Immigration Officer, Barbados Immigration Department

Mr Jackson Bright, Director, Barbados Licencing Authority (BLA)

HE Balwin Tullock CMG, British High Commissioner to Barbados and the Eastern Caribbean

Mrs Andrea Tullock, British High Commissioner's wife

Miss Gina Crosby, Media Liaison, British High Commission – Barbados

Miss Barbara Lane, Consular Assistant, British High Commission – Barbados

Ms Zoe Markowitz, Consular Officer, British High Commission – Barbados (also Secret Intelligence Service – MI6 officer)

Sir Thadeus Theolophus Thomas KCMG, Head of Secret Intelligence Service (MI6, UK), code-named 'Elgar' – a.k.a. Mr Tommy Connell, Managing Director, UK Trading Co. Ltd

Cindy Lady Thomas, Sir Thadeus's wife

Major Digby Moorhouse LVO, Private Secretary to Her Royal Highness Princess Rowen, UK

Inspector Brian Swetland MVO, Royal Protection Unit, Metropolitan Police, UK

HE Stephens Rowley III, Ambassador to Barbados and the Eastern Caribbean, USA Embassy – Barbados

Mrs Mona Fisher, secretary to the US Ambassador, USA Embassy – Barbados

Ms Amarouse Busbee, Cultural Secretary, USA Embassy – Barbados (also Central Intelligence Agency – CIA officer)

Major Ashford Rice, US Marine Corps, Defence Advisor, USA Embassy – Barbados

Mr Tom Huney, Special Agent-in-Charge of Miami and Surrounding Districts, Federal Bureau of Investigation (FBI), USA

Mr Xui Kung Pei, Minister, Chinese Embassy – Barbados (also China State Security officer)

Mr Jose Jesus Sanchez, Trade Secretary, Mexican Embassy – Barbados (also Mexico's National Security Service officer)

Sergeant Peter Eversley, Close Protection Officer to the Prime Minister, Close Protection Unit (CPU), Royal Barbados Police Force (RBPF)

Constable Jack Marshall, Driver/Close Protection Officer to the Prime Minister, CPU, RBPF

Mr Willoughby Peter Jeremie, Commissioner, RBPF; *P.A.A.N.I.* member

Mrs Sandra Jeremie, Commissioner's wife

Miss Jasmine Boyt, Commissioner's secretary

Mr Jethro Smith, Assistant Commissioner – Administration, RBPF

Station Sergeant Robert 'Bob' Black, Officer-in-Charge, Worthing police station, RBPF

Chief Superintendent Johnny Vickers, Head of Crime, Special Branch, RBPF

Inspector Byron Moss, Special Branch, RBPF

Mrs Pearle Moss, Inspector Moss' wife

Sergeant Billy Browne, Close Protection Officer, Visitors' CPU unit, Special Branch, RBPF

Sergeant Malcolm Holder, senior officer on PR, RBPF

Constable Paul Reece, police escort vehicle driver on PR, RBPF

Constable Roosevelt Dryer, Desk Officer, Oistins police station, RBPF

Station Sergeant Donald Avery, officer-in-charge, Oistins police station

Superintendent Barry Walford, Operational Commander, RBPF (at football match and international concert)

Inspector Melanie Gray, Public Relations Officer, RBPF

Detective Philbert Fontain, RBPF

Detective Flynn Rice, RBPF

Mrs Jacklyn 'Jackie' Motby, Prime Minister's wife

Captain Michael 'Mike' Motby, Senior LIAT ATR aircraft pilot; Motby's son

Miss Kimberley Motby, banker; Motby's daughter

Mrs Jenny Wisdom, Kimberley Motby's best friend; anticipated Matron of Honour

Mr Anton Zendon, Kimberley Motby's fiancé

Mrs Gillian Nowell, Motby's sister-in-law

Mr Franklyn Nowell, Mrs Nowell's husband

Mr Ronald 'Ronny' Withers, Motby's close friend

Hon. Richard Preston Dawson MD MP, Leader of the Opposition Progressive Barbados Party (P.B.P.) / Managing and Medical Director, The Dawson Clinic

Mrs Dawn Dawson, Dr Dawson's wife

Miss Sherry Trotby, Leader of the Opposition's Executive Assistant

Colonel Trevor 'TB' Xavier Burke, Director (a.k.a. 'chief'), Barbados Intelligence Bureau – BIB (code number B1); *P.A.A.N.I.* member

Mrs Diane Burke, Colonel Burke's wife

Mr Sherman Broome, the Burke's home help

Mr James 'JJ' Johnson (a.k.a. 'boss', 'De Ole Time General'), senior leader – 'Gold' and 'RED' teams, BIB operative (code numbers P3 / RED 1)

Mrs Vanessa Johnson, JJ Johnson's wife

Mrs Carmen Richards, Vanessa's friend

Miss Angela Johnson, JJ Johnson's daughter (aged 13)

Master Andrew Johnson, JJ Johnson's son (aged 10)

Mr Mark Egwell, JJ's best friend outside of BIB

Mr Roger Dane a.k.a. 'Uncle Roger', Johnson's neighbours

Mrs Mindy Dane a.k.a. 'Auntie M', Johnson's neighbour

Mr Alfred 'Fred' George, leader – 'Blue' team / 'RED' team member, BIB operative (code numbers E5 / RED 2)

Miss Charlotte 'Charlee' Nadine Piggott, Intensive Care Unit Nurse, Queen Elizabeth Hospital / Fred George's fiancée

Miss Kylie 'Joe' Callendar, leader – 'Black' team / 'RED' team member, BIB operative (code numbers S11 / RED 3)

Dr Stephan 'Stef' Simmonds, dentist; Joe Callendar's boyfriend

Mr Riley Morris, BIB operative (code number C16)

Mr Steve Rogers, BIB operative (code number T30)

Mr Ivan Forde, BIB operative (code number Y50)

Dr Samuel Atkins, BIB operative; Head, secure intelligence room (SIR) (code number V70)

Miss Margaret Pearson, BIB operative; Assistant Head, SIR (code number A18)

Mr Mohammed Carr, BIB operative (code number F40)

Miss Jayne Bixley, BIB operative code number U21)

Mr Bruce Jordan, BIB operative (code number X60)

Captain Rodney 'Rod' Selwick, pilot, Boeing 777-200 aircraft, British Airways (BA)

Mr Harold Oliver, CEO, Grantley Adams International Airport Inc. (GAIA)

Mr Keith Henderson, CEO, Queen Elizabeth Hospital (QEH)

Mrs Roslyn Jacks, Secretary to QEH's CEO

Dr Ronald 'Ron' Hayes, Chief of Surgery, QEH

Mrs Joan Hayes, Dr Hayes' wife

Brigadier Michael 'Mike' Tenton, Chief of Staff, Barbados Defence Force (BDF) / *P.A.A.N.I.* member

Commander Edward 'Ted' Madley, Head of Coast Guard, BDF

Commander Bruce Alleyne, Special Task Force unit, BDF

Captain George Collins, Head of Air Wing, BDF

First Officer Annette Taitt, Air Wing, BDF

Sergeant Jim Pugh, aircraft master mechanic, BDF

Rt. Hon. Algernon 'Toby' Walker MP, Prime Minister of St. Vincent and the Grenadines / university friend of Colonel Burke

Mr Aubrey Gaynor, Commissioner, Royal St. Vincent and the Grenadines Police Force (RSVGPF)

Chief Inspector Terry 'TG' Gomez, leader of search team #3 and Head, Response Task Force (RTF), RSVGPF

Sergeant Casper Arnold, leader of search team #1 and second-in-command, RTF, RSVGPF

Corporal Montgomery 'Monty' Conway, leader of search team #2 and third-in-command, RTF, RSVGPF

Sergeant Rolf Boorman, RSVGPF

Corporal Mitch Papos, St Vincent and the Grenadines Defence Force (SVGDF)

Mr Astor 'Brotherman' Delaney, Rasta group leader, St Vincent

Ms Jasmine 'Sister Jas' Huey, female Rasta group member, St Vincent

Leading Fire Officer Maxwell Ferogie, St. Vincent and the Grenadines Fire & Rescue Service (SVGFRS)

Mrs Veronica Ash, hijacked victim of Power

Mr Jenson Parchmore, taxi owner

Mr Cornelius Pickett, Head of News, Star News Corporation Inc. (SNC)

Mrs Barbara Jarvis, Head of News, Barbados News Corporation (BNC)

HE Sir Livingstone Murray KA, Governor General of Barbados

Kathryn Lady Murray, Governor General's wife

Mrs Harriette Joseph, Resident Housekeeper, Government House

Dame Laura Sprigg, Chief Justice of Barbados

His Honour Martin Taylor, Chief Magistrate

Mr Pierre 'Double P' Pilgrim, Owner/Proprietor of P's Disco

Mr Grover 'GP' Price, Resident disc jockey (DJ), P's Disco

Miss Zelda Hughes, Waitress at P's Disco

Mrs Rita Goodridge, Owner/Proprietor, Rita's Kitchen

Ms Sarah McPiers, President, New Beavers Cricket Club (NBCC), UK

Mr Glyn Aitken, former England cricketer; boyfriend of Ms McPiers

Mr Timothy Rickson, cricketing all-rounder, NBCC, UK

Miss Rhonda Ziegler, sports reporter, The Daily Dispatch newspaper, UK

Mr Hubert Mustard, recently retired England Test cricketer, Cricket Correspondent for another leading UK national newspaper

Mr Ron Francis, taxi driver in St Lawrence Gap

Mr Neal Butler, President, Barbados Cricket Association (BCA); Director, West Indies Cricket Board (WICB)

Mr Orville 'Orrie' Moore, Head Groundsman, New Kensington Oval

Mrs Jeannette 'Jean' Cushion, Head Hostess, Government Headquarters

Mr Donald Rice, security guard, Government Headquarters

The Very Reverend Dr Boyd Mercer, Dean and Rector of the Cathedral Church of St Michael and All Angels, Bridgetown

Mrs Mary Jones, secretary to Dean Mercer

Miss Betsy Hefton, young lady with Dean Mercer at the Cathedral

Miss Emma Pilessar, Head, Greater Americas' Corporation (*The Organisation*)

Mr Benedict Shepherd, Pilessar's Barbados driver

Mr Royce Thomas, Number Two in the Greater Americas' Corporation (*The Organisation*)

Mr Rhohan Castille (a.k.a. 'The Principal'), enforcer and Number Three in the Greater Americas' Corporation (*The Organisation*)

Frieda, Aisha and Sean, Castille's R&R friends in Miami, USA

Senior Max Frequente, Mexican employee of *The Organisation*

Miss Maria Soares, Frequente's secretary

Dr Sharon LeKasha Gladwell, prominent dentist / underground businessperson

Mr Demario 'Spend Big' Wharton, Leader, Pressure Group gang / Owner, SBB&G

Mr Norbert 'Nobby' Kirton, Pressure Group member (self-employed tiler)

Mr Keith Lee, Pressure Group member (handyman relief night watchman at a private school)

Mr Arnold Rowe, Pressure Group member (unemployed former truck driver)

Miss Iris McCarthy, Mr Rowe's partner

Mr Jasper 'Stabs' Power, Barbados prisoner (gun importation, drug lord, wounding arrests)

Miss Marcie Leach, one of Power's girlfriends

Mrs Jessica Lynch, Barbadian prisoner (jewellery shoplifter)

Miss Franchesca Moradi, Italian prisoner (drug trafficker)

Mr Orrin Foulkes, UK prisoner (drug trafficker)

Mr Warren Field, Barbadian prisoner (child support payment defaulter)

Mr Jenson Clarke, Attorney-at-law for Field

Lt. Colonel Simon Innis, Head, Barbados Prison Service (BPS) / Superintendent, Her Majesty's Prison (HMP) Dodds; *P.A.A.N.I.* member

Miss Melba Bodie, Innis' secretary, HMP Dodds

Mr George Telford, Deputy Prison Superintendent, BPS

Mrs Alanya Telford, Telford's wife

Mr Clarence Rouse, lead prison officer on PR, BPS

Mr Randolph Perch, driver of prisoner transport vehicle on PR, BPS

Commander Junior Samuel, Co-ordinator; Executive Director, Regional Security System (RSS)

Mr Miles 'Sugar' Roberts, informer (snitch)

Mr James 'Jimmy' Rochester, Chief Fisheries Officer, Barbados

Mr Floyd Best, Comptroller of Customs

Dr Rollerick Edwards SCM, Governor, Central Bank of Barbados (CBOB)

Mrs Joyce John, Dr Edwards' secretary, CBOB

Mrs Gloria Griffith, Mrs Joyce's retired sister

Dr Albert Maurice Lewis, Deputy Governor, CBOB, Barbadian; US national; music lover

Mrs Marjorie Ruck, Dr Lewis' secretary, CBOB

Mrs Betty Lewis, Dr Lewis' wife

Mr Bertram Lewis, Dr Lewis' son; Attorney-at-Law, New York, USA

Mrs Roni Garcia, Mr Lewis' secretary, USA

Mrs Caroline Lewis-Greenidge, Dr Lewis' daughter; University Lecturer, Texas, USA

Mr Jack Greenidge, husband of Caroline Lewis-Greenidge / Dr Lewis' son-in-law

Mrs Ava Prescod, maid to the Lewis family

Mrs Claire Parnell, Head of Research Department, CBOB

Miss Evadne Scott, Secretary, Precision Laboratories

Mr Oswald King, Sky Sports television reporter, UK

Mr Brent Norbury, England Test Match captain, UK

Miss Leamore 'LP' Phillips, Canadian pop, jazz, rhythm and blues chart-topping artist/actress

Mr Magnus Hunter GCM, retired Permanent Secretary, Ministry of Defence & National Security / former Head of the Public Service

Mrs Anna Hunter, Hunter's wife

Mr Charles 'Corey' Miller, retired Chief Medical Officer, Ministry of Health

Mr Kenrick Hyman, attempted robber, St Lawrence Gap / robber, St Michael service station

Mr Virgil Procter, attempted robber / shooter, St Lawrence Gap; robber, St Michael service station

Mr Desmond Alli, Duty Manager, Rising Sun hotel

Mr Selwyn Gay, coach, Barbados senior soccer team

Mr Mick Wayne and Mr Lorburn 'Lorbee' Wayne (brothers), Dr Lewis' kidnappers

***

Significance of the Twelve BIB Operatives' Codes Stations in Life's Journey:

Bravo 1 (B1) – Birth

Papa 3 (P3) – Pre-School

Echo 5 (E5) – Primary School

Sierra 11 (S11) – Secondary School (Eleven +)

Charlie 16 (C16) – CXC / O Levels

Alfa 18 (A18) – CAPE / 'A' Levels / University

Uniform 21 (U21) – Work

Tango 30 (T30) – Family

Foxtrot 40 (F40) – Life begins (again)…

Yankee 50 (Y50)– Celebrate half a century (Grandparent?)

Xray 60 (X60) – Early Retirement

Victor 70 (V70) – Enforced Retirement